All
Stirred Up

All
Stirred Up

A Novel

BRIANNE MOORE

alcove
press

Copyright © 2020 by Brianne Moore

Published in the United States by Alcove Press, an imprint of The Quick Brown Fox & Company LLC.

Alcove Press and its logo are trademarks of The Quick Brown Fox & Company LLC.

Library of Congress Catalog-in-Publication data available upon request.

ISBN (hardcover): 978-1-64385-531-8
ISBN (ebook): 978-1-64385-532-5

Cover design by Tsukushi

Printed in the United States.

www.alcovepress.com

Alcove Press
34 West 27th St., 10th Floor
New York, NY 10001

First Edition: September 2020

10 9 8 7 6 5 4 3 2 1

*For my brilliant husband, Adam,
who makes it all possible, and our beautiful
boys, Jamie and Alex, who are the reason
I do everything*

Chapter One
Going . . . Going . . . Gone

෨

"So, this is it."

Susan cringes inwardly at her own words, which seem as flaccid and tasteless as raw squid. Before her stand over forty people now looking for work, and all she can say is "This is it"?

They deserve better. She wishes she could offer more, but there is no more. Elliot's Regent Street, the jewel in the crown of Napier Hospitality, is going out of business, and there's nothing anyone can do about it. And Susan certainly tried. She'd fought—dug her nails in, clung, clawed, pleaded, begged—but she'd been too late to save it or any of the other Napier restaurants, which had shuttered one by one over the past two years. She watched, alarmed, as it happened. As her grandfather's hard work gave way to waste, disaster, and ultimately bankruptcy. She pleaded with her father to let her step in, as her grandfather had always intended. It was why she'd gotten a business degree. It was why she—

Well, best not to think about that. Not now, as a swarm of eyes stare her down. "I—we—my family—we want to thank you all for everything you've done," she continues. "And to say that we're so sorry it's come to this. Believe me, if there was any other way . . ."

It's no use. They're getting restless. They want to be off to one of their favorite haunts—maybe that slightly grubby place "with

1

character" in Camden Town—to commiserate and reminisce and talk about who's hiring.

Susan wants to be off too. Put London, and all its failures and unhappy memories behind her. And she will—tomorrow. Tomorrow's a new start for all of them. A last chance to save her grandfather's legacy in the place it all began: Edinburgh.

"I'm sorry," she repeats. "It's been a great pleasure working with all of you, and you'll be missed."

She doubts *she* will be, despite having been on friendly terms with most of them. Now they look at her and only see the reason they'll struggle to make rent for a while. The sense of misplaced failure weighs heavily on her.

They all stare for a few long seconds. Waiting for some sign of what to do. What *should* she do? Dismiss them? That seems so arrogant. Her grandfather probably would have gone around the room and hugged each and every person, and they would have hugged him back and probably wiped away a few tears. But then, everyone loved Elliot. And he could hardly be blamed for any of this: he and Emily, his equally talented and hard-working wife, had built a good business, a solid, well-respected one. Spent their whole lives at it and died thinking it would be in good hands. Susan's hands. But she was too young when he died, and her life too complicated. And so it wound up going to her father's old school chum instead.

"It makes no sense for me to manage things. You know I've never had a head for this business—even my father said so," Bernard had pointed out when the question of who would run the business first came up. "It's better this way. Sozzy can manage. Why, he was secretary of the Plimsopps for three years when we were at school, and he was brilliant at it."

(Bernard Napier saw no difference between a school social club and a multimillion-pound restaurant empire because he was equally uninvolved in running both.)

But Sozzy hadn't managed. All he *had* managed to do was escape at just the right time. He took early retirement (with full pension, of course) just as things went downhill. And now he's living it up in a villa in the south of France, immune to the rot he planted in the business he'd been responsible for.

It's Susan who faces the carnage now. Who tries to make this a dignified ending for their former employees. She isn't the cause, but she's the face of the failure, and their resentment creeps toward her like a chilly mist. It wraps around her, and she shivers.

The sommelier is the first to sense that there's nothing more to be said, and he turns without a word, heading for the door. The others take their cue and follow. In five minutes, Susan is left alone.

The stillness of the place! She's never been here when it's been empty. There have always been people in Elliot's. Loads of people! In the dining room, those who enjoyed looking down on their fellow man fought over tables on the grand mezzanine. In the kitchen, ambitious and talented comers pursued careers, knowing the cachet of the name would carry them far ("Oh, you trained at *Elliot's*. Well, well, let's see what we can do . . ."). They filled the place up with their clatter and their chatter.

But then, just like that, they were gone. A recession makes you think twice about paying more than two hundred pounds a head for dinner. Especially when what arrives on the plate is not at all what you expected.

Susan douses the lights, room by room. Farewell, gleaming kitchen, with your mirror-shine, stainless-steel tables and massive ovens, now unnaturally still and cold. Goodbye, dining room, the site of countless big-business deals, budding romances, and damaging affairs. So long, bar, where dozens of bankers gathered as the hammer came down, wondering if their employer—or they themselves—would go next. Praying they were too big to fail. But is anyone really too big to fail? Once upon a time, they'd thought Elliot's was safe, nestled in its reputational cocoon. But it doesn't take much to ruin a great thing, does it?

She pauses, taking one last look at the darkened dining room.

I'm sorry, Granddad, Susan thinks as, with a sigh, she locks the door and turns her back on Regent Street forever.

* * *

She walks home, avoiding the rush-hour Tube. People squeezed like sausage meat into a subterranean metal casing—she won't miss that. There is no Underground in Edinburgh. And it's a small city: you can walk just about anywhere. That suits her down to the ground—she prefers walking. Her father, on the other hand . . .

"I'm not selling the Aston Martin," he informed her as she laid out the drastic plan necessary to save them from bankruptcy.

"Dad, we need to cut back," she insisted, not for the first time. With each repetition, it became harder to keep her voice even. "We've talked about this—no unnecessary expenses."

"A car is *not* unnecessary! How am I supposed to get around?"

Susan hadn't even bothered bringing up public transport. The mere notion probably would have killed him on the spot.

At last, Kay intervened. "All right, Bernard, if it means that much to you, keep the Aston. But Julia's car will have to go."

Julia gaped at her aunt. "That's not fair!" she screeched.

Bernard reached over and patted Julia's hand. "Now, now, Julia, sacrifices must be made."

He listens to Kay because she's famous and beautiful. Susan is neither—and so is ignored. She'd almost given up asking to take some role in the business, having been rebuffed so many times, but after Sozzy left, she and Kay joined forces.

"Just think, Bernard, what a burden running the restaurant will be," Kay coaxed. "Eighteen-hour days, all those decisions to make—you'll get worry lines."

Bernard's hand fluttered to his forehead in alarm.

"Susan's perfect for the job," Kay continued. "She's had years of management experience, and it was always the plan for her to take on the business. Let her take this load off your shoulders, Bernard. You've earned a good rest."

All the skills that won Kay two BAFTAs and four London Evening Standard Theatre Awards had gone into that little speech. And it worked. Bernard beamed, agreed that the business *was* a terrible burden, and all right, then, Susan could have it. Kay shot Susan a triumphant look over her brother-in-law's head and later, as they said good night, hugged her tightly and whispered, "Make your mother proud, my dear."

And now they're going north, where Susan will run the only Napier restaurant still holding its head above water: The original Elliot's, on the Royal Mile. For financial reasons, it's been decided that Susan's father and her older sister, Julia, should go as well. Edinburgh's not cheap, but it's much more affordable than London.

One last stand.

A fresh start, Susan tells herself. It's a relief, in many ways, to be leaving London.

Her cozy flat has been sold along with the townhouse where Susan and her sisters grew up. There will be one last night there for her, Julia, and Bernard before Susan catches a morning flight, and her father and sister take a more leisurely trip by car.

When Susan arrives at the house, she finds Julia watching movers wrap the last of their furniture in plastic and cushioned covers.

"Be careful with that—it's Chippendale!" Julia barks at one of them before turning to her sister. "How'd it go?"

Susan shrugs. "It went. Like all the others."

"Unpleasant, but someone has to do it," Julia sighs. "Nice of you to take it on. You know how uncomfortable Dad is with confrontation."

"Nice" had nothing to do with it. Susan had asked—or, rather, *very* strongly suggested—that her father come with her to address the staff today. But he just shook his head and said he couldn't possibly, because he had *so* much to do ahead of the move and people he had to see and *so* many of the men at the club wanted to stand him one last drink . . . And so Susan stopped arguing about it, because it was useless and even if he did come, he'd probably just sulk and make it all worse.

"Where is Dad? Still at the club?" Susan asks Julia.

Julia shakes her head. "One last appointment with Dr. Keegan."

"To say his sad farewells, I'm sure." Susan rolls her eyes. "He sees more of Dr. Keegan than he does of us."

"Now, now," Julia murmurs, "you can't blame him for wanting to look good. And he does. Keenan's the best."

Bernard should look good, she thinks, *considering what Keegan charges. He should look* spectacular. *His wrinkles should be filled with platinum. His face alone could have saved two restaurants.*

Just thinking about it ignites a hot little jet of anger in Susan's chest. Her father could have done more. Done anything. Could, at least, have acknowledged that his idiotic friend caused this whole mess, with his insane expansion plans, disastrous cost-cutting attempts, and line of ready-meals that raised the blogosphere to new heights of poetic condemnation ("Excellent for those who find airplane food a little too posh and flavorful," ran a particularly memorable one.).

Susan would never have done any of that. And she would never have hired that dishwasher who turned out to be a journalist working on a story about unfair pay practices in high-end London restaurants. He got so much more than he expected because he also discovered that the organic, imported, Wagyu beef Elliot's was selling at eye-watering prices wasn't organic at all. Most of it wasn't even beef. And then there were investigations and boycotts and petitions and reporters phoning constantly or turning up at the house, looking for a comment. Even Julia got tired of all the attention.

But then, to be fair, Bernard himself admitted he had no sense for the business. And any work ethic he might have had was probably ruined by the incredible spoiling he received, growing up as the only child of successful parents who had both had to go without when they were children. Bernard was under no illusions about his abilities. It's why he handed things over to his wife right after his father died. Things might have been all right if she hadn't . . .

I should have done more, Susan thinks. *I should have fought harder all those years ago. Pulled myself out of my mess faster and stepped into Mum's shoes before Sozzy ever got a chance.*

But there's no use crying about it now.

"Maybe I should have gone to Dr. Keegan too," Julia frets, turning away from the movers and running her fingers over a cheek. "I swear all the strain is giving me worry lines."

"You're fine," Susan reassures her, trying to keep her voice bright. The salon Julia frequents is bad enough without piling on more Keegan fees. Though, like Keegan, the salon does a great job: you'd never guess Julia wasn't a natural blonde. She's forever after Susan to do something with her own hair, but Susan can't be bothered to spend hours in foils at a salon. She's content with her natural brown, which curls to her shoulders.

Julia drops her hand from her cheek and goes back to watching the movers work. Susan notices her eyes flickering over the room, and the one adjoining it. Julia's spent nearly a decade redoing this place. She started just after she climbed out of her alcoholic haze, following their mother's death. Buying new rugs and curtains and paintings and ripping down wallpaper. Over and over, until there was nothing left of the home Susan once knew. "Can't you leave anything alone?" Susan once implored, after seeing what her sister had done to Susan's childhood bedroom.

"We need change, Susan," Julia responded. "I can't bear to look at any of it anymore!"

This house is Julia's magnum opus, just as Regent Street was their grandfather's, and now they're losing it. Her grand project, handed off to strangers who will probably bring in a new decorator to undo it all.

Susan sees her sister's chest rise as she takes a deep, silent, steadying breath. She wraps an arm around Julia's shoulders and gives her a quick squeeze. "You're handling all this very well."

Julia shrugs. "Well, there's no use making a fuss. Anyway, a change of scenery is good, right? Edinburgh's on the up and up. And I'll have a new house to do over."

Oh God. Susan cringes, thinking of the expense. *And* thinking about the new house.

"A five-bedroom townhouse in the City Centre?" Susan screeched when Julia first told her about the purchase. "What were you thinking? We're supposed to be cutting back! You were supposed to find a nice flat somewhere. What do we need five bedrooms for? There are only three of us."

"But we'll have *guests*, Susan," Julia responded in a voice that bit. "Well, *you* probably won't," she added.

But now Susan puts aside her irritation and smiles thinly. "Right. So I'll pick up the keys from the solicitor's office, then?"

"Yes, that's right." Julia side-eyes her, waiting for further judgment over the extravagance of the house. Susan keeps her face studiously neutral. She and Julia have to live together for the time being. Best to get started on the right foot.

"I've ordered you a takeaway from that place around the corner you like," Julia continues, grimacing as the movers manhandle an Eames chair.

"Thanks." Susan isn't hungry at all. The memory of those blank faces and the dead, empty restaurant still haunts her. She wishes her baking supplies weren't already packed and sent ahead—this was just the time to make a batch of biscuits. Or, even better, bread. Something she could manhandle. "Are you having anything?"

Julia recoils. "Do you know how much *butter* and *oil* they use in their food? No, thank you." She turns back toward the movers. "Oh, for God's sake, don't you know what you're doing? That's an *original.*"

Susan takes the opportunity to slip away. She goes to the kitchen and picks at the food for a while, listening to Julia scold the movers. When things start to quiet down, she heads upstairs to her old bedroom. It was a cheery, cozy room until Julia got her hands on it. Now the sunny quilt and daisy cushions sewn by their mother have been replaced with a commanding canopy bed and heavy toile curtains that match the bedspread. It feels like a hotel room, and Susan hates hotels. Thank God it's only for one night.

Her overnight bag sits on a chair, along with an old photo album she accidentally found in a pile of things Julia decided would be donated or thrown away.

"You're not getting rid of this!" she cried, incredulous, hugging the album to her chest, as if Julia might tear it away.

Julia glanced over, shrugged, then quickly looked away. "Those pictures are ancient, Susan. And God, I look *so fat* in them!"

Now, Susan flops onto the bed and flips the album open.

The first several pages are pictures of her and her sisters as children. Splashing in the pool at that villa in Spain they used to have. Decked out in fancy dress—Julia in a big hat and fur stole of their grandmother's, Margaret in a fairy princess costume, and Susan in a suit of armor she'd made out of cutup cardboard boxes and silver paint.

No pictures of her father—he hates to be photographed unless it's with someone important—but five pages in, the pictures of Susan's mother start. Marie laughing while sunning herself by that pool. Smiling as she pretends to read a book. Giggling as she poses on a windy castle rampart with Kay. Mum always seemed to be laughing or smiling, even at the very end, when she must have been in so much pain.

And there, on the second-to-last page—there it is: a photo Susan had forgotten all about. Her, her mother, and Elliot, in the kitchen. Susan remembers that day.

"We're going to teach you to make the *best* brownies," her mother declared. And they did.

Susan's head to toe in chocolate in the picture, getting ready to lick the spoon. Her mother and grandfather laugh and applaud and show off the fruits of their labors. It's the first of many times Susan joined them in the kitchen, learning her grandfather's secrets with her mother's encouragement. Her sisters had no interest: Margaret once burned herself and refused to go near a stove again, and Julia had more or less been on a diet from the age of ten. Elliot used to shake his head as he watched her pick at her plate.

"She'll never be any good with food," he would murmur to Susan. "To make great food, you have to *love* food. You can't just like it or tolerate it. It's a bit like marriage in that way."

Susan *does* love food. It's why she'll never look good in skinny jeans. And she's fine with that.

She turns to the last page in the album, and every last bit of her body clenches. Her heart rate picks up just a little. No family picture this time, but a photo of Elliot, already looking frail, his arms slung over the necks of two much younger men in chef's whites. The one on the right—cocky, smirking straight into the camera—went on to become the head chef at Elliot's Regent Street. It's thanks to him they wound up serving horsemeat as prime rib. The other man—broad shouldered, russet haired, hint of a lantern jaw, nose slightly crooked after having been broken once, smiling admiringly at Susan's grandfather—is Chris.

Susan snaps the album shut, swallowing hard against the lump in her throat. It shouldn't be this hard after all these years. It's ridiculous to still feel this way. He's long gone, on to bigger and better things.

But still . . .

She buries the album at the bottom of her bag, changes into her pajamas, and climbs into the silly bed, which is so soft it's like trying to sleep on a marshmallow. She draws her knees up to her chest, trying to distract herself with thoughts of Edinburgh and work, as she's always done.

It will be a relief to get out of London.

* * *

There are many things Chris will miss about New York, but the international departures lounge at JFK Airport is not one of them. He speeds through it, past the places selling ludicrously overpriced, soggy sandwiches and I ♥ NY snow globes, and settles in at the bar in the British Airways First Class Lounge.

"Talisker, please, mate," he says to the bartender. "Neat."

As the bartender serves his drink, a woman a little farther down begins eyeing Chris. He studies her out of the corner of his eye. Conventionally pretty. Blonde. Thin as seaweed. Not really his type. Women like her remind him of Julia Napier, and try as he might, he can't forget the look she gave him that one time Susan brought him home for dinner. Like he was dog shit someone had just tracked into her house.

This woman smiles, which immediately sets her apart from Julia. Chris smiles back instinctively. She takes that as encouragement and approaches.

"Sorry for staring, but you look familiar," she begins. "Are you on TV?"

Chris's smile stiffens a touch. "Yes." He steels himself for the inevitable follow-up.

Her eyes widen. "Oh, are you the guy from *Outlander*?"

There it is. Not that he can blame her—or any of the others who have made that exact same guess. The resemblance is deliberate. His producers realized that they, too, had a well-built, medium-height, red-headed Scotsman they could capitalize on. They encouraged him to bulk up ("Your viewership is eighty-six percent female; you need to give them something besides the food to drool over") and grow his hair out. He'll chop that off before getting back into the kitchen. Maybe then people will stop thinking he's Sam Heughan.

"No, sorry," he tells the woman.

She recovers quickly. "I should have known that," she purrs. "You're much better looking."

He guesses she's a couple of glasses of wine in, but nevertheless lifts his whisky in thanks.

"But you *are* on TV?" she confirms. "Which show?"

"I hosted a cooking show," he admits. *Chris's Cookout* isn't something he's enormously proud of, but he does owe a fair bit of his success to it and supposes he should be grateful.

"Oh. Oh, right! That one where chefs are dropped in random places and have to collect ingredients and cook over fires and in caves and stuff? I *love* that show!"

Loads of people do for some reason. The producers were outraged when he told them he wanted to stop after four seasons.

"But it's a *hit*!" one of them wailed. "We were about to start merchandising you! We had baking tins and everything all lined up. We were thinking about Iceland next year!"

Much as he loved the idea of freezing his balls off while watching a bunch of publicity-hungry chefs try to start a fire on ice, he had to decline. He has his own dreams, and they do not include six more seasons of *Chris's Cookout*.

"So, you're not doing it anymore?" The woman sighs. "Shame. Guess I'll just have to binge-watch it on Netflix or something. Or pick your brain on the flight over. You always had the best cooking tips." She looks up at him through her eyelashes. Her voice turns husky. "Is London your final destination?"

He polishes off the whisky and sets down the glass. "No," he answers. "Edinburgh."

Chapter Two
Baggage Claim

～

The plane dips beneath a thin scrim of cloud, and Susan presses up against the window as Edinburgh reveals itself below.

The Firth of Forth glitters invitingly in the peek-a-boo sunshine, which is reliable enough today to call boats out to the little islands: Inchkeith, with its lighthouse; Cramond and Inchmickery, with their hunkered down, wartime fortifications that refuse to give way to time and tide. Just ahead, the spiderweb spans of the bridges link Edinburgh to the whimsically named Kingdom of Fife.

And there, to the left: the city. Susan's been here before, but now she looks at it differently, feeling a sort of proprietary excitement and pride in her new home. She watches as farm fields and kelly-green hills give way to rows of shops and terraced stone houses. Unlike London, there are no skyscrapers here, just a few ugly council block towers looming defiantly over Victorian-era semi-detatched houses and 1920s bungalows. Susan spots Edinburgh Castle on its jutting, craggy perch, looking out over its domain.

She marvels at the city's many guises, packed together and changing in the blink of an eye. The pleasant seaside promenades of Portobello swiftly give way to the commercial docks and old warehouses of Leith, which just as quickly transform into South Queensferry, easily identified by its proximity to the sunset-orange Forth Rail Bridge. The tide is low, revealing large expanses of sand, rock, and muck in some places, temporarily spoiling the view for those with waterfront properties. Beyond those shores lie the thickly clustered buildings and perplexing warren of hilly streets that defy any sort of grid pattern and beg to be explored.

London has its history, of course, but so much of it feels new. Edinburgh clings to its past; lives in it. It pools around an ancient castle and packs into narrow streets and old buildings. It clings to its cobblestones and turns genteel Georgian town-houses into office buildings with Escher-esque interior layouts. The Scots are an admirably thrifty people. They see no need to build new when what's there already will do perfectly well, thank you very much.

The plane lands and Susan retrieves her bag from the overhead, feeling the firm, sharp corners of the album nudge the canvas sides. She inches down the aisle of the plane, a maddening crawl past harassed fellow passengers and plastically smiling cabin crew. Once free, she surges forth, speeding toward the exits just beyond the baggage claim. There's so much to do: house keys to be collected, the restaurant to visit, the chef to catch up and make plans with. She aches to be free of airports, of London; to get started, to set things right—they can't wait another moment. Not another Regent Street.

At last! She reaches the escalator, gets stuck in the bottleneck there, but at least the exit is within sight. So close!

But then she sees, just up ahead on the escalator . . . No. It can't be. Can't *possibly* be. His shoulders seem broader, his arms far more muscular. And . . . it can't be.

The auburn-haired man who transfixes her turns at the bottom of the escalators and makes his way to the baggage carousels. A few minutes later, Susan, too, reaches solid earth and makes for the exit, convincing herself, *It can't be.*

But it is.

As she passes the carousel for her own flight, she sees him again, and there is no mistaking him. Yes, he's definitely fitter (his physique now speaks more of hours in a gym than hours in a kitchen), and his hair longer, pulled back from his face in a low, short ponytail at the nape of his neck. His clothes are simple but clearly expensive, as is the artfully distressed leather satchel at his feet. He stands with his arms crossed, watching the carousel turn. As Susan passes, however, he turns his head and looks straight at her.

Chris Baker.

Every part of her freezes, heart included, it seems, at least for a moment. But then that one bit starts beating very fast, and her mouth feels dry and her skin hot. She stares at him, wondering what she should do or say. Apologize? Try to explain herself? Just greet him as an old friend? ("Wow, fancy meeting you here! Small world, eh? How've you been?" As if nothing ever happened.)

She stands there, clutching her bag, for what feels like eons but is really only a second or two. Then Chris turns away, back to the luggage carousel, as if he hadn't seen her at all.

* * *

Twenty-two Moray Place is not the home Susan would have chosen for herself. It's one of a series of nearly identical, four-story, Georgian-style buildings set in a ring around a viciously fenced central garden accessible only to residents. These have always been homes for the rich; they bear the hallmarks of refined ostentation: decorative columns across the front, and enormous windows with tiny, curlicued balconettes on the three central floors.

The Napiers' new home is one of the few in the area that is still fully intact: most have been carved up into offices or luxurious flats. Susan's first thought, when she opens the front door, is that it's overwhelmingly beige. Not a hint of color or personality to be seen in any of the public rooms except the dining room, which, for some reason, is royal purple. She can see why Julia was excited by it. A blank slate for her to play with. She'll probably start by painting the entryway the same gray color that features in the London house. Something by Farrow and Ball that was all the rage among *Town & Country* readers ("It's not *gray*, Susan, it's *Mole's Breath*. Can't you see the blue undertones?")

The beige, even the Mole's Breath, Susan could live with, but the kitchen! She groans at first sight. It's a kitchen for people who don't cook. Reflective white cabinets that will show every fingerprint, and an unforgiving slate floor. She makes a mental note to pick up some rugs from IKEA to put down and steels herself for the bedrooms.

Not beige. A riot of color, in fact. She chooses the one with wallpaper least likely to give her a headache, plunks her bag next to the door, and retreats.

*　*　*

A private hire car collects Chris from the airport and deposits him on his new doorstep on Mill Lane in Leith. His flat is one of six built in the shell of a Victorian office building. History on the outside, modern on the inside. How very Edinburgh. How very *Leith*. Edinburgh's former docklands, now experiencing a resurgence. Not quite the place that produced Renton and Sick Boy anymore.

It hasn't fully left behind its grubby past, so quaint cafés peddling flat whites and oversized scones to yummy mummies sit alongside cheap chippies with faded, gap-toothed signs and lurid yellow, plastic interiors that date to the eighties. There are still plenty of people here with accents so thick you could spoon them up like custard. But former warehouses are now restaurants and posh flats, and shiny new residential towers at the waterfront try to make everyone forget about Leith's working-class background.

Chris's flat, like so many others, is brand-new and so still lacking personality. The blank white walls feel cold and stark, but it's only a place to sleep. He mostly liked it for its plentiful natural light and location just a few blocks from his restaurant.

Leith is his home territory. Cables Wynd House, the "Banana Flats" made famous (for all the wrong reasons) by *Trainspotting*, is just around the corner. He grew up there. Sam too.

But Chris tries not to think about that.

Why here? He could have opened his restaurant anywhere. Why Edinburgh? Why *Leith*? It's not as if he has very many fond memories of the place. His most recent time here *definitely* wasn't great. What brought him back? Is it that he does, in a begrudging, Scottish sort of way, love this city, with its vibrant clash of old and new, rich and poor? Its neighborhoods like little towns in themselves, clustered around a sort of high street with the obligatory butcher, baker, and newsagents where you can buy the latest gossip rag, a bottle of cheap plonk, and freshly made samosas, all in a space roughly the size of Chris's bedroom.

Or maybe it's not the city, but the people in it that drew him home. He's never encountered anyone else quite like the Scots. These are a people who refuse to let go of the past entirely, squeezing awkwardly into old buildings and maintaining a grudge against the English that everyone else thinks they should have let go of centuries ago. But to a Scot, Culloden may as well have happened yesterday. The Scots are people of stone, they are. They remember, and they refuse to budge. They withstand, and though you may think you've beaten them, you haven't. You never will. They'll play their banned instruments and wear kilts unironically in the most inhospitable weather and just *dare* you to say anything about it. They will rise again and again and again, holding tight to their traditions even as they maneuver themselves into position as a modern society worth paying attention to.

Maybe it's neither of those things. Maybe Chris has come back to give an emphatic middle finger to the neighborhood that once almost ruined him. He's returned successful and famous, and the restaurant will just be the capper to it all. *You see, a boy from the Banana Flats can make good. We council house kids can rise to the top, and to hell with all the people like the Napiers who used to look down on us.*

Damn. He'd hoped to keep Susan from his mind—he's managed so well these past several years. But here she is again, rising like a wraith. Invading *his* city (how very English of her!). As he wanders over to a window and looks out at a collection of buildings turned sullen gray by centuries of soot and industry, he wonders: *What the hell is Susan Napier doing in Edinburgh?*

Seeing her younger sister, maybe? The one who was up here, at Edinburgh University, when he and Susan were together? He's never met that sister, but Chris imagines she's just like Julia. Susan had seemed such an odd one out in her family. He'd sort of loved that about her. And he'd definitely loved the fact it didn't seem to bother her.

He digs his nails into his palms and tries not to remember the things he'd loved. The time she showed up for a date with a massive box of biscuits in half a dozen different flavors ("I was experimenting today") or how she frowned and bit the left corner of her bottom lip as she really concentrated on getting something right. Or the feel of her hair, or the smell of her . . .

Chris forces himself to dredge up another memory: of coming home, after a double shift and the worst news of his life (up to that point), to find her standing beside two packed bags. No warning, no explanation. That was it, she was gone. It hurt even worse than he'd expected, and then what happened next . . .

Chris closes his eyes and digs his nails in harder. He had risked everything for her and got nothing back. And that's when he realized he'd been nothing to her. A taste of something exotic: a rich girl slumming. Someone to distract her when her life got hard. And when she was done with him, she'd dropped him without a thought and never looked back.

Maybe she's more like Julia than he thought.

And now, here she is again. Wandering back into his orbit, just when he truly believed he'd put all that far, far behind him. Seeing her at the airport had been like a leap into a steaming pool that turned out to be freezing. It was such a shock, he hadn't known what to do, so he flailed, bewildered. Looked away to collect himself, and then she was gone.

Maybe she hadn't really been there at all. Maybe he'd just imagined it. It would make sense—she looked exactly as he remembered her, and who doesn't change in ten years? That dark, wavy hair cut short, framing a heart-shaped face with skin as smooth and pale as milk. There was a scattering of freckles over her nose and cheeks—how many times had he tried to kiss each and every one? How many times had he tried to come up with a better way to describe the color of her eyes than "mackerel belly"?

But it *was* her. He knew it was. She has changed, subtly. Her face is a little thinner. Her eyes a little sadder. And she seemed just as shocked to see him. Nothing you conjure up is going to seem surprised to see you.

Hopefully she's just in town for a quick trip. A couple of days with her sister, and then she'll be gone.

The sooner the better, Chris thinks.

He has a restaurant to open and a book coming out. He has his hands more than full, *And anyway,* he sternly reminds himself, *Susan's a bitch.* She used him, got what she wanted or needed, and then dropped him. And when he needed her, she hadn't been there. Even today, in the airport, she hadn't had the grace to come over and speak to him. And really, she should make the first move, right? After all, she was in the wrong.

Of course, she was shocked too. Maybe she *will* make the next move, if given the opportunity. Does he want to give it to her?

Without allowing a chance to talk himself out of it, he pulls out his mobile and dials a number.

"Yes, hi, it's Chris Baker," he says to the bright voice on the other end of the line. "I just want to leave a message for Russell Cox. Could you please tell him I'll do his event?"

Chapter Three
All the Delight of Unpleasant Recollections

❧

Edinburgh smells of porridge. It's the first thing Susan notices, as she steps outside. *Is that something they do for the tourists?* she wonders, bemused. It isn't: there's a brewery or a distillery—she can't remember which—outside the city, and so some days the pleasant, toasty, quintessentially Scottish smell permeates parts of the city.

Chris first told her about that.

"Can't smell it in Leith, though," he'd added with a slightly bitter smile. "Different sorts of smells there."

Chris. She spent the entire taxi ride from the airport trying to calm herself down and wondering what the hell he was doing in Edinburgh. Yes, he'd grown up here, but she had always been under the impression he was happy to have left. Maybe he's just visiting friends. Or his sister—he mentioned a sister a few times. Beth.

A visit, of course. But it seems so bizarre, seeing him just after finding that album. It was as if she'd conjured him up. Maybe she had. Maybe that hadn't been him at all, just some other man with a similar build and coloring. Scotland is full of muscular redheads, if popular culture and Highland Games are to be believed. It was seeing that photograph; it put him in her head, primed her to see him where he couldn't be. Because, surely, if it had been him, he'd have said something?

Then again, maybe not. Not after what she did.

She grimaces just thinking about it, as she turns down Forres Street and begins the steep climb past Charlotte Square. Locked up tight now, in two months the Square will throw open its gates for the Book Festival. Every available space in the city will open itself to the grand August festival triad: Book, International, Fringe. The city will swarm with people, and no one will want for entertainment at any hour of the day or night. And they'll all need feeding.

Strangely enough, Susan's never been to Edinburgh for the festivals. She was meant to come up years ago. The tickets were bought, the hotel room booked. But then her grandfather died. It was just a few weeks after that picture of him and Greg and Chris was taken.

That photo! She wants to kick something in frustration. How long will she keep circling back to it? Maybe it would be better to destroy it, like banishing a bad talisman. But she can't do that; it's one of the last photos taken of Elliot.

She'd taken it.

It was Chris's and Greg's first day in the kitchen at Regent Street. Chris had only arrived the day before. Elliot offered to give him a day or two to get settled, but all Chris wanted to do was get in there and start working. He was a proper chef now, no longer a trainee, and he was eager to make his mark.

"My wonder boys!" Elliot declared, laughing as he slung a bony arm around both of them. "Come on, Susan, take one for posterity. One day, we'll both say, 'We knew them when.'"

Susan obliged, hoping the camera hid her blush. Greg smirked, thinking it was for him, but he wasn't at all her type. Chris grinned, and she could have sworn he reddened just a little bit too.

A month later, Elliot was dead. Bronchitis, which he couldn't fight off anymore. Even though he had been in poor health and they'd been steeling themselves for this for months, it still hit hard. Susan cried more than she ever thought she could. Her mother cried with her, but not the others. Her father was too busy being baffled by all the business decisions now coming his way, and Meg and Julia were never close to their grandfather.

The day of the funeral, Susan managed to hold herself together long enough to be polite at the reception. But as soon as she could, she slipped away into the kitchen, where she found Chris. He was still in his funeral clothes, with his sleeves rolled up and tie tucked into his shirt, to keep it out of the way of the enormous pile of vegetables he was reducing to mirepoix.

"I'm sorry," he said, setting down his knife as soon as he saw her. "I just . . ."

"It's okay," she responded, joining him. She understood. He needed to stay busy. Keep his mind occupied somehow. "I thought that I might bake something."

He looked up at her, and she saw the puffy, reddened eyes that had been her own constant companions the past week. He, too, had loved her grandfather, a man who took a gamble on the kid who showed up at the Edinburgh restaurant one day, eager to do any work so long as he could learn. And learn he did.

She smiled at him, a gentle, sad smile of camaraderie in distress, and he responded in kind. He made a soup, and she baked Elliot's brownies, and they sat and talked for hours with their simple feast. And that's how it all began. A bittersweet beginning, perhaps, but that soon changed as they fell into it and into each other.

And then, oh, how sweet it was! Susan wasn't like Julia: she didn't have boys lining up to flatter and compete for her. She hardly knew how to react to Chris's attention, and it bowled her over. She reveled in it—the dinners at his shabby flat, with wonderful food and cheap wine and his roommates good-naturedly teasing them. The late nights out with the kitchen brigade, drinking too much and laughing and making rude jokes. The charming little gifts and the hungry kisses that inevitably led to more. It was dazzling and dizzying, and she loved every minute of it.

And then her mother died, and everything went right to hell.

* * *

Susan hauls herself out of her memories long enough to realize she's reached the end of genteel George Street. To the right, the road slopes down toward the Scott Monument: a bit of overblown, soot-soaked, Gothic insanity wrapped around a statue of a seated, exhausted-looking Sir Walter. With its spikes and arches, it reminds Susan of something out of Mordor. Does Sauron's eye appear after dark?

Just ahead of her is St. Andrew Square, where a slightly more subdued statue perches on a fluted column, looking down on passersby. Susan stops for a flat white at the Costa Coffee in the square, then cuts down to Prince's Street and onto North Bridge, one of the major conduits between the Old Town and the New(er) Town. North Bridge spans the vast glass roofs of Waverley Train Station, which nestles in the hatchet-shaped gully that splits the city. On one side, the New Town, which looks like it stepped right out of a Regency novel. Prim Georgian terraces in gray or sand-colored stone that conjure up images of ladies in poke bonnets and gentlemen on horseback strolling along.

Across the bridge: the Old Town. A fascinating jumble of genteel and sometimes overly decorative 19th-century architecture and tall, narrow, austere buildings of rough-hewn stone that seep history and untold stories.

"Oh, aye," those buildings seem to say, like craggy old men watching the visitors wandering by. "Aye, I could tell you a thing or two, that I could. Things that'd make your toes curl. Seen much,

I 'ave. Could tell you about the bonny Queen Mary and her lover, who murdered her husband *right down there*! Rode past me hundreds of times, she did. Oh, aye, and both the gentlemen, that fateful night. There's been blood in these streets often enough—stabbings and battles, fights and squabbles. There's been filth, and fine ladies and gentlemen on horses picking through it. Rough lives and soft ones. Stolen bodies, burned witches, whores, pickpockets, religious reformers—oh, I've seen 'em all, that I have. But you don't want to hear about any of that. On your way, then."

*   *   *

The Royal Mile runs in a steep decline from Edinburgh Castle to Holyrood Palace, drawing visitors from the craggy fortress at the top to the fairytale royal residence and the jarringly modern Parliament building at its base. The more adventurous explorers venture down the cramped, dark closes and wynds that branch off the Mile, enticed by names that hint at ancient purposes: Old Tolbooth Wynd. Fleshmarket Close.

Elliot's is about halfway down the Mile, in an area saturated with cafés and restaurants. Just across the street is a cute bakery specializing in sponge cakes and charming afternoon teas, flanked by a pub on one side and a sandwich place on the other. Just a little ways down, a Mexican restaurant faces a Turkish café that serves a confusing mix of Middle Eastern mezze and Scottish favorites.

It wasn't at all like this when Elliot used a modest inheritance to buy his first restaurant. Back then, the Old Town was still thought of as fairly grubby, even a little dangerous. Well-heeled diners stayed, literally, on the other side of the tracks. But Elliot had been born here, and he saw the possibility. He threw himself into his little ten-seater place, doing remarkable things in the kitchen while his wife ran the front of the house. (Grandmother Emily was, by most accounts, a tough and astute businesswoman, and an excellent cook in her own right. Susan was always sorry she never had a chance to know her, but Emily died the year Julia was born.)

Gradually, word spread that Elliot's food made it worthwhile to risk the Old Town, and the right people started to come.

And then the Fringe exploded. Like Elliot, it rooted itself in the area of its birth, even after becoming famous, and so hordes of tourists began flooding the Old Town every August. That rising tide lifted the area, and Elliot's rose too. It expanded into two adjacent buildings, and Elliot and Emily started thinking about opening new restaurants. Glasgow first, just ahead of its own resurgence. Then York. Finally, London. By that time, Bernard had come along, and the family relocated to the south, to be nearer Emily's aging parents and the grand new flagship restaurant.

Susan pauses at the front door and takes stock of the area. Notes the knots of tourists pausing in the middle of the sidewalk to examine maps or take pictures of double-decker buses, oblivious to the glares of irritable locals just managing not to run into them. It's lunchtime, and the cafés and restaurants are filling up, but everyone seems to be passing Elliot's by. Susan's work is definitely cut out for her.

Well, good. She needs a project.

* * *

"Table for one?" The perky hostess smiles at Susan, even as she hastily stashes her mobile phone beneath the podium.

"No, I'm not here for lunch. I'm Susan Napier."

The hostess blinks a few times. "Susan . . .? Oh. Oh!" The smile remains, but now the eyes widen in alarm. "Right! You're—we didn't think you were coming in today."

"I saw no reason to wait," Susan explains, glancing around the dining room. There's only one occupied table that she can see: a young couple reviewing their photos over two barely touched plates of salad that look heavy on the iceberg lettuce. "Seems slow for lunchtime," she observes. "Is it usually like this?"

"Well . . . it's a Tuesday." The girl giggles. A high-pitched, nervous sound.

Susan smiles, hoping to put this girl at her ease, at least a little. She won't get anywhere by alienating staff. "What's your name?" she asks.

"Jen."

"How many reservations for tonight, Jen?"

"Six." There's that giggle again.

"*Six?*" Unless they're all for parties of ten, that won't even fill a third of the restaurant. "How many covers is that?"

"Twelve," Jen squeaks.

Six two-tops. "How many walk-ins do we usually get?"

"On a Tuesday night . . ." Jen's grimace says it all.

Twelve guests. Even if they all order the most expensive food and wine on the menu, there's no way Elliot's will break even tonight.

Susan sighs. "I think I'll go talk to the chef now."

*   *   *

Despite being down in the basement, the kitchen, with its antiseptically white walls, gleaming metal prep tables, and bright lighting, is literally dazzling. Noisy, too, since the exhaust fan is blasting, ferrying away cooking smells. Or it would be if anything was actually being cooked.

To Susan's left, at the bottom of the stairs, are two electric dumbwaiters for ferrying food up to the dining room. Immediately opposite them is the pass: a long, flat table with a shelf above, where food receives finishing touches before going out to the diners. During a busy service, an expediter (often the executive chef) will run the pass, ensuring everything is completed on schedule. But right now there's nobody there. No point, really.

Just beyond the pass are two further prep tables. The sous chef, Paul, stands at one of them, sharpening his knives in a lazy, bored-seeming way. At the other, a short, stocky woman, with blonde hair tightly pulled back in a bun, fillets fish at lightning speed. Nearby, a pair of young trainee chefs chop vegetables, telling jokes about their girlfriends. One of them cackles loudly enough to startle the pastry chef, at work in a separate room with a window that overlooks the main kitchen. He scowls and bangs a warning on the window before going back to folding cream into a chocolate mousse.

Against the farthest wall, a spare, hatchet-faced chef carefully stirs what looks like a pot of béchamel sauce on the stove. Another pot of cullen skink soup bubbles gently on a back burner.

Yet another chef emerges from a passageway to the left of the stove, carrying two cases filled with eggplant. He slams them down next to the trainees, then looks into one of their plastic prep tubs and curses a blue streak about what they've done to the Chantenay carrots.

"The fook am I supposed to do wi' this, eh?" he demands. "Pair o' tits, you are. Start over." He smacks one of them on the back of the head, sweeps the offending vegetables into the garbage, and disappears into the storage room, muttering.

"Told you 'e'd lose his shite," says Paul, without looking up from his knives. "Did you listen? Nooooo. So after you're done, you can go clean the fifteen pounds of sole that just came in. My gift tae you."

The trainees roll their eyes, anticipating a long, unpleasant afternoon, elbow-deep in fish guts. The blonde chef rolls her eyes as well, as she finishes the last of her fillets, tosses it into a tub with the others, and hauls it off toward the walk-in refrigerator.

The door to the dining room opens, and a waitress comes pelting down the stairs, stopping short just behind Susan, who still hovers at the bottom.

"Javier, where the hell is the soup for table fifteen?" the waitress yells over the din.

The chef at the stove jumps, as if startled out of a daydream, and begins ladling cullen skink into a bowl.

The waitress turns her glare toward Paul. "I shouldn't have to do this," she sniffs before turning and clattering back up the stairs.

Paul rolls his eyes. "Yer lucky you've got such a nice arse, missy," he mutters, just loudly enough to be overheard. The trainees titter and nod.

Javier wanders over to a dumbwaiter and carelessly sets the soup in it, sloshing a little over the side of the bowl and onto the presentation plate. He ignores that, closes the dumbwaiter door, and presses a button on the side. It slowly starts to rise.

Paul finally notices Susan standing there. "You lost, lass?" he asks. "Toilet's back upstairs and to the left."

"Thanks, but I'm not looking for the loo," she answers. "I'm looking for Dan."

He snorts. "I'll bet you are."

"I'm Susan Napier."

He stops sharpening immediately and looks up again. "Oh. *Oh.* Yeah. Sorry. Dan's in the office." He points with a knife in the right direction.

"Thank you." Susan crosses the kitchen and just manages to avoid being smacked in the face by the door to the walk-in when it flies open to let out the female chef.

"Oh, sorry about that!" the woman says cheerily.

"Don't worry about it." Susan knocks once on the office door and lets herself in.

* * *

Dan looks up from some paperwork as she enters, and unlike the others, his face indicates he knows exactly who she is.

"Hello, there," he greets her, without getting up. "Didn't expect you today."

"I gathered that," Susan returns, forcing a pleasant smile. She's a bit shocked by what she's just seen both in the dining room and the kitchen, but, as with the front-of-house staff, she's determined to take a friendly approach.

Susan pulls up a chair and sits, continuing, "I thought it was best to plunge right in."

"I'm sure you did."

It's impossible to miss the hard edge in his voice or the way his lips purse a little as she settles in. He'll need a lot of buttering up.

"The kitchen seems really well staffed," she comments.

"Thaaaaanks."

All right. Buttering wasn't going to get her anywhere.

"I wonder if it might not be a little overstaffed, for a Tuesday lunchtime," she says. "Jen says Tuesdays tend to be slow. Is that true?"

He shrugs. "Some days are slower than others. Hard to say which ones those'll be, you know?"

"It's *not* hard, though," she rejoins, struggling to keep her voice even and pleasant. "All you have to do is look at the receipts over time. Patterns emerge."

"Look, I'm a chef, not a statistician."

She wants to scream—or throttle him. Doesn't he care? No, of course he doesn't. This isn't *his* restaurant. This isn't *his* legacy. This isn't the *only* good thing he has left in *his* life. He could pack up and go elsewhere—he doesn't need to prove anything. If this place fails, he won't have let down anyone who matters to him.

And he's been spoiled, too, in the four years he's been in charge here. He's never had to answer to anyone. He's gotten everything he ever asked for, every fancy bit of equipment he insisted they needed. Of course he'll resent having someone looking over his shoulder now.

Once again, Susan forces herself to smile. "Of course, Dan. That's why I'm here, to take over the boring things, like number crunching, so you can focus on the food. Together, we can lift this place back up."

His eyes narrow as he considers what she's just said. "Lift it *back* up?" he repeats. "You think it's fallen, then? And you've come swooping in to save it?"

"Let's be realistic, here—we have an overstaffed kitchen and only twelve covers for dinner. We can't keep going at this pace; we're hemorrhaging money. I don't want to come in here and start firing people, but economies will have to be made somewhere. Maybe we'll close on Tuesdays, if they tend to be slow. Maybe we'll reconsider staff hours or renegotiate with suppliers. This is what I'm here for. I'm not here to tell you how to do your job, Dan, I'm here to *help* you with it. I promise. I want us to work together. Do you think we can do that?"

She holds his gaze and also holds her breath, wondering what he'll do. He might just leave—he's well trained and could probably find another job. She really doesn't want to have to recruit for a new head chef right now.

"All right," he says at last.

Susan breathes out, relieved, and hopes he doesn't notice. "Good. I'm glad to hear we're on the same page. I'll start working some numbers, and why don't you and Paul put your heads together over the menu?"

Now she's done it. She may as well have just called one of his children ugly. He bristles, sensing encroachment on his territory.

"What's wrong with my menu?" he demands, drawing himself up so he's just a little taller than her.

Susan, too, sits up straighter and looks him dead in the eye. He's hardly the first chef she's faced down.

"The food here is very good," she tells him, "but I think the menu would benefit from a refresh. It hasn't changed in years;

some of the dishes are the same ones my grandfather was serving when we first opened."

"Those dishes made this place famous."

"*Innovation* made this place famous," she points out. "But now everyone is doing these dishes. We need to be better. Diners are more discerning than ever. We need to give them something they can't make at home or get anywhere else. It's the only reason they'll come here."

He shakes his head. "You've been in Edinburgh for—what? A few hours? Let me fill you in on a few things you probably don't know yet. You own a restaurant on the Royal Mile, which means that about eighty percent of the customers who come through the door will be tourists who just want 'something Scottish.' They don't care about innovation; they just want to go home and tell their friends they had shortbread and haggis. That's as adventurous as they want to get."

"Thank you," Susan says coolly. "I'll keep that in mind. There's no reason we can't have those things on the menu. I just want them presented in a way people can't get at a dozen places between here and Edinburgh Castle. We have to distinguish ourselves so we get both the tourists *and* the locals, who actually live here and might come back. But they'll only do that if there's something here that entices them."

"Fine," he grunts, swiveling his desk chair away from her and back toward his paperwork. "I'll talk to Paul."

"Good." Susan takes a deep breath. "I really do want us to work together, Dan. We both want the same thing, right?"

"Right."

She presses her eyes closed and counts to ten, to calm herself. Otherwise, she might yank that paperwork away and smack him over the head with it. *You catch more flies with honey,* she reminds herself.

Dan will take some work, definitely. But they'll get there. They have to. Susan stands and extends her hand. He pretends not to see it for several long seconds, then glances over, takes it briefly, and says, "I've got the payroll to do."

"I'll leave you to it, then."

Susan makes her way back through the kitchen and up the stairs. The dining room is empty now, the soup-and-salad pair having already left. She pauses by the bar and looks around, taking the place in.

She doesn't like what she sees.

Like many buildings along this part of the Mile, it's fairly dark, only having windows at the front. And the interior design doesn't help. The woodwork is deep walnut, the carpeting and upholstery maroon. Lighting is low, atmospheric, some might say, but Susan knows that most people like to at least see what's on their plates. And this would do no favors for those who like to Instagram every last bite. The brass trim and fixtures make the place seem dated. She feels overwhelmingly like she's in one of those pubs that try to make people think they're getting some sort of authentic Victorian experience, minus the typhoid. People might like that sort of thing with their pints, but not with venison medallions and velouté.

More than the menu needs to change. Much more. They need to make a splash—no, they need to *explode* back onto the scene—if this tired place is going to regain any attention in a restaurant scene as crowded as Edinburgh's.

Susan Napier is going to have to blow some shit up.

But first: family.

Chapter Four
All Happy Families Are the Same

~

"Thank God you're here!"

Before Susan can react to this unusual greeting, Meg has pulled her inside the house, closed the door, and pointed to a spot just below her chin. "Feel there. Is there a lump? I swear I feel a lump."

"Hi, Meg." Susan obligingly leans forward and probes her sister's neck. "I don't feel anything. I think you're fine."

Meg emits an exasperated yawp, turns on her heel, and marches toward the kitchen at the back of the house. "It's there, I swear I feel it!" she insists.

Susan closes her eyes and takes a deep breath. From the family room to the right come the sounds of video game gunshots and theatrical deaths. She pokes her head in and finds her two older nephews, seven-year-old Andrew and three-and-a-half-year-old Alisdair, engrossed in a first-person shooter.

"Hi, boys," she greets them.

"Hey," Andrew grunts, without looking away from the screen. He frantically punches a few buttons on the controller, and the person in his sights seems to explode, spattering the screen with gore. "All right! Got 'im!" Andrew cheers, punching the air triumphantly .

Alisdair turns away just long enough to reward his aunt with a sweet smile. "Hi, Auntie Susan," he says, waving, before turning back to the game.

Susan continues on to the kitchen, dropping her overnight bag by the door.

"Isn't that game a little . . . old for them?" she wonders aloud.

"Oh, don't you start," Meg snaps. "It keeps them out of my hair for a little while, okay?" She leans against the wooden countertop, engrossed in a tablet. Her youngest ("And last—I mean it this time!"), Ayden, is nestled in a bouncy chair near the propped-open French windows, gurgling up at the moon and stars dangling from a mobile just out of his reach.

"See?" Meg shoves the tablet, which displays the WebMD symptom checker, into Susan's hands. She jabs at the picture. "See? Lump on the neck—thyroid *or* throat cancer."

"Or swollen glands," Susan points out, indicating the list of nearly ten conditions all associated with a bump in the neck.

"Yes, and swollen glands can be associated with *cancer*!"

Susan sets the tablet aside and begins gently but thoroughly checking every last inch of Meg's neck while her sister holds her chin up, sniffling and biting her lip.

"Meg, I really think you're okay," Susan reassures her once she's done. She switches to rubbing her sister soothingly on the back. "I honestly don't feel anything."

"That's what William said this morning. He said I was just dreaming things up because I don't want him to go golfing tomorrow. Like I care if he goes golfing! Though, of course, it does leave me here, alone, with the three little hooligans to deal with."

"You're not alone," Susan reminds her. "I'm going to be here." Meg's generously agreed to house her sister until the furniture arrives at Moray Place later in the week. "And Russell and Helen are just around the corner," she adds.

Margaret rolls her eyes at the mention of her in-laws. "I can't send the boys there. Helen spoils them. Gives them candy all day long and then sends them here to bounce off the walls for hours. Oh, the noise, noise, noise, *noise!*" She groans, squeezing her head between her palms.

"Why don't I make us some tea?" Susan offers. "Maybe something herbal."

"Just not peppermint," Margaret implores. "It was all I could drink when I was pregnant with Ayden, and now I can't even think about it without my stomach turning." She nevertheless turns to smile at her youngest, who drools a little and smiles back.

"Oh, he's got teeth now," notes Susan.

"Four. All came at once. They do come on fast," Margaret sighs. "I only hope I get to live to see the next stage." She reaches up and massages her neck again, making fretting noises.

"Meg"—Susan catches and clasps her sister's hand—"it's okay. You'll be here to see them grow up."

"We used to think that about Mum," Meg retorts. "And then she got a cough—a cough!—and that was it." She and Susan know, better than most people, how horrifyingly fast someone can be there—and then gone. Six weeks they'd had. Barely enough time to arrange hospice care, let alone say or do everything that needs to be said and done. They all sat and watched, helpless, as their mother was devoured. Because she didn't get a cough checked early enough.

Julia had coped (if you could call it that) by partying twice as hard as she ever had and existing seemingly on nothing but champagne and cocktails. Her fledgling interior design business foundered. Meg, at first, escaped from home and traveled, embarking on expensive trips to Thailand, New Zealand, and Kenya. When she was finally persuaded to return to her studies at Edinburgh University, she'd done the same thing Susan had and found someone to cling to. Someone she felt could offer comfort and stability. Unlike Susan, she'd stuck with him.

"If it worries you, call your GP," Susan suggests, filling the kettle and hunting for teabags in the cupboard. "I'll watch the boys while you go."

"I did call. They don't have any appointments until next week, and they didn't believe it was an emergency." Margaret huffs. "I swear, no one cares if I'm alive or dead!"

"You know that's not true." Susan retrieves a box of chamomile teabags and accidentally closes the cupboard with a bit more force than she means to. The sound of it slamming startles Ayden, who jumps and begins to wail.

Meg rolls her eyes again. "Thanks, Suze," she says, turning to unbuckle him from his seat. "Thanks *so much*."

Susan closes her eyes. Surely something will go right today? Eventually? "I'm sorry. Why don't we have our tea outside? It's a nice afternoon."

Meg gathers up Ayden and a rabbit-shaped soother and steps through the French doors, jiggling him on her hip and talking baby talk to him. Susan can hear him laughing again as she fills the teapot, gathers mugs, and joins them outside.

* * *

Two cups of tea and a relaxed chat about London and how the boys are getting on are enough to distract Meg. She forgets about her imaginary lump (for the time being), allows herself a single biscuit, and goes to fetch a hat for Ayden.

Susan cups her mug and settles back in the chair, closing her eyes and turning her face to the sun. The baby laughs and there's a distant rumble of traffic, but otherwise it's fairly quiet. The stillness, after the rush and noise of London, both astonishes and soothes her. It creeps in and pokes at the hard knot in her middle, the wrapped-up anxieties of these past years. There is peace here.

She opens her eyes and looks at Ayden, now playing with a plastic caterpillar that lights up and plays music when he presses buttons. He seems particularly fond of the blue button, which plays "Old MacDonald." His face brightens as he makes it work again, and he waves the toy at Susan, who grins back and thinks of how much he resembles his father.

Meg mollusked herself onto William Cox with a ferocity that made any escape seem impossible. William, a member of a patrician family that could trace its lineage all the way back to John Balliol, met with Bernard's wholehearted approval. The couple married as soon as Meg received her degree (in music, but never used). He took over the family's investment firm, and soon enough the boys came along.

Now, watching Ayden, Susan can't help but wonder how things would have been if she'd held on to Chris the way Margaret had William. Would she be sitting in a garden, watching her own baby playing?

Probably not, she tells herself. Not here, at least. Meg lives in Stockbridge, one of the plushest areas of Edinburgh. Guidebooks keep bafflingly referring to it as "bohemian," which suggests the word is as meaningless as "artisanal." The high street is populated by chic boutiques, cafés, and high-end specialty food shops. On Meg's street, Inverleith Row, tidy stone Victorians look out over the Royal Botanical Gardens. Three of the city's most expensive private schools are within easy walking distance.

No, this is not Chris's sort of neighborhood, Susan decides. He'd hate living here, among the bankers and solicitors and professors. She remembers how uncomfortable he was the one time she took him home for a family dinner. Like he was afraid to touch anything. Or say anything. And she remembers how Greg and the other chefs used to mock him for his rough Leith accent

"Oh, aye, ye braw wee bairn," they'd bray nonsensically. On Chris's first day at Regent Street, they dubbed him Oour Wullie, after the comic strip character. He'd smile, pretending to go along with the joke, but Susan could tell it bothered him. When they all gathered for drinks, and Greg really got going, Chris would clasp his hands under the table and clench them rhythmically. Susan guessed he was imagining he had a good grip on Greg's throat as he did it.

His accent and cheap clothes hadn't played any better at the Napier home. Susan's mother, of course, was warm and kept him engaged with food talk, but Julia and her father sat by, keeping out of the conversation and oozing contempt and disapproval.

"Jesus, Susan," Julia hissed once Chris was gone. "A line cook? Are you *kidding* me? Why not the dishwasher while you're at it? Why not a *plumber?*"

Even Susan's mother sighed and said, "He seems like a very nice boy, Suze, but beware of anyone in the restaurant business. Their hours are . . . not always conducive to a healthy relationship."

What about someone who does nothing? Susan thought sourly. *Is that the recipe for a happy marriage?*

But she bit her tongue. Her mother was already so frail.

* * *

Meg emerges from the house, a blue sunhat in one hand and Andrew close behind, dribbling a football. He gives it a good kick as soon as he's clear of the door, and it sails past Ayden, who's briefly distracted from his caterpillar.

"Mind your brother!" Meg hollers after her eldest, who leaps down from the patio and goes after the ball. He pauses long enough to pat his baby brother on the head as he passes. Meg sighs and good-naturedly shakes her head as she bends and jams the hat onto Ayden. He squeals in protest and then begins to wail as she smears him with sunscreen.

"I know, I know, love, but you'll thank me for it, believe me," Meg soothes. "A big red bus, a big red bus . . ." she sings in a bell-clear soprano.

"Aunt Susan, what'siss?"

Susan turns and sees that Alisdair has dragged her overnight bag to the door, rummaged through it, and found the photo album, which Susan had brought so Meg could see the old family pictures. Susan's clothes and underwear are strewn about the floor at his feet.

"Oh, Ali, don't go through Aunt Susan's things. That's not nice, is it?" says Meg, now massaging sunscreen into Ayden's arms. "Say you're sorry and tidy up."

Instead, he repeats, "What'siss?" and holds the photo album aloft.

"It's pictures, darling." Susan joins him, shoving her things back into the bag. She pauses long enough to open the album to a picture of herself, Julia, and Meg when they were small. "That's me, your Auntie Julia, and your mummy," she explains, pointing to them each in turn.

He looks skeptical. "No, it's not," he says, wrinkling his nose, grinning, and vigorously shaking his head. "*That's* Mummy," he adds, pointing to his mother.

Susan smiles. "Yes, it is," she agrees, patting him on the arm. He drops the album on the floor and joins Andrew. Susan reaches for her last pair of scattered panties just as her brother-in-law, William, comes in.

"Hiya, Suze," he greets her, quickly looking away from the underwear in her hand.

She shoves the pants into her bag and rises to hug him. "Hi, William, how're things?"

"Oh, you know." He shrugs, grins, gestures to his family. "Is she still on about the neck lump?" he asks sotto voice.

"I think we may have moved on." Susan pats him on the arm.

He shakes his head. "I can't tell you how glad I am you're all coming up here. Especially you. Good to have some sense around."

He strips off his suit jacket and tie, tossing both over a nearby chair, and unbuttons his collar.

"Is she getting worse, do you think?" Susan asks, nodding toward her sister.

"I don't know," he admits. "Maybe she's just frazzled. It's a lot with the three. We have a nanny, but she's only part time. And Dad's talking about standing in the next National Election, which he's pretty sure is going to be called soon, so he and Mum have been busier than usual. And work's been a bit mental because of all the upheaval in the Asian markets, but never mind all that." He grins again, this time at Susan. "It'll be fine—it always is. And having all of you nearby'll help, right?" Without waiting for an answer, he walks out onto the terrace. "Take the shot, Ali—you've got him!" he calls.

"Dad!" Andrew and Alisdair shriek, abandoning the football and barreling toward their father, who squats down to embrace them both.

"You're home early," Meg notes, gathering up the baby and going to greet her husband. He stands and kisses her, then takes Ayden and swings him in the air. "Had a meeting cancel," he explains between Ayden's joyful screams. "Thought I'd come home and enjoy some of the beautiful day with my family."

"Mm-hmm," Meg murmurs, glancing Susan's way.

Susan wonders if Meg knows about that Christmas five years ago, when William (very drunkenly) confessed to Susan that he wished he'd met her first.

"It all coulda been very different," he'd slurred, swirling whisky around a glass.

"William, why don't I make you some coffee?" she'd suggested.

He'd never mentioned the conversation again, which made her suspect he didn't remember it.

Susan considers slipping away to allow the family their time together. But then William turns and gestures for her to join them.

"Suze, come on."

Susan smiles and heads toward them, pausing only to jam the album back into her bag and kick the whole thing under the kitchen table.

Chapter Five
Family Dinner

❧

By the time Julia and Bernard arrive on Thursday, the movers have been swarming for over an hour, and Moray Place is an *Ideal Home* obstacle course of chairs you're not really meant to sit on and mirrors too decorative to use. Susan hovers at the foot of the staircase, afraid that if she moves, she'll knock over a lamp worth thousands of pounds.

"Ugh, you did the right thing, flying," Julia declares, shimmying past four boxes marked "layering china." "If you ever find yourself considering a drive from London to Edinburgh, Susan, then slap yourself. *Hard.* Here, I've got your . . . uncle, or whatever." She thrusts a jar of beige goop toward her sister, holding it only by the very tips of her fingernails.

"The *mother*," Susan corrects, snatching the jar and cradling it. This is precious stuff: the sourdough starter, or "mother," that her grandfather began the year he opened Elliot's Edinburgh. He kept it going for decades, regularly feeding it flour and water, and after he died, Susan took it on. It makes the most amazing bread: dense and moist, with a crisp crust. .

"Hallo, Susan, dear," Bernard greets her, leaning over a low bookshelf for a kiss. "Shame about all the chaos. But it's all right, this, isn't it?" He stands back and looks up through the wrap-around staircase to the skylight three floors up, which keeps the hall from feeling gloomy. "We'll do all right here, don't you think?"

"It's nice, Dad," Susan agrees.

"'Nice,' she says." Julia snorts. "There's gratitude. You know part of the reason we got this place was because I thought you might like the kitchen. You just think it's 'nice.'" She sighs as she crosses her arms.

Bernard gives Susan a "fix this" look she remembers well from her childhood.

She takes a deep breath, then smiles. "It's wonderful, Julia. And the kitchen is very . . . roomy."

That seems to appease her. Julia unwinds her arms and begins exploring the rooms, muttering about paint and wallpaper and new throw pillows.

"Good girl." Bernard pats Susan on the shoulder, then smiles proudly after his eldest. "She'll do the place up right. I heard all about her plans on the way up. It's good for her to stay busy, I think. Idleness does no one any good. So, what've you been up to these past few days?"

"I've been at the restaurant mostly."

Bernard blinks in such a way that Susan wonders if he forgot they even have a restaurant in Edinburgh. "Ah, right! Of course! Good. Everything shipshape, I assume?"

"Not quite." She's been trying her damnedest to unscramble the books while Dan hovers nearby, sighing loudly and telegraphing annoyance.

"Well, I'm sure you'll manage to sort it." Bernard's examining the crown molding in the hall, then poking his head into the nearest room.

"And I've been spending time with Meg, of course," Susan adds.

Bernard drags himself away from the woodwork. "How is little Bambi?" he asks. "Still taking fright at every loud noise?" He chuckles.

"She's . . ." Susan wonders if it's worthwhile telling Bernard about Meg's anxiety, which has begun to concern her. She finally settles on, "She seems tense."

"Oh?" Bernard has strolled over to the window and stands looking at the quiet street outside. "Well, it'll be nice for her to have you and Julia around, then. She can talk to you."

"And you," Susan suggests.

Bernard chuckles softly. "Oh, I don't know about that. I'm rubbish at comforting. That was your mother's—" His shoulders sag, almost imperceptibly, and he clears his throat, still staring out the window.

Susan joins him and says quietly, "You know what they say about practice making perfect."

"Hmm." Bernard turns his face away from her just a little, and Susan realizes she'd better change the subject.

"We've all been invited to Sunday lunch at Russell and Helen's."

Bernard turns to her, his usual pleasant expression back in place. "Ah! Good! Nice to catch up with family."

Julia reappears, rolling her eyes. "Do we have to go? There's so much to do here and . . . Russell." She huffs. "He's so . . . Tony Blair-ish."

"Now, now, Julia, of course we'll go. They are family, after all. And if we're to live here, we really must establish ourselves with the right sort of people. I wonder if Russell knows of a good replacement for Keegan? Surely a man in politics gets a little brightener every now and again? And if we're meant to be economizing, I feel I shouldn't be dashing down to London too often."

Julia's eyes slide toward her sister, as if she's waiting for Susan to explode, but Susan's smile only tightens a little as she replies, "That's an excellent plan, Dad."

Julia wanders off toward the dining room and kitchen, and Susan joins her father at the window. "It's a beautiful city, Dad," she says, her smile returning to a genuine level as the two of them look out. "I don't know how you were ever able to leave it."

"Yes, I suppose it's all right here. But, well . . . *London*." Bernard sighs, drooping a little at the thought of what he's left behind.

Susan pats him on the arm. "It'll be better here," she promises. "The festival season is coming. You and Julia will be in your element."

Julia's shriek carries all the way from the kitchen. "Are these brown IKEA mats? Oh, Susan, what am I going to do with you?"

* * *

At two o'clock on Sunday, bearing bottles of wine and wearing mostly forced smiles, the Napiers arrive at Russell and Helen's for lunch. William's parents live right around the corner from their son and daughter-in-law, in an enormous house the color of digestive biscuits that overlooks Inverleith Park.

Russell answers their ring with a hearty "Bernie! Girls! Come in, come in!" Red-cheeked, paunchy in the way of well-cared-for middle-aged men, dressed in khaki trousers and a pink windowpane-check shirt with the top button undone, Russell Cox, Member of the Scottish Parliament, is the very picture of upper-middle-class comfort. He speaks in a soft Scottish burr, which he apparently had to learn before he went into politics. Although he was born in Scotland, he went to the kind of schools that rigorously train regional accents right out of their pupils, leaving them all speaking like members of the royal family. But Scottish voters would almost certainly reject anyone with a posh English accent, so now he speaks like, well, a member of the Scottish royal family.

Russell claps Bernard (who tries not to flinch both at the man-handling and the nickname he never asked for) on the shoulder and bellows over his shoulder, "They're here!"

A pair of Labradors gallop in from the kitchen, and Lauren, the twenty-year-old daughter of the house, races down the stairs, shouting, "Hiya!"

Susan notices that Lauren, as usual, is experimenting with her hair. Last time they'd met, it was a pixie cut, but now it's grown past her shoulders and is dyed a red so dark it's nearly purple.

The dogs launch themselves at the new arrivals, barking and wriggling and wagging. Julia shrinks from the threat of hair or slobber on her pristine silk blouse. Susan hands Julia the tart she brought and diverts the dogs' attention by kneeling down and scratching them each behind one ear. They both lean into it, groaning in pleasure, and Julia is forgotten.

Helen Cox—blonde, smiling, fit in the way of well-cared-for middle-aged women—follows the dogs. Wiping damp hands on a floral-patterned tea towel, she leans over the animals to kiss everyone on both cheeks, greeting each with, "You all right?"

"How was the trip up? Not too bad, I hope?" Russell is asking Bernard, while Lauren raises her voice above the din of parents and pets to tell them all how lucky it is that they came just before the summer got into full swing.

"You'll have time to settle in and get to know the city before all the craziness," she says, hauling the dogs away. "But the Festival! If you want my advice, don't bother with the International Festival— it'll be stuffy. Well, there's *one* show at the International I'll go see, but we'll talk about that later. But the Fringe! It's amazing! Oh, and I've got all sorts of news—Julia, I love your boots!—and I know all about how to get the best tickets. See the free comedy shows, they're fab—the comedians haven't gotten all full of themselves yet, you can see it all really raw. Oh, come on, you two!" She begins hauling the dogs away, herding them, with little success, toward the door open to the back garden.

"Lauren, let them catch their breath, darling," her mother urges. Glancing past the guests, she brightens, waves, and halloos: "Boys!"

Susan turns to see William, Margaret, and the boys coming up the front walk. Meg deflates a little at being overlooked, but

William shouts back, "Hi, Mum! Dad! Napiers all!" and Andrew and Alisdair tumble through the front door, tangling with the dogs and hurling themselves into their grandmother's arms.

"Ah, my little hooligans!" crows Russell, play-boxing with Andrew for a moment before tossing Alisdair in the air.

"Have you got sweeties?" Alisdair asks his grandmother before even saying hello.

"Not before lunch," Meg says, bringing up the rear with an armful of Ayden. "Hi, Jules." She leans over to kiss her sister, but Julia takes one look at the drooling baby and manages only an awkward one-armed hug that keeps her well clear of bodily fluids.

"Hey, Megs," she responds.

Meg turns expectantly to her father, who smiles fondly and reaches over to tickle the baby under the chin, saying, "You've got your hands full there, Meg!"

"Here," Susan offers, taking Ayden so Meg can embrace their father without putting his linen jacket at risk of infant slobber.

Bernard immediately embraces his youngest and kisses her on the cheek. "You look lovely, Bambi, really well."

"Oh, thanks, Dad." Meg's tone makes it seem as if that's the best compliment she's received in a while.

"In, in, come in, everyone," Russell urges, herding everyone along into the sitting room, which looks like a headlong collision between William Morris and Cath Kidston. Florals everywhere, not all of them matching. Julia actually blanches at the sight, but Susan rather likes it. The colors are bright, the furniture soft and inviting. And there isn't a hint of Mole's Breath gray anywhere.

"If you don't mind, I have to see to the roast," says Helen.

"I'll help," Susan offers, setting Ayden down on the floor and following her and the dogs to the kitchen.

"You're a darling," Helen bends down in front of the Aga and pulls out a beautiful roast beef. The rich smell of it fills the kitchen and, like Pavlov's dog, Susan's mouth waters. The actual dogs plunk their bums on the floor in unison, as if they think that, by being good, they'll be rewarded with the whole joint.

"You'll get yours at the end, you two," Helen says to them without even having to look up. She probes the meat with one finger and nods. "I think that's ready for its rest." She moves it to a cutting board, covers it with tinfoil, and leaves it so the juices can redistribute.

"It smells wonderful, Helen, what do you do to it?" Susan asks.

"Not much," Helen admits, now poking around a roasting tin filled with vegetables. "A little oil, salt, pepper, and good, strong mustard. Dijon, not English, but don't tell anyone," she adds with a mischievous smile. "I find that sometimes simpler is better. Especially when you start with good ingredients. We're rather blessed with places to get them, in this neighborhood." She pushes the vegetables back into the oven and closes the door. "If you haven't already, you should visit the Sunday farmers' market. There are wonderful stalls selling meats and fruit and jams. And cakes too, but you're already an expert there, aren't you?"

"Hardly an expert."

"Oh, come now." Helen gestures to the lemon tart Susan brought along. Like the roast, it's simple and classic, but undeniably delicious. Susan smiles her thanks at the compliment.

"Here, would you mind chopping these for the salad?" Helen asks, rummaging in the fridge and producing a bunch of radishes and a knobby cucumber.

"Of course." Susan fetches a knife and small cutting board and begins chopping away.

Helen moves to wash her hands and hovers at the window near the sink for a little while, watching her next-door neighbor. The woman's hacking away at some bushes so venomously that Susan wonders if they've personally offended her in some way. Helen shakes her head and sighs. "If she paid as much attention to her marriage as she does to those hedges, maybe Mark wouldn't have to 'work late' quite so often," she comments.

Susan isn't sure what to say to that. Luckily, Andrew and Ali come running in.

"Mum's gone upstairs to feed the baby," Andrew announces.

"Oh, all right," says Helen, reaching into a cupboard and retrieving two chocolate biscuits. She hands one to each grandson with the admonition, "Don't tell your mother!" Both boys nod solemnly, grab their biscuits, and run outside, where they began kicking around a football while cramming the biscuits into their mouths.

Helen sighs, watching them. "Poor lads. It's quite a strain on them sometimes, with their mother the way she is."

Susan catches Helen's sideways glance but keeps her face neutral. She's not about to be forced into taking sides against her sister, despite her concerns about Meg's hypochondria. Every little thing—a sharp pain, a headache—sets her off. Susan can only imagine what it's like when one of the boys gets sick. They're probably on a first-name basis with every nurse at the children's hospital.

"You've heard about this latest nonsense with the baby, I suppose?" Helen asks, face darkening just at the thought of it.

"No, what's that?" Susan asks, setting the vegetables aside.

Helen pauses, watching the boys a little longer. "Well, I'm not one to gossip," she finally says. "Let's go and pick some lettuce while the meat rests, shall we?"

* * *

They sit down half an hour later at a table barely large enough to hold all the food. There's the meat, and a mass of roasted potatoes, carrots, swede, beets, and onions, lavished with rosemary and thyme. Gravy, and mustard, and some sort of hot-pepper jelly that Helen insists is absolutely perfect with beef—"you have to try it! Just a little."

"No, no thank you," Bernard replies, leaning away from it. "I'm prone to heartburn, you know."

The salad, and a casserole of green and yellow summer squash topped with crispy breadcrumbs. Crusty bread, sliced tomatoes with basil. ("Bought tomatoes, I'm afraid," Helen explains apologetically as she sets the plate down. "Mine won't be ready for a while yet. Too rainy.")

No rain today; the windows and back door are all open to the patio, to catch the fresh breeze that ripples the lilac bushes, unleashing the flowers' heady scent.

Susan understands now why William laughed when she wondered if having three extra people to Sunday lunch might be an imposition.

"Mum doesn't know how to cook for fewer than thirty," he'd answered. "Sometimes I think she secretly believes constituents might come by and need feeding. Bring friends, if you like. Hell, bring strangers—Dad would love it."

Russell stands to carve the roast while the rest of the Coxes fall on the dishes, talking over one another while the Napiers sit back, blinking and trying to take it all in.

"Oh, Susan, you really must try the summer squash—they're so sweet this year. Here, let me give you some."

"—Did you hear that Leonardo DiCaprio's going to be filming a new movie in Glasgow? A friend of mine's managed to get a job as an extra and she says she can get me onto the set."

"—Andrew, for God's sake, don't take *all* the potatoes. Give some to your brother, will you?"

"—So I said to him, Bob, we really can't keep having this discussion week after week after week. Either you're in favor of making people earn their benefits, or you're not. We just aren't in a position, as a country, to tolerate layabouts, now are we? Rare, or medium, Bernie?"

"What? Oh, well done, if you have it."

"We don't, sorry. Medium it is."

A deep pink slab of meat, oozing juices, lands on Bernard's plate. Julia, sitting beside her father, looks sick.

"Just salad for me, please," she whispers.

"Oh, my dear, you must have a little more than that," Helen implores.

"No, no, it's all right, it's just—"Julia casts about for an excuse. "Just I've recently gone vegan."

Half the table actually stops talking. William blinks at her as if she's just spoken in a foreign language. Russell wonders, "Why would anyone want to do such a thing?"

"Oh, dear," Helen flutters, sensing a dire hostessing failure. "I wish you'd said something, Julia, I would have gotten you one of those tofu-burger thingies. They have some at Waitrose that Mary next door says are quite edible."

"It's all right," Julia reassures her, helping herself to some salad.

"I was thinking about going vegan," Meg pipes up. "Is it hard? Do you have any recipes you could send me?"

Julia, realizing this particular lie is about to get out of hand, buys herself some time by stuffing a few bits of rocket into her mouth and chewing far longer than she needs to.

Susan turns to Lauren. "What other news is there, Lauren? Did I miss anything while I was in the kitchen?"

"No, I saved some of it because I thought you'd be interested," Lauren says. "Do you know who's coming here to do a play during the Festival? The International Festival, that is—and I may actually have to go to this play just because he's in it."

"Philip Simms," Julia supplies.

Lauren droops. "How did you know?" she shrieks. "Do you read *Arion Nation* too?"

Now *all* conversation stops. Seven pairs of adult eyes bore into Lauren. Andrew takes the opportunity to spear more potatoes.

"Sorry, what?" Julia asks.

"Rufus Arion's blog," Lauren clarifies. "What?" she asks the table at large. "Why are you looking at me like that?"

"Is that seriously the name of his blog?" Susan asks, amazed that, even in an era of shock value and historical ignorance, anyone would consider that appropriate.

Lauren waves her hand. "Oh, yeah, I know—terrible, right? Part of me feels like I shouldn't read it just on principle, but he does have a lot of really good information, and he's a lovely writer, so I just try not to think about it too much, you know?"

"I think that's a stance that's used with that particular name too much already," Julia mutters, only just loudly enough for Susan to hear.

"Kids, eh?" Russell chuckles. "Social media." He reaches over and ruffles his daughter's hair. "Best not to go bandying about that you read that blog, all right?"

"Dad, come on." She ducks away from him, even as she smiles. "I'm not an idiot. I know to be careful so I don't harm your career. Anyway, how do you know about Philip?" she presses Julia.

"My aunt told me. She's in the play as well." Julia glances at Susan. "It was supposed to be a surprise. Sorry."

"Oh, wow!" Lauren's eyes widen and her face lights up. "Do you think she could introduce me to Philip? My friend Sarah too? Sarah's a huge fan—practically obsessed! He'll probably want to take out a non-harassment order against her." Lauren giggles.

"Then I'll make sure she's the first one he meets," Julia promises.

Lauren misses the cool tone of Julia's voice and chatters about how now she'll actually see something at the International Festival, because you *have* to support family, and also *Philip Simms*! And she doesn't care that Liam will roll his eyes and tell her she's *so* middle class.

"Now, Lauren, Liam's a nice boy, and it's not nice to talk about people when they aren't there to defend themselves," her mother chides.

Out of the corner of her eye, Susan can see the slight tightening of Julia's jaw whenever Philip Simms is mentioned. Julia's left off toying with her salad and is now glaring at a cherry tomato so hard Susan half-expects it to combust.

Years ago, Julia actually met Philip at some fancy club in London. And she made a *very* hard play for him, only to find herself rebuffed (an extreme rarity for her). And then, outrageously, she was escorted from the club by some polite security who called her a taxi and suggested she call it a night. It was a drama Susan almost certainly never would have been aware of except that, as it unfolded, Julia was energetically texting about it, having mixed up Susan-the-sister with Susan-the-friend. So Susan-the-sister was a rather baffled distant witness to the whole thing. Once she'd sobered up, Julia was mortified to discover what she'd done. Susan was never sure which had stung her sister worse: Philip's rejection or her own knowledge of it.

"A matinee might be best," Lauren muses. "Fewer people, probably. You don't want to be crowded in with a bunch of old ladies complaining about the weather. Oh, and they *do*. Everyone complains about the weather here, even when it's good. 'It won't last,' they'll snip. Why can't people just be happy? I can probably get a group of friends to come to the show, and that'll be fun. Even if the play's boring, Philip's pretty yummy, isn't he? Maybe he'll take his shirt off or something. That'd be all right, wouldn't it, Dad? If I take an afternoon off to see the play?"

"Lauren's helping out in Russell's office for the summer," Helen explains. "We thought it would be good for her to have some real-world experience. And to stay busy over the break," she adds with a slightly strained smile.

"Course it's all right, sweetheart," Russell answers. "You see as many shows as you like; you're only young once. Besides," he adds, noting the subtle raise of his wife's eyebrow, "it's educational. Cultural education. Broadens the mind, like travel."

"I totally agree," Bernard chips in. "Did I ever tell you about that wonderful little museum I stumbled across the last time I was in Mallorca? Changed my life, let me tell you—"

"I've got some other news," Lauren interrupts. "You might be interested in this one, Susan. You know Chris Baker, the chef?"

Susan goes hot and cold in quick succession, and her heart thumps hard. Now it's Julia's turn to give her a side-eye.

"Chris Baker?" Susan squeaks. Does Lauren know about her and Chris? She can't possibly—that was long before Meg married William.

Lauren nods. "Yeah, the chef. You know, he had that television show in America? And oh, talk about yummy!" She giggles. "He's opening a restaurant. Here, in Edinburgh."

Susan's body repeats the hot-cold-thump. She blinks at Lauren. *Act normal. Act normal. Actnormalactnormalactnormalactnormal!*

"Oh?" she manages to respond, before turning her attention back to her plate.

"Yeah! Isn't that great?" Lauren beams.

"Did you read that on *Arion Nation* as well?" Julia asks.

"No, I got it from the man himself. Well, sort of. Dad heard through someone that Chris was coming back to Edinburgh to open a restaurant, so he asked about Chris doing the food for some political event thing in two weeks—"

"'Political event thing' indeed," her father chuckles. "I'm only entertaining the top Westminster Tories, including the Chancellor of the Exchequer."

"Are you really?" Bernard breathes.

"Yes. Oh, and you must come, all of you. Going to be a good time, I promise."

"No one knows a good party like the Tory inner circle," Julia observes.

"Whatever." Lauren flaps her hand at Russell, who pipes down so she can continue her story. "His publicist didn't think he'd do it because he's super busy just now, of course, and he's only just arrived, but then the other day he telephoned and said he'd do it after all. And I took the call and had a really nice talk with him. He sounds sexy."

"Didn't he used to work for us or something?" Meg wonders, wrestling a roll out of Alisdair's hand and jamming it into Ayden's. "The name's familiar."

"If he did, I certainly don't remember," Bernard replies sharply. Susan frowns at him across Julia, puzzled. She'd brought Chris home to dinner. Had her father really forgotten that? And even if he had, Chris is famous and good looking, which means he ticks two of her father's most important boxes. Surely Bernard, of all people, would remember and cling to a connection with a now-famous chef.

But Bernard is staring down at his plate, lips pursed in a way that would only encourage wrinkles. Susan's never seen him look like that.

Julia closes her eyes in one long blink, then says, "Of *course* you remember him, Dad. He was Granddad's pet." She glances meaningfully at Susan. "Wasn't with us long, though."

Bernard clears his throat and runs his fingers across his lips, smoothing them. He looks back up at Russell. "Well, then, Russell, does this mean we can expect you to make a run for Westminster soon? Surely you're not going to waste your talents up here forever?"

"Oh, now, now." Russell grins and taps the side of his nose with his forefinger.

"You know what? I forgot to bring out the peas!" Helen cries, half-rising.

Susan springs out of her chair, grateful beyond measure for the forgotten veg. "I'll get them."

In the kitchen, she finds the peas, still in the strainer, fetches a bowl for them, and then decides to get some mint from the pots just outside the back door. Once out in the air, with the noise of the dining room reduced to an indistinct murmur, she leans against the wall of the house, closes her eyes, and breathes. Rubs her palms against the rough stone, gathering herself.

Chris is not in Edinburgh for a visit, as she'd hoped. He's going to live here. He's opening a restaurant here.

The high-end restaurant world is a small one, and incestuous, especially in a city this size. Staff move between a handful of places, go to the same events, drink at the same bars. Everyone knows one another, or has at least one friend or acquaintance or former colleague in every other restaurant of note in the city, and even beyond. There's no way Susan will be able to avoid him. Jesus, she'll be eating his hors d'oeuvres at Russell's party in two weeks! How awkward will that be? She supposes she can plead off, but that seems disloyal. Sometimes, you have to do things you don't want to, for family.

Julia sticks her head out the door. "You're taking a very long time with those peas. Helen's starting to think you got lost."

"Sorry." Susan bends down and snatches a handful of mint out of the nearest pot. "Just came out for some mint and air."

Julia narrows her eyes. "You all right?" she asks. "You seemed a little strange when Lauren brought up Chris Baker."

"God, Julia, that was years ago," Susan replies, slipping past her, back into the kitchen, hoping she sounds convincing. "I'm just not happy to hear we'll have more competition, that's all." She grabs a knife and begins shredding the mint.

Julia watches her for a little while, arms crossed, then says, "I know you saw the photo in that album."

Susan pauses in her chopping but doesn't look up. "Is that why you were going to get rid of it? To protect me?" It surprises her that Julia should be so considerate, even in a fairly misguided way.

"No." Julia's voice is a little strangled. "There were a lot of other pictures in there, and I—" She clears her throat and Susan looks up, startled, remembering all the photos of them as children. And their mother. Happy, sunny days.

Julia's concentrating on a ring on her right hand, centering the stone just so on her middle finger. "Anyway," she shrugs, "with that, and now him being here . . . just thought it might have thrown you off. But you say you're fine, so I'll just go tell Helen you're still in one piece, then. Oh, and Meg says could you please mash some of those peas up for the baby? Apparently peas and bread are almost all he'll eat."

Chapter Six
How the Sausage Is Made

~

The furniture placement has displeased Julia, and so new movers are brought in early on Monday to spend the day getting Moray Place just as she wants it. Susan guesses they'll be returning in a week to start shifting it all again. And then again in a month, once Julia has decided on new wall colors and window treatments.

Bernard takes one look at the chaos of men and furnishings and decides: "I think it's best I not be underfoot. Julia, darling, phone my mobile when peace is restored, will you?"

Julia issues instructions and then heads to the kitchen to make coffee. Susan is already there, piling some freshly baked cardamom buns on a cooling rack.

"Don't worry—they're not for you," Susan reassures her, noticing Julia's wary look. "I thought the movers might appreciate some elevensies." It's a likely enough excuse. In truth, Susan's been on a baking binge ever since they returned from the Coxes' the previous day. The biscuit tin is now full of cranberry-pecan biscotti, and a sourdough loaf is enjoying a nice, slow rise in the fridge.

"What *is* that?" Julia wonders, prodding at the fleshy bulge of dough swelling above its bowl.

"Don't poke it, please—you'll let all the air out," Susan warns.

Julia snatches a bag of ground coffee from the top shelf of the fridge and goes to fill the kettle. "Suppose I should start ordering paint samples," she muses, measuring coffee into a large cafetière. "Or maybe I'll wallpaper this time . . ."

"Julia, I want to run something past you," Susan says, sidling up to her sister and offering her a cup of tea.

Julia looks guarded. "Do you?"

"I do. I'm planning to refurbish the restaurant and then do a full relaunch with a new—well, fairly new—look and menu."

Julia sips her tea. "Sounds expensive. I thought we were meant to be tightening our belts."

"I don't want to spend money unnecessarily, but this *is* necessary, I think. The place is floundering; we have to do something big to kick it back on track."

"And how is this going to be paid for?"

Susan takes a deep breath. "That's the thing. I'm going to have to dip into the family funds for it."

"The family funds! What're we going to live on? We're already cutting right back to the bone as it is. Practically on bread and water!"

Hardly, Susan thinks, eyeing the specialty coffee from Artisan Roast, and her sister's Stella McCartney dress.

"Jules," she implores, "you've been really great about all this, and I appreciate it. It won't have to be too much. And if the restaurant recovers, then so will the investment."

Julia leans against the countertop, arms crossed, eyes narrowing. "How much?"

"That depends on you."

"How so?"

"I want you to take charge of the refurbishment."

Eyes un-narrow. Julia now blinks at her. "Me? You want *me* to redo the restaurant?"

"I do. If you're not too busy with the house, that is."

"No, no, the house can wait!" It's been so long since Julia had anything other than her own sitting room to do over. A restaurant is a whole new challenge. Susan can practically see the ideas ticking over behind her sister's bright blue eyes.

Susan smiles. "So you'll back me up with Dad, then, when I ask for the money?"

"Of course!" Julia nibbles her bottom lip for a moment, then says, "You know, it might be best if I ask him." She pats her sister on the shoulder. "You know how hard it is for him to say 'no' to me."

"Oh, I know," says Susan. "We'll *both* talk to him. In the meantime, why don't you come by the restaurant and have a look around? Start making plans."

"Yes, all right. I'll see how things go here and let you know."

The teakettle starts whistling for attention. Julia turns back to the coffee, and Susan packs up some of the buns.

"Where're you off to?" Julia asks her.

"Thought I'd take a walk and then get to the restaurant early," Susan explains. "See you later."

* * *

Susan hikes up Calton Hill, a curious, monument-dotted rise with spectacular views, located at the east end of Prince's Street. On the northern side, you can stand in the shadow of the unfinished National Monument (modeled on the Parthenon, the project ran out of funds before more than a series of columns could be erected. It looks like a very large, very heavy piece of theatrical scenery). From there, you can look across Leith and the Firth, to Fife, hazy in the distance.

To the east, the tall tower of the Nelson Monument provides an exclamation point termination to Prince's Street. Beyond that, Arthur's Seat, an ancient, long-dormant volcano, rises high over Edinburgh. A grassy giant lying in great humps, jutting its rocky chin at the city, it reminds the genteel Georgian terraces that this used to be a much more violent and dangerous place. Now it's frequently dotted with tourists and furred with mustard-yellow flowers on the gorse bushes that grow wild on its slopes.

To the south is the gracious, temple-like memorial to Dugald Stewart. It enjoys one of the most iconic views of the city, overlooking the Castle, the old and new towns, the Balmoral Hotel's commanding clocktower, and the mist-topped peaks of the Pentland Hills in the distance.

Susan makes a full circuit of the hill, absorbing the views, stopping by the National Monument and spreading her arms. Stretching, expanding her lungs, she breathes Scotland in and London out and hopes—believes—convinces herself—that things will be better here.

She looks over the city, toward Leith, and thinks of all the work ahead of her. And the uphill battle she's facing with her chef.

She has no time for that.

Out there is a city crowded with restaurants, from fast-food takeaways to Michelin-starred destinations. Elliot's needs to elbow its way back in, find its place. *Compete.*

Somewhere down there, in Leith, yet another restaurant is poised to open. She imagines Chris is already in the kitchen. He will be—she knows he will be—hard at work. Perfecting recipes, teaching them to his fellow chefs, finalizing details. Ready to leverage his fame and his incredible talent into creating the sort of restaurant that will crush places like Elliot's.

The clock is ticking. She can't play nice forever. There's work to be done.

While she considers her next move, scattered clouds over the Forth suddenly clump together, race to Calton, and dump rain, as Scottish clouds are wont to do. Susan laughs—Scotland, after all!—descends, and walks the short distance to the restaurant.

The blonde chef (Gloria Przybylski, Susan has now learned—a name that seems at odds with her very Edinburgh accent) is checking in some orders when Susan arrives. She takes one look at Susan and laughs.

"See you got some Edinburgh sun!" she says, tossing Susan a kitchen towel.

"Thanks," says Susan, drying her damp face and setting the bag of cardamom buns on a prep table. "Some breakfast pastries, if you want."

"Aye, I do!" Gloria helps herself to one, taking a moment to appreciate the beautifully knotted little bread before taking a bite. "Ooh, someone stopped by Soderberg Bakery."

"No, I made them."

"A baker! Ace!" Gloria grins and goes back to checking the deliveries.

"Are you the only one in?" Susan asks, glancing around the curiously quiet kitchen, as if that would somehow make chefs appear.

Gloria shrugs. "It's like this most mornings. The apprentices are here. In the walk-in, putting things away."

"And Dan?"

"Office."

"Paul?"

"Gets in later."

"*He* should be checking in supplies," Susan mutters, lifting the lid on a box of onions.

Gloria smirks. "He and Dan agree that this is good for my career development."

Susan looks up with a raised eyebrow. She's read Gloria's CV: she doesn't need this kind of career development. She's spent more than a decade working in some of the best kitchens in Scotland and the North of England. "And what do you think?"

Gloria lowers her clipboard and looks Susan right in the eye. "I think I'm doing this so Paul can sleep in and Dan can update his Tinder profile."

Susan nods. "How does everything look?" She gestures to the food Gloria's checking.

"I sent back some of the fish, but the rest of it's all right."

Two of the apprentices appear, and Gloria directs them to some boxes filled with produce.

Susan reaches into a large plastic bag lying on one of the prep tables, and pulls out a roll. Just by looking at it, she can tell it's going to be lousy. It has no crust to speak of, and the sides are wrinkled, which suggests there's no structure inside. Sure enough, when she tears it in half, the interior is gummy and underdeveloped. "You should have sent these back too," she grunts.

"We'll not get anything better. Not from that supplier," Gloria answers, grimacing in agreement.

"There's no excuse for lousy bread nowadays," Susan declares, setting the roll aside.

"I've suggested other places to try, but Dan says most customers don't know the difference."

"Well, he's wrong about that," says Susan, crossing her arms and leaning against the prep table, mentally preparing herself for an argument with her chef.

"Preaching to the choir, you are," Gloria singsongs. "Everybody's starting sourdough cultures and watching Paul Hollywood wail about gluten structure on *The Bake-Off*. They know their bloody bread."

"They know a lot more than that." Susan shakes her head. There's a hot spurt of anger building in her chest. "Right—I'll be back." She straightens her shoulders and strides to the chef's office, reminding herself that, while she wants this relationship to be a partnership, ultimately she owns this place and Dan is her employee.

She tries to ignore the fact that the rain has left her hair stringy and her top a bit more clingy than she'd like.

"Have a nice weekend?" Dan asks, hastily closing a browser window on the computer as she enters his office.

"I did, thank you. And you? I'm looking forward to seeing the receipts from the last three nights. You told me on Thursday the weekends tend to be busier."

"Riiiight. Yeah, it was busier." He's looking everywhere but at her.

"Was it really?"

"Yeah. A bit." He's toying with a fake cactus on his desk now.

"May I see the receipts?"

He takes his time, fussing around with various paperwork, but finally hands them over. It takes Susan all of a minute to go through them and discover that "busier" means "we had ten tables on Saturday night." That hot spurt builds to an actual flame, fueled by his indifference.

Susan sets the receipts aside. "Dan, this isn't enough, and you know it. How's the new menu coming along?"

"Paul and I are talking about it."

"And when can I expect to see some ideas? When do you plan to start testing new recipes?"

"Soon."

She wants to scream. And cram that stupid fake cactus right down his throat. Instead, through tight lips, she says, "We really have to talk about some changes, and that starts with the running of the kitchen."

She can see his protest gathering in a deep frown and blazing eyes. At least now she knows what it takes to light some kind of fire under him. Before he can form an argument and try to drown her out, she continues, "I realize the running of the kitchen is meant to be your department, but it's all part of the overall running of the business, and that's my job. And I have to say, I'm a bit disappointed with what I've been seeing. Gloria should not be checking in all the supplies; that's your job or the sous chef's job. And why isn't Paul in yet? It's nearly ten and there's a lunch service to prep for."

"We did a lot of our prep last night," he explains, getting to his feet so he can stand above her.

Susan stiffens her spine but keeps her tone even. He won't provoke her. "Even so, he should be here to organize the supplies. It's not Gloria's job. If you want it to be her job, since she's doing so well with it, then promote her to sous chef and send Paul packing."

"I can't do that!"

"Then make him do his job! You're chef de cuisine, so get out of this office and run your kitchen!

His glower actually seems to be giving off heat. She imagines he's trying to sear her with it, force her to give up, tuck tail, and run.

She won't run.

"Dan," she says, switching to a different tone. Conciliatory. "I really don't want to tread on your toes, but surely you agree that changes need to be made." She gestures to the receipts. "We're simply not breaking even, and it's not because it's the off-season, because there isn't really an off-season in Edinburgh anymore. There are always people around who need feeding, and we simply can't afford to slack off and just hope they wander through the door. The restaurant scene in this city is competitive, and we need to compete. If we don't"—she takes a deep breath, remembering those blank faces at Regent Street, staring up at her as she stumbled through her speech—"then we'll have to let people go." *Starting with you,* she doesn't add.

"Maybe we should just convert to a chippie," Dan sniffs. "The students and the Americans will love it, and all we'll need is a fry cook."

"Let's not be dramatic, please; it won't help," says Susan, barely suppressing an eye roll. "Change will. And on that subject, we're going to be closing down the restaurant for a little while and refurbishing."

He blinks at her. "What? When? You're shutting the place down without consulting me? All that nonsense about this being a partnership! I knew you were full of shit!"

Stand firm, stand firm. "I'm sorry to blindside you, but it needs to be done, and ultimately it's my decision. You see to the running of the kitchen—there's clearly plenty of work to be done there. I mean, my own family didn't even think to come to us for food. Something's going wrong here, and we need to fix it quickly, and the only way to do that is a complete overhaul."

"I thought you said dramatics wouldn't help," he spits out.

"It's not dramatics; it's plain fact. And I don't have the time or the capacity right now to coddle a kitchen diva, so you need to get on board or we'll have to consider a change." They stare each other down for a few long, silent moments. "Now," Susan says, "do you want to tell the rest of the staff what's happening, or shall I?"

"You may as well do it," he answers. "You're dying to be in charge."

"I *am* in charge," she informs him. "We'll be closing down and announcing the refurbishment by the end of the week. And I want you and Paul to have a new menu proposal by then as well, so you can start testing recipes. Oh, and Dan? If I see Gloria doing the inventory again, I'm going to assume it means Paul no longer works here."

* * *

"Feeding Tories!" Calum Walsh punctuates this exclamation by sinking a butcher's knife deep into the side of a half pig lying on the butcher-block table in front of him. "I know we were bound to sell out, mate, but did we have to do it before we even opened?"

Chris is focusing on a delicate sauce that's in danger of breaking, and takes his time answering. "I was on television," he says at last. "Selling out is second nature to me now. And I hate to break it to you, but the prices we're charging, we're going to be feeding a lot of Tories."

Calum laughs and, with another whack of his knife, separates the pig's shoulder from the rest of the body.

"Besides, they can be our guinea pigs," Chris reminds him. "We'll try out some of our ideas on them, and if they boak, we'll know not to serve 'em to anyone else."

"Excellent business strategy there," says Calum. "Nothing like a load of politicians spewing up your food two weeks ahead of opening."

Two weeks. Chris can't quite believe it's only two weeks away. Or that he's standing in his own kitchen, which he's planned and laid out himself, overlooking a dining room that will soon (so soon!) be filled with diners eating his food.

Well, his and Calum's. Chris's sous chef came over from Ireland back in the day to work at Elliot's. He and Chris started and came up at the same time. But while Chris unexpectedly went on to fame, Calum languished and wasted his talents at a country house hotel in Cornwall. He was only too eager to give up endless chicken liver toasts and overdone beef to return to Edinburgh.

"I swear, the menu at that place hasn't changed in twenty years," he moaned. "Mind you, neither has the clientele—more blue hair than a Katy Perry concert and *far* less hot."

Calum turns to Rab, the pale, gangly apprentice meticulously chopping onions on the adjoining table.

"I know why he agreed to it," Calum says to the boy, with a knowing look Chris's way. "The cute daughter."

Rab's head snaps up.

"Mind what you're doing!" Chris says, gesturing to the boy's knife, which is still slicing through the onion, even though Rab's attention is elsewhere. "And don't listen to a word this numpty says." Now he gestures to Calum, who laughs again.

"Say what you will, but that girl'd make me agree to most anything. You saw her, Rab, what d'you think?"

Rab turns bright red and hyper-focuses on those onions.

"Leave him be," Chris warns his friend.

Chris hates to admit it, but Calum's right: Lauren's just the sort of girl to make you turn and stare. She's petite, but lithe as a willow branch. Her hair, which curls at the ends, frames a sweet oval face with green eyes and cupid's-bow lips. She doesn't wear much makeup. He likes that. Susan never wore much either.

Lauren, he realizes, is attractive the way many healthy, carefree young people are: full of energy and enthusiasm, still seeing the world as a place of opportunity instead of one of striving and struggle. Life is still sweet for her, her optimism and good nature unblunted by the pressures and realities of adulthood.

She bounded into the restaurant that morning to choose the menu for her father's party. Trailing behind was a staid staffer who clearly felt she had better things to do.

"Dad sent me because I know what he likes," Lauren explained, galloping toward Chris to shake his hand. "And he sent Rachel to make sure I don't do anything crazy," she added, indicating the staffer. "So nice to meet you," Lauren continued, grinning in a way that lit up her whole person. "Face-to-face, that is. But it was really nice talking on the phone the other day. I love your show. And this restaurant. It'll be great once you open. I'll bring some friends and we'll all sit right there." She pointed to the bar that ran along one side of the open kitchen. The "Chef's Table" they're calling it, and charging an extortionate fee for people to sit there and have a special meal cooked just for them by Chris himself. Chris hates the idea of having to take time to schmooze people there, but these are the things you need to do to pull ahead. And if they all look like Lauren, he might not mind.

Lauren kept up a steady stream of chat all through the tasting, exclaiming over the food and talking about her father and her friends and her plans for the summer and asking Chris what it was like living in America and being on TV, and did he miss it? And how did he like being back in Edinburgh? Was it a wonderful homecoming? Must have been, because this is a nice city, isn't it? Nothing like New York, of course, but more laid back, you know? Which is nice.

Nice. Yes, it is.

He found himself smiling at her—really smiling, which he rarely did anymore, outside the kitchen. No polite, close-lipped smile like he had given the woman at JFK, but an actual honest-to-God grin. He was sorry when she and Rachel had to go.

"You liked her," Calum teases, finishing up the last of the pig carcass and sorting pieces into various bins for storage.

"She's a bit young for me," says Chris. "More Rab's age."

"How about it, Rab? Fancy dating a Tory's daughter?" Calum asks the boy, who blushes yet again. "I can't say how she'll age, since she's half her dad and Lord knows he's nothing to look twice at, but her mum's quite fit, so it may be all right. I've always heard that if you want to know what a woman will look like later in life, have a look at her mum."

Chris wonders if his sister looks anything like their mother at the same age. They have no way of knowing: Mum disappeared when he was six and Beth nine. They came home from school one day, and she was just gone. Their father never said anything about it, never mentioned her again. It was as if she'd never even existed. If he hadn't been able to confirm it with Beth, he'd almost have thought he made her up.

"Speaking of fit women," says Calum, as if he's just read Chris's mind, "is Beth coming to the opening?"

"She is," Chris answers, gesturing for Rab to join him so he can demonstrate how to make the sauce he's working on.

It took some doing, convincing Beth to come.

"What, me come all the way there tae eat dainties with a bunch o' bankers? Are ye aff yer heid?" she'd bellowed into the phone. Curiously, as Chris's accent went "posh" (Beth's words)—a necessity if he was to be understood by an American TV audience—hers thickened like hollandaise. So much so that even Chris struggles to understand her from time to time. It's as if she thinks she has to be Scottish enough for the both of them.

"Beth, please, I'd really like to have you here," he begged, even though he knew she'd come no matter what he said. Still, he knew she'd appreciate feeling wanted. "I promise, there'll be no bankers. It's just family, friends, and a few critics."

"Critics! Bunch o' richt bawbags, if ye ask me!"

"I didn't," he replied, clenching his teeth and reminding himself that he loved his sister and she loved him, and this was just her way. "And I need them. And I need you, Beth. Please come. Mollie will be here."

A pause, then: "Mollie? Mollie Wilson?"

"Of course, Mollie Wilson."

Another pause. "She still talks tae you, then? Always was a good 'un, Mollie. Weel, that changes things, dunn it? Can't leave her alone there with all 'em . . . critics."

Even so, he had to agree to arrange all her travel from Aberfeldy and put her and the dogs up at his flat for the duration of her stay. He doesn't mind, really. He likes the dogs. And he wants Beth there.

"Oh!" Calum now leans back and dramatically clutches his heart. "Beth's coming! The best news I've heard all day!" He turns to Rab. "That, my friend, is a fine woman. A fine, fine woman.

Take note when she gets here, my boy—find someone just like her. She will always be honest with you, won't take or give any bullshit, won't play games. That's what you need in a partner, amirite, Chris? Especially a partner in this business."

"Honesty's the best policy?" Rab tentatively supplies.

"Right you are, lad!" Calum grabs a tub filled with pork. "Now, why don't you come with me and see how the sausage is made?"

Chapter Seven
A Certain Uneasy Gloom

Susan senses trouble as soon as she comes through the door at Moray Place. Pausing, her key still in the lock, she assesses. Is it some tension in the air? A certain uneasy gloom?

The movers are gone; all the furniture is in its place (for now). The house is quiet. Except for . . .

There it is! Dan's voice. A murmur floating her way from the sitting room to her left. Not the sulky tone he uses with her, but a jovial, convivial one. The sort you use on job interviews, when you're trying to win people over and convince them you're just right. And her father's voice, answering. A light tone as well.

Susan yanks the key out of the lock, closes the door loudly, and pushes into the room.

As she thought, Dan is there, sitting on the very edge of the sofa, leaning toward Bernard, who is ensconced in the precious Eames chair. Both men look up as she comes in. Dan smiles, but in a way that seems dark to her. There's something in his face that says, "I've got you." Bernard's smile is tight with irritation.

"Oh, Susan," Bernard says, "the chef has come to talk to me." His tone adds an unsaid: "Why is this person talking to me about restaurant things?"

"Has he, indeed?" Susan says, turning to Dan. She does not smile. And both Dan and her father notice that the tension is steadily ratcheting up as she stands there. "And what's so important, Dan, that you have to bother my father? You know he's retired, don't you? Which means he has nothing to do with the running of the business?" She directs that as much toward Bernard as at Dan.

"He was just telling me that you plan to close down the restaurant," Bernard answers. "I thought we moved here so we wouldn't have to close the restaurant down. Wasn't that the whole point?"

"It was," Susan reassures him. "It's a temporary closure while we refurbish and overhaul the menu. Did you not have time to get to that bit, Dan?"

"Well, I've only just arrived," Dan excuses.

"Still, though. Closing down . . ." Bernard murmurs, shaking his head, "and refurbishing? Won't that be"—he lowers his voice a little—"expensive?"

"Julia's going to handle the redecoration," Susan explains. "She had a look this afternoon and doesn't think it'll be too bad."

That's half true. When Julia first arrived, she looked around, face mostly impassive, only her widening eyes revealing particular disgust now and again. Susan guessed that interior designers had to perfect the art of not looking horrified. It was probably a whole class they had to take at design school.

"We should tear everything out and replace it with new," Julia finally declared. "Move the bar in there"—she gestured to the dining room on the right—"so people sitting at it don't get a cold blast every time the door opens. And put up some sort of a wall here"—now pointing just to the left of the door—"to protect the diners in the main room. A glass wall, I think, so the space still feels open. Rip up the carpeting and go for a wood floor. All new lighting, of course, and new upholstery. Maybe get something bespoke; it can be part of the branding. And speaking of branding, that'll need an overhaul too. New logo, new menu covers. And new plates and glassware. Should we see about installing a fireplace we can light in the winter? I think we should. It'll give the space a focal point."

"We can't move the bar," Susan told her. "Not now. You can have your wall, but no bespoke textiles, and the fireplace isn't happening just now either. But I agree with you on the lighting."

Julia nodded. Obviously negotiation was important in this line of work too. "At least let me *ask* about some kind of a fireplace. A gas one—something people can gather round in the cold months. People love that sort of thing; it'll be another selling point. I'll just inquire, okay?"

"All right," Susan agreed. "But we'll be setting a firm budget, you and I, and all expenditure goes through me."

"You're the boss," Julia responded with a sarcastic smile, but her eyes were already gleaming at the challenge.

Bernard is less excited by this whole prospect.

"*Julia's* going to do over the restaurant?" he gasps. "But"—he looks around at the beige walls—"she's meant to be redoing the house. We might have guests here during the Festival, and we can't have people over with the dining room that horrible purple color. What will they think?"

Dan's looking down at the floor, turning red. Susan gets the feeling he's trying hard not to burst out laughing.

"We can talk about that when Julia gets in," she replies. "In the meantime . . ."

But then the front door opens and Julia blows in, hugging a book of fabric samples.

"Suze! I think I've found just what we need," she announces, joining them in the sitting room. "Who's this?" she asks, looking Dan over and clearly deeming him unworthy to be gracing her sofa.

"This is Dan, the head chef," Susan answers. "He's come all the way over here to tell Dad about the plans for the refurbishment."

"Oh no, Dad, let me tell you all about it." Julia bounds over to her father and flips open the swatch book. "Look at this—it's such a lovely color, isn't it? 'Thistle Field' they call it. I think it'll really brighten up the space, especially against the blonde wood I'm going to have put in. No more of that ugly dark stuff. Suze, don't look at me like that. You know the paneling needs to be redone, okay? Oh, and I've got a meeting with three contractors this week; one of them just got finished with the interior for Chris Baker's place. Don't know if that really recommends him, but we'll see."

Bernard smiles softly at his eldest, pats her hand, and agrees that Thistle Field is lovely and he's sure it'll make a real difference in the space. (*As if he would know,* Susan thinks.)

"But Julia, darling, what about the house?" he asks. "Remember, you promised me you'd do it over as soon as we arrived."

"Oh, Dad, I'll get to it when I can, of course, but this is important. It's for the *business*, which is for the *family*. And it'll be so good for me to spread my wings a bit, don't you think? Oh, please let me do it. I promise, once everything's underway there, I'll get to work on the house, okay? *Please?*"

"Well," Bernard sighs, "if it'll make you happy, Poppet. I suppose we can hold off until next year to have Festival guests."

"Aw, thanks, Dad—you're the best, you know that? Now, I'm going to look into some graphic designers for the menu and logo," Julia goes on. She glances Dan's way again. "I suppose you're here to discuss the changes to the menu? Because Susan's right: it's dreadful."

Bernard looks at him expectantly. Dan just blinks, clearly unsure how this has all gotten away from him so quickly. "Oh yes," he agrees. "Yes, we'll be making changes."

"Good. I'm off to make some calls, then." Julia drops a kiss on her father's cheek and disappears.

The silence in the room is a heavy one.

"Dan, could you give my father and myself a moment, please?" Susan finally requests.

Dan rises slowly and leaves the room. Susan closes the door behind him, then walks over to her father.

"Dad," she says, lowering herself onto the sofa Dan's just vacated. "I need you to answer something honestly for me. Do you want to be in charge of the business and its day-to-day running? Because if you do, I need you to say so now, and I'll go back to London and find another job."

Bernard's horrified face is enough answer. But even so, he gasps, "Run the business? We all agreed it was for the best that I not do that. And anyway, I'm busy now: I've been asked to serve on the boards of two charities and joined the Malt Whisky Society. This is supposed to be *your job*, Susan."

"So we're agreed I'm in charge, then?" Susan presses. "I need to hear you say it, please."

"I already *have* said it! Yes, you're in charge, all right? And much joy may it bring you!"

"And may I borrow some family funds to pay for the refurbishment?" Bernard looks even more alarmed, so Susan hastily adds: "It'll disappoint Julia terribly if we called it off. She's already put in so much effort . . ."

"Right, of course. Shame to waste all her talents. Yes, all right, Julia can redo the restaurant."

"Thanks, Dad." Susan pats her father on the shoulder, then goes out to the front hall, where Dan loiters on an antique bench. Susan can hear Julia on the phone in the study, already interviewing a design firm.

"This is going ahead whether you like it or not," Susan informs her chef. "Don't think I don't know what you were trying to do here. Thought you'd go over my head and convince my father to overrule me? Nice try, but unsuccessful." She steps a little closer, standing over him, arms crossed. "It's clear you don't see us as being on the same team here, Dan, and I need my chef to be on the same team as me. I don't have time to fight someone every step of the way."

He smirks. He knew this was coming. If she didn't fire him, he'd quit. But still, he won't go quietly. "You think you can just wander up here with your London accent and attitude and just start running this business? You don't know anything about the restaurants up here—or the suppliers. You're not part of this clan."

"Not yet, but I'm working on it," she coolly replies.

"Who's going to help you, huh? Gloria?" He snorts. "I know she's been saying things about the restaurant, and you've lapped it up. You think she's not playing you? You think she doesn't have ambitions and is using you to get ahead?"

"I don't fault people for being ambitious if they're also good at their jobs."

He shakes his head. "You skirts always stick together."

"Keep talking, Dan, really. You think we don't know restaurant people up here? We do. You don't want us poisoning your well, or you'll find yourself looking for jobs at B&Bs in the Orkneys because that's the only place people will still hire you, and that's because they won't know your name. I suggest you get up, walk out of here, and go register on S1jobs, because you're fired."

* * *

Susan got almost no sleep that night.

Immediately after closing the door behind Dan, she realized her heart rate was reaching alarming levels, and her knees were shaking slightly. With any luck, he hadn't seen that or sensed it.

And then she realized she'd have to recruit a new head chef. And that chef would need time to give notice at their current place, get acclimated to the new restaurant and the staff, and then set about redoing the menu. This was going to push things back. *Way* back. It had to be done, of course, but this was not at all ideal. She wondered if Dan guessed that and would hover around for a while, hoping she'd telephone, apologizing, begging him to come back, hence giving him all the power.

Like hell she's going to do that. He can sit by his phone until he starves. She'll make this work. Somehow.

Just after five she gives up tossing and turning and goes down to the kitchen to bake something. The bread she made the day before is sitting on a cooling rack on the countertop, its thick crust cracked and lovely, jagged ridges ripping through the neat swirled pattern the proofing basket left on the dough. She cuts a thick slice and pops it in the toaster, makes some tea, and eats the bread spread generously with marmalade. Sour, nutty, sweet, fruity, bright, citrusy—a wake-up and a joy in a single bite.

She polishes off the first piece and, while a second toasts, decides to try out a cake idea she had, which she thinks will work best with a genoise sponge. While she's watching the eggs beat up into a thick, primrose-colored froth in the stand mixer, Julia comes in, eyes ablaze, hissing:

"It's *six o'clock* in the morning, Susan! What the hell are you doing down here?"

"Sorry." Susan sheepishly turns off the mixer. The sponge will have to wait.

"God! Most people just read books or watch TV when they can't sleep!" Julia storms out, muttering about how this was going to give her *bags* under her eyes.

Susan stands in the middle of the kitchen, afraid to make any more noise. It's been so long since she's lived with anyone, she's forgotten how sensitive people can be to it. Chris never minded her late-night baking binges. But then Chris almost never slept himself.

She dumps out the half-whipped eggs and heads out, deciding it's best to leave the house to her father and sister.

It's light out already—the sun sleeps as little as she does at this time of the year—and the sky is watercolor-washed in pale pinks and blues. It's quiet, no one about, and few buses and cars on the road at this hour. She likes the peace. She can think here. Sometimes (like, when her mind wanders to Chris and those memories) she'd rather *not* be able to think so much, but it's good today. The day is fresh and, despite the lack of sleep, her mind is too.

She goes to the restaurant because she can't think of anywhere else to go at this hour, and there's work to be done anyway. An advertisement for the chef's position will have to be written up and posted. And Paul will have to be dealt with. She knows instinctively that he'll feel entitled to the top job. But if he wants it, he'll have to work for it.

There are other things that will need her attention today. Budgets to be balanced, suppliers to be contacted, jobs to be reviewed. Possibly some tough decisions to be made. And it all has to be done soon.

She unlocks the door and trots down to the kitchen, where she manages to scare the hell out of Gloria.

"Jesus!" Gloria gasps, nearly dropping the foam canister she's holding.

"Sorry," says Susan. "I didn't expect anyone else to be in." The chefs aren't due in until around half past eleven, since the restaurant has put a hold on its abysmal mid-week lunch service. "What are you doing here?"

"Oh," Gloria gestures to the plates arrayed in front of her, "just working on some things." She shakes the canister and very carefully pipes a creamy, snow-white mousse onto a thin charcoal-colored biscuit.

Susan eases over to the table to watch her work. "What sorts of things?"

"Just a few ideas," Gloria answers without looking up. She places some salmon roe on top of the mousse with the delicate precision of a jeweler setting diamonds.

Susan waits until she's done before saying, "I guess you heard about Dan, then?"

"Oh, we all heard." Gloria smirks. "He came blasting in here yesterday to get his knives and whatever else from the office. He took Paul back there and the two of 'em yelled about how ridiculous the whole thing was. They closed the door, but we could still hear it. I learned at least eight new variations on 'fanny,' which is impressive, because I thought I already knew 'em all." She shakes her head, grinning. "Dan left after that, banging every door he could find on the way out. He didn't tell us he'd been sacked, but he didn't have to, did he? Paul spent the rest of the night strutting around in that smug way of his, and after service he took a bottle of whisky back to the office while the rest of us cleaned up."

"And now you're here, at the crack of dawn, experimenting," Susan murmurs, facing Gloria over the chef's new concoction.

Gloria's face is set. "Are y'askin' if I'm goin' to make a bid for the executive chef post? Hell yeah, I am. Why shouldn't I? I've trained up and down the country and spent three years here working every station, handling inventory and purveyors, training apprentices, and being ordered to fetch drinks and coffee. I'm hungry and qualified. And you don't seem like the type to hand a job to a sous chef just because he's next in line. So yeah, I'm making a play here."

The two women stare at each other, taking the other's measure. After a few moments, Gloria asks, "You hungry? I've got some eggy bread keeping warm in th' oven."

"Honestly? I'd rather try this." Susan gestures to the plate on the table.

Gloria grins. "Have at it, then."

Susan picks up the fragile biscuit. "What is it?"

"Try it and find out."

Susan places the whole thing on her tongue and swirls it around her mouth. What it is is amazing: a fresh burst of sweet, briny crab flavor, beautifully complimented by just a hint of lemon, followed by a soft crunch from the biscuit, which dissolves more slowly than the mousse and has a slightly salty, vegetal flavor. Susan's sorry when it's done; she could happily eat a dozen of these, or just a bowl filled with that mousse.

But she doesn't want to show her hand, so she keeps her face as still as she can manage and just makes a little "hmm" noise as she wipes a little mousse off her fingers with a kitchen towel (hard to resist licking them clean). "Is that seaweed?" she asks, indicating a tray of the biscuits, lined up nearby. Without the mousse topping, she can see that they weren't really biscuits at all, but many layers of paper-thin seaweed, pressed together to form a semi-firm base.

"It is," Gloria confirms. "Foraged from Scottish coasts, with Orkney crab mousse and Scottish salmon roe. Scotland's waters, on a plate."

Susan nods, thinking. "Gloria," she says at last, "I'm going to go do some work. But I'd like you to make me lunch today."

Gloria grins, lighting up like Bonfire Night, and nods. "Thanks! I will. Any time in particular?"

"Let's say eleven," Susan answers. "Before the rest of the brigade gets in."

"Right you are!" Gloria turns away, begins pulling out tools and hurrying toward the walk-in, ready to work.

*   *   *

While Gloria preps, Susan reacquaints herself with the chef's CV. Gloria has indeed trained in some of the country's best kitchens, and her references are more than glowing. Quite effusive, actually, for chefs who tend to be fairly to the point. "Driven," "innovative," "soulful." Susan guesses the torporific state of things at Elliot's has been killing Gloria. No wonder she pounced on the chance to do something different.

In the kitchen, Gloria has turned a radio to an oldies station and is singing along.

"I love you baaaaybe, and if it's quite all right, I need you baaaaybe, to warm a lonely night," Gloria belts.

Susan smiles, unable to help herself. How nice to have someone there who actually seems to enjoy what she's doing.

Susan spends the rest of the morning going over budgets and figures, reviewing suppliers' invoices, and writing up the advertisement for the chef's position, just in case. The mousse that morning was outstanding, certainly, but what if Gloria chokes when asked to present a full meal? Unlikely, yes, but it's best to be prepared. And it makes Susan feel like she isn't just taking the easy road, although promoting from within would simplify things.

Promptly at eleven, Gloria raps on the door and announces, "Lunch is served."

Susan follows her into the space across from the office, which serves as a sort of staff room. There are lockers on one side for personal items, cardboard boxes filled with clean aprons and chefs' uniforms, and a rectangular table where staff gather for the preservice "family dinner."

It's Susan, now, who seats herself at the table.

Gloria places a bowl in front of her. "First course—haggis, neeps, and tatties. And a 'tattie scone' on the side." She disappears to prepare the next course.

Susan takes a moment to note the presentation. "Eat with your eyes first," Elliot used to say, placing everything just so. Gloria's soup is the same creamy white as her mousse, and dotted with crispy haggis croutons arranged in a half-moon shape. The "tattie scone" isn't the classic tattie scone, which is a flat potato-and-flour pancake fried crisp in a pan, but more like the risen scone you have with afternoon tea. Susan picks up the spoon and dips into the soup.

Ohhhhhh. The soup is perfect, smooth and luscious, with a slight tang from the turnips (the "neeps" of the title) that keeps it from being too heavy. The finishing flavor is smoky, peaty. A little whisky, perhaps? The haggis croutons crunch as she bites into them, and the burst of spice further tames and complements the velvety richness of the soup. She devours every bit, sopping up the last of it with the scone, which is surprisingly fluffy for something made with potato. Like that morning's amuse-bouche, she's sorry when the dish is finished.

But then Gloria appears, whisks the bowl away, and replaces it with a plate of seared trout with a lime-green sauce. On the side is rainbow chard and a small potato, split open, insides fluffed, topped with tuna tartare—a cheeky nod to a favorite Scottish meal of tuna salad–topped baked potato.

"Trout with a lemony samphire sauce," Gloria explains, turning to leave.

"No, stay," Susan invites, gesturing to the seat opposite. "Doesn't every chef want to know how a diner's reacting to their food?"

"Oh, the hidden cameras will tell me that," Gloria says. "Kidding!" she adds, when Susan looks up at her in alarm. She plops down on the chair, smiling, folds her hands, and watches as Susan takes her first bite.

It only takes that one bite for Susan to decide to offer her the job. She'd be crazy not to. But she still keeps her face as neutral as she can (she slips up a time or two, closing her eyes and making some sort of cooing noise as that first bite of crisp, buttery fish and powerfully salty sauce hits her taste buds). She finishes the dish and pushes the empty plate to one side.

"How do you like working here?" Susan asks.

"It's an excellent kitchen, and the restaurant has a good reputation," Gloria carefully responds.

"But . . .?"

"But it's coasting on that reputation, and that's harming the place." Gloria leans in, dark eyes shining intensely, cheeks pinkening as she becomes more animated. "The kind of customers you want to bring in—the ones who'll pay the prices we charge? They *know* about food. They're not impressed by the same old—they want something new. Not necessarily something completely crazy, but something that seems familiar with a new spin."

"Like haggis, neeps, and tatties in soup form?"

"Exactly! We're not giving that to them now. The menu almost never changes, and what we offer isn't even remotely out of the box. There are a hundred places within a mile of here where people can get some haggis and mash on a plate. We need to do more! Give them something to talk about on TripAdvisor and Instagram and get some of the locals buzzing too. We can't cling to the same dishes that this restaurant was founded on just because they were popular back then. We need to be sharks and move forward."

Susan can't resist smiling. "Sounds like you've been waiting a while to get that out."

"Oh God, yes!" Gloria flops back in her chair. "It's a relief, believe me." She straightens up, face serious. "Don't think I was bashing your granddad just then. That's not what I meant at all."

"It's all right—I know what you meant," Susan reassures her. "So tell me, Gloria, what is it that brings you into the kitchen? What brought you here at seven in the morning? I've been looking at your past experience, and I know it's not just this one opportunity that lights a fire under you, so to speak. You've been driven from the get-go. What do you think of when you cook?"

"My parents," Gloria answers immediately.

Susan is taken aback. Usually people answer questions like that with some long-winded rhapsody about how seasonal ingredients are just *so* amazing they can't wait to get their hands on them. But Gloria doesn't really need to say that: her love and respect for food shows in everything she makes.

Her surprise must have shown a little, because Gloria continues. "I'm first-generation Scottish; my parents came over from Poland six months before I was born." She smiles ruefully. "When I got stroppy as a kid, Mam used to remind me how she battled morning sickness all through that awful trip, just so I could be born here. She an' my dad, they settled down, worked hard, did everything they were supposed to do, so that I could be whatever I wanted. They dealt with some really awful shite—people can be such racist arseholes, you know? But they put up with it. I think about what they did, and I think—how shameful would it be if I repaid all that by being lazy and just coasting along, ya know? They did all they could so that I could succeed, so I'd damn well better succeed—or kill myself trying."

Susan absorbs that, then says, "Gloria, you've succeeded. Go phone your parents and tell them you're now the executive chef at Elliot's. The kitchen's yours."

It seems to take a very long time for this reality to sink in for Gloria, but once it does, a slow smile spreads across her face, widening and widening until it nearly splits her cheeks.

"Thank you, thank you, thank you!" she says, jumping up, grabbing Susan's hand, and pumping it. "Really, thank you so much."

Susan laughs. "I have faith in you, Gloria. And your food is outstanding. I hope we'll work well together."

"I hope so too. This is a team, right?" Gloria says, gesturing between Susan and herself.

"Yes. It needs to be."

Gloria nods and her smile fades. She chews her lip, thinking. "Paul isn't going to work under me," she says at last.

"Won't he?"

"I doubt it. He calls me 'Double-E.'" Gloria gestures to her generous bust.

"He calls you what?" Susan demands, flabbergasted. She knows restaurant kitchens, being pretty male dominated, often lean toward the misogynist, but straight-up sexual harassment is definitely unacceptable.

Gloria shrugs and rolls her eyes. "Some boys never stop being boys," she sighs. "Sometimes he changes it up. Uses 'Girl' or 'Polack' or something."

"Well, I'll have a word with him, and we'll see what happens," Susan suggests. "If it doesn't work out, then we'll have to recruit for a sous." *Easier said than done, but if need be . . .*

"All right." Gloria nods. Out in the kitchen, they can hear the clatter of feet on the stairs, the chatter of voices as the rest of the brigade starts to arrive. "Will you announce, or should I?" Gloria asks.

"I'll go out with you, but you take the moment. You've earned it," Susan answers.

Gloria heads back into the kitchen, with Susan trailing several steps behind. Paul passes them as they reach the main kitchen area, he on his way to the staff room to change.

"Coffee, will you, Girl?" he says to Gloria, without even looking at her.

"That's *Chef,* Paul, not 'Girl,'" she barks after him. "You will address me properly."

Paul stops and very slowly turns to face her. "Excuse me?"

The rest of the brigade clumps near the pass, silent, watching. Gloria turns toward them. "Tom," she says to one of the trainees, "What does 'chef' mean?"

"Uh, 'chief,'" he replies.

"That's right. Chief. The person in charge. I have just been appointed executive chef, which means I'm the number one in charge here, and I'm now announcing that a few things are going to change. First off—Paul, listen up here—we will treat each other with respect. So that means no more names that you pretend to think are cute and funny but that we all know are incredibly shitty. If I hear anyone throwing around racial or ethnic or sexist slurs, there will be consequences. And those consequences may or may not include me pinning your willie to that bulletin board." She gestures to the corkboard where schedules and messages are posted. A few of the men in the crowd wince. "Understood?"

Everyone nods.

"Announcement two," Gloria continues, "we are relaunching. This is a fresh slate for us. It means a new menu and new opportunities for staff members to advance. If I can move up, then you should too. Hard work and good ideas will be rewarded, and this goes for everyone from the sous chef"—she gestures to Paul with a sweet and very fake smile—"to waitstaff and dishwashers. It goes the other way too—I do not have time for coasters. If you don't contribute and pull yer weight, you'll be cut loose. Got that?"

More nods.

"I want ideas, people. Dazzle me. Let's make Elliot's great again, a'right? Someone turn that radio on. Find something motivating. We've got work to do."

Staff begin to move, but Susan is frozen, feeling a little shell-shocked. *Well,* she tells herself, *you wanted fireworks, right?*

Boom.

Chapter Eight
The Long Fall

~

To the surprise of exactly no one, Paul quits before the week is out. Doesn't even hand in notice, just packs up his knives and walks out the door, brandishing one last middle finger at Gloria, who smiles, shrugs, and yells, "Bye, Felicia!" as she waves at his retreating form. "I told you he wouldn't work underneath me," she says to Susan, "but don't worry. I've got someone in mind. His paella will make you weep."

"You already have someone in mind?" Susan repeats warily.

"Yeah." Gloria puts her hands on her hips. "I didn't plan this, if that's what you're thinking. I would've been perfectly happy to have Paul stay if he'd been willing. This is for the best. Let me call Rey in and you can see for yourself."

Susan agrees, and yes, his paella is amazing. And Reynaldo himself is definitely a more colorful personality than Paul.

"Sit down, honey, and watch me work," he tells Susan the day he makes his trial dish, rushing off to grab a chair from the staff room and setting it down at his prep table. He unrolls his knives with a flourish and proceeds to chop vegetables at a blinding speed, talking almost as fast, tossing jokes and anecdotes and occasionally a bit of raw veg Susan's way, like he's working in a Hibachi restaurant. *It's a shame we don't have an open kitchen,* Susan thinks. She laughs at the jokes, catches bits of pepper, and learns that, for all his showmanship, the man knows his business inside and out.

"We were at Gleneagles together," Gloria said when introducing him. Susan phones Gleneagles after she eats. The chef there begs her not to take Rey. She does.

So they'll have a sous chef in a few weeks. And Julia has secured a contractor, agreed to (and argued over) a budget with Susan, and begun looking over paint and upholstery and fixings. The restaurant is officially closed until the end of July, and Gloria's already working on new dishes, with input from the rest of the staff. Susan feels a steady pickup in energy at Elliot's, and she smiles a lot more now. It feels like something is finally getting done. All the activity distracts her and makes her forget, for a little while, all about Chris and his proximity. Until Meg reminds her.

"You're coming, aren't you, to Russell's party on Friday?" Meg suddenly asks late one sunny afternoon. They're standing in the playground at George V Park in Cannonmills, watching Andrew and Alisdair climb to the top of a huge slide built into the side of a steep hill. There are stairs to get to the top, but the slide itself is flanked on both sides by a slope of pavers, with stones poking out here and there, presumably to serve as hand- or footholds. It looks to Susan like a parental nightmare, but Meg isn't overly concerned and has been talking animatedly about how she's decided to give up both gluten and potatoes because she heard the starch or something in potatoes can make your cells turn cancerous all of a sudden, as if root veg are creating a rebel army right in your body.

". . . so I told Russell that I'd need options at this party of his, or I wouldn't be able to eat a thing, and he just smiled in that way of his and said, 'Sure, sure,' so now I *know* I won't be able to eat a thing. You are coming, aren't you? To Russell's party on Friday?"

"His . . . party?"

Meg looks exasperated. "Suze! Honestly! You all said you'd come, and he's already given final numbers to the caterer. And God, what that man is charging! These so-called 'celebrity chefs.' Lauren just won't shut up about him, goes on and on about how nice he is and what amazing food, and she can't wait to go to his restaurant with all her friends, because he's as yummy as the food is, and soooo nice!" She flutters her eyelashes mockingly. Ayden, from his pram, makes a protesting squawk, as if he senses his mother's poor mood. Meg begins rhythmically pushing and pulling the pram back and forth to soothe him.

The party. The party Chris is cooking for. A room full of rich political types. And Chris. A heavy pit forms in Susan's stomach.

"So you have to come," Meg continues. "I want none of your excuses about being too busy. I'll need someone else to talk to— the place'll be crawling with politicians already practicing their campaign speeches on each other. More spending cuts and austerity! Fewer immigrants! Isn't Brexit amazing!" She does some jazz hands at the end, and Susan laughs despite herself.

"It won't be that bad, will it?"

"Of course it will be. You've never been to one of these things, but I've been to more than my fair share. All MSPs, MPs, and rich donors and everyone's bored spouses. And the Chancellor of the Exchequer because he and Russell go way back. Oh, Suze! It'll be so boring."

"Maybe the chancellor will bring his wife."

Meg pauses. The chancellor, a widower for some years, had recently remarried a moderately famous model-turned-television presenter. Amongst Lauren's gossip at the most recent Sunday lunch was the tidbit that the chancellor's wife is expecting their first baby.

"He might," Meg murmurs. "She would be interesting to talk to. Think of all she's done! She used to be one of the faces of

Alexander McQueen—I heard she was some kind of muse to Sarah Burton and practically designed Kate Middleton's wedding dress."

Susan smiles and wonders if she's found an escape from this torturous evening. "Just think how much you two would have to talk about," she says, "now she's expecting. It's uncharted territory for her, but you're old hat." She gestures to Ayden, who's gnawing on a giraffe-shaped toy, and to Andrew and Ali at the slide. Ali is perched at the top, watching his brother attempt to climb up via the treacherous pavers. Susan nudges her sister and points to Andrew. "Should he be doing that?"

"Oh, it's fine—he says he does it all the time with the nanny," Meg answers, as Ayden throws his giraffe on the ground and begins to wail. "Oh, sweetie, have you dropped Sophie?" Meg murmurs, bending to fetch it and rub it clean on the leg of her jeans. "Do you think she still gets some sort of discount at McQueen?" she wonders aloud, handing Ayden back his toy (which he promptly tosses on the ground again). "She might even be able to extend it to close friends. I've heard some designers will do that. Oh, but you'll still have to come. Really. Russell's expecting all of you, and Helen says she's counting on it because she doesn't want the house to look too empty in case of last-minute cancellations, and Dad already promised you'd all be there."

Well, there it is. Now Susan feels stuck. Maybe there'll be an emergency at the restaurant that'll give her an excuse not to have to dress up and shovel Chris's food into her mouth in the company of a bunch of rich people while he toils in the kitchen not ten feet away.

Neither of them are quite sure how it happens. She and Meg are both looking away from the slide, so they miss it. But as Susan starts to answer, Andrew shouts, and the women's heads jerk toward him just in time to see the boy tumbling down the pavers, crashing into the ones poking out, unable to stop himself. He lands at the bottom a second later, and a silent moment balances delicately as everyone in the park freezes and stares.

Then he starts screaming.

Screaming and wailing, a high-pitched sound that means one thing: pain. Lots of it.

Ali, still at the top, gazes in horror at his brother; then he, too, begins to wail. Susan kicks into action, springing toward Andrew, who has managed to pull himself to a half-seated position. His arm sticks out at a funny angle, and he's bleeding from a gash in his forehead. He screams and screams.

"Meg! Call an ambulance!" Susan yells, crouching beside her nephew. But Meg remains in that frozen moment, eyes wide, shaking, mouth agape. The baby is crying now too, along with a few children nearby. Other parents hurry them away for comfort, shooting Susan and Andrew concerned and pitying looks. "Meg!" Susan bellows.

"I'm on it!" a nearby dad volunteers, waving his mobile.

A mother sprints to the top of the slide and scoops up Ali, carrying him down, soothing him. "There, there, love, it's all right. You've had a fright, now, haven't you?" she murmurs. "Your brother's going to be fine, just fine. Come over here, love." She carries him over to Meg, who is now wailing almost as loudly as her firstborn. A few other parents are trying to calm her.

Susan is dealing with Andrew, who's turning dead-fish gray. "Andy, you're going to be all right. We're calling for help now," she says, in the bright, fake tones one uses in situations like this. She examines the gash on his forehead. It doesn't look too deep, but cuts to the head always bleed like crazy. She read that somewhere. Why is that? Is extra alarm really necessary when your head's wounded? She pulls a tissue out of her pocket and dabs gently at the cut. She expects Andrew to flinch, but he doesn't. He's stopped screaming and is now shaking and staring into the distance. Shock.

"Andrew," she says, her voice now firm because some instinct tells her she has to keep him conscious and aware. "Andrew, tell me about your day at school. Or your favorite film. What did you see last at the cinema?"

"That Lego movie," he murmurs. "There were superheroes, I think."

"That's good, that's good." Another slight dab at the head wound. "Did you like it?"

"'S okay."

"What's your favorite film?"

"I liked *How to Train Your Dragon.* The dragons are cool. Wish I could have a dragon."

"You're very brave, Andrew," she reassures him. "Very, very brave. It's all right—the ambulance is coming." She looks over his head and catches the eye of the dad with the mobile. He nods to her.

"On their way!" he reports. "I'll go to the gate and direct them." He sprints away. Susan guesses that he, like the others who are coddling Meg and frightened children, are enjoying this just the tiniest bit. Excitement and variety in what has otherwise been another fairly dull, routine afternoon at the park. She can just imagine this scene being relived over half a dozen dinner tables that evening, parents and kids comparing notes.

The ambulance arrives, sirens screaming, and Andrew is loaded onto a gurney and taken to the Royal Hospital for Sick Children. They offer to let Meg or Susan ride with him, but Meg's still hysterical, and Susan doesn't want to leave her in that state, with the little ones to deal with on top of it, so instead they follow in a taxi. Meg sobs. The boys wail. And Susan has her hands full tending to the three of them while also telephoning Will to tell him what happened. He was playing tennis at the Meadows and arrives at the hospital just behind them. Susan has never been so grateful to see her brother-in-law.

"Hey, hey, big man," he says to Alisdair, who's cried himself exhausted. "It's all right—your brother will be fine." He sweeps the boy up in a hug, then says to Meg, "What the hell happened?"

"It was an accident," Susan explains, quick to defend her sister against his perceived judgment. "He was climbing up to the top of the slide, and he slipped and fell."

"You're a godsend, Suze," he says. Still holding Ali with one arm, he drapes the other over his wife's shoulders and pulls her close. "Come on, let's go in," he murmurs.

"Why don't I take the boys home?" Susan suggests. "No sense keeping them here."

"That would be great," Will says, handing Alisdair over. Ali makes no protest. He's limp, and his head rests heavily on his aunt's shoulder. "Thank you so much—we really owe you one."

"You don't owe me anything," says Susan. "This is what family does."

Alisdair settles his head in the hollow of her shoulder and snuggles in against the curve of her neck. Susan lets her own head rest gently on his, finding his warmth and weight against her body soothing. He's worn out. They all are now the emergency situation adrenaline is ebbing. Susan feels exhausted and wants nothing more than to collapse onto a sofa with a cozy blanket. Even the baby seems pretty relaxed as the taxi stutters toward Stockbridge through heavy afternoon traffic.

Ali falls asleep about halfway home, and the taxi driver kindly helps Susan get both boys into the house when they arrive. She tucks Ali into his little race car–shaped toddler bed and settles Ayden on a blanket in the playroom with some stacking cups. He's as fascinated by them as if the secrets of the universe were contained in their plastic shells and he could get to them if he just gets the order right. Susan smiles, watching him. Thinking how nice it is when life's that simple. When complete happiness can come just from figuring out that the blue one goes on top of the red one.

Ayden completes half a stack and applauds, looking to Susan for approval. She duly gives it, just as the front door opens and Lauren swirls in.

"Hiya!" she crows, breathless. "Sorry—just ran over. Mum texted something about Andy being in hospital? She thought I should come over and see if you needed help. She'd come, but she and dad are making an appearance at the constituency. Got to keep those voters placated, you know."

"Oh, thanks, Lauren," Susan answers. "It's a broken arm probably, and maybe a concussion. Meg and Will are at Sick Kids with him."

"Glad it's not serious," says Lauren. "Must have been a thing, though! Did Meg cry? I'll bet she cried."

"Of course she cried! He's her son!"

"You know what I mean. She makes a big drama, doesn't she? But like you said, it's her kid and all. You want some tea? I'll go make some tea." She clatters about in the kitchen for a while, occasionally singing some pop song off-key, then reappears with the teapot, some mugs, and a plate of biscuits. "These are gluten-free nonsense, but it's all I could find," she announces, pointing to the biscuits.

Susan shakes her head. "I'm fine."

Lauren takes a biscuit, bites into it, and shrugs, apparently finding it edible. "Will he have to stay overnight, do you think? In the hospital? Mum'll want to know. If he does, she and dad'll turn around and come right back."

"That's sweet of them," Susan murmurs.

Lauren smirks. "It'll seem that way." She flicks a lock of purple hair over her shoulder. "Dad does like to seem the devoted family man. I mean, I guess he is—it's not like he's a lousy dad or husband or anything, but he tends to play it up when he needs to. You remember when Meg was pregnant with Andy? There was a by-election that year, and Dad never missed an opportunity to have her with him at photo ops and things, so he could smile proudly and pat her belly. You'd have thought *he* was the dad, the way he fussed over her. She lapped it up. And then Andy was born right before the election and Dad made sure he was holding him when his victory photos were taken. So very wholesome. It's why they keep trying to drag me up to the constituency, so we can all smile together. Dad almost had a stroke when he saw what I'd done to my hair." She giggles. "Turns out, it was my ticket out of all that nonsense. And there'll be a *lot* of that sort of nonsense now, because Dad says another general election is coming, and he's going to make a run for Westminster.

"Oh!" she sits up straight, and her eyes sparkle. "Did I tell you I went to Chris Baker's restaurant? Seòin." She pronounces it "shown." "He told me it means 'feast' in Gaelic. The press will probably love that. You think that's why he did it? It's really all about marketing, isn't it? No matter what business you're in. It's why I just went ahead and started on a marketing degree, seemed the best thing to do. Of course, Liam told me I'm just studying to be a sell-out, but he's getting a philosophy degree, so he *would* say that, wouldn't he?" She rolls her eyes and finishes her biscuit.

"Who's Liam?" Susan asks, struggling, in her worn-out state, to follow Lauren's stream-of-consciousness chatter.

"Oh, just some guy I was seeing for a while, and then not seeing, and then seeing again. He's a pompous little arse, but hot and, you know, *good at things*." Lauren raises her eyebrows momentarily. "So sometimes we're together and sometimes we're not."

"And now?"

"Now we're not. We thought it'd be better to take some time apart over the summer. Well, *I* did. He's in Greece or something just now. Keeps phoning me. But anyway, Chris—the restaurant's really nice, and the food's fab, so it'll be really good at Dad's party, I made sure of it. He's a nice guy too—really friendly. You always think that people on TV will be really snobby and full of themselves, so it's nice when they're not. You used to know him, didn't you? What was he like?"

Like? Susan briefly allows herself to look back on their time together. She thinks of times they spent cooking together—the happy times, those brief weeks between her grandfather's death and her mother's diagnosis. Ingredients and suggestions flying back and forth. Playful tastings, tongues lapping rich sauces, lips closing on luscious bites.

And those bleak days, after she sought refuge in his little flat, seeming, like her sisters, incapable of facing the family home without her mother in it. Those days when she cried and cried, and he held her, stroked her hair, said nothing. Just let her cry.

"You're right, he was nice," she croaks. "Know what? I think the baby needs his nappy changed." She scoops up Ayden, who squawks in protest at losing the stacking cups, and rushes upstairs with him, to the silence of the nursery.

Chapter Nine
Top-Shelf Secrets

❧

A broken arm, but no concussion. Two stitches in his forehead ("Poor child, he'll have a *scar!*" Bernard groans, when he hears). And now, Andrew's injuries have thrown Meg's presence at Russell's party into question.

"I really shouldn't leave him," she fusses, two hours before the party is scheduled to begin. "What if something goes wrong? I've heard of situations where someone's broken something, and bone marrow gets into their bloodstream and goes to their heart or their brain or something and kills them."

William blinks at his wife, then looks helplessly at Susan, whom he's called in, hoping she can talk sense into her sister. But what can you really say to that?

"Meg, that's really rare," she tells her.

"But it *happens,*" Meg insists.

"Meg, this is important," Will chimes in. "We told Dad we'd be there. They're counting on us to show some support."

"Our *child* is important, William! Or, at least, he is to me."

"Margaret . . ." he begins.

Meg throws her hands up. "Oh, *here we go.* Now he's going to lecture me on proper behavior, like one of the boys. How very, *very* important it is for us to put in an appearance and smile and make nice with all his dad's friends and colleagues."

"Jesus, Margaret, you're acting like this is some kind of torture!" he cries. "You've been talking for weeks about how nice it'll be to see some of the other wives and tell them all about this paleo thing you've decided to try out, and then you just turn around and cancel the babysitter!"

"My son has just been through a *trauma*! You don't think I'm going to leave him with some teenager he barely knows, do you?"

"He wouldn't have to be with a stranger if you hadn't fired the nanny," he flings back through clenched teeth.

"They weren't safe with her! She's the one who let him start climbing up to the slide that way in the first place. And I'll have you know that she was letting them eat Twiglets when she *knows* I insist on the Ella's Organics snacks at all times!"

The raised voices have traveled from the kitchen to the playroom, where the boys are watching a Disney movie. Susan glances in that direction and sees Andrew's pale little face peeking around the door.

"I'll stay with them," she offers. "I'll stay with the boys tonight. It'll be fine. They know me, I'm a responsible adult, and I'm first aid trained, so I can handle any situation."

William looks like he could kiss her, which makes Susan almost want to take a step away. Meg, however, hesitates.

"I-I feel like I should be the one to stay," she says.

Susan smiles and strokes her sister's arm. "Meg, go on out and enjoy yourself. Spread the paleo good news to the wives of the Tory ministers. It's been a stressful week; you deserve a little break. And don't forget about the chancellor's wife. You'll have loads to talk about. You'll have so much fun."

"Aren't you sorry to miss it?" Meg asks.

With some effort, Susan keeps that smile going. "I'll live. I'm sure there'll be other parties at your in-laws'." But, hopefully, no others catered by Chris. It's childish, but the longer she can put off having to face him, the happier she'll be.

"If you're sure," Meg says, easing toward the door. "I guess I'd better go get ready."

"You go right ahead, Meg—I've got things here," Susan urges. She glances at Andrew, still peeking around the door, and thinks it's probably really wrong to be this relieved by a small child's injuries.

* * *

William and Meg are waved off by Susan and Andrew (the only one of the boys who can be tempted away from *The Lion King*). Once the door closes, Susan turns to her nephew.

"Don't want to watch the movie?" she asks.

He shrugs the one shoulder not encumbered by a cast. "It's a baby movie," he sighs.

"Okay." Susan bends down so they're eye to eye. "Wanna bake?"

He considers that. "Bake what?" he finally asks.

She grins. "I'm going to teach you to make the best brownies."

He trails her into the kitchen. "Mum doesn't keep chocolate in the house," he says. "She says it's toxic and exploitative."

"Uh-huh," Susan says, dragging one of the chairs from the kitchen table into the pantry. Balancing on her tiptoes on it, she can just see onto the top shelf, where Meg has stashed several bars of Green & Black's behind two half-used bags of flour. "Still hiding your hoard in the same place, Meg," she murmurs, remembering all the times, growing up, she'd stumbled onto her sister in this same position: balancing on a chair, arm digging into the back of a shelf, alarmed at the thought that the person she heard coming might be Julia. "Don't tell your mother I let you see that," she says to Andrew, hopping down from the chair with two bars in one hand and a bag of flour in the other.

Andrew's eyes widen and he grins, nodding. "I won't."

"Grab me a couple of eggs, please?" she requests, pulling out a pot and a heatproof bowl. The pot, filled with an inch of water, is placed on the hob with the bowl on top to form a makeshift double boiler. "Never put chocolate directly on heat by itself," she tells Andrew as he hands her two eggs. "If you do, it'll burn and scorch before it melts."

He nods, attentively watching what she's doing. Susan breaks the chocolate bars into chunks and tosses them in the bowl as the water comes to a simmer.

"Here," she says, handing him a spatula. "Give it a stir now and again, so it melts evenly."

Andrew very carefully stirs the chocolate, which quickly dissolves into a heavenly goo. The aroma is powerful enough to tempt Ali from the playroom. Susan lifts him onto the countertop so he can watch what his brother's doing.

"Choc-lit," Alisdair declares proudly, pointing to the bowl.

"Yes, but it's very hot, so don't touch," Susan warns him.

"Very hot," he repeats with a solemn nod.

Susan adds butter to the melted chocolate, then starts mixing the eggs with salt and brown sugar. As she measures out flour, she watches Andrew and notices he's got an expression she can only describe as melancholy. She's never seen a kid look at a bowl of melted chocolate in such a sad way.

"You okay, little man?" she asks, nudging him.

He shrugs.

"Your arm hurt?"

He shakes his head.

Alisdair gets tired of watching chocolate melt and demands, "I get down now!"

Susan sets him back on the floor, and he gallops off. She takes the chocolate off the heat and sets it aside to cool a little. "You want to talk about it?" she asks her nephew.

He considers that, then asks, "Is it true, what Mum said? About bone getting into my blood?"

"Oh, sweetie." Susan reaches over and pats his good arm. "No, you'll be fine. Your mum's just worried about you."

He's silent for a little while. "She's always worried," he says at last. "And it makes her and Dad fight. They were fighting about me tonight."

"They fight a lot?" Susan asks, not because she wants the dirty details about her sister's marriage, but because she's concerned about the effect it's having on their children.

"Usually they go upstairs and close the door," Andrew replies. "They think we can't hear them. But we can. Mum always thinks she's dying. Is she?" He turns to his aunt with a pinched, concerned face.

Susan reaches out and hugs him close. "No, love, your mum's not dying. Your mum's fine. She's going to be here for a long, long time."

"Am *I* dying? Because she says these pains and things that she has mean she's dying. *I* get pains sometimes."

"Andrew, sweetie, we all do."

"And she doesn't let us eat things. She says they're poison."

"To be fair, some things are poison." He looks up at her and then down at the chocolate, and she hastily adds, "Not this, though."

Andrew nods. "Okay." He goes back to his stirring. "If mum asks where these came from, you have to tell her it was your idea," he says, a few moments later.

Susan laughs. "Don't worry, little man," she says, patting him on the shoulder. "I'm happy to take the heat."

* * *

Meg and William return late, long after the boys are in bed. Meg comes in laughing and glowing, rhapsodizing about the evening.

"Jane Howell came!" she announces as they walk through the door.

It takes Susan a moment to realize she's talking about the chancellor's wife. "Oh, great! Did you get to talk to her?"

"I did. And she was so nice, but just as I was getting around to telling her everything she really should know about labor, she had to run off to the loo. Pregnant ladies—we have to go all the time." Meg laughs.

"The food was really nice too," William adds. "Lauren dragged the chef out of the kitchen and made him do the rounds. The restaurant will probably be booked for months now. She's not a bad marketer, that sister of mine."

"Great," Susan says through a tight smile. "Hey, Meg, can I ask you something?"

Meg is sniffing the air, not paying attention. "Is that . . . chocolate?" she asks.

"Yeah, the boys and I made brownies."

"Not . . . *the* brownies?" William asks hopefully.

Susan nods.

"Please, please tell me there are some left," he begs.

"There are."

"Where'd you get the chocolate from?" Meg wonders, her eyes narrowing.

"I owe you a couple of bars of Green & Black's," Susan answers.

"God, Susan, you didn't let the boys see where that was, did you? They'll be in there all the time, trying to get to that chocolate, and they'll end up breaking their necks trying."

"Meg, it's fine—listen: I'm a little worried about Andy."

"Wait, what? Why?" Meg's eyes widen. "Did something happen? Did he spike a fever? Start feeling strangely? Did you check his pulse? Call the doctor?" Her voice escalates: "William, get the car—we're going back to Sick Kids. Oh Jesus! It was the chocolate, wasn't it? I knew we shouldn't have gone out tonight!"

"Meg! Breathe! He's fine!" Susan reaches out, grasps her sister by the shoulders, and shakes her a little. Out of the corner of her eye, she sees William roll his eyes so hard his head rolls with them.

"Then what? What is it?" Meg demands.

"It's *this*—" Susan releases her sister and gestures toward her. "This anxiety over everyone's health. I think it's starting to affect him. And maybe the others as well."

Meg crosses her arms and purses her lips. "Did he tell you that?"

"Kind of. He thinks you're going to die and that everything is filled with poison."

"Everything *is* full of poison," Meg spits. "You know what I was reading recently about vaccines? I'm seriously considering holding off on Ayden's next round."

"Oh God, let's not be on about that again," William groans, materializing from the kitchen with a brownie in each hand. A few telltale crumbs are sticking to his lower lip. He licks them away before offering one of the brownies to his wife. "Eat that; you'll feel better."

"I will not," Meg huffs, folding her arms and glaring at both husband and sister.

William shrugs. "Your loss," he says and crams both brownies into his mouth. "Mmm, delicious, delicious poison!"

Susan closes her eyes for a moment, silently castigating herself for starting this mess. Andrew was already upset about his parents fighting, and what does she do? Starts a fight!

"Meg, I'm sorry I brought it up, I didn't mean to upset you," Susan soothes. "I just hate to see you so stressed out. And the boys see it too, and it worries them because you're their mum and they love you. And it worries me and William because *we* love you." She turns to her brother-in-law with a smile and a fierce look in her eyes that says, "Your cue!"

William takes his time brushing crumbs off his hands, but then looks up with a smile of his own. "Course I do," he says.

"I guess I can't really expect you to understand," Meg sniffs to Susan. "You don't have kids. And you couldn't possibly love mine the way I do."

"Meg!" William admonishes as Susan draws back, stung.

"Sorry," Meg says insincerely.

"Don't worry about it," Susan says quietly, gathering up her things. "It's late; we're all tired. I'll see you soon, Meg. Will." She drops a perfunctory kiss on both their cheeks and leaves, choosing to walk home despite the fact the weather has turned suddenly and is unexpectedly damp and chilly.

*　*　*

Just up the street, Lauren wanders into the kitchen as Chris is preparing to pack up his knives. She hops up on a countertop, crosses her legs at the ankle and swings them, watching as he scrapes each knife down a honing blade, tests the edge with his thumb, and then carefully tucks it into his knife roll.

"Do you have to do that every time you use them?" she asks, two knives in.

"You don't *have* to do it every time, but I do," he answers. "It's an end-of-the-day ritual, like brushing your teeth."

She smiles. "How do you know when you've got it right?"

"You get a feel for it." He spent time in Japan—quite a bit of time, actually—and was drilled in knife skills. He can sharpen them in his sleep now and slice anything paper thin without having to think about it. Muscle memory.

"The other thing you can do," he continues, "is test it. It should be able to slice through a sheet of paper."

"It will not," she scoffs.

"No, really—I'll show you." He reaches for the nearest piece of paper—the breakdown of tasks for the evening, now no longer needed—and hands it to her to hold up. She does, at arm's length. He smiles playfully at her as he lifts his chef's knife. "Ready?"

She grins and nods.

Lightly holding the handle, he lets the knife slice neatly downward through the paper, splitting it precisely in half. Lauren's eyes widen.

"Wow! That's so . . . Jedi!" she exclaims.

"It's not," Chris says, sliding the knife into the roll with the others and tying it up. "Just a skill."

"Will you teach me how to do that? The sharpening thing?"

"Sure."

She hops down, grabs a knife from a magnetic strip near the stove, and rejoins him.

Chris hands her the honing blade and says, "Turn around."

With a little smirk, she turns, nestling her back against his chest. Chris takes her knife hand in his right and the honing steel hand in his left and helps her scrape the blade down the steel. *Scritch, scritch, scritch.* He focuses on that, trying not to be distracted by her warm body snuggled up to him. *Scritch, scritch.*

Lauren giggles. "Can I convince you to stay and help me do all of Mum's knives?" She looks up at him with a flirtatious wink.

Chris releases her hands and steps away. "I would, but tomorrow's a busy day, and it's late."

"Right." She rehangs the knife and hands back the steel. "You've got your opening soon. And after tonight, you'll probably have a full house for a while. Tell me"—she springs back onto the countertop—"did you enjoy the party?" She tilts her head, grinning, daring him to tell the truth.

"It was really nice," he answers. Once, he wouldn't have been able to say that convincingly. But he's developed the ability to smile and ingratiate and seem like he's having the time of his life, even when he feels like he wants to jab himself repeatedly in the eye with a pickle fork.

"Oh, come on, you were bored to tears!" she scoffs. "*I* was bored to tears! Anyone would be except for Dad and some of the others who really make this their lives. I thought the chancellor's wife was going to make an escape through the bathroom window. But I couldn't blame her, the way Meg was going on and on." She rolls her eyes. "She's sweet and means well, Meg does, but God. Shut up already!"

Chris smiles, even though the mention of a Napier annoys him. They were all there—Meg (at least three glasses of wine too many), Julia (sneering at the champagne because it wasn't *actually* champagne, but an English sparkling wine), and Bernard (laughing a little too loudly at every politician's joke). All of them except Susan, and her absence irks him even more than the others' presence. He thought this might be a chance to see her when he was at less of a disadvantage. He psyched himself up for it, thought of all sorts of things to say to her, clever and cutting things, so he could get some of his own back, finally, after all these years. It's why he agreed to do this stupid party in the first place.

But she didn't come. The coward! She stayed away; he'd done all that planning for nothing. And on top of it, he had to endure an evening of being dragged away from his cooking by Lauren, who paraded him around, accompanied by her father, who introduced him to friends and colleagues as "that celebrity chef I've been telling you about. Really great, isn't he? Did you try those scallops? And that beef thingy? Opening up his own place now— got to admire that! Quite a risk to take, in a market as crowded as that. When do you open again?"

"A week," Chris answered, wishing to God he had a pickle fork on him.

"A week! Get those reservations in now, lads!"

A week. There were a dozen other things he could be doing, but instead he was tripping over Calum in a domestic kitchen that wasn't at all suited to catering, listening to his sous chef curse a blue streak about the oven, the flooring, and the twee decorations that took up precious counter space. And it was all for nothing.

Lauren is still chattering on about something, and Chris tries to drag his attention away from his frustration and back to her. He focuses on her bright smile and the animated way she gestures with her hands as she speaks. Her hair is curly tonight, bouncing with her energy. Her skirt, cut to mid-thigh, shows off her long, slender legs, which she's swinging again.

"Will there be a party to celebrate the restaurant's opening?" she's asking. "There usually is, isn't there? My best mate, Chelsea, is working for a PR firm this summer, and she's been to at least half a dozen openings—restaurants, bars, all sorts of things. Her job sounds much more fun than mine, but then, I did get to meet with you and plan all this, so it's worth it," she adds, smiling coyly. "So, is there going to be a party?"

"There is," Chris answers. "Would you like to come?"

Her face lights up. "Would I? Can I bring some friends?"

"Why not?" It's not as if there won't be plenty of food. And Lauren and her pals might brighten up what might otherwise be a staid gathering of critics and overawed friends and family members.

"You're ace, Chris!" She notices his phone lying nearby and grabs it, typing away. "I'll give you my number, okay? You can text me with the details. Or," she looks up at him through her lashes, "we could meet up for a drink, and you could tell me in person."

Tempting, he has to admit. Her happiness and excitement are infectious, as is often the case with the young. Part of him wants to say "yes" and see what happens, but a slightly more practical part answers, "Maybe after the opening."

"Course." She finishes off her typing. "You'll be too busy this week. But you'll send me the deets, right? I'll be *very* disappointed if you don't."

"I wouldn't dare disappoint you," he says, reaching out to take the phone back. She holds onto it for a second or two, giggling, then releases it to him.

"You'd better not," she says, hopping down from the counter and sashaying toward the kitchen door. "Night, Chris. Sweet dreams."

Chapter Ten
Find Yourself a Girl, and Settle Down

⁓

Twenty-four hours to launch. Chris's kitchen is humming: delivery-men coming and going, extractor fans blasting, whisks scraping frantically around metal bowls. Calum is on the phone with their fish guy, who called to say he won't be able to get the oysters they need after all, and could they just substitute some Shetland mussels instead?

"No, the whole dish is built on *oysters on the half shell!*" Calum bellows. "Mussels on the half shell? Come on! Oi!" he shouts to a deliveryman bringing in crates of carrots. "Ya daft? Not there—does it look like we've got room to be tripping over those? Joe, show him to the walk-in." He turns back to the phone. "You'll get me oysters, or you'll get my foot up yer backside, 'kay?"

Chris is showing a line cook and an apprentice how to make the smoked bacon–flavored droplets that are meant to be going over the missing oysters. He looks up at Calum and says, "Relax. If they can't get oysters, we'll make do with the mussels. I'll come up with something new."

"Right, because you have time for that," Calum scoffs.

"I'll make time," Chris answers. "Rab, y'all right, there?"

Rab is trying his hand at puff pastry under the tutelage of the pastry chef, who's also working on the savory ice creams. Chris notices a sheen of nervous sweat on the boy's forehead.

"Yeah, aw'ight," Rab mumbles, concentrating on folding, rolling, and refolding the pastry.

"Too much flour!" the pastry chef snaps. "And look—your butter slab is poking through." He gestures to a spot where a bit of bright yellow is peeking through a tear in the pastry. "It won't rise now. Ruined!" He sighs and shakes his head.

Rab sags.

"It's fine," Chris reassures him. "This is how you learn. Why don't you show him how to fix it?" he adds to his pastry chef.

"You can't fix it!" the pastry chef snaps back. "You won't get a proper mille-feuille out of that."

"But it'll probably do for the mini haggis rolls," Calum suggests. "Saves me the trouble of making rough puff. Thanks, lad!" He claps Rab on the back, and Rab revives a little.

The pastry chef shakes his head and mutters as he scrapes the ice creams into tiny half-sphere molds.

A sharp female voice cuts across the chaos. "You lot know how tae make a mess, I'll give 'ee that!"

Chris looks up and sees his sister standing where the crate of carrots just was. Like Chris, Beth is tall and sturdily built, with deep red hair worn short. She's dressed in her typical uniform of worn jeans, plain T-shirt that's starting to fray a little at the neck and hem, and trainers so old you can't tell what color they used to be. Her right hand is planted on her hip as she surveys the chaos. In her left hand is a leash attached to a ginger-colored bulldog pup who's hopefully sniffing the air.

"Beth, my love—here at last!" Calum crows, swooping in to give her a hug.

She grins and thumps him on the shoulder with her free hand. "Ah, ya numpty," she affectionately greets him. "You stayin' oot o' trouble, eh? And keepin' 'im straight?" She nods toward Chris, who's wiping his hands on a towel and coming over to embrace her.

"You're early," Chris notes. She was supposed to come in after six. Leave it to Beth to do her own thing.

"Is that any way to greet yer only sister?" She rolls her eyes. "Charmer, him. How d'ye manage, Calum?"

"I just ignore him," Calum answers.

"Oh, aye? Seems the ticket. Y'all right, then, Rab? Yer gran's been asking after you."

"Yeah, all right," Rab answers, ducking his head and blushing.

The pastry chef sighs again and shakes his head, which does not escape Beth's notice. Chris can see her narrowing her eyes and opening her mouth to say something.

"You can't have that dog in here," Chris cuts in.

"We'll scarper," she says. "I'll take 'er for a walk to Bladigan's and see some o' th' folk there."

"You can't. It's gone," Calum informs her with a grimace and shake of the head. "It's a yoga studio and juicery now."

Beth narrows her eyes. "Whit the bleedin' hell is a *juicery*? Right, we'll find summat to do."

"My keys are in the desk in the office." Chris points the way. "You can just let yourself into the flat."

"Right." She heads to retrieve the keys, then returns. "See you there, then, brother. Ta, loves." She grabs a few slices of Iberian ham from a prep station and tosses one to the dog on her way out.

Chris wails after her, "Beth! Do you have any idea what that costs per ounce?!"

"Ach! It's just *posh bacon*, Christopher!" she bellows, slamming the door behind her.

Calum chuckles. "You think she'll ever love me back?"

"Only if you grow a tail and two more legs," Chris sighs, getting back to work.

It's nearly one in the morning by the time Chris drags himself home and is let into his own flat by his sister.

"Thought you'd be asleep already," he says.

"Well, I'm not." She flops down on his sofa, which is already stippled with ginger hair from the dog, and looks around at the bare, stark white walls. "Ya sure know how to make a place home-like," she observes with a raised eyebrow. "'Bout as cozy as living inside an IKEA cabinet. Is this that hygge thing I keep hearing about? Or is this what New York does to ye?"

"It's just a place to sleep," Chris tells her, setting his knife roll on the kitchen counter and joining her on the sofa.

"You cannae do much else here," she says.

Seeing it now, through her eyes, he realizes it is a bit unwelcoming and under-furnished. There's the sofa (charcoal gray—chosen because it's a color that hides stains well and therefore requires little upkeep), two overpriced, industrial-style lamps that a (short-lived) New York girlfriend insisted he *had* to have, and a pair of birch wood stools at the kitchen island. The only beauty spot is a coffee table fashioned from a slab of fallen oak, edges left jagged, just as nature intended. It was an impulse buy from a craftsman at the weekly Leith market.

Even the kitchen is sparse because he does nearly all his cooking at the restaurant. There's a tiny soup pot, a spatula, a colander, and that's about it.

It's sufficient for him, but Beth pats the dog on the head and remarks, "Needs a woman's touch, this. What do the girls think when you bring 'em 'ere?"

He snorts. "There are no girls."

"Are there no? Then 'oo's this Lauren creature who's been textin' ya?" Beth holds up his phone.

Chris gapes at her. "Did you steal my phone?"

"Course I did," she replies, now scrolling through his text messages. "Can you blame me?" Chris tries to yank the phone out of her hand, but she has a grip like a bear trap. The dog, not loving being caught in the middle, hops off the sofa and snuffles around the kitchen cabinets. Beth flicks through the messages and raises an eyebrow. "Chatty one, this. So, who is she?"

"A nice girl," he answers, finally wrenching the phone away from his sister.

Beth gives him a skeptical look. "They're always nice at the beginning, aren't they?" She sighs and tucks both feet under her. "You should get out more, Chris. All work and no play makes you . . ." She gestures to the bare room.

"I'll get out after the opening."

"No ya won't. You'll throw yersel' into that place twice as much as you already 'ave."

"Work is good," he excuses. "Work keeps me busy. We want me to be busy, don't we? Keeps my mind occupied. Keeps me out of trouble."

"Oh, aye, but so do people," she says. "Nice people. I can't stay around always and look after ye, and Calum can't do it on his own. Ye'll need others." She sighs again. "D'ye like this girl?"

"Sure. She's nice. Really nice. Happy."

"So go out with her, then."

"She may be a little young."

"Is she legal?"

"Yes, Beth, of course she is."

"Ach, well, it's fine, then. Nobody thinks twice about an eligible man with a younger girlfriend. And my friend Carole's fifteen years younger than her man; they get on a treat. Age is just a number, so they say. Nobody's sayin' marry her. Just a drink or summat. What've ya got to lose?"

Chris says nothing. Just watches the dog stop and scratch itself behind the ear and thinks of a long-ago day when he came home late and found Susan sitting on his sagging sofa. Pale, sad, packed bag at her feet.

"Ye've had bad luck," Beth sighs, as if she's reading his mind. "We both have. I've found my peace, and you need to find your'n."

"I *have* found mine. I've got a restaurant to run now. I have two dozen employees relying on me not to mess it all up. If that's not enough to keep me on the straight and narrow, I don't know what will."

"Restaurants are what caused the problem in the first place," Beth points out. "And bein' back here can't be helpin'—ya must be black 'n' blue with all the memories flyin' yer way. Ya need real creatures lovin' and relyin' on ya, and ye relyin' on them. It's why"—she gestures to the bulldog, who is now chewing on her right back foot—"I brought you this."

"What?" Horrified, Chris turns to his sister. "Beth! I can't have a dog! Do you have any idea what sort of hours I'm working now?"

"And she'll keep you from driving yourself back into the ground, Christopher. Dinnae fuss—it'll be good fer ye to have summat to come home to every day. If ye've got a creature relyin' on ye, you're more likely to stay straight. Besides," she adds, with a wry smile, "the girls'll like it."

"I can't keep the dog," he tells her.

"If ya don't take her, she's goin' to the Edinburgh Dog and Cat Home," Beth flings back. "She doesnae get on with the others. So take yer pick." She glares at him for a moment, then sighs. "Chris, you need a bitch in yer life who won't leave you."

Chris rolls his eyes and lets his head drop onto the back of the sofa. After staring at the ceiling for a moment or two, he asks, "What's her name?"

"Dug."

He brings his head back up. "You named the dog 'Dog'?"

Beth shrugs. "Yer job now to name her proper. I cannae be bovvered with silly names for 'em—you know that." She pats her brother on the knee and stands. "Call this Lauren, if she's so nice. Maybe she'll come up with a name fer the creature." She kisses her brother on the cheek, then walks into the guest room and closes the door.

Chris looks at the dog, who has finished feasting on her foot and now comes to sit at his feet, looking up at him as if she expects him to do something. She's leggier than most classic English bull-dogs, mostly a dark fawn color, but with a large white patch over one eye. She has those droopy bulldog eyes that can look, by turns, sad and judgmental. But now she stands and cocks her head and wags her tail, and Chris finds himself smiling, begrudgingly, and patting the sofa cushion Beth just vacated.

"All right, up you come." The dog hops up, and Chris begins scratching her behind one ear.

"You going to put up with me?" he asks. She grunts and leans into his hand. "Right"—he picks up his phone—"where should we take Lauren?"

* * *

She's supposed to be sitting in on meetings between Gloria and the other chefs. She's supposed to be making sure Julia does not choose the most expensive light fixtures. She's supposed to be going over lists of purveyors, but no; instead, Susan is spending her afternoon in Inverleith Park, entertaining two-thirds of her nephew contingent.

Andrew has a follow-up appointment at Sick Kids, and the babysitter cancelled, so Meg phoned in a bit of a panic.

"I can't take all of them! They'll run riot! And the in-laws are at their constituency *again*. William's in a meeting he can't get out of, and Lauren has a date or something. So I'm all alone."

"Meg, I can't," Susan told her, just as she walked into the kitchen at Elliot's. "Gloria and I are meeting with the chefs—"

At that, Gloria looked up, shrugged, and said, "Go ahead, I can handle the meetings. What is it—a couple of hours? You and I can deal with the suppliers then."

"Susan, *please*!" Meg wailed. "I need you!"

And so, here she is, watching Ali kick a football around while she pushes Ayden in a swing.

"Look at me! Look at me!" Ali crows, tripping over the ball as he chases it, landing flat on his face. Susan braces herself for wails and tears, but Ali just pops back up and goes back to kicking the ball around.

At least it's a nice day to be out, and Susan begrudgingly admits she's glad not to be stuck in a basement kitchen. A few clouds scuttle across the sky, but otherwise it's sunny and mild. The park is full of people taking advantage of the weather (any time the mercury creeps above single digits and the sun comes out it's officially "taps aff" weather in Scotland. There isn't a sidewalk or green space in the city that isn't full of people quaffing fruity cocktails or neon orange Irn-Bru, trying to soak up a year's worth of vitamin D in a single afternoon).

The playground, of course, is packed with kids clambering over slides and climbing frames designed to look like a shipwreck. Parents chat while sipping lattes bought from the blinding aluminum coffee truck parked nearby. Beyond the playground fence, dog owners fling balls and Frisbees for their pets; joggers trot along the paths; and lemon-yellow, open-topped tourist buses make their leisurely way up the road to stop just outside the Botanics. On the opposite side of the park, the grand, chateau-like spires of Fettes School slice across the bright blue sky.

Ayden begins to fuss, reaching toward his brother, so Susan stops the swing, lifts him out, and decides it's snack time.

"Ali! Let's get a snack!" she hollers.

Ali obligingly begins dribbling the ball toward the truck, and Susan follows behind, jiggling Ayden up and down to make him smile and laugh.

"Right, what'll it be?" she asks Ali as they step into the shade of the truck.

"Organic," Ali answers, standing on tiptoes to try and see the cakes on offer. "Mum says."

"Oh, it's all organic," Susan tells him, catching the eye of the barista, who grins and winks. "How about a flapjack?" They have oats in them: practically health food.

"Okay," Ali agrees.

She pays for their treats and they head for a nearby bench.

As she sets Ayden down, Ali looks up at her and says, "Kneel down, Auntie Suze, kneel down!"

"Okay." She sets her coffee on the bench and kneels in the grass. Ali backs up a few paces, grins, and runs at her full-force, knocking her flat on her back.

"Rugby tackle!" he gleefully announces, putting his face right in hers and cackling.

"Oof!" Susan catches her breath and laughs. "You got me! You got me! You got me!" She lifts him up in the air with each chant. He screams in delight, and Ayden claps his hands and laughs.

Susan rolls back up onto her knees, blinks, and sees Chris, accompanied by a golden bulldog, standing on the nearby path, watching them.

The sight of him is even more of a sudden smack than Ali's recent assault.

"Hi," she manages to say.

Screaming, "Rugby tackle!" Ali hurls himself at his aunt, laying her out once more. The fall (she tells herself) is what's knocked the wind out of her, and this time she just lies there for a second, staring up at the toddler's smiling face and the blue sky above, wondering (yet again) if she's just seen Chris or imagined it.

But then Alisdair is being gently lifted off her, and Chris's voice is saying, "Easy, wee man—you'll hurt your mum!"

Chris sets Ali back on his feet before turning to Susan, still on the ground, and offering her a hand to help her up.

"Thanks," she mumbles, flustered. She overlooks his hand and rises under her own steam.

"She's not my mum," Ali informs Chris, reaching into the paper bag beside Susan's coffee and retrieving the flapjack.

"Is she not?" Chris asks.

"They're my nephews," Susan explains. "I'm just babysitting."

"Ahh." They blink at each other. Then he says, "I thought you didn't like kids."

"Why would you think that?" she asks, confused. He's never even seen her with children. It was barely even a subject of conversation for them; they were both far too young to be thinking of that sort of thing. He'd mentioned, once or twice, wanting them, but Susan had brushed it off because the way things were for her at that time, the thought of being completely responsible for another human being was overwhelming. She'd hardly been able to look after herself.

* * *

Chris flounders a bit, realizing he's wandered into strange territory, but unsure how to get back out of it. He shrugs. "I don't know. I guess I just assumed."

He thinks of the one time he brought the subject up. It was an offhand comment—they were talking about traveling and all the places they wanted to visit, and he said something about having to visit some of them "before we have kids, of course." It had just popped out. But the look of absolute terror that came over her face when he said it . . . that was the end of *that* conversation.

Ali has polished off the flapjack, and now he and Ayden are inspecting the dog. Chris hunkers down, smiles, and the tone of his voice lightens.

"You like dogs, do you?" he asks. "Do you have dogs at home?" Ali says no, but his grandparents have some. "I know. I met them," Chris tells them. "Nice dogs, those."

No need to tell the kids how annoyed he and Calum were with those dogs, the night they catered the party. They were nice creatures but seemed to have a knack for always anticipating where you were going to turn or step next, and planting themselves right in your path. The two chefs spent most of the evening tripping over and cursing at the poor things, until finally the lady of the house came in, laughing, and said, "Oh, they're not in your way, are they? Naughty babies! Out you go!" as she shooed the dogs into the garden.

"We want a dog, but Mum says no," Ali announces. "They shed and track mud, and we track enough mud in for five dogs." He seems proud of that.

"I'll bet you do," Chris agrees heartily. "You play football, little man?" He nods toward the abandoned ball.

"Yeah. Dad says he'll take me and Andrew to see the Hibs play."

"Ah, a Hibernian fan! Man after my own heart!" Chris claps a hand dramatically over his chest. Ali giggles.

Susan smiles and says, "I didn't know you were such a fan of the little 'uns."

Chris squints up at her and shrugs. "Sure. Who doesn't like kids?"

"Plenty of people."

"Yeah, well, I guess if you lack some sort of nurturing instinct . . ."

She responds sharply, "Or you just don't like kids. Some people don't like dogs or roses—not liking something doesn't make you a freak."

Ali looks up. "Do you like us, Aunt Susan?" he asks.

"Of course I do, sweetie," she replies warmly, bending down to hug him. He wriggles away and goes back to his football. Susan sighs.

Chris straightens. "Sorry," he says.

This isn't how he imagined it would be, their first meeting. He'd planned all those things to say—nasty, hurtful things—but the second he saw her today, they all vanished. His mind went blank, and all he could do was stare at her like some creep. And some of the rancor he felt disappeared, too, at the sight of her on the ground, laughing, playing, tangled up in toddler limbs. It reminded him of the last time they were happy together—really, truly happy. Regent's Park, a day like today. Before her mother got sick. He with a beer and she drinking Pimm's, which stained her upper lip red. He'd rubbed it off gently with his thumb, kissed her, and tasted it . . .

He clears his throat and looks away, fiddling with the dog's leash.

Susan seems to feel the awkwardness too. She glances around and settles on the dog. "What's her name?" she asks, bending to scratch behind the dog's ear.

"Dug," Chris replies, cringing inwardly with embarrassment.

Susan responds with a raised-eyebrow look. "Doug? For a girl?"

"Not 'Doug.' 'Dug,' as in . . . uh, 'Dog.'" Oh God, he sounds like an idiot. He should've renamed the poor dog by now, but when the hell does he have time to come up with a dog's name? He doesn't even have time to put pictures on his walls! "She came with that name," he adds, as if that excuses it.

"Ah. Well, she's lovely." Susan straightens. "The color of a ginger biscuit." She laughs, a little nervously, the way he remembers her doing whenever she felt embarrassed. "Congratulations on your opening," she says. "I hear it went really well."

The press was salivating over the place. The opening went brilliantly—better than anyone expected (breakout dish of the night: the mussels. "I never ever would have thought of doing that with a Shetland mussel," one reviewer swooned. "This is a whole different way of looking at classic dishes.") Even Beth was extraordinarily complimentary ("No bad, no bad," she nodded, examining a half-eaten pheasant pastry. "Ya know what? I'd eat this again. Wouldn't even share it with the dugs.") They've been going full tilt in the three weeks since the launch. This is the first chance he's actually had to get away, and it only happened because Calum essentially banished him from the restaurant for the afternoon. ("Just go out and get some fresh air, will you? You look wan, mate.")

"Thanks," he says to Susan. After another painful silence, he adds, "I'm sorry about Regent Street. And . . . all of it."

"Yeah," Susan sighs. "We got . . . really unlucky."

He can't help but smirk, even as he shakes his head. "You got screwed by your head chef, mostly. He always was a dick."

"Yeah," Susan agrees. "He really was, wasn't he?"

The pair of them share a chuckle despite themselves. Then Chris asks, "I hear you're redoing the Royal Mile restaurant. How's it going?"

"Oh, it's going," Susan sighs. "These things always end up being bigger jobs than you expect, right?"

"Yeah."

"We're hoping to reopen in about three weeks."

"Good."

They stare at each other for several long moments.

"What brings you to this part of town?" she finally asks.

"I'm meeting someone for a drink at the Raeburn," he answers, gesturing in the direction of the restaurant, which lies on the other side of the park's duck pond.

"Oh well, don't let us keep you," Susan says, looking relieved to have an excuse to end this uncomfortable encounter. "I should probably get the boys home soon anyway. Their mother'll probably kill me for letting them have refined sugar, so I may as well face the music. Good seeing you!"

"Yeah," he says. "You too."

She flickers a smile, then runs after Ali, growling, "Fee-fi-fo-fum! I'm coming to get you!"

Chris watches them for a little while, then turns to the dog, saying, "Come on, Ginger," and is on his way.

* * *

Susan resists—*strongly* resists—the urge to turn back around and see if he's watching her go. Of course he isn't. Why would he? She's nothing to him. Clearly.

She concentrates instead on buckling Ayden into his pram. He wriggles and shouts in protest. "Ali! Time to go!" she calls after nephew number two, who's once again running after his ball.

"Just a minute!" he calls, as her phone chirps at her.

"Oh my God, Susan, you won't believe this amazing thing that happened over here," Julia cackles as soon as Susan answers. "It's hilarious—you have to hear it. Oh, and also? There's dry rot in the walls, and the pastry chef just walked out."

Chapter Eleven
The Curse of Crème Brûlée

❧

How is this happening? How? How?!

Susan stares, horrified into speechlessness, at Julia's phone while her sister laughs and says, "Just wait—the best bit's coming up now."

This is not how today was supposed to go. She had a plan: up early, good breakfast, and off to the restaurant to get work done. The plan did not include babysitting or an excruciating surprise face-to-face with her ex, and it sure as hell didn't include having the pastry chef walk out. And yet, here she is, getting the story from Julia, of all people.

Julia pelted toward her almost as soon as Susan came through the front door of the restaurant. "There you are! You missed it! It was amazing! But here—I got most of it." She skirted some workmen looking gravely at a bit of the wall, pulled out her phone, and pressed the "Play" button on the screen. A second later, a recording of Gloria's voice spilled out.

"Crème brûlée? *Crème brûlée?* I asked for innovation, and that's what you came back with?" Gloria shrieks.

"It's cranachan inspired!" the pastry chef counters in a wounded tone. "With Madagascar vanilla, and a raspberry sorbet."

A sigh, from Gloria. Then: "I don't think 'innovation' means what you think it means. It doesn't matter how nice the vanilla is; it's still vanilla. The flavor that actually *defines* boring.

"Now, don't get me wrong, crème brûlée is delicious, and it's a classic for a reason, and twenty or so years ago, you could really impress someone by putting it on a restaurant menu, because they had no clue how to do it themselves at home. But now! Now we have cable TV with whole channels devoted to showing you how to up your home baking game. Now, we have the internet full of videos where Nigella and Delia will lovingly show you exactly how to make the perfect crème brûlée every time. And you can finish it off with the nifty little torch you picked up at Sainsburys for five pounds because it was just too cute and isn't it fun to have this wee little torch in your kitchen?

"People brûlée *everything* now! They brûlée their *porridge*, for god's sake! So when they come to a restaurant like this one, they expect a little more—you get me? They definitely expect slightly more than what they sling out for breakfast on a Thursday morning. They want to be surprised. They want to be intrigued. They want to wonder how the hell we did that. They are not going to think any of those things if we plunk a vanilla crème brûlée down in front of them. They're going to wonder why the hell they just got charged twelve quid for that. It won't matter if those raspberries were foraged by Hugh Fearnley-Whittingstall himself, they're still going to leave here brassed off, because they'll know that that dessert was a massive middle finger to them.

"We are trying to relaunch this place as a destination. If we're going to serve crème brûlée, then I may as well just be out there deep-frying haggis and chips, because it won't matter how amazing the starters and main course were—all anyone'll remember is how crap the dessert was. Please tell me your other ideas were better than this. I mean, they weren't a chocolate lava cake with salted caramel or something, right?"

There was a very long silence.

"Ohh," Gloria says, and the recording ends.

Julia cackles as Susan stares at the phone, stunned.

"Oh my God!" Susan finally yells, drawing stares from more than a few of the workmen.

"I know—it's amazing, isn't it?" Julia giggles. "I wish there was video—I'd put it up on YouTube." She begins scrolling back through the recording. "I love that bit about brûlée-ing porridge—so true! Lord, even my friend Kerry can do that, and she once set her flat on fire boiling water."

Susan takes several deep breaths, wondering if this day can get any worse, and trying not to tempt fate by even considering it. A headache is hammering away at the walls of her skull, as if demanding release. They're supposed to relaunch in three weeks, and now they'll have to recruit and settle in a new pastry chef. There's no way there'll be time for that. But they can't afford to push the opening back much further.

Julia's still giggling, listening again to the recording. "This made my day. Dad'll get a kick out of it."

"Julia, don't you *dare* play that for him!" That's just what she needs: for her father to think she's incompetent and made a terrible decision, promoting Gloria. After that scene with Dan too. The last thing they need is for Bernard to appoint yet another of his friends to manage the restaurant. "And don't play it for anyone else either." Not that it would matter if she did, really. The staff must have overheard this if Julia did. And the pastry chef himself will be out there, telling the story, spinning it so he sounds like the one in the right. This will be restaurant-circle gossip in no time. Dan will be vindicated. Everyone will be talking about how Elliot's is completely falling apart. On her watch.

"Lighten up," Julia huffs. "A little viral marketing would do this place some good. But I won't post it. Can't do much with just a voice recording anyway. I should have live-tweeted. Oh"—she tucks the phone into her pocket—"the contractor needs to see you. He says there's dry rot in one of the walls, but since *you* control the budget, I told him he'd have to speak to you about getting it sorted. And we can't continue with any cosmetic work until that's fixed, so make sure you speak with him today, all right?"

Bad things always come in clumps. Choosing to tackle one crisis at a time, Susan closes her eyes for a second, then says, "I'll talk to him in a minute." She holds out her hand. "May I borrow your phone?"

"Just for a few minutes," Julia says, handing it over. "I'm expecting a call."

"Fine." Susan takes it and heads down to the kitchen.

Salsa music is blasting downstairs, and Gloria and Rey are laughing, swaying back and forth, chopping vegetables in time with the beat.

"You've got the hips, honey, you got it!" Rey declares, hip-bumping Gloria. It's his first day in the new post, and his excitement is palpable, crackling in the air like static electricity. There's been a noticeable difference in the energy in the kitchen since Gloria took over: the languid, sluggish feeling of Dan's days has been replaced by something brighter, more vigorous. The employees, from fellow chefs to waitstaff, to dishwashers, now chatter among themselves and offer up ideas, which Gloria genuinely listens to, nodding, encouraging, saying, "That's good—really good. Maybe if we also do this . . .?" And so new dishes and a new way of working are developing. The employees smile now, to Susan's relief.

"Make sure everyone likes coming to work every day," Elliot used to say. "Depressed people make depressing food."

"I don't know: I think it depends on the food," Susan once countered. "When I'm sad, I make good comfort food."

"You might *think* it's good, but it's not as good as it could be," Elliot insisted. "Good comfort food needs love in it. Think—when you're sad, would you rather have boeuf bourguignon you've made or one that *I* made?"

"You, definitely," she responded immediately. "Though I think I'd prefer a spaghetti bolognese."

"Good girl." He kissed her forehead.

The new energy in the kitchen had given Susan hope. But now this had to happen.

"Gloria, I need to speak to you!" Susan shouts over the music and general cooking din.

Gloria looks up. "Oh, hey, how were the kids?"

"In the office. Now." Susan moves in that direction and waits for Gloria to join her. A moment later she does, wiping her hands on a towel. Susan closes the door behind her, crosses her arms, and demands, "What happened with the pastry chef this morning?"

"We had a difference of opinion," Gloria replies, sitting in the desk chair.

"I'll say." Susan brandishes Julia's phone and plays a few seconds of the recording. "You think browbeating employees is the best way to get good work out of them?"

"Oh, come on," Gloria scoffs. "He wasn't even trying!"

"Maybe he would have if you'd had anything encouraging to say. Instead, you just yelled at and humiliated him. Of course he walked out!"

"This is a good thing," Gloria insists. "He was lazy, like the others."

Susan sighs deeply and pinches the bridge of her nose between two fingers, willing that headache to go away. Instead, it just redoubles its efforts.

"Gloria, listen—I put you in charge here because I thought you were ready for it. I thought you would be a better leader than Dan was, and to your credit, you have been."

"High praise indeed." Gloria smirks.

"Until now," Susan continues in a tight voice. "This is not good leadership. Bullying someone is not acceptable. I won't tolerate it here, understood? Staff should be treated with respect. We need them. We need them to do good work and to want to come and do good work here. What we don't need are enemies. I think we're pretty well set there already, don't you?"

Gloria sighs, looks down at her hands for a moment, and looks back up. "You're right, and I'm sorry," she says. "I got carried away. It's just . . ." She purses her lips and clenches her hands. "You know how I feel about this place and this job. We're getting some good, solid ideas down, but none of that'll matter if we serve shite puddings. If you fall at the last hurdle, it doesn't matter if you jumped clean the rest of the round, right?"

Susan responds with a baffled look.

"Sorry. I thought that all rich girls were into horses. I was trying to speak the language," Gloria explains.

"I'm allergic to horses," Susan grumbles. Begrudgingly, she agrees with what Gloria's saying, even if she doesn't agree with how it was communicated. "So what're we going to do now? We relaunch in three weeks; that's not enough time to get someone new in post at all, let alone get them testing ideas and recipes."

Gloria sighs again, and the two of them contemplate this dilemma in silence. Then Gloria brightens a little and says, "*You* can bake."

"Excuse me?"

"No, really—didn't you train in Paris or something?"

"During my gap year. That was ages ago."

"But you haven't forgotten it. You learned all the techniques, and you've kept up with it—I've had some of the things you've brought in."

"I'm just a home baker, Gloria. It's something I do for fun."

"Do you know of anyone else who can step in at short notice?" Gloria asks. "I mean, I'll ask around, but I don't know of anyone off the top of my head." She leans forward, eyes snapping, gesticulating. "Look, we can put out the call and start recruiting, but in the meantime, you've got a few weeks to work on some things and iron out the kinks so at least we'll have *something* when we launch, right? Better than ordering in from somewhere."

Susan groans. She has a needy sister and a business to run—when is she going to have time to do this? And what if the things she makes aren't good enough? What if they're the boring, crappy desserts everyone walks away sneering about? The restaurant might fail entirely because of her inability to make a decent babka.

But she can't see any other solution. Not in the short term, at least. So, she nods. "All right. As you said, we'll start recruiting, and I'll start coming up with ideas. But Gloria, if anything like this happens again, you're done here. I mean that. I won't have a bully running this kitchen."

Gloria slowly nods. "Fair enough. Can I get back to work now? Rey and I have an idea we're working out."

Susan nods, collects Julia's phone, and follows Gloria out into the kitchen. The music is still playing, though at a slightly lower volume, and Rey is showing one of the dishwashers how to make the spice mix for his paella.

"You think some cayenne might be good in there?" the dishwasher suggests.

"Not in this one," says Rey. "Too overpowering. But maybe we'll work on another version, yeah?" He looks up as Gloria rejoins him, and she gives him a quick nod before getting back to separating eggs. Rey visibly relaxes.

Susan heads back up to the dining room, where Julia is demonstrating to the contractor the exact height at which she wants the new lamps to hang. Susan joins them, handing the phone to Julia, and says to the contractor, "Tell me about this rot."

Chapter Twelve
Radio F-U

❦

Susan is doing battle with sea buckthorn.

She wants to make this work: everyone's going mad for the stuff because apparently it's a superfood. And it's local—harvested from wild plants right in East Lothian—so it fits their new goal to source at least three-quarters of their ingredients from within fifty miles of the restaurant. Even the flour is coming from a farm just outside Drem, only twenty miles away. And she, Rey, and the head waiter spent part of this morning at Mr. Eion's, a coffee roaster in Stockbridge, sampling blends concocted just for Elliot's, choosing which one would be served in French presses and delicate espresso cups at the end of the meal. They'd sipped and quizzed Mr. Eion himself (a warm and enthusiastic man with the full hipster glasses-moustache-beard combination) on bean origins, roasting times, and Fair Trade status before declaring blend number three the runaway winner.

And sea buckthorn. Susan got it into her head to turn some of its juice into jellies to serve alongside a rich pound cake flavored with thyme, but she's having trouble getting the consistency right. One batch of jelly refused to set, and another set so hard you'd need a hatchet to get through it. She wonders if there's something in the chemistry of the juice that's interfering. Baking is a delicate chemical science; the littlest thing can throw a whole recipe off. Or maybe it's her. Maybe jelly is her Waterloo.

There's a bag of coral-colored buckthorn berries in the refrigerator, which she considers turning into a sort of jam. Perhaps she can do a nutty tart crust to go with it—a spin on a linzer torte. Or maybe she's overthinking this and needs to get away from the buckthorn for a while. After all, there are other recipes that need her attention.

She's been at this for a week now. Holed up in the pastry kitchen, making ice creams and tarts and meringues. Experimenting with flavors, tweaking classic recipes, and getting a handle on the incredible array of gadgets at her disposal. Because Dan and the pastry chef were given free rein to buy whatever toy they wanted, both kitchens are loaded with the latest thing, whether it's useful or not. Gloria isn't quite sure yet what to do with the sous-vide machine, but another gadget that cold-pickles just about anything is proving to be a source of inspiration. For her part, Susan was a bit horrified by the bread machine in the pastry kitchen, but intrigued by the candy-floss maker. Her attempts to make chocolate-flavored floss haven't worked because the cocoa burns too easily, but she's having better luck with peanut flavor and trying to think of what could go with it.

She whisks some agar into the sea buckthorn juice, pours the liquid into a lined pan, and pops it into her refrigerator to set (hopefully). It shares a shelf with four bowls, each containing a different flavor of sourdough bread, slowly rising. The sourdough mother now lives on a pantry shelf, happily bubbling away after its feed the previous afternoon.

Susan turns her attention to strawberries. They're easier. Who doesn't like a strawberry? And they're excellent right now: a cold, damp spell in May delayed the season, but the more recent, prolonged good weather means they're exploding all over, rich and sweet. She's trying them out on a cloudy pavlova flavored with pink peppercorns, mixing the strawberries with mint and lemony sumac. Getting the flavor balance just right is tricky, but she's nearly there, and once she has it, she can sign off on at least one dessert.

Then on to the next: she has dinner and lunch menus to fill with delectable, seasonal delights. There need to be at least four desserts for each meal—five, if she can manage it, plus breads and anything else that needs baking. Gloria will need crusts for quiches and pies; puff pastry for various dishes. She and Susan have been putting their heads together on the menu, and now Susan is experimenting with flavored pastry crusts—there's a vibrant orange carrot pastry relaxing in the refrigerator just above the jelly and bread dough. Susan worries about what color it'll be when baked—it won't stay that bright and might very well turn an unappealing brown. They may have to consider a carrot nest instead, if they want to keep that visual appeal.

She chops strawberries and mint, humming along to the music pouring through her propped-open door. Today it's classic Motown. "I need something with a little soul," Gloria insisted as she tied on her apron that morning.

"You got it, honey," Rey answered.

Their daily music choice sets the tone and pace of the kitchen. Everyone chops and stirs and cooks in time with it. Gazing through the window that overlooks the main kitchen, Susan sees Gloria and Rey swaying their hips, even as they keep their heads down, focusing on their work. Gloria is tweaking presentations on the dishes Susan has already approved, and Rey is developing a new accompaniment to their scallop dish. An apprentice works alongside him, learning how to get just the right sear on the scallops so they caramelize, but don't burn, and remain tender and just barely cooked inside.

"Otherwise, you'll get rubbery scallops, and nobody wants that," Rey tells him, gesturing for the young man to flip the creamy mollusks.

The other apprentice is making buckwheat crepes for one of the starters they're testing. With a cocky smile, he tries flipping it in the air with a flick of his wrist, but he misses the catch, and it lands draped over the side of the pan, clinging for a second before disintegrating and landing on the open flame of the gas burner. The kitchen briefly fills with the acrid smell of burning before the extractor fan manages to whisk the stench away.

"Hey, don't get fancy, here; there's no one to impress with that kind of trickery," Gloria scolds him, glancing up from her painstakingly placed microgreens. She catches Susan's eye and they exchange a "kids, you know?" smirk.

There's a good feeling, a good energy, but it feels like time is running short, even though they've pushed the launch back *yet again*. That's mostly thanks to the dry rot in the walls upstairs, which is proving extra tricky because they're in a listed building, and the Council needs to sign off on any structural work. They don't seem to be in any particular rush to do that, because what do they care if Elliot's ever reopens?

There's still so much to do, and now Susan is gazing down at her pile of precisely diced strawberries and wondering if this is enough. Will *they* be enough? Will *she* be enough? Will the critics and the Instagram-loving diners they're going after take one look at her desserts and think, "Pavlova? Really? Welcome back to 1986, amirite?"

She needs a break. She's been at this since half past six, and now, Susan realizes, it's past two. She puts the strawberries to one side and steps into the main kitchen, stretching her arms above her head and trying to get the kink out of her lower back.

Gloria glances up and smiles a hello, then catches sight of the clock on the wall and yells, "Ah, shit—Rey, the interview's on."

Rey switches from the music to BBC Radio Scotland, where a pleasant female voice is saying, ". . . today we're sitting down with Chris Baker, who's followed up his rapid rise to culinary television stardom with the much-acclaimed opening of his first restaurant, Seòin, in Edinburgh. And he'll be following that with the publication of a new book in August. Quite the busy man! I feel fortunate he had the time to sit down with us. Chris, thank you so much for being here today."

"Not at all—thank you for having me." Chris's voice, light and warm, roots Susan to the spot.

"Tell us a bit about your restaurant," the presenter urges. "It seems like you're pulling from a lot of different culinary traditions, but tying them in with classic Scottish cooking."

"You have it exactly," he agrees. "I've been fortunate enough to travel and study all over the world, and I've sort of stolen the best bits—or my favorite bits—and used them to play around with some of the dishes I grew up with."

"Yes, that's right, you grew up in Edinburgh, didn't you?" the presenter says, as if Chris has only just reminded her.

Gloria snorts. "What? Like she didn't know that?"

"These things are always so fake," Rey agrees.

"I did," says Chris. "I grew up a bit rough, on one of the council estates in the city. I . . ." There's a pause so long that Gloria and one of the line cooks look up at the radio, wondering if it died. Susan frowns, wondering what Chris is thinking of. "I knew more than a few people—young people—who got into trouble. And honestly, I probably would have been one of them if it hadn't been for cooking." His voice takes on a self-deprecating tone. "I know that must sound incredibly cliché, but it's true. The kitchen saved me, and I want to do the same for other lads—and lasses—who need direction. So, Seòin is also a sort of social enterprise. I'm hiring at-risk youth and young offenders and giving them a chance for a different sort of life."

"That's very noble," the presenter purrs.

Rey rolls his eyes and makes a "jerking-off" motion with one hand before getting back to the vegetables he's pickling.

"Just do him already, why don't you?" one of the apprentices joins in.

"Shh!" Susan hisses. She doesn't care much for this presenter either, but she thinks Chris's plan for the restaurant deserves a little respect. Some people would do something like this purely for a marketing angle, but she senses he's in earnest. She can hear it in his voice. He's excited about this.

"And you're helping out fellow chefs as well, aren't you? Helping them get started?" prompts the presenter.

"Not just me. There's a team of us—the Kitchen Lab. Established Scottish chefs who've been fortunate enough to find success. We've bought a space in the Arches, near Waverley Train Station, and turned it into a restaurant that up-and-coming chefs can use as a pop-up for a month at a time. It helps them get exposure that may help them establish themselves more permanently on the Scottish restaurant scene."

"Aren't you worried about potentially creating competition?"

Chris laughs softly. "I welcome it. Competition keeps you sharp. Keeps you innovating."

"Speaking of getting started in cooking—it was Elliot Napier who gave you your first job in a kitchen, wasn't it? At his flagship restaurant?" the presenter continues.

Susan's heart thumps and her stomach twists.

"That's right, he did," Chris agrees. "Back when Elliot's was still producing halfway decent food."

The kitchen goes dead quiet as everyone stops what they're doing and stares at the radio.

The host chuckles. "Don't think much of it now, I suppose?"

They can almost hear Chris shrug. "Oh, you know, he let it go corporate, and it lost its soul. It used to be one of the best restaurants in the city, but now . . . Well, the tourists like it, at least. They're planning a relaunch, I hear, but honestly, at this point it'd take a miracle to make that place any sort of destination again."

"Ouch," Gloria says with an exaggerated wince. "Thanks a lot, wanker."

The dishwasher flips a middle finger at the radio, and Rey shrugs. "Imagine how surprised he'll be," he says, finishing up with the vegetables, "when he has his first meal here . . . Mmm!" He smacks his lips. "He won't know what hit him." He looks up at Susan and cocks his head. "You okay, honey?"

Susan is still standing in front of the door to the pastry kitchen, anchored to the spot. Her emotions are so all over the place she isn't quite sure what she's feeling. Shame? Rage? Embarrassment? A certain determination to deliver a massive culinary "F--- you to Chris I'm-so-famous-now Baker? Maybe all of those things?

Gloria, too, glances up and her brow furrows. Susan realizes she must look awful. She takes a stumbling step back toward the pastry kitchen, mumbling about having a lot to do. Once safely inside, she closes the door, shutting out the rest of the interview. She crosses to the refrigerator and yanks open the door, letting the cold air soothe her for a few seconds. Then she returns to her strawberries.

*   *   *

The perfect end to the day: the goddamn jelly hasn't set again. Susan glares at it. It glistens in its sheet pan, a mocking, gelatinous, Agent Orange–hued symbol of failure.

The rest of the staff has long since gone. She hardly noticed them trickling out, but now she looks up and realizes the main kitchen is silent, cleaned, and empty. And no wonder: it's almost half past eight.

As she stands there, struggling not to cry, Gloria walks into the kitchen, spots her through the window, and does a double take.

"Still here?" she confirms, sticking her head through the door to the pastry kitchen.

Susan continues to brood over her ruined jelly. "It won't set," she mutters.

Gloria joins her, cocks her head, puts her hands on her hips. "Time to throw in the towel on this one, I think," she concludes. "You gave it a good try; no use wasting more time over it." She pats Susan on the shoulder. "Maybe we can reduce the juice down to a sauce or something, or use it in a vinaigrette."

"Sure," Susan agrees dully, taking the pan over to the dish-washing station and tipping the mess into the sink.

Gloria follows and watches as Susan hunches briefly over the sink, closing her eyes and trying not to get so worked up over something as stupid as a jelly. She realizes she's sore all over from standing and bending for hours. Even her eyes are sore—they feel sandy when she blinks.

"Let it go, Suze," Gloria urges in a gentle voice. "No use crying over spilt jelly."

Susan barks a laugh.

"Right," Gloria decides. "You need to replace jelly with alcohol. Come on—let's get a drink."

* * *

They settle in at a bar farther down the Mile. Gloria knows the bartender well enough to exchange nodding greetings with him and to request "that thing you make that I like so much? She'll have one." She indicates Susan before continuing, "And I'll have an IPA. The one the hipsters all like right now."

"Right," Gloria says once the drinks are in front of them. "So what's really up? Are you letting nerves get to you?"

"Of course I am," Susan answers. "I'd be crazy not to. We are up against it, and if this place fails, that's it. *And* we've got to find a way to create an entirely new reputation, which is pretty damn hard to do, especially when famous people are slagging you off on live radio."

"Oh, there it is." Gloria nods, sipping her beer. "The interview. Yeah, I have to admit I was a bit scunnered by that one as well. Bit of a low blow, that."

"A bit! Calling my grandfather a sellout when Chris owes him his start. You know he just showed up at the restaurant one day and asked for a job? I'm serious—my grandfather went to open the restaurant one morning, and there was this kid there, lying in wait for him. And he somehow managed to convince my grandfather to let him come in and cook something, and he didn't know any-thing—nothing at all. I think he made bacon rolls or something like that, but my grandfather was impressed enough by his enthu-siasm to take him on as an apprentice and teach him what he knew. Chris owes my granddad everything!" Susan takes an angry swig of her drink, which tastes of about eight different kinds of alcohol.

Gloria waits for the end of the tirade, then comments, "He's got some balls, Chris does. You have to give 'im that." She sips her beer, then asks, "So, what happened? He and your granddad fall out or something?"

Susan toys with her glass and takes another sip while Gloria waits. Gloria's face transitions from "What's up?" to "Oh, I *see*," just in those few seconds. Even so, Susan steels herself and says, "He didn't say those things because of Grandad. It was because of me."

Gloria nods. "It all comes together. Didn't end well, I take it?"

Susan closes her eyes for a few seconds, wishing she could will away the past decade. But nothing can do that, and the universe seems determined to keep throwing it back in her face.

"No," she admits in a voice that barely breaks a whisper. "No, it really didn't."

How to explain to someone who wasn't there?

Elliot's death had been a blow, but her mother's was a bomb detonated among them, leaving the family torn and ragged, scattered and hollowed out. Without her to rally around, they fled, finding comfort where they could. For Susan, it was Chris, who felt like the one good thing left in her life. And he'd tried so hard to be there for her—she knew that now, looking back from the perch of greater maturity. He had also lost a parent; he understood. He held her when she cried all night and endured her silences, her clinging, her constant presence in his cramped, dingy flat.

But he had his own life. He had a career he was desperate to establish, and restaurants are as demanding as a grieving partner, if not more so. He came home later and later, as she lay in bed, staring into the dark. Panicking, imagining him dead or hurt somewhere, bleeding into the pavement. Or not dead—just tired of her. Out enjoying himself with some blonde with perky breasts, who smiled and giggled and cooed over his accent. And why shouldn't that be the case? He was young and good looking—*far too good looking for me,* Susan always thought. Why shouldn't he be out with happy young women, instead of dragging himself home to a depressive sad sack who could barely function?

After all, Chris seemed to have energy to burn. Most chefs got tired after endless double shifts, on their feet in hot kitchens simmering with urgency, but Chris seemed to thrive on it. He came home hyperactive, even on the days he was out until dawn. Susan, sleep deprived herself, found his energy exhausting. She was hardly able to take it in as he quick-fire chattered about his day and new dishes he was coming up with, new techniques, plans to travel. He hopped from one thought to another, pinging around from subject to subject, a pinball ricocheting faster than Susan could follow.

"Thailand!" he announced one day, bursting into their bedroom at three o'clock one morning. "We should go, don't you think? You and I? Not the beachy bit that all the tourists go to, but the real Thailand, where actual Thai people live and work and eat. Wouldn't that be great? You know, I think I might order some Thai. You hungry? I'm starving. You think that place we like is open? Nah, probably not. Are there others? Maybe pizza instead? Or I could go to that kebab place down the road—they're always open. You think that guy ever sleeps? It's the same guy there all the time—did you ever notice that? Last time I was there, they put some sort of sauce on the kebab. I really need to ask what was in that, because I think I could do something with it. Not on a kebab, of course, because we don't serve kebabs at the restaurant, which is just snobby, I think. We should do a kebab. A really good one, with that sauce. I wonder if that guy at the kebab place makes the sauce too, or if they bring it in? Or I could get Thai food. How about we go to Thailand?"

"Thailand?" Susan repeated, struggling mightily to follow him.

"Or somewhere else! Japan, India, some of the Middle East, the States—there are so many amazing places we could go. We could just eat our way across the globe! Let's do it!"

In her state of mind then, the thought of planning a trip so intricate—sortingoutvisasandhostelsandadozendifferentlanguages— overwhelmed and intimidated her, so she'd just stared at him as he leafed through takeaway menus, gabbling about kebab sauce. But later that day, when she met her aunt for lunch, and Kay innocently asked how things were going, Susan burst into tears.

Babbling almost incoherently about plane tickets and Chris's hours and her fears, she scared the hell out of Kay. Scared her enough that Kay unearthed herself from her own grief and stepped in. She found a counselor—one of the best—and sent Susan to her (and, not long after, Julia as well).

Kay had dealt with the loss of her sister by throwing herself into her work; taking a role in a film that was shooting in New Zealand. But with principal photography nearly finished, she told the director she was done and settled back down in London, turning down offers of work for the time being, so she could always be available to her nieces. The counseling and having this one steadying influence helped get Susan back on an even keel. At Kay's suggestion, she moved out of Chris's flat and into her aunt's. No longer waiting for the sound of Chris's footsteps every night, she started sleeping better.

Once it was clear Susan was improving, Kay sat her down for a serious talk about her future.

"He's a nice boy," Kay allowed, "but you know how this business is. You'll be waiting up nights forever. Is that what you want? To always be waiting? You have your own future to consider—you had plans, Susan, and your mother was so excited about them and so happy you were doing so well at school! She'd be so disappointed to see you throw it all away just to sit around, night after night, in some Tottenham flat."

She pulled Susan close and hugged her. "This whole relationship was formed when your emotions were very high, my dear," she murmured. "Believe me, I know how that can be—it's happened to me dozens of times! I'm not saying you have to throw the whole thing away, but perhaps simply take a step back. Give yourselves some space and time to . . . develop a bit. Grow up, even. Let your life calm down. You're both so young! You're just getting out in the world. Let him climb that restaurant ladder, if that's what he wants to do, and you go back to Cambridge and finish your degree and start your career. And just . . . see where you both end up."

Kay toyed for a moment with a cup of tea, then added, "It's so challenging for a young man in this business to balance those hours with a relationship. He'll probably thank you for this."

But—

"He didn't thank me," Susan concludes in the story for Gloria. "He really, really didn't."

"Well, he should have understood, right?" Gloria asks. "I mean, like you said, he lost a parent, and it's not like he didn't know you were grieving. And he must've thought you'd go back to school eventually."

"It wasn't just that," Susan sighs. "I handled the whole thing horribly. *Really* horribly. I went back to his place and packed up the last of my things and just waited for him. I had this whole speech prepared, but when he came through the door . . . I don't know, it just went out the window. And I didn't know what to say, so I just babbled something about space and told him I was sorry, and I just left. I didn't even have the guts to tell him I was breaking up with him—I didn't say anything. And he kept trying to phone and text me, and I ignored him, and eventually he stopped."

"Oh, man," Gloria breathes, cringing. "You ghosted him?"

"I know! I'm such a bitch! It's just . . . I was such a mess. There was all this confusion in my life already after my mum died, and Chris and I—our thing—it was just really, really intense and amazing, and I wasn't prepared for it and didn't know how to manage it, so I just ended up fucking the whole thing up." Susan finishes off the drink, which is definitely not meant to be drunk all in one go. She feels almost instantly tipsy.

"Oh please, everyone's an arsehole in their twenties," Gloria reassures her, patting her on the back. "Some never get past that stage, so you're already doing better than them, right? Aw, don't beat yourself up. I mean, this was—what, ten years ago? If he's still holding a grudge over a fling that ended badly a decade ago, he's got some serious issues."

"It wasn't just a fling, though," Susan sighs. "It definitely wasn't for me."

The bartender whisks her empty glass away and immediately replaces it with a full one. Susan knows she shouldn't, but she starts drinking it anyway.

Gloria scrunches her face sympathetically. "Aw, man, he was your first, wasn't he?" Off Susan's look, she nods. "Yeah, those're tough to shake. Like a bad lurgy, right? Make you feel all sick and dizzy, even after they're gone. Took me ages to get over my first. Seeing him with another man really helped."

Susan laughs despite herself.

"You'll shake him eventually. We all do," Gloria continues. "We have to, don't we?"

"Suppose so," Susan agrees, staring down at her drink.

A moment's silence, and then Gloria asks, "You want him back?"

Startled, Susan stammers, "No! I mean, I-I don't know. I don't really know him anymore, do I? I knew him ten years ago, and he's done so much since then, he must be different now. And he hates me. Clearly."

"Maybe he's just trying to get your attention."

"By insulting my grandfather's restaurant?"

"Worked, didn't it? And I have t'admit, it lit something of a fire under *my* arse. Don't you just want to prove him wrong now? I sure as hell do."

"Yeah," Susan murmurs, nodding. "Yeah, you know what? I do!"

"Attagirl! And while you're at it, get out there! Nothing clears a bad dating history like a new one. Go date! Or don't—just take someone home. That guy at the end of the bar keeps looking at you. He's cute. Go for it!"

Susan glances toward the end of the bar. A young man with ridiculous cheekbones and brown hair that waves far too perfectly for him to be entirely mortal is having a lively conversation with the bloke sitting next to him. He's way out of her league.

"You're seeing things," Susan says.

"I don't think so." Gloria cocks her head and squints. "He look familiar to you?"

Susan looks again. "Kind of. It's a small city, though. We've probably run across him somewhere."

"I'd remember if I'd seen *him* somewhere around." Gloria smirks. "If you won't have a go at him, I might."

"You do that, and have fun," Susan says, slowly getting down from the bar stool and trying not to visibly sway. The room is tilting just a little, and her hands are tingly—a sure sign she's hovering on the edge of having drunk too much.

"Oh, I would," says Gloria. "Seriously, though—forget Chris Baker. He thinks he's hot shite because everyone keeps telling him he is. But you know the truth, right?" She leans toward Susan with a wicked smile. "I mean, you'll know about all those times he burnt the toast or laughed so hard he farted, right?"

Susan laughs, a little more loudly than warranted, and the man at the end of the bar looks up and grins. His smile is as dazzlingly superhuman as his hair. She feels herself blush and fumbles with her purse.

"Don't worry about it," Gloria says. "I got this one."

"Thanks, Gloria," Susan says. "Not just for the drinks, but—"

"I know, it's all good," Gloria answers, taking her second beer. "You know I'm here, okay? We women in this business need to stick together."

"In any business," Susan agrees. "See you tomorrow. And don't forget we've got that interview with *The Scotsman* on Sunday."

"I remember." Gloria's eyes twinkle over the bottle. "Maybe we'll give Baker a little of his own back."

"Let's not." Susan's not prepared to tackle a full-on war. She can't even make a berry behave. "See you tomorrow."

"See you." As Susan walks away, Gloria looks at the man standing at the bar next to her, who seems to have his eyes affixed to her generous breasts. "Sorry," Gloria says, gesturing to his drink, "were you looking for something to put that on?"

Susan laughs again as she sidles out the door and hails a cab.

Chapter Thirteen
Played

～

It is most definitely not Lindsay Howard, *The Scotsman*'s new deputy head of content, who saunters through the door of Elliot's on Sunday morning.

Susan, caught unawares, is expecting a petite forty-something woman with honey-colored hair. Instead, in comes a young man with black hair and a ruthlessly waxed and styled French handlebar moustache. He looks around, seeming amused, emits a low whistle, and observes, "You're really doing a number on this place, aren't you?"

"Can I help you?" Susan asks. In his white, popped-collar polo shirt, seersucker jacket, skinny jeans, and Toms slip-ons, he looks like the sort of person who parades around the city just hoping to run into someone taking photographs for a Street Style spread. It seems odd that he'd wander into a restaurant so clearly under construction.

"I sure hope so," he answers, approaching her and extending a hand. "Rufus Arion. Lindsay sent me." He shakes her hand, then produces a card.

Rufus Arion

Journalist

Arionnation.com

"Oh, you're *that* Rufus Arion," Susan can't help but say, passing the card along to Gloria, who raises an eyebrow and pinches her lips together.

He brightens. "You've heard of me!"

"My sister-in-law's mentioned your blog." Susan forces a smile, even though the idea of having to entertain someone with such a repulsive blog moniker makes her skin crawl.

"Oh, right!" Rufus grins. "That's Lauren, right?"

"You know her?"

"I know *of* her, of course. Not exactly a shrinking violet, is she? And now she and Chris Baker . . . kinda fun, innit? Complicated for you, though, right? But we'll get to that. Shall we?" He swoops down on a table, setting out his phone and a pad and pen.

Gloria swallows hard and gives Susan a "good luck with this one" look before vanishing into the kitchen. As she goes, the bartender approaches the table with a bubbly, coral-colored cocktail in a champagne glass.

"Buckthorn fizz." He sets it down in front of Rufus and winks at Susan.

The previous day she'd handed him the sea buckthorn juice she'd been unable to use and told him to do whatever he wanted with it. This pretty brunch cocktail is his answer.

"Oh, *very* nice," says Rufus. "The hen parties'll love it."

"We hope so," Susan responds, taking a seat across the table from him.

Rufus raises an eyebrow. "Really? You'd welcome the hens, would you?"

She knows what he's doing. Hen parties are notoriously raucous, and plenty of restaurants won't have them or their male counterparts, the stag dos. But she won't have Elliot's known for snobbery.

"We welcome everyone," she replies. "This is a restaurant, not a members-only club."

"Well, that's a bit of a turnaround," he observes. "I went to Elliot's on Regent Street once. All bankers and their second wives. Hoping to attract a different sort here, then?"

"We hope to attract people who appreciate excellent food."

"Ah yes, the food. There's been some debate about that, hasn't there?" He makes a sympathetic clucking noise. "Chris Baker was really rough on you the other day, wasn't he? Naughty boy, going after the very place that gave him his start."

"He's entitled to his opinion," Susan answers in a tight voice and with an even tighter smile. "But let's talk about the food."

"Oh, we'll get to that." Having been cut off from a gossipy story about a potential rivalry between the restaurants, he's clearly searching for another angle. His eyes flicker around the chaotic interior, taking in the walls that have been reduced to studs, the tables and chairs that have been bunched near the windows, the open box of lighting fixtures that don't match the ones that have already been hung (Julia had had a fit over that and gave the supplier an earful). The brass that has not yet been removed. "Going industrial chic with your decor, I see." He chuckles. "You should know that's out now. We all want some Scandinavian thing."

"I promise you'll get it," says Susan, "but I'm sure you know any major refurbishment takes a fair bit of work."

"Especially when you're dealing with council red tape." His eyes flash, waiting for her response.

Susan heads him off with "I didn't know you were a food writer. I got the impression your blog was more . . . news based."

"It's a gossip blog—no need to beat about the bush." He smiles, unperturbed by any judgment. "I'll write about nearly anything. Freelance life, you know. But I asked for this assignment. Seemed juicy." He knocks back the Buckthorn Fizz in one go. "Oh, that's quite refreshing." He sits up a little straighter and catches the bartender's eye. "Don't suppose you have anything in the line of a

Bloody Mary, though? More Mary, less bloody, if you know what I mean?"

The bartender glances at Susan, who nods briefly. They need to keep Rufus sweet, after all. It's been hard enough to get this story. She had leaned hard on the deputy editor and mentioned her connections to both Kay *and* Russell when it became apparent that Elliot's name alone wasn't enough to interest the paper. The (potential) resurgence of a high-end restaurant doesn't scan with newspaper editors, who are after clicks and ad revenue. Susan hates having to play those family cards, but she'll hate not having any customers far more.

"Shame about the flame-out in London," says Rufus, wrinkling his nose in sympathy. "Bad luck, that. Well, some of it was bad luck, eh?"

"It's rough on luxury brands when the economy takes a turn," Susan agrees.

"Luxury? But it wasn't really a luxury brand anymore, was it? More Kardashian than Cartier. You think opening the door to hen parties is going to help that?"

Susan glances away, trying to stay calm, keep the rage from building. It's not rage toward Rufus, as unpleasant as he is. It's only fair that he should ask these sorts of questions. She expected it and told herself she was ready for them. She was wrong.

"There were regrettable decisions made," she allows. "We experimented. Took some risks. They didn't pay off. Sometimes that happens. All you can do is learn from it."

He nods. "So no risk taking here, then?"

"We're committed to getting back to our roots. Elliot's was always about excellent food and a great experience—"

"Kind of lost its way, though," Rufus clucks, shaking his head. "The stuff that was being served here . . . I don't know anyone who's been to Elliot's. They all want to hit Aizle or The Kitchn or Baker's new place. Speaking of that"—Rufus leans forward and lowers his voice to a conspiratorial murmur—"you and Chris Baker have a history, I hear."

"Who told you that?" Susan asks, pulling away from him.

"Oh, come on now—I have sources. No need to be coy."

"I'm not going to discuss my personal life or Mr. Baker's," Susan responds primly.

Rufus sighs, and for the first time, his expression changes from one of overeager wickedness to something more genuine. Almost like sympathy.

"Listen," he tells her, "I'm trying to help you, believe it or not. No one is going to read an article that's all 'the food here is good.' They want more. Trust me, I know. I'm the perfect person to write this whole thing up. You want to build some excitement and bring feet through that door? You'll need clicks on this article, okay? Give me a juicy angle to work with. Now, you and Chris Baker—I'm guessing it didn't end well, considering that interview and the fact he's backing your former chef's new venture."

"He's what?" Susan hisses, feeling like she's just had ice water thrown at her.

That previous expression, the one that almost made Susan like Rufus, is, for a second, replaced by a smile that slithers. "Oh," he says, "you didn't know?"

"Who's hungry?" Gloria and a waiter appear at the side of the table, arms piled with dishes.

Rufus straightens and rubs his hands. "Oh, me! I've brought my appetite."

Dishes are set before him: grilled pheasant and pomegranate salad; the haggis, neeps, and tatties soup; a savory doughnut stuffed with fresh crabmeat; lemon, zucchini, and Anster cheese soufflé; a slab of moist sourdough bread with a pot of freshly made crowdie and preserved lemons to spread on top; and, of course, the pudding.

This one was born from Susan's childhood memories: after-school treats of bananas split in half and spread with peanut butter, and her mother's chocolate chip–studded banana bread, lavished with butter or dripping with honey. This pudding starts with a cake: the bottom layer is a rich, dark, fudgy chocolate as luscious as velvet. On top of that a layer of banana honey cake laced with cinnamon—just sweet enough to balance out the bittersweet bottom layer. And finally, a peanut butter mousse that dissolves as soon as it reaches your tongue, melding creamily with the other layers like a slightly salty, addictive sauce. Shards of honey and peanut praline decorate the cake, and it's accompanied by a little peanut-flavored candy-floss "lollipop" on the side.

Rufus snaps photos with his phone, murmuring, "Oh yes, that'll do nicely. Looks delish!" At last, he takes a bite of the salad, followed by some of the soup. "Yes, this is *much* better than what you served here before. Edible, even!"

"Thaaaaaanks," says Gloria, joining them at the table.

Around a mouthful of bread, Rufus tells her, "I was just telling Susan here that your former boss is opening a place just around the corner. Dan—that's his name, right? Well, he and the sous chef and the former pastry chef here took a place in Waverly Arches, with support from Chris Baker. What do you think about that?"

Gloria gapes at him for a moment, then looks at Susan, who is similarly shocked. The Arches! That is literally around the corner from Elliot's—a set of cave-like hollows from the Victorian period that were revamped into retail and dining space. And now their disgruntled former employees are opening a place there!

"We wish them luck, of course"—Susan manages to cover—"as we would wish anyone luck. This is a tricky business."

"Yes, indeed, as you yourself have found," says Rufus, reaching for the doughnut. "Seems you," he says to Gloria, "have ruffled more than a few feathers."

"Women who speak their mind and take a tough line tend to," Gloria flings back. "People hate an uppity girl."

"Not me!" Rufus chuckles. "I like 'em feisty!"

Something about the way he says that makes Susan shudder. Out of the corner of her eye, she could swear she saw Gloria do the same.

"Kind of a gamble on your part, putting an untried chef in charge of a restaurant you're trying to pull back from the brink," Rufus comments to Susan.

"She's not an untried chef. She's highly qualified and has been working here for years. And I think the food speaks for itself," Susan replies.

Rufus nods. "Oh, I agree!" He starts in on the soufflé.

"We're interested in fostering talent here," Susan presses on, hoping to regain control of the interview and maybe find that angle Rufus says he needs. "We've always been interested in identifying and nurturing promising up-and-comers, even when others would consider it a risk."

"Like Chris Baker," Rufus supplies.

Susan inwardly curses herself for walking into that. "Yes." Tightly, through her teeth.

"And that's the kind of comeback to bite you in the arse, isn't it?" Rufus shrugs and begins sucking up the Bloody Mary through his straw.

"We'll just have to see," Susan says.

"Oh, come on. He's funding a restaurant run by your angry former chefs, just around the corner from here." Rufus clucks, shaking his head. "I mean, really! What else does he have to do, actually walk up and punch you both in the face?"

"I don't think that'll be necessary," Susan coolly replies.

Rufus sighs. "He really has it in for this place. Just the other day, I was talking to my friend, Babs, who runs the Foodies Festival, and she said Chris floated the idea of doing a wee head-to-head competition at the Festival this year—you know, to give the crowd a little thrill and raise some money for charity? And she suggested he go up against a team from Elliot's, but he just laughed and said you'd never compete against him because you'd be afraid of being humiliated. And you *would* be humiliated because he'd wipe the floor with you. His words, not mine. He said this place was all washed up, and your chef was just some woman no one's heard of. He told Babs not to waste her time." Rufus leans forward again, peering into Susan's face. "Jesus, what did you *do* to him?" he asks.

"Nothing to warrant that," Susan growls as Gloria demands, "He actually *said* that?"

Rufus slathers his bread with crowdie. "Of course, I *could* tell Babs the man was talking out his arse. It's not too late, you know, to schedule this whole thing. You could show him what Elliot's really has to offer." He gestures with the bread to the remains of the food.

Susan narrows her eyes. Something about this doesn't quite gel. She's never known Chris to be so, well, cruel. It all sounds a bit cartoon villain to her. But then she clearly doesn't really know him anymore. Would the Chris she knew say those things about her grandfather's restaurant on the radio?

Rufus sets the bread aside after two bites, digs a fork into the cake, and scoops some into his mouth. "Oh yes!" He closes his eyes, savoring it. "Now *that* is pudding," he declares before devouring the rest of it. "So, ladies, what do you say? Should I tell Babs you're game? It'd be great publicity," he adds, as if he senses they need further persuasion.

"Yeah," Gloria answers before Susan can get there. "You do that."

A Grinch-like grin spreads once more over Rufus's face. "Excellent. I'll phone her today."

* * *

Service! Just the thought of it is enough to get Chris's blood pumping. That frantic run-up to the opening of the front doors—a flurry of chopping and last-second prep. His last turn around the kitchen to sample sauces and soups, and make sure the meats and fish and vegetables are all correctly portioned out. A reminder to the waitstaff to push particular dishes. That brief period, just after the first guests are seated, when the chefs correct any last-minute errors ("too much salt in that dressing, mate—let's do something about it") and Chris takes his place at the pass. A breathless moment, and then the computer spits out the first ticket. Chris bellows, "Service, please!" and calls out the orders to a chorus of "Yes, Chef!" from the line cooks.

And from then on it's a marathon and a dance, all of them doing a dozen things at once—sautéing and saucing and plating and finishing, stepping around one another in a dangerous choreography as they juggle knives and crackling pans filled with spitting fats. Every plate is set in front of Chris, who finishes them off, wipes the edges, makes sure they're perfect before placing them on the pass to be whisked away by the waitstaff.

They do this for hours, until the tide of customers begins to ebb. They see the orders drop off, and finally it's only the puddings left to plate. A few people linger over coffees and after-dinner drinks as the kitchen staff shut down and clean up. Then the door is locked, and they can all breathe again. Work the kinks out of their muscles and notice the sore spots for the first time. Chris has noticed recently there are more sore spots than there used to be.

"Right, bacon rolls!" Calum announces at the end of Sunday night service. This is their tradition: proper bacon rolls for the whole staff at the end of the night, before everyone disperses to beds or (more often) bars. Sunday is a particularly popular night for partying, as the restaurant's closed Mondays and Tuesdays.

Calum tosses thick slices of smoked back bacon on the hot grill, where they sizzle away, while Rab slices soft buns and the staff crowds in, popping open bottles of beer, swapping stories about the evening's more interesting customers, and making plans for the night and the next two days. Bacon comes off the grill and is slapped onto buns, then slathered in bottled brown sauce and distributed. Chris always gets his last: it only seems right to him.

"Thanks for another great night, everyone!" he shouts before sinking his teeth into the roll. His reward is a spicy-sour gush of brown sauce, mixed with the mellow smokiness of the bacon and barely there bun.

People keep trying to posh up the bacon roll. They put fancy meat on rich, buttery brioche buns and pile on homemade chipotle-red-pepper-Sriracha ketchup or something, and a handful of arugula as if they're trying to fool everyone into thinking it's healthy. They charge eight pounds, and people pay it and talk about how great these rolls are and isn't it amazing how far food's come these past few years? But Chris hates those sorts of rolls because to him they miss the point of the bacon roll entirely. It's supposed to be cheap and comforting and satisfying. You aren't supposed to get all nuanced with it.

A proper bacon roll, like the ones they make for the staff, takes him back. His dad used to make them sometimes as a treat. The bacon and buns were equally cheap, usually bought at a dodgy corner shop, but Chris and Beth loved them. They'd watch as Dad flipped the bacon into the air and caught it (sometimes) in the pan, like pancakes, and they'd all dig in together, munching and licking dribbles of brown sauce off their fingers. Those rolls were the first thing Chris learned to cook.

His one concession is to use really good bacon in the rolls now, but the buns still come from a corner shop, and good old-fashioned HP Sauce is slathered over the bacon.

"And what're you up to on your days off?" one of the waitresses asks Chris as he swallows his first bite.

Chris shrugs. "Might go out to Dunbar and forage some seaweed."

Calum rolls his eyes. "D'you ever do anything that's not work?" he asks.

"I'll play with the dog too," Chris replies. "She likes the beach."

"You should come up my way," the waitress invites. "I'm just outside Musselburgh. It's nice up there. Quiet." She winks.

Chris pretends to be very focused on finishing his roll.

"Oh, Chris, I forgot—there's a message for you." The hostess reaches into a pocket and retrieves a slip of paper. "Some journo. Said it was urgent."

"They always do," he says, wiping his hands on a dishtowel and tossing it in a hamper with the other dirty kitchen linen. "Too late to call back now," he adds, glancing at his watch.

"No, no, I told him you couldn't get back to him until after eleven, and he said that'd be fine, that he'd still be up. He said something about Susan Napier."

Chris frowns, wondering why a journalist would be calling him about Susan. He catches Calum's eye, and Calum gives him an "aren't you curious?" look back. He *is* curious. But he makes a show of rolling his eyes and telling the others he'll catch them up before heading to his tiny office at the back of the restaurant.

Ginger is curled up on a pillow beside the desk, snoring. She wakes when she hears the door open and comes over to snuffle Chris's hand (which still smells of bacon roll) and paw at his leg.

"I've not forgotten you," he promises, holding up a piece of bacon he saved for her. She plunks her bottom on the ground and receives her reward.

Chris drops into the chair at the desk and dials the number on the slip of paper.

"Chef Baker!" an excited voice trills after the second ring. "*Delighted* to hear from you. I see you got my message. May I say, your hostess has a lovely phone manner. She hardly lets you feel it when she's giving you the brush-off."

"It's why I hired her," says Chris. "What can I do for you?"

"My, isn't that a tempting question? Don't worry, I won't take much of your time. Only, I'm working on a wee story for *The Scotsman* about Elliot's—you remember, that little place you don't think much of?" Chris cringes. He regretted saying that almost as soon as it came spilling out of his mouth during the interview. "Anyway, I have to say, I do agree with you—or, rather, I did, but I was there today, and their food has *vastly* improved. At least, the bits I tried were excellent. I'm sure it's the best they have to offer, but even so . . ."

"I can't really offer opinions on someone else's food, especially when I haven't tried it," Chris curtly reminds him, hoping to wind this up quickly because Ginger is starting to get anxious, and he doesn't want a puddle on the floor. Plus, he hates talking to journalists.

"Of course, and I'd never ask that, but that's why this is such a marvelous opportunity, you see."

"What are you talking about?" Chris opens the office door and finds Calum lurking there, leaning against the opposite wall, arms crossed. Chris gestures desperately to the dog, and Calum rolls his eyes but pats his leg and takes her outside.

"The competition. Don't tell me . . . oh, she's a sly one, that Susan Napier, isn't she? She told me it was all sewn up, that the two of you were going to have a head-to-head at the Foodies Festival next week, with the proceeds going to the charity of the winner's choice. I thought she might be bluffing, because I hadn't seen it on the schedule, and the organizer is a dear friend of mine, but I phoned Barbara up and sure enough, it's a late addition. I guess Susan thought she'd try to get a bit of her own back."

"Well, that was stupid of her," Chris snaps before he can stop himself (again!). He doesn't like being maneuvered in this way. "She's mistaken—there's nothing arranged between the two of us."

"Oh. That's a shame. Because like I said, Barbara's already put it on the schedule, and it's up on the Festival website already. And there's something about it going out in *The List* tomorrow morning. It'll be a shame if you back out now. Might look a bit like you're . . . not quite confident you'll come out on top. And it never goes over well when someone cancels a charity benefit just because it seems like he can't be bothered."

Chris mulls this over as Ginger and Calum reappear. He could just say he's too busy for this, except he long ago agreed to do a cookery demonstration at the Festival anyway, so he'll already be there. And what harm could it do? It's a crowd-pleaser; they'll both get some publicity out of it. If he wins, he can put the money toward a good cause. And it might be fun. But still, he feels manipulated, and that pisses him off. And he isn't going to allow this Rufus person to run the show.

"I'll talk to Barbara about it tomorrow," he says curtly. "Good luck with your piece." He hangs up before Rufus can say another word.

"The hell was that about?" Calum asks as Chris douses the lights and grabs Ginger's leash.

"Apparently Susan Napier wants to do a head-to-head at the Foodies Festival."

Calum snorts. "Sounds desperate."

"Very. But we may as well go ahead and do it. She's already worked the whole thing out with them."

"Course she has. Wants to make sure she's got all the advantages."

"Yeah, well, we'll see about that."

The staff are gone, already on their way to the bar for drinks. Chris figures he'll stop by for his usual single stout, nursed for just long enough so the others don't think he's trying to avoid them. He isn't; he's just tired of the long, raucous after-hours drinking. He wants to go home and crawl into that nice, comfy bed and just sleep. Maybe he's getting old.

But now he's got an event to plan for, which means he's unlikely to get much sleep tonight. Chris flicks the kitchen lights off a bit harder than is strictly necessary.

"At least you've got time to think it over," Calum says, as if reading Chris's mind. "It'll keep your mind occupied while you go trekking for seaweed. Unless, of course, you decide to take someone along, and I think you should. Lyddie seemed keen."

"I don't date staff," Chris reminds him.

"Lauren, then. She's fit. Bet she wouldn't mind a quick dip in the chilly sea." Calum waggles his eyebrows suggestively. "And a nice warm-up afterward. Go on and take her. I'm sure she can show you all the best spots."

"You're a filthy creature." Chris shakes his head, chuckling. "Anyway, she's out of town. Some music festival in Berlin or something."

"Ah, mate, you live like a monk, you do," Calum teases as Chris opens the back door, then pauses. "What's up?"

Chris holds up a hand for quiet, listening. Did he just . . . Was that some kind of rustling he heard in his kitchen? Jesus, they don't have mice, do they?

He flips the lights on and strides back into the kitchen. No telltale rodents scurry out of sight (thank God), but he can still swear he hears something. Is he going crazy?

His eyes slide toward a small storage room just off the kitchen. He yanks the door open and there, sitting on a pile of freshly laundered chefs' whites, is Rab, looking sheepish.

"Jaysus, boy, what're you up to?" Calum asks, grabbing his chest dramatically. "You'll give us all a heart attack."

"What're you doing?" Chris asks. "Don't you want to go home?" His mind starts conjuring up all sorts of nightmare scenarios: abuse, drink, drugs, gangs.

"It's—it's—I—" Rab stammers. His face, normally as pale as those whites, reddens, and the port wine birthmark that runs from just below his left eye to the top of his neck turns a livid purple.

Calum's voice is steel. "There's no cash left here overnight, you know," he reminds the boy. "If it's theft you're after, you're out of luck."

Rab looks up at them in panic, shaking his head. "No, no, no! I really—I just wanted to practice."

The two chefs stare at him, baffled.

"Practice?" Chris repeats.

"What do you need to practice in the middle of the night? You did fine on salads tonight. Get yourself home, boy," Calum says, rolling his eyes but seeming relieved he doesn't have to deal with some hardened thief.

"I wasn't going to practice salads. I was going to work on pastry," Rab mumbles, looking down at his hands, clenched in his lap. "It's . . . I like doin' it, but I don't seem to be doin' great with it, ya know? I keep wreckin' the puff. And then I mixed up salt and sugar in the crème pat the other day and thought Chef Martin was gonna kill me."

"Don't worry about that," Chris reassures him. "We all screw up at some point. When I was your age, I somehow mixed up olive oil and truffle oil. Made the world's most expensive batch of completely inedible vinaigrette dressing."

Rab smiles in spite of himself, and so does Chris. Amazing, really, that Elliot hadn't fired him for that. But instead the old man tasted it and said, "Experiments are good, lad. That's how you'll know what works and what doesn't. This doesn't. Now you know. And so do I."

It's a shame his pastry chef doesn't have that sort of equanimity. Martin's a good guy, and a great chef, but he's not a natural teacher. Rab's not the only apprentice who's struggled with him, but he is the only one who's persevered with pastry. And despite the salt/sugar disaster, he's been doing a good job with it.

"So, you love doing puddings, eh?" Chris asks.

Rab looks up at him and shrugs. A tiny smile appears. "Yeah. It's no' easy, but it makes people happy, eh?"

Susan used to say something like that, Chris recalls. *And Elliot too.*

"You do seem to have a talent for it," Chris observes. "I'd say your short crust puts even Martin's to shame. And that mousse you made the other day . . ." He glances at Calum, who nods in emphatic agreement. "We'll see about getting you more training, if that's what you want," Chris promises. "But we can't have you banging around in here after hours."

"Can't you practice at home?" Calum wonders.

Rab gives him a rather withering look. "I have four younger siblings, and the kitchen's the size of this closet," he answers, indicating the storage cupboard.

"Fair enough," Calum allows.

"Come on," Chris says, patting the boy on the shoulder and getting him to his feet. "You can come to my place. Get your practice in there, or at least get a good night's sleep, and get here bright and early tomorrow morning. And I'll see what I can do about finding someone who can train you. And also, maybe get you out of the kitchen here for a bit, and we'll see what you can really do."

Rab's face brightens. "Thanks, Chef!"

"Ach, it's after hours. Call me Chris."

Chapter Fourteen
Oh, Kay

∾

"Darlings!" Kay folds first Susan, then Julia into tight embraces as soon as she's through the door at Moray Place. "And Bernard! You're looking unnaturally youthful," she adds, offering up a cheek for him to kiss.

"Kay, how lovely you look," Bernard declares, peering a little too closely into her face. "How do you do it?"

"It's not so difficult," Kay replies. "I walk, Bernard. And I work. Amazing how rejuvenating some honest, hard work can be. Just look at how wonderful Susan's looking these days."

She gestures to Susan, who blushes. She doesn't think she looks all that great—she hasn't even bothered with makeup, beyond a hurried slick of mascara. And she's been so busy she's sure she looks worn out. But neither Julia nor Bernard offer any arguments, so maybe there's something to it.

"Well, do walk this way—we've got a beautiful little pinot grigio waiting on the terrace," says Bernard, offering her an arm with a flourish. "Unless you want a tour first? How do you like the place?"

"Oh, very nice. So roomy," Kay replies, giving the entryway a once-over as she straightens the flowered silk scarf draped around her neck. "You seem to have changed your style, Julia," she notes.

"I haven't had time to work on this. I've been busy at the restaurant," Julia announces.

Kay crooks a perfectly groomed eyebrow. "Have you indeed?"

Julia's almost childlike in her eagerness. "I'm doing the whole thing over. It needs it."

"Oh, you clever girl," Kay says, glancing in Susan's direction.

"Thank you," Julia replies. "Just wait until you see it! But you have to wait until it's finished. It's been such a fuss, really—there was an issue with the lighting fixtures, and I had to rethink my whole concept, and Susan's always on me about the budget, which is impossibly tight, but I'm managing despite her."

"I'm sure you are. Your patience, Julia, is remarkable." Kay pats Julia on the arm, and Julia glows.

"Shall I tell you about the—"

"Later, dear," Kay says to Julia, slipping a hand around Susan's waist. "I want to hear all about what Susan's doing at the restaurant. Shall we go open that wine, and you can tell me all about it?"

Julia droops and Bernard pats her on the arm.

"Yes, the wine, excellent idea," he says, leading them all toward the terrace. "Kay, I do wish you'd stay here with us. I'm sure we could squeeze you in. You didn't have to go taking that little flat for the month."

"Oh, Bernard, you're a dear, but you know how I like having my own space," Kay excuses as they emerge into the sunshine. "Besides, the flat is much nearer the theater, and I'm going to be very busy there for the next few weeks. Rehearsals start in two days." She leans over to examine the platter of snacks Susan has put together. Olives, four different types of cheese from Mellis's in the Old Town, cured meats, and an assortment of homemade chutneys and flavored crackers. Susan also baked a focaccia that morning, spongy inside and crisp outside, topped with garlic and sweet cherry tomatoes, and lavishly drizzled with olive oil. Kay spears an olive and helps herself to a slice of the focaccia.

"Now," says Kay, settling back with her snacks, "tell me how the restaurant's getting on. New chef all settled in?"

"She seems to be," Susan answers. "We hope to reopen in a few weeks, and Gloria and I are doing a competition at the Foodies Festival next Saturday."

Kay's eyes widen. "Are you? That sounds fun! Who are you competing against? Not each other?"

"No. Chris Baker," Susan answers. She pretends to be very interested in her glass of wine as she glances through her lashes at her aunt. Kay is looking right at her. Serious. Getting a read on what Susan's feeling.

Am I such an open book, Susan wonders? *Can Kay really suss out what I'm feeling, when even I'm not sure?*

"Well," Kay murmurs, exchanging a meaningful look with Bernard, "there's a name from the past. I had no idea he was here."

"Just opened his first restaurant," Julia supplies. "It's good. I had dinner there the other night."

Susan's astonished. "You did?"

Julia shrugs. "Sure. Everyone's going there. And it's good to know the competition, isn't it?"

"What was the food like?" Susan asks. "What did you have?"

"It was all right. Looked nice. I only had a salad, and it wasn't that memorable. Someone else had the fish; a couple of people had puddings and seemed to like them. I was mostly looking at the design of the place. Inspiration, you know. Oh, Dad, you'd love the wine list."

"Everyone has a good wine list these days," Bernard responds curtly. "That's hardly a reason to go to a restaurant. Kay—tell us about this play of yours."

"What, *Oedipus*? It's hardly new, Bernard."

"Yes, but it's new to *us*," he insists. "We've never seen it with you. And Philip Simms—did he fly up with you?"

"No, no, Phillip's been up here for a while now. He came for the Film Festival and just stayed on. He's never been to Edinburgh before and says he loves how down-to-earth it is. Hardly anyone bothers him. Refreshing for him, I take it. He's a darling; I'll have to bring him round, or have everyone over for drinks or something."

Bernard glances at Julia, who shrugs. "Sounds nice," she drawls. "Is there more wine, Dad?"

Bernard hands her the bottle.

"What a pretty garden you have here!" Kay declares. "Is that a lilac over there? I do love a lilac. Susan, let's go look at it." She rises and strolls toward the lilac bush in the far corner of the garden. Susan obediently joins her.

"As you can see this is a fine . . . lilac," Susan says, gesturing to the bush.

Kay smirks. "I hate lilacs. The smell reminds me of old ladies, and I don't like old ladies, even though I am one. Now, my dear, I want to know how you are."

"I'm well," Susan answers. "As well as can be. Working all hours, but it's good. It keeps me busy, keeps my mind working." Her mind's been working overtime the past few days. She's been firing on all cylinders, her brain churning out new ideas faster than she can write them down. It's exciting. She's going to be doing a *lot* of experimenting this week.

"And keeps your mind occupied, I take it?" Kay asks with a knowing look.

"Oh, don't worry about Chris—that was ages ago." Susan hopes she sounds convincing.

"It *was* ages ago, dear, but it was such a tumultuous time, and I know how upset you were over the whole thing." Kay sighs and contemplates the bush for a little while. "I may not have handled things the best way I could. I hope you know that I only wanted to help you and make sure you were all right."

"Of course I know that," Susan says warmly, taking her aunt's hand and squeezing it. "Why wouldn't I think that?"

Kay smiles and pats Susan's hand. "Have you seen him?"

"Once. He happened upon me in the park when I was out with Meg's boys. It was . . . fine. A little awkward, but that's to be expected."

"And now you two are competing against each other? How did that come about?"

"It's a long story."

"Usually is. Are you nervous?"

"A little."

"Good. Nerves drive you on. I try to get myself good and terrified before I go on stage. That way I'll overcompensate and be great instead of just good enough. But you were never satisfied with just good enough. I'll bet anything you've been turning yourself inside out over the desserts at the restaurant."

"Inside out and back again. You should have seen me with this stupid sea buckthorn."

Kay laughs. "You'll knock everyone's socks off, my dear," she declares. "Fear not! But do leave yourself some time for fun, all right? I was serious about inviting you all to meet Philip. I think he'd rather like you."

"I'm hardly the type movie stars go for, Aunt Kay."

"Oh, nonsense! I'm a movie star, and I adore you."

Susan chuckles and gives her aunt a fond pat on the arm.

"Really, though, Susan, don't sell yourself short. Just because you don't look like Julia doesn't mean you don't have merit. And I'll be honest with you: I think you're really blooming up here. You look and seem . . ." Kay steps back, shaking her head, searching for the words. "I don't know—happier. Brighter. It's good, it really is. I was starting to be afraid you'd never recapture that, and it broke my heart. I'm so glad to see it back again." She glances back toward the house and sighs. "Oh, here comes your father now. Our time is done. Hello, Bernard!"

"Still examining the lilac?" he asks, looking at the bush as if it confuses him.

"No, we were talking about this food festival Susan's going to be competing in. Of course, we'll all be there to cheer her on?"

"Yes, yes, of course!" Bernard agrees. "But I thought you'd have rehearsal?"

"Don't be silly: they can rehearse a scene without me that afternoon. This is important! Is there any of that wine left, or has Julia drunk it all? Come on, you two, those tasty nibbles won't eat themselves."

* * *

Kay was serious about that cocktail party. With the same efficiency she'd displayed when rescuing Susan from her grief many years before, she has a date set, hors d'oeuvres ordered, and a waiter and bartender lined up to make sure nobody has to bother doing anything for themselves. The entire cast of the play is coming, and some of the crew, and Kay's theater and film friends who are in town, ahead of the opening of the festivals in just a week's time. Bernard is beside himself.

"She said David Mamet might be there!" he gushes to his daughters over breakfast the day of. "And Kenneth Branagh has practically promised to poke a head in!"

Susan has too much on her mind to get excited about theoretical Branagh sightings. The Foodies Festival is just a few days off, and she needs a perfect sweet for it.

"Pastry is not Chris's strong suit," she informed Gloria, recalling with a smile the time Chris attempted to make a quiche for their dinner. The crust was so tough it was almost impossible to cut, and when she tried driving a fork through it, she managed to shoot the bite halfway across his flat. It smacked his roommate's sullen cat in the rump, and the thing leapt a good four feet in the air, yowling indignantly as they laughed. They wound up ordering a curry that night, and binned the quiche.

"He might have improved," Gloria pointed out. "Or he might bring his pastry chef."

"He isn't. Rey told me he's bringing one of his apprentices."

Gloria was clearly impressed by Susan's use of the kitchen underground. "Look at you, spy girl!"

Susan shrugged. "We need to win this, Gloria."

"Yeah," said Gloria. "I know. Believe me."

So, the day of Kay's party both women have been chained to their stations, tweaking and swearing when something goes wrong, allowing little gasps of delight when it doesn't. Upstairs, the last of the dry rot is being removed and the contractor promises the walls will be finished by the following week, at the latest. Susan can't wait for the restaurant to stop echoing with the pounding of work boots and hammers and the shriek of saws, though the workmen have helped her add considerably to her swear vocabulary. And they're nice guys: she regularly bakes them biscuits and brownies, which they receive with a "Cheers, luv!" and down in a gulp with their massive mugs of builder's brew during their morning break.

No biscuits today, though. Susan's too busy trying to solve the mystery of a weeping meringue, one that is still unsolved when Gloria lifts her head and shouts, "Hey! Suze! Don't you have to be somewhere?"

"Damn it!" Susan hastily dumps mixing bowls and spatulas in the sink at the dishwashing station, stashes fruit and tarts in her reach-in, slaps on some mascara and lipstick, and decides it'll just have to do.

"Have fun!" Gloria calls as Susan skitters past her station, takes the stairs two at a time, and rushes to Kay's flat.

Kay has taken a penthouse in a new building not far off the Royal Mile. The building has the antiseptic, colorless feel of a place that's meant for people just passing through, but Kay's decorated her flat with gorgeous wall hangings made from embroidered silk she bought in India, and the dull gray furniture is livened up by Moroccan cushions in poppy red and saffron yellow. There's a terrace with a spectacular view of the monuments on Calton Hill, and since it's a mild night, the French doors opening onto it are thrown open and guests with drinks are already mingling out there, leaning oh so casually against the railings.

Those guests, Susan assumes, are the actors and actresses. They're uniformly beautiful, tall, dangerously lacking in body fat, and dressed in clinging, expensive clothes and uncomfortable shoes. They keep to their own little cluster.

Inside—right next to the kitchen—are the nonactors. They're less glossy, and they greet one another with big hugs and laugh loudly at their inside jokes. They load up every time an hors d'oeuvre tray passes, as if they're hoping this will be their dinner. (It seems Kay realized this would be the case: the hors d'oeuvres are more substantial than one would expect at a cocktail party, and there's a small mountain of bacon rolls at one end of the bar.)

Kay flits between these two groups, air-kissing the actors, joking with the crew, and stopping in the middle to speak to the nontheater people, such as Susan's family, who seem uncertain whom they should approach, or how. Only Bernard and Julia have made an attempt to sidle up to the people on the terrace. One actor easing into his dignified salt-and-pepper years smiles tolerantly and nods at whatever Bernard is saying, even as he shoots one of his fellows a "save me" look. Julia has apparently run out of things to say to an actress with waist-length blonde hair, so she joins Susan at the bar, to have her glass refilled.

"I was starting to think you weren't coming," Julia says as the bartender hands Susan her glass of white wine.

"Lost track of time," Susan explains, reaching out to snatch a miniature sausage roll from the waiter's passing tray. She hasn't eaten all day; it vanishes in an instant.

Julia wrinkles her nose at the sausage rolls and then wrinkles it further, sniffing. "God, Susan, you *reek* of the kitchen!" she hisses. "You couldn't be bothered to shower before you came?"

"I didn't have time!" Susan answers plaintively as she lifts a corner of her shirt and sniffs. Does she really stink? All she smells is sweet: cake batter and sugar and fruit. But maybe she can't smell the worst of it?

Julia rolls her eyes. "I hope you find a new pastry chef soon; this isn't dignified."

"Don't hold your breath," Susan says. Their search for a pastry chef has been suspiciously futile, and she suspects someone out there has been poisoning the well.

Julia accepts her champagne cocktail from the bartender and leans against the bar, sipping and watching Kay as she stops to have a word with Meg and William.

"Aunt Kay is not aging well," Julia declares in a whisper. "I mean, just look at her skin. And that hairstyle! And what is she wearing?"

"I think she looks amazing," Susan answers. She can only hope to age as gracefully as her aunt, though she seriously doubts she will. She'll certainly never have her style: tonight Kay is wearing a long white caftan with bell-shaped sleeves, embellished along the neckline with blue beads and embroidered white flowers. It flows as she walks and delicately lifts with every breeze that comes through the open windows. On most other women her age it might have looked a bit much, like Norma Desmond trying out beachwear, but somehow Kay makes it work.

"You *would* think she looks amazing," Julia sniffs.

"What's got under your skin tonight? Ohh," Susan grimaces sympathetically. "Is Philip Simms here?"

"He is," is Julia's clipped response. "I said hello."

"That was nice of you."

"He acted like it was the first time he'd ever seen me."

"Well, Jules, it was a long time ago. He may have forgotten."

Julia's face clouds over at the very thought she might be forgettable, so Susan hastily adds, "Or it may be that he's just embarrassed by what happened. Maybe he's trying to cover up. Awkwardly."

To Susan's relief, at that moment Kay looks up, sees her, and beams.

"Didn't hear you come in, darling!" Kay abandons Meg (who pouts), floats over, and folds Susan into a hug. "Oh, you smell delicious! What've you been baking today?"

"Roasted strawberries and rhubarb for a mascarpone ice cream. Lemon tart pastry, mint meringues, sundried tomato rolls, honey cake." Susan reels off each item, counting them on her fingers and feeling like she must have forgotten something.

"Sounds divine!" Kay grins and gestures to the waiter, who comes over with his tray of miniature quiches. Kay helps herself to two.

"I was just saying to Susan, Aunt Kay, that I really love your dress," Julia simpers, taking a quiche and setting it on a napkin on the bar.

Kay smiles. "That's sweet, dear, but no you weren't. If you're going to lie, at least be good at it." She slips an arm through Susan's and pats her niece's hand. "Susan, I want to introduce you to someone. You don't mind if I steal you away, do you?"

Susan, halfway through a quiche of her own, shakes her head and tries to swallow. Kay steers her toward the crowd on the terrace, which has bunched around one man in particular. He has wavy brown hair, a lean frame that's just muscular enough to be fashionable, and an easy, brilliantly white smile. This is Philip Simms: actor, face of Versace watches, and recent Academy Award nominee. (He lost, alas, to someone who played a former POW who picks up the pieces of his life by helping a polio-crippled boy train a troubled horse to win the Kentucky Derby. Nobody can beat that.)

As Kay and Susan approach, Philip sniffs the air and his eyes widen in delight.

"Who brought cake?" he asks.

"Oh, sorry, that's me," Susan mumbles, dying a little inside but also thinking how hilarious Gloria will find this exchange when Susan tells her about it in the morning.

Philip's smile broadens, and he says, "You smell like *cake*? That's amazing!"

"It's because I've been baking all day," Susan explains, noticing that the actresses clumped nearby are eyeing her. They back away slightly, as if she's oozing calories and they'll put on half a pound every minute they're within her range.

"Philip, this is my niece Susan," Kay introduces. "The one I was telling you about."

"Yeah, yeah! The one with the restaurant." Philip hops forward and shakes Susan's hand. "I've heard loads about you. Glad you could make it tonight—you sound super busy."

"I am," Susan admits.

"Well, we are honored." Philip puts a hand on his chest and inclines in a slight bow.

Susan smiles, unexpectedly charmed. "Well, you should be," she rejoins. "I've abandoned weeping meringues for this."

"Weeping meringues—the tragedy! Do tell me how one moves a meringue to tears."

"I wish I knew," Susan sighs.

Philip smiles again, and Susan has a sudden sense that she's seen him before. In person, not on a commercial or poster at the cinema. It takes her a few moments, but then she realizes he was the man Gloria claimed had been checking Susan out at the bar not too long ago. How could she not have recognized him then? Was seeing someone out of context really that confusing?

She blushes and feels foolish, but he leans against the railing and gestures for her to join him.

"I love a good pudding, but I'm hopeless at baking," he admits. "Kay says you're amazing. What've you been baking today?" He cocks his head, waiting for her answer. He isn't just being polite—he seems genuinely interested. Or he's an excellent actor. Either way, Susan finds herself slipping easily into a conversation with him, detailing her adventures with the meringues and the sea buckthorn and the pudding she served Rufus.

"Oh God, that sounds amazing, and I don't even like bananas. Will you make it again soon, so I can try it?" Philip says after she describes it.

"Sure," she finds herself promising.

The party continues to buzz around them as the sun inches toward the horizon. It won't really set until after ten at this time of year, but the light dims enough for Kay to begin lighting strategically placed pillar candles.

Susan and Philip drift toward a rattan sofa on the terrace, talking about food and traveling and the new play. They do not discuss the television role that made him famous or the Oscars or his upcoming film, which hasn't even opened yet but is already being touted as the one that will surely, surely sweep the awards next year. And before they know it, the terrace is nearly empty, the actors having departed (taking Julia with them, Susan assumes, judging from her sister's absence).

The crew members, too, are gone; the platter of bacon rolls now completely empty; and only one solitary, half-squashed mini-quiche remains of the hors d'oeuvres.

Bernard has deflated onto a chair: apparently neither Branagh nor Mamet came, and he failed to make a friend of the salt-and-pepper actor.

Meg and William are sighing and making noises about having to go relieve the babysitter, but yes, all right, just one more drink, they're taking a cab home anyway because parking in the city center is the *worst*, isn't it?

Philip, having just finished up one of his funnier stories about researching a role as a Maine lobsterman, realizes it's time to make a graceful exit. He looks around and murmurs, "Well, we've shut the place down."

Susan chuckles, realizing she's sorry to have to say good night. The two of them rise as one from the rattan sofa and wander inside.

"Kay, I can't thank you enough for a beautiful night," Philip says, warmly embracing his costar. "And you know what? I don't think you've even begun to do Susan justice. I expect better from you, Kay."

"Well, I thought I should let her personality speak for itself," Kay says, as Susan stands there, blushing.

"And it certainly did," says Philip, turning back to Susan. Kay discreetly pulls out of hearing range. "Listen," Philip murmurs to Susan, "I know you're incredibly busy, but if you ever get some time off, I'd really like to continue our chat. It's been fun."

"I'd like that," Susan replies, grinning. "I've got a thing on Saturday, but how about Sunday? If it's nice we can take a walk along the Waters of Leith."

"Yeah, that'd be great." He whips out his phone. "What's your number?"

Susan tells him, and he thumbs it into his contacts, puts the phone away, and takes her hand, gallantly kissing the back of it.

"Until Sunday, then," he says. "Good luck with the sad meringues!"

"Oh," Susan sighs, rolling her eyes, "thanks. I'll need it."

Chapter Fifteen
The Competition

⌒

Saturday is clear but windy. High gusts buffet people out walking their dogs in Inverleith Park, where the Foodies Festival takes place. The huge tent where the main events are held snaps and sways alarmingly with the wind.

"Hope it doesn't come down on us," Gloria comments as she and Susan unload large plastic tubs full of ingredients.

Honestly, Susan wouldn't mind if the tent was carried off, because then they'd have to cancel this thing and she wouldn't be risking humiliation. Because she knows that if she and Gloria lose, they'll just be proving Chris right, publicly. Elliot's *is* behind, and they're not catching up. Their relaunch will be sunk before it even happens.

This competition is a stupid idea.

She watches Chris as he sets up, assisted by a teenager with very bright red hair, the blindingly white skin that typically accompanies it, and a startling birthmark that covers half his face. He's lanky in the extreme and has a certain sunken-faced, bug-eyed look that speaks of several generations worth of struggle and poor nutrition. Every now and again, he glances warily at Susan and Gloria, before Chris gets his attention and directs him where to place cutting boards and mise en place. Chris, too, occasionally casts an eye Susan's way, with a look so chilly she actually shivers, despite the fact the tent is warm to the point of stuffiness.

"What's the other table for?" Gloria wonders, jerking her head in the direction of a third table, set between theirs and Chris's. Ingredients and utensils are already set up; clearly someone's going to be cooking there.

Chris seems to be curious about it too, because he calls over one of the organizers and has a few words with her, gesturing to the table. Susan continues unpacking, until she hears Chris bellow, "That's not what we agreed!"

She jumps and both she and Gloria freeze. Barbara, the woman in charge of organizing the event, is talking fast, trying to manage a situation here, as Chris stands back, arms folded over his chest, shaking his head.

"What's up?" Gloria calls.

"There's a third competitor," Chris spits. "A mystery."

"No. No, no, no. It's bad enough we got roped into this in the first place," says Susan, putting her boxes down and joining him. "What's the plan? A big reveal? Trot this person out once the audience is in place?"

"I—um," Barbara stammers. Clearly this actually *was* the plan.

"Forget it," says Chris. "I've already been forced into this, and when we spoke, Barbara, I made it very clear this was a straightforward head-to-head. No last-minute tricks."

"Wait, please, wait just a minute!" Barbara sprints away and gathers a few of her fellow officials for a quick chat at the far end of the tent.

"What do you mean you were forced into this?" Susan murmurs. "I thought this whole thing was your idea."

"Why the hell would I suggest it?" he asks through clenched teeth. "You think I don't have enough to do, I need to waste time with nonsense like this?"

"Oh, thank you very much," she hisses.

"I don't mean you—I mean the whole thing. It's just a silly bit of theater, and I have enough on my plate without taking time out for it."

"And yet, you did," she points out.

"Only because it felt like I didn't have much choice. I was told you'd already set the whole thing up, so if I refused to play along, I'd be the bad guy."

"Well, I *didn't* set this up," she informs him.

"Yes, I realize that now. And *I* sure as hell didn't set it up either!"

The two of them glare at each other for a second, and then something changes. Some pressure releases suddenly, like a small balloon popping, and she can see a tiny smile tugging at the corners of his mouth. She, too, wants to burst out laughing at the absurdity of the situation and the stupidity of the two of them for believing Rufus Arion, of all people.

Just then, the organizer group breaks up and Barbara returns.

"I'm really sorry," she pants. "Poor decision on our part, we realize that. It's okay— we'll bring the third team out now. Just, please, don't leave! We've already issued tickets for this and it's a sellout."

Now, Susan and Chris direct their glares at her.

"I'll stay until we see what you've got up your sleeve here," Chris decides. He turns to Susan. "Totally up to you whether you stay or leave."

Obviously. "We'll stay," Susan replies. They've both crossed the Rubicon.

"Right. Okay." Barbara disappears again.

As Susan returns to her station, Gloria murmurs, "I'd lay good money this was all his idea." She jerks her head in the direction of Rufus, who has just slipped into the tent. He catches her eye, smiles, and waggles his fingers at Susan in greeting. "Little shite."

"Not much we can do about it now," Susan sighs. She resumes setting up, glancing in Chris's direction. He's talking to his assistant, who looks even more nervous now there's another player in the game. Chris pats the boy on the shoulder, smiles encouragingly, and Susan can imagine him murmuring, "Hey, it's all right—you've got this! We've practiced this, just do what your instincts tell you, all right? One more team doesn't make any difference."

"Okay!" Barbara pops back into the tent. "They're here." She waves to someone just outside, and in strut Dan and Joe, Elliot's recently departed executive and pastry chef.

"What the actual fuck is this?" Gloria explodes.

"Nice to see you too, Double-E," Dan smirks. "I see you haven't changed much."

Out of the corner of her eye, Susan can see Chris shaking his head in disgust. He sets his knives down, glares at Barbara, and says, "You are railroading her"—pointing to Susan— "and I don't like it. Springing a surprise team on us was one thing, but this is something else entirely." He turns to Susan. "It would be totally understandable if you decided to leave. "If you go, we'll go too," he says, gesturing to himself and his assistant, who looks completely unnerved.

Barbara's panicking, stammering, throwing alarmed looks at Rufus.

Rufus calmly watches the ruckus unfold, probably mentally composing his next blog post on this very fracas. "That won't play well," he comments. "It'll look like you're both running scared."

"Hardly," Chris scoffs. "Believe me, I'll make sure everyone knows just what happened here."

"Thought you'd be a bit more welcoming, now we're partners and all." Dan sulks before sending a sly look Susan's way. "You hear we're going to be neighbors soon? Funny how these things happen, right? I mean, you did this totally shitty thing to me, but it probably ended up the best thing that ever happened. So I guess we should both thank you." He indicates himself and Joe, who looks a little embarrassed.

"You are most welcome," Susan replies, beaming. "I'm so glad you agree that your firing really was the best thing."

Chris doesn't even attempt to hide his smile.

Susan exchanges looks with Gloria, whose smirk clearly says, "We can take them."

Susan crosses the stage to Dan and holds out her hand. He hesitates, as if he's afraid it might be dipped in poison, but then takes it, weakly. "I'm glad you're here, Dan," Susan tells him with a sickly smile. "It'll be really satisfying to hand you your ass so publicly." She turns on her heel and marches back to her station, practically feeling another, wider grin from Chris. She looks up, catches his eye, and they smile at each other. And now they aren't competitors, really, but chefs ready to make some amazing food, and two teams united in showing up some asshole.

"Well," Rufus gushes, "This is *fun*! I can't wait to see the show!"

"Don't you start. We know this is all down to you," Gloria snaps, jabbing her chef's knife in his direction.

Despite the fact he's a good five feet away from her, Rufus cringes and shrinks away from the blade. "Oh, come on," he says. "A little extra tension and drama adds to the fun of the thing, don't you think?"

"No," Chris flatly responds.

Dan and Joe shake their heads, muttering, and go about their business as the audience begins crowding into the tent. Susan notices several women putting their heads together, eyeing Chris, fluttering lashes and giggling. He doesn't seem to notice. He's directing his assistant and seeing to his prep. Susan, too, tries to ignore them and focus on what she needs to do.

Each team has forty-five minutes to produce two courses of their choice. They've been permitted to bring along up to three items that absolutely needed to be prepared ahead of time. Susan notices that Paul and Joe have brought along some very elaborate garnishes—carved radishes and fruits—and a small cooler filled with wobbly snot-yellow blobs. Chris has something that looks like salmon roe at his station.

The tent fills, and the heat and stuffiness increase. Susan can feel sweat beading up on her forehead, and she follows Gloria's lead and ties a brightly patterned kerchief around her forehead like a headband. She sees Kay come in, followed by the rest of Susan's family, including all of Meg's boys, who already look bored. Kay grins and waves to her niece, who waves and smiles back. Susan notices Chris's mouth tighten momentarily at the sight.

As the last people take their seats, Chris and his assistant leave their station and cross the stage to Susan and Gloria's.

"Good luck to you both," Chris says, extending a hand. "This is Rab, by the way," he adds, gesturing to the boy, who turns bright red.

"Nice to meet you, Rab," Susan says, shaking both their hands. "Good luck to both of you as well."

Chris leans forward and whispers, "I really hope you're doing those brownies of yours. Nobody'll beat those."

His warm smile sends a jolt up her spine and takes her right back to those days in his old flat. The two of them cooking, weaving around each other in a complex, instinctual dance. Tasting and laughing and touching and creating. She swallows hard, smiles back, and says, "You'll just have to see, won't you?"

Dan and Joe look uneasily at each other, then reluctantly join the other two men at the station. Handshakes all around, and they're back in their places as the judges—a venerated chef, a young woman who smiles a lot and has a Saturday morning cooking show, and a semi-famous food blogger who looks to be about twenty years old—take their seats. Barbara, clearly relieved and probably looking forward to a very stiff drink after this, bounds up on stage, welcomes everyone, and introduces the judges and the chefs (everyone smiling and waving as the crowd cheers—loudest for Chris, of course).

"All right, chefs, are you ready?" They all nod obediently. "Let the games begin!"

They spring into action. Susan dumps rhubarb, sugar, and water into a saucepan and sets it boiling as Gloria fires up some music.

"Aw, no fair—they've got props!" Chris calls out good naturedly, bobbing his head in time to "Percussion Gun."

"Everyone can use them; they're equal opportunity!" Susan yells back, waggling her hips and whisking in time to the music.

"Hope you take requests!" Chris shouts back.

The crowd loves it and starts clapping along, as Chris laughs and makes a show of flambéing something in a pan. The audience oohs. The judges grin and chat. Dan and Joe smile gamely and try to get into the spirit of things. Barbara ping-pongs back and forth between the tables, asking the chefs questions, because as if this isn't already difficult enough to pull off, you have to be charming too.

"What're you doing today?" she asks Chris. "Something savory? Or sweet?"

"I'm a savory man, I'm afraid," he replies. "Despite my name, pastry's not my forte. She can tell you." With a self-deprecating smile, he gestures to Susan with a whisk. "Ask her about my quiche."

Susan laughs. "You should've let your pastry rest," she says. "I told you! But you never listened to me. Chefs!" With an exaggerated roll of the eyes.

"So it looks like you're doing something sweet here," Barbara says, coming over to Susan and gesturing to the array of sugar, spices, and fruit in front of her.

"That's right," Susan confirms, tamping down the urge to say something snarky. "Pastry *is* my forte."

"And who taught you?"

"My mother and my grandfather. They taught me nearly everything I know about cooking and kitchens." She and Chris exchange a quick smile.

"That's something the two of you have in common, isn't it?" Barbara asks them.

"That's right. I owe Elliot Napier a lot," Chris confirms, shucking scallops at lightning speed.

"Didn't sound like that on the radio," Gloria comments.

"Ah, words spoken in the heat of the moment." Chris shakes his head. "You often end up regretting them later, right?"

Susan looks up and catches his apologetic look.

"Oh, that's nice," Barbara gushes, moving toward Dan and Joe's table. "What's that you're doing there, crème brûlée?" She bends over some shallow ramekins of custard Joe's arranging on the workspace.

"Come on, *really*?" Gloria cackles. Both Joe and Dan glare at her.

"Well, this is interesting," Barbara goes on, returning to Chris, who has a dozen bottles and several halved citrus fruits arrayed in front of him. "Mirin, yuzu . . . something written in Japanese that I can't even pronounce." She titters. "You like your Asian influences!"

"I collect influences from everywhere," Chris tells her. "I spent a bit of time in Asia, learning techniques and discovering ingredients, so yes, there's a lot of that, but there's also quite a bit of Scotland in my cooking"—an appreciative cheer from the crowd, which he acknowledges with a heartthrob grin—"and I've learned from other chefs, of course. There's this great technique for cooking fish that one of the contestants on my show came up with, and afterward I asked him to teach it to me. We use it in the restaurant. It's important to remember that you shouldn't ever think you're too good or too important a chef to stop learning from others."

"Words to live by indeed," Barbara agrees.

"He's *good*," Gloria murmurs to Susan.

"He is," she whispers back. Chris has definitely developed the skill of playing to the crowd, but she knows it's not just lip service: she can tell he's sincere about everything he's saying.

The clock is counting down fast. Gloria's hands become a blur as she finishes arranging short ribs and snatches chips from the deep-fat fryer. Susan pipes custard and puts the finishing touches on her puddings. They plate up, arranging things just so, garnishing, drizzling sauces, wiping edges.

"And that's *time*!" Barbara shouts. Chris and Rab spring back, hands flung dramatically in the air. Susan and Gloria laugh and embrace. Joe and Dan look at their handiwork, hands on hips, nodding, as if they have to convince themselves they've done really, really well. Dan pats Joe on the back. Chris slings an arm around Rab's neck and pulls him in for a quick man-hug.

"All right, chefs, time's up! Chris, would you like to bring your plates forward first?" Barbara invites.

Chris and Rab deliver their plates to the three judges and step back.

"Starter and main," Chris announces. "For your starter, there's a seared scallop with preserved lemon and sea buckthorn 'caviar.'"

Susan almost groans aloud, wondering how the hell he managed to get that damn sea buckthorn to set in perfect, tiny spheres. *Damn him,* she thinks, without rancor. As he said, there's always something you can learn from another chef.

"This scallop is perfect," purrs the TV presenter.

"And the lemon and buckthorn really keep it nice and fresh and light," the chef agrees.

"For your main," Chris continues as the judges reach for their second plates, "homemade rice cavatelli with a spicy kimchi sauce."

The judges devour in silence. Then the blogger sits back, looks at his empty bowl and says, "I want a lot more of this. Like, a *lot* more."

Chris grins and nods encouragingly to Rab, who clasps his hands behind his back, ducks his head, and smiles at the floor.

"The only criticism I can think of, and it's a little thing, is that the presentation could be a little more interesting," the chef adds. "We all want something a little theatrical nowadays, you know?"

"Noted," Chris says. "Thank you." He and Rab return to their station.

Joe and Dan are up next.

"We have a main and a pudding for you," says Dan. "For your main, we have a lamb Wellington with locally foraged mushrooms and Serrano ham, accompanied by asparagus and nettle mash."

"Locally foraged mushrooms?" the blogger says. "Ace! What kind of mushrooms?"

"Uh, it's a mix," Dan answers.

As one, the judges frown.

"So you're bringing them in, not foraging yourself?" the blogger presses.

"Mushroom foraging's something best left up to the experts," Dan explains.

"Sure, but you should know what type of mushrooms you're getting and using," says the chef. "You should always know your ingredients."

There's not much Dan can say to that.

The judges dig in, and after a minute the TV presenter says, "It's a beautiful Wellington. Very flavorful, excellent pastry. You did make the pastry yourself, right?" She glances meaningfully at Joe, who nods.

"Yes, of course, I make all our pastry," he replies.

"Well, it's great. It's a very nice dish, but at this time of year it feels a bit heavy."

"I'd agree with that," says the chef. "May I ask, why did you put nettles in the mash?"

"Nettles are really good for you, and we felt the grassy flavor helps balance out the richness of the meat," says Dan.

"Eh, not sure I agree with you on that." The presenter shrugs.

"Pudding?" the blogger suggests, pushing aside the Wellington and reaching for the crème brûlée.

"Yes, this is a Cranachan-inspired crème brûlée," says Joe, seeming relieved they've moved off the main. "Whisky-infused custard with raspberries, burnt sugar top, and a sprinkling of crisp meringue."

The judges break through the tops of their puddings and dip spoons into the smooth custard underneath.

"Crème brûlée is one of my favorite desserts, and this is an excellent one," says the presenter. "It's really, really nice. Very smooth and creamy and rich. I can taste the smokiness of the whisky. It's lovely."

The other two nod. "It is," the blogger agrees. "Really nice."

Dan and Joe seem relieved, and as they turn back to their station, Joe gives Gloria a smug look.

"Last but not least!" Barbara gestures for Susan and Gloria to come forward.

"Main and pudding," Gloria announces. "Nothing about this is healthy, but we definitely know where it all came from." She smirks at Dan. "For your main, there's a tea-glazed short rib with hickory-smoked-salt chips, cornbread soufflé, and braised greens."

"Ah-may-zing," the blogger declares, halfway through his dish. "Tastes like the best summer barbeque you've ever had in your entire life."

"These chips are like crack," says the presenter, holding up a small handful of them.

"You could maybe bring down the smokiness a bit," the chef suggests.

"No, I love that! Don't change a thing," the presenter counters.

"Ah, to each his own!" The chef laughs, eating a few more of the chips. "It's an excellent dish, though I'd say maybe choose between either the soufflé or the chips. Having both tips it a little to the heavy side."

"Noted. Ready for pudding?" Gloria asks, stepping back so Susan can present.

"Our take on a rhubarb and custard," Susan announces. "Rhubarb sorbet on the bottom, topped with whipped custard and a candied rhubarb sweet."

It's served in small egg-shaped glasses, so you can see the layers: bright pink sorbet on the bottom, rich lemon-yellow custard, whipped to airy delicacy, topped with a wafer-thin, jewel-like disc of rhubarb that's been roasted, pressed flat, and encased in rhubarb-flavored praline.

The chef takes two bites of it, then sits back, sighs, and looks at his plate for a while. Susan feels like melting into the floor. He hates it! What went wrong? Is it too simple? She worried about that. Maybe she should have done a tart or a mille-feuille.

"This tastes of summer," the chef says at last. "Every bit of it is delightful and delicious—it's so light and airy and enjoyable."

"I totally agree," says the presenter. "It's the perfect follow-up to something as heavy as those ribs, and the flavors remind me of rhubarb and custard sweets, which really takes me back."

"Yeah, me too." The blogger nods. "Raiding the sweet shop after school."

"Which was what—just last week for you?" the presenter kids him. "It's lovely, thank you," she says to Susan, who's practically exploding from the praise.

As Susan turns away from the judges, she catches Chris's eye and beams, so caught up in the moment the smile bursts forth naturally, the way it used to. To her shock, he stares back at her with a look she remembers well from those days long past. It was an astonishing look that always made her feel like the most beautiful woman in the world. *But that's silly,* she thinks, because she knows she's flushed and sweaty, and her hair is frizzy from the humidity. Still, his expression makes her blush and stumble as she follows Gloria back to their table.

The judges confer for what feels like a very long time while the chefs pack up their supplies and tidy their stations. The crowd grows restless, now there's no action to divert them.

Chris calls to Gloria, "Do you have any of those ribs left over?"

"Only if you've got some of that pasta," she answers.

"It's a deal." He scoops the last of the kimchi pasta into a pair of bowls and delivers it to Gloria and Susan, who obligingly hand over two servings of ribs and a pudding.

"You want any?" Susan asks Joe and Dan.

"We're fine," comes Dan's clipped response.

Susan shrugs and digs into her bowl. It's amazing. The delicate pasta seems to dissolve soon after it hits her tongue, melding with the salty-spicy sauce. The crunch of the cabbage and carrots keep the whole thing from feeling like mush.

"Did you do this?" she asks Rab in between bites.

"Oh, um, I—" He ducks his head, looking anywhere but directly at her, shying toward the side of his birthmark, as if trying to hide it, "I didn't come up with the idea, but yeah, I made it."

"It *was* your idea," Chris counters. He turns to Susan and explains, "He mixed kimchi with some rice noodles for family dinner and everyone devoured it, so I told him to keep at it and see what other pasta shapes he could do. He's got the touch, this lad."

"You do," Susan agrees, patting Rab on the arm. "It's amazing!"

Rab finally looks up at her, as if astonished to receive praise. She smiles warmly, and Chris suddenly says, "Can I ask you something?"

"All right, everyone, we have our results!" Barbara announces, bounding back onto the stage. Susan finds herself unexpectedly contemplating actual bodily harm at the interruption. It's not as if she's short on weapons.

"After," she murmurs to Chris, who nods and returns to his station with Rab.

"Right, this was a close one, everybody. Really, really close," Barbara continues. "But one team has prevailed. Second runner up, scoring seventy-five out of one hundred points, is . . . Team Escape!"

Dan and Joe try hard to look pleased.

"Escape? *That's* what they named their restaurant?" Gloria shakes her head, laughing.

"And in second place, with eighty-seven out of one hundred points, it's . . . Team Seòin!"

Susan freezes, even as Chris claps Rab on the back, nodding, looking as happy as if they'd won. But they didn't win. She and Gloria did. They've done it!

"Which means the winner, by two points, is Team Elliot!"

Gloria shrieks and throws her arms around Susan's neck, then drags her to the center of the stage, where Barbara and the judges are gathered with their trophy: a glass plate inscribed "Foodies Festival Cook-Off." Susan is still too stunned to do much more than smile automatically and shake hands. She manages to notice Chris and Rab applauding, and some of her family standing and cheering, while the others (Julia, her father) keep their enthusiasm to a minimum.

She stumbles back to their station, clutching the plate, as the crowd streams out of the tent. A few women fight their way to the front so they can ask Chris to take selfies with them; he obliges, of course. And then Susan looks up and suddenly Chris is there, saying, "Well deserved. I'm glad you decided to stay now."

"Yeah, so are we," Gloria responds, taking the plate from Susan and grinning at it. "Would it be crass to put this on the wall at the restaurant?"

"You mind if I ask you something?" Chris asks Susan again.

"No, of course not." Her heart begins to speed up.

"Well, it's—it's about Rab." He glances toward the boy, who's still clearing away a few things at their station.

"Oh." Susan tries not to sound as disappointed as she feels. But, really, what was she expecting? A date? A confession of love? She knows that ship has sailed. Sunk, really.

"He wants to learn pastry," Chris goes on, "but my pastry chef—well, he's not the best teacher. I was wondering if you might . . ." He trails off as he looks at her. He must sense her distancing herself just a little, to hide her unexpected disappointment. "Forget it, you're too busy," he finishes briskly, stepping back.

"No! No, sorry, I'm just a little out of it still from all this." She chuckles awkwardly and gestures to the stage. She *is* too busy, but she finds herself looking at Rab, who glances up and smiles at her, suddenly not so shy, and she looks back at Chris, who seems to be pleading, and finds herself saying, "I can make time."

Chris looks relieved and waves Rab over. "Rab," he announces, "Susan is going to teach you how to do pastry. Make sure she shows you how to do those brownies of hers."

"Ah no, that's a family recipe," says Susan. "You'll have to marry me to get it."

What did I just say? Susan's so horrified, she cringes.

Gloria laughs and announces, "The gauntlet has been thrown, Chris!"

Thank God, Susan's family chooses that moment to make their way to the stage. Most of them anyway: William and the boys have long since disappeared.

Kay throws her arms around her niece. "Oh, Susan! Your mother and grandfather would be so proud. Well done, you!"

"Yes, well done, my dear. Knew you could do it!" Bernard drops a kiss on his daughter's flushed cheek.

"That'll be some nice publicity," Julia comments. She turns to Chris and adds in a cool tone, "Congratulations to you too, on today and the restaurant."

"Thank you," he says, sounding surprised at receiving a compliment from her.

Susan can't help but notice the way her father purses his lips and only barely manages to give Chris a curt nod.

"Sorry, the boys got bored," Meg explains. "William took them to play in the sand pit near the beer garden. It's nice, this festival, isn't it? I didn't really know what to expect—we're forever getting people from Pilton down to this park, and I was afraid there'd be loads of them here today, but I suppose charging admission really helps."

"Eat this, Meg," Susan says hurriedly, shoving a spare pudding into her sister's hand. She notices Rab ducking his head again, and Chris is looking daggers at her sister.

"Is this vegan?" Meg asks, examining it.

"Yes, Meg, it's a vegan custard," Julia says dryly, looking up from a text she's drafting just long enough to roll her eyes.

"Such things do exist, you know!" Meg huffs. "Have I told you I'm going pesce-vegan?" she says to Susan, spooning up a bit of the custard. "I'm totally vegan, except I still eat fish. And sausage. And bacon."

"Meg, darling, I really must buy you a dictionary for your birthday," Kay says before turning to Chris. She gives him an icy appraisal, then extends her hand. "I must congratulate you on your new restaurant, Mr. Baker. I hear it's doing very well. And you are looking quite well. Much better than the last time I saw you."

Chris's mouth tightens as he takes her hand, clamping down a little harder than is necessary. "Thank you. I hear your play is going to be quite something. Seems you've found your niche, playing a woman destroying her own family. I wish you well with it."

She smiles in a way that suggests she'd love to do him violence. Susan notices Rufus hovering nearby, taking it all in. In a bid to distract everyone, she says to Chris, "Let me give you my number—Kay, do you have a pen?" She scrabbles for a slip of paper, tearing one off the edge of one of Gloria's prep checklists. "Just send me a text or phone me to make arrangements for Rab." She nods in the direction of the boy, and everyone glances his way. He notices and blushes at the attention, fumbling a box he's holding and tipping ingredients all over the table, which makes Susan feel terrible. So does Bernard's whispered "Good *God*" at the sight of the boy's birthmark.

"Gracious, Susan, how in demand you are!" Kay declares. "A date with Philip tomorrow, and this as well."

Susan blushes as dark as Rab. "It's not a date," she insists as Julia's head snaps up from her phone so she can demand, "Philip? Not Philip *Simms*?"

"Philip Simms? Really? You kept that quiet, you sly thing," Gloria laughs, clapping Susan on the back.

Rufus is practically drunk on this.

"It's not a date. He just wants to see the city," Susan repeats, seeing Chris draw away.

"I'll be in touch," he says, turning his back on her and going to help Rab.

"Call it what you will. You young people don't 'date' anymore, do you? There'll be some other term for it," Kay purrs. "Come on, celebratory glass of champagne in the VIP tent, eh? You too, Gloria, of course."

"Thank you," says Gloria.

"Susan? You coming?" Kay beckons her niece from the door of the tent.

"Yes," Susan answers, slinking after them, wondering how she's gone from elated to deflated in roughly the amount of time it took her sorbet to melt.

Chapter Sixteen
Water, Wander, Wonder

Reluctant as she is to admit it, seeing Philip the next day definitely lifts Susan's mood. It's hard to be glum when a beautiful man is standing on your doorstep with flowers.

"I hear congratulations are in order." He proffers a bouquet of gerbera daisies. "Kay said you blew the competition out of the water."

"I wouldn't put it quite like that," Susan demurs, accepting the flowers with a grateful smile. "It was actually fairly close."

"Nevertheless, I'm going to stand you a celebratory drink. Or cake. Your choice."

"Let's see how we feel after our walk," Susan suggests. "A wander along the Waters of Leith?"

"Yes, please."

Susan turns and sees Julia standing behind her, wearing a bright, false smile.

"Hello," she says to Philip. "Didn't expect to see you again so soon."

"Here I am," he says unnecessarily with a self-deprecating grin and a spread of his hands. "You can't get rid of me. I just keep cropping up."

"Mmm, like a stinging nettle or athlete's foot." Julia gestures to the flowers. "Would you like me to put those in water for you?"

"Yes, thank you." Susan hands them off and steers Philip back out the door, wondering if she'll return to a vase filled with nothing but decapitated stems.

"She seems . . . nice," Philip offers.

"She can be if she's handled properly."

"She sounds like my ex, then." He chuckles as they cross Queensferry Road and wind down into Dean Village, a quaint collection of old stone mill buildings clustered around the glittering, gushing Waters of Leith. "I've decided I'm done with high-maintenance girls."

"Oh?"

"God, yes. No more actresses for me. The demands! The constant need for attention! And the scheduling challenges! My last girlfriend—we dated each other for over a year but were only actually in the same place together for a total of three weeks. That's three weeks spread out over an entire year. I added it up. She was shooting in South Africa while I was doing a play in London, and then I was shooting in Croatia while she was doing a promotional tour in Asia. We only really saw each other at awards ceremonies, and you're always on show at those things, so that wasn't, you know, real." He shrugs. "I probably could have handled things better with her. But screwing things up now and again is how we learn, right?"

"I guess that's one way to look at it."

They pass St. Bernard's Well, a circular temple with a statue of Hygieia built over a natural spring that was once said to cure everything from bruises to blindness. They pause to look at it, and Susan can't help but notice a few people glancing twice at them as they pass. She knows they're wondering: "Is that the guy? No, surely not; what would he be doing *here*?" They almost certainly aren't looking at *her*, but all the same, she feels conspicuous and suggests to Philip they move on.

They pass through Stockbridge and pick up the path just opposite Inverleith Park.

"Tell me about the play," she suggests.

"Sure. What do you want to know? Your aunt's brilliant, of course. You know, I took the role because she was going to be in it. I mean, a chance to work with Kay Ashland? You'd have to be crazy to pass that up."

"Even if it means poking your own eyes out on a nightly basis?"

"Totally worth it!"

Susan laughs.

They pass the rest of the walk with anecdotes, mostly his. He talks about the play and the behind-the-scenes mishaps, which leads to more stories of trip-ups hidden from audiences past: a memorable tour with the Cambridge Footlights where the costumes were forgotten, so they had to improvise with bedsheets in a performance of *Julius Caesar*. A film where, on the last day of shooting some complicated action sequences, the actor playing the villain showed up drunk, which led to some very interesting ad-libbing and almost cost a stuntman his left arm and the director the last, frayed bits of his sanity. A famous actress's insane beauty rituals, which were apparently based on Joan Crawford's, "but dialed up to eleven." An entire film crew sent to a different island than the actors ("At least I had time to get a tan!") and an actor who threw a fit and held up production for nearly a month when he discovered his trailer was four inches smaller than Philip's.

"I mean, I offered to trade with him, of course, because who cares about something like that? But apparently it was the principle of the thing." Philip rolls his eyes. "Film actors can be so crazy.

Give me theater folk any day. They can be divas, but in the end I find we all pull together. It's the art that matters. Films are so much about ego."

"Everything's about ego," says Susan, trying to ignore two girls openly staring at them, whispering to each other and pulling out their phones. "We all assume that everyone cares about every little tiny thing we do."

"Except you, it seems," says Philip. "Kay tells me you don't even do social media."

"I don't have time, and who cares what I'm up to?" Susan shrugs. "I probably should do more of it, for the business's sake. Start up an Instagram account and post glorious pictures of artfully arranged butter and wooden spoons. But again, I don't have time for that."

"That's why most people hire someone to do that kind of thing for them. Even I outsource it sometimes."

"Really? Philip Simms's famously hilarious Twitter account is outsourced?" She pulls an exaggerated shocked face. "See, now I *have* to start up a social media account because I actually have something to report!"

"It's not all outsourced." He laughs. "I promise, some of it's me. The funniest bits, of course. But when I'm deep into filming or doing a play, I just don't have time for funny little comments. So, I've got this nice twenty-two-year-old kid who does it for me. He works with a lot of well-known actors; it's his full-time gig. Pulls down more than six figures a year doing it."

Susan shakes her head. "We're all in the wrong business. Well," she amends, "you're not. But the rest of us, shuddering along, trying to pull in our average twenty-six thousand pounds sure are."

"Never too late to reinvent."

"Yes it is. Nobody wants to hire a thirty-something to craft their tweets. All we'd come up with is complaints about the council tax going up or the people next door having more than six people over and it's after eleven on a Friday night, and OMG, what are they thinking? This is the boring age."

"Only if you let it be. I don't feel particularly boring."

"Yes, but you're famous, and that makes you an exception to the rule. You and your life are glamorous."

"You don't need glam to be interesting. I feel like you're proof of that." He cringes, even as Susan bursts out laughing. "I'm so sorry; that came out totally wrong!"

"No, no, it was totally right!" she snorts. "I'm not glamorous, and I'm fine with that. I'm perfectly happy to wear loose jeans and smell like cake."

"Good. You make loose jeans and cake pretty sexy."

Startled, Susan looks up at him, wondering if he's having her on. He must be because who would honestly think something like that?

Judging from his warm smile and the look on his face, Philip Simms does. Philip Simms, movie star and lauded actor. Possessor of perfect hair and sculpted body. Philip Simms, with his million-plus Twitter and Instagram followers and his NSFW Google Image Search results (Photoshopped, of course) is interested in *her*. Despite what Kay said, Susan genuinely hadn't thought this was a date. No one except for Chris has ever overlooked Julia in favor of Susan. That's just not how the world tends to work.

"Sorry, didn't mean to make things awkward there," Philip says.

"You—you didn't," she lies, telling herself she's being utterly ridiculous. After all, can you really trust what a talented actor says to you? They can make you believe anything; it's their job. "Cake. We talked about having cake." Susan tries to collect herself, grasping for something familiar and comforting. "Mimi's Bakehouse is near here. They do a nice tea and cake. Or a scone, if that's more your thing."

His smile remains in place, and it makes her feel less flustered. "Sounds delicious." He reaches out and takes her hand.

Susan smiles back and tries to ignore the passersby. And the strange, nagging tug in her belly, which she's not quite naive enough to believe are the first pangs of love.

Chapter Seventeen
Queen of Puddings

~

On Tuesday, Susan's heading back to Leith, swaying as she clings to a strap on a packed double-decker bus. She's heading to Seòin for her first session with Rab, wondering if that awkward tension she felt from Chris at the end of the Foodies Festival will still be there. She still can't account for that—she asked Kay about it, but Kay just shrugged and said, "He didn't take to me when we first met, I suppose." Susan knows there's more to it than that, but she certainly isn't going to get any more out of her aunt. Probably won't get anything out of Chris either.

All Kay wants to talk about is the date with Philip. It's all anyone wants to talk about—even Lauren telephoned to breathlessly ask what it was like.

"I'm so jealous!" she gushed. "I go away for a couple of weeks and look what happens—you and a *movie star*!"

"It's not as exciting as it all sounds," Susan mumbled into the phone, warily watching Julia, who was pouring herself a cup of coffee. Holding her mug with just the tips of her fingers, Julia leaned against the countertop and raised an eyebrow as she sipped her drink. "It was just a walk," Susan continued, as much for her sister's benefit as for Lauren's.

"Along the Waters of Leith! And there was cake too! What kind of cake did he get? I couldn't tell from the pictures."

"I—pictures?"

"Yeah, it's all over Arion Nation. Didn't you see?"

As Lauren spoke, Julia tapped away on her phone, then held it up for Susan to see. There she was, photographed through the window at Mimi's Bakehouse with Philip seated across from her, laughing. Pots of tea and thick slices of cake between them.

"Who the hell took that?" she wondered, aghast, taking the phone and staring at the picture.

Simm-er down, ladies! the caption read. *Looks like this one's off the menu! Is it any wonder that a man who clearly loves his cake would go for Susan Napier, pastry chef/owner of Elliot's on the Royal Mile?*

"Not exactly Shakespeare, is he?" Susan had grumbled, returning the phone.

"Does he have to be?" was Julia's rhetorical response.

Susan couldn't help but notice the high—*very* high—share count underneath the picture. She was grateful she didn't do social media now. "Lauren, I have to go."

"But wait! Are you and he going to—"

Bleep! Susan cut off her sister-in-law mid-sentence, facing instead a pristine kitchen filled with a heavy silence.

"You going to see him again?" Julia asked, seemingly nonchalant, coolly staring down her sister.

"Yes," Susan admitted. "He asked to take me to dinner sometime soon." She sighed. "Listen, Jules . . ."

"Don't worry about it." Julia tossed her mostly undrunk coffee in the sink and put the mug in the dishwasher. "I mean, it all makes sense now. *Obviously* I'm not his type."

"Okay." Susan tried not to be offended. "So, we're all right, then?"

"Course we are. All publicity is good publicity, right?" Julia flicked her hair back over her shoulder and headed out of the kitchen. "Oh, the contractor says they should finish plugging all the holes in the walls today, and they can pick back up the cosmetic work by the end of the week, once the plaster's dry. And it turns out the wallpaper I'd originally gone for has been discontinued, so I had to order the more expensive choice. I'm meeting a friend for coffee; I'll be by the restaurant later. Byeeee!"

There seems to be a tenuous peace in the house now, though Susan is careful not to mention the date or give Julia a hard time about the wallpaper. Let her have her bloody wallpaper; Susan already has enough on her hands and mind.

The bus to Leith jerks to a stop and disgorges Susan, along with a mass of camera-clutching tourists and exasperated locals. It's August now, and the city is bloated with people. Tourists, performers, actors, authors, critics, artists, and harried daily commuters all jamming in, flooding and clogging the roads, the trams, the buses and trains. The visitors have a bad habit of drifting down the streets in clumps, stopping unexpectedly to take pictures of who-knows-what, oblivious to the fact they're blocking everyone's way. Those with places to be dodge past them as best they can, and weave past street performers, theatrical groups begging for audiences, and the ubiquitous bagpipers, who seem to quadruple in number this time of year. The Royal Mile, epicenter of the Fringe, hums with shouts, soliloquies, taglines, confusion, and piped renditions of "We Will Rock You," competing with the more traditional "Amazing Grace." Every night, at half past ten, the crack of the fireworks that close the Military Tattoo at the castle echoes across the city.

The Royal Mile gets the worst of the crowds, but no part of the city remains untouched: in typical Edinburgh fashion, everyone wedges into whatever space they can find, making it work as best they can. Shows are staged in enormous tents in the city's parks, in gardens, clubs and function rooms; in proper theaters, museums, bars, restaurants, and elaborate spiegeltents brought over from mainland Europe. It means you can find yourself attending events in some very incongruous surroundings: a series of free shows for small children, for instance, is held in rather dark, grubby rooms belonging to a pub in the Cowgate.

Susan has mixed feelings about the Festival season. She finds the daily struggle through the throng draining, and she's already been whacked on the head twice by carelessly wielded selfie sticks. But as a business owner, she recognizes the visitors as a gift, and she wants to scream at how slowly the work at Elliot's seems to be going. She glares at the plasterers, who take their time, and why shouldn't they? They're paid by the hour. Meanwhile, just outside, hundreds of prospective customers pass by their locked door, drifting down the cobblestones toward Holyrood.

Escaping to Leith for a little while is something of a relief despite the packed bus. The tourist crush is slightly less up here, and she's always liked being near water. It was Chris's idea to have Rab's first lesson at Seòin. "Rab's comfortable here," he explained. "He'll be less tense. And the restaurant is closed on Tuesdays, so it'll be quiet."

She agreed, telling herself it would be good to get away from the frustrating slowness of the workmen. Anyhow, it's good to get out of your usual surroundings. Stimulates the mind. That's what she tells herself as she takes a deep breath and pushes through the back door of Seòin, ready for whatever might lie on the other side.

"Morning," Chris greets her, glancing up from some prep work with a welcoming smile. "Not too much trouble getting up here, I hope?"

"No. There was enough room on the bus to breathe, which is all I need," she replies.

His smile shifts to one of gratitude. "Thanks for coming. I know how busy you are."

"I'm sure you do, having just opened a place of your own." Unable to help herself, Susan has a look around. She's seen pictures of the restaurant in features that ran in local magazines, but hasn't seen it in person.

Seòin is housed in an old stone factory. Not a huge one, but it's definitely larger and more open than Elliot's. There are immense windows along the two longest sides of the building, filling the place with light, which helps soften the look of the exposed stone walls. Near the entrance is a circular bar with a base of river stone and a polished top in warm, honey-colored wood that matches the tables. The floor is stained a slightly darker color, and the chairs are all upholstered in cream, with cozy red-and-yellow tartan wool blankets slung over the backs, inviting a chilly diner to snuggle down.

The open kitchen is toward the back of the building, opposite the bar and behind a stainless-steel counter with eight chairs arranged in front of it. The chef's table.

"How do you like having this?" Susan asks, indicating the chef's table.

Chris glances up again and shrugs. "Depends on who's sitting there. Some people just want to watch me work and that's great—I just get on with things—but others keep asking idiotic questions or just want to talk and talk about the show and New York, and 'Oh, do you know so-and-so? I'm sure he used to work in New York at some restaurant, sometime. Or maybe it was Brooklyn? Or New Orleans?'" He chuckles. "Everyone always thinks all chefs know one another."

"To be fair, it is a fairly small club, especially at your level. No wonder Dan went to you when he wanted a business partner."

Chris frowns. "He didn't come to me. Not for that, anyway. Just after you fired him, he tried to convince me to hire him as my sous chef, as if I would just replace Calum. But you know a group of us chefs bought a restaurant to offer as a pop-up to up-and-comers?"

Susan nods, recalling the tidbit from Chris's radio interview.

"Well, he put in an application with the group. And I'll have you know I voted against giving him our funding and restaurant, but I was overruled by the majority." He shakes his head. "You really think I'd go into business with him and put him just around the corner from you? That's daft, that is." He sounds both hurt and incredulous.

"Is it?" Susan wonders aloud.

He puts his work down and looks right at her. "It is. That's . . . mean."

"Some might say that's business."

"Not how I want to do business." He shakes his head. "You think I don't know about him? About how he treats staff members and how lazy and uninspired he is? Like you said, it's a small world, the restaurant one. And did I mention he tried to convince me to fire my best friend?"

"He's a dick," Susan agrees with a smirk.

"A right fannybaws, as my sister would say."

Susan bursts out laughing, and after a moment he joins in.

"She's got the best insults now, Beth does," he adds. "What was that one she used when someone cut her off in traffic? Ah, right—a 'boaby-faced, lavvy-heided bum splatter'!"

Susan laughs herself helpless. Laughs far more than the line actually deserves, but she's just so relieved this is turning out to be less tense than she was expecting.

"I was tempted to use it on that Arion git at the Festival," says Chris, dashing away a laughter tear with the palm of his hand. "I hate being played."

"Who doesn't? But I have to confess, the competition was sort of fun."

"Yeah," he agrees, smiling. "It was, actually. Mostly." His smile falters and he turns to slide the tray of prepped food into the refrigerator, shutting the door a little harder than is necessary. Susan feels a chill seep in and struggles to banish it.

"Rab did amazing work on Saturday," she says. "It was a good idea to bring him."

"Thought it might do him some good," says Chris, taking his time turning around. "Get him away from the kitchen, maybe build up his confidence a bit."

"Did it work?"

"I think so. He kept throwing ideas at me all the way home. Most I've heard him talk since he started here."

"How did you find him?"

Chris finally returns to his prep table. There's still an expanse of stainless steel between them, but at least he's facing in her direction, which is an improvement. "Beth, actually," he explains. "Rab's gran is her neighbor, and when Beth told her I was coming back to Edinburgh to open a restaurant, his gran asked if I'd be willing to take him on as an apprentice. I wasn't going to say 'no' to Beth"—he smirks—"but it turns out it was a good thing. The boy has talent, as you saw."

"And you're continuing a grand tradition of nurturing new talent," says Susan. "My granddad would be proud."

Chris looks up and smiles at her in a way she hasn't seen since their days together. It's the sort of smile that goes right to the core of her and hurts in a deep, longing, achy way.

They stare at each other, and a thick mist of unsaid things rises between them as they both struggle to think of a way to disperse it.

And then the back door flies open and Rab tumbles in, jabbering apologies for being late as he tries to tie on an apron while running toward Susan.

"Easy, lad, take your time—she's not rushing off," Chris reassures him. "You all right?"

"Yeah, yeah, just got held up and missed the bus." Rab is red-faced, wheezing from having run full-tilt from the bus stop. "Dad's offshore and Mam needed help gettin' all the bairns fed and dressed and—"

"I only just got here. It's fine," Susan chimes in. "Go ahead, catch your breath while I get myself situated." This thing with Chris will have to wait.

She wanders over to the pastry station, tying on a clean apron, taking a few moments to orient herself and find the tools and ingredients she needs. By the time Rab joins her, still apologizing, ducking his head in an ashamed sort of way, she has butter, flour, sugar, ice water, lemon juice, a bowl, and a pastry cutter laid out before her.

"Before we do anything, here's the first lesson in dessert making: don't stint on any of the good stuff. Fill it up with butter, and cream, and sugar, and fruit. All the things we want loads of but really shouldn't have. It should feel decadent."

That's her grandfather talking, of course. "Pudding is an indulgence; it should feel like it," he used to say. She could recall one day, in the kitchen of their house in London, when she was maybe nine or ten, helping her mother frost a birthday cake for one of her sisters (Meg, surely; Julia had given up cake, by that point). Elliot sat on a stool at the kitchen island, watching them, guiding Susan's technique: "Take off just enough of the frosting to give a smooth appearance, but don't scrape it all off. The whole point of cake is the frosting, isn't it? You don't want a bare cake."

"Julia would," Susan commented with a wry smile.

"Julia doesn't appreciate things like this" was Elliot's response.

"Now, now," Susan's mother gently remonstrated with a warning look at her father-in-law.

"Well, I worry about Julia," he said. "If you can't indulge in a little cake now and again, what sort of joy do you have in your life? Can you indulge in anything? And yes, cake is an indulgence. You don't *need* it, but you *want* it. It should feel celebratory and just a little delightfully naughty when you have it. It's the same with any dessert."

"We want it because it's full of fats and simple carbohydrates," Mum chimed in, handing Susan a small bowl full of hundreds and thousands and indicating, with a smile, that she should feel free to sprinkle them over the cake. "All the things that trigger pleasure centers in the brain. We want them because, back when we had to be ready to flee from predators or keep from freezing to death in our caves, quick sources of warmth and energy were useful. We haven't quite evolved past that caveman ideal. Pudding is primal."

"Rule number two," Susan now tells Rab, "you don't need to make it too complicated to make it amazing. Most times, something fairly simple, something that taps into your childhood, will be the winner. Now, ready to get started?" Rab nods. She gestures to the table. "Lesson one: pie crust."

She guides the boy through her recipe, which she learned in France. It produces a crust so flaky it's almost like puff pastry. Chris works quietly at his prep, glancing up every now and then to smile at them. While the pastry's resting in the fridge, they move on to fillings: lemon curd and vanilla custard, both of which make Rab anxious. She can see it on his face as he stirs and stirs, and she knows what he's thinking: *Why isn't it thickening? What've I done wrong? I screwed it up!*

"Patience," she murmurs, reaching out and slowing down his hand, which is starting to whisk the curd a little too frantically. A froth of fine, glossy bubbles is gathering on the surface. "Rule number three: Take your time. Rushed pastry is sloppy pastry and wasted ingredients. You've done it right; it just takes time for the eggs to cook enough to thicken the liquid. It always takes much longer than I expect it to," she adds, with a bright smile. "Ah, there, you see?" She points at the sunny, viscous liquid in the pot, which has, in the space of a moment, gone from a runny juice to a thick spread that holds back for just a moment when she drags a spoon through it. Susan holds the spoon up, marveling at the alchemy one can produce in kitchens. "See how it's coating the back of this spoon? That's ready now. Through the sieve and into the bowl it goes, and now you've got your lemon curd."

A grin—the first smile of the day—breaks out across Rab's face. "I never done it before!" he says, dumping the curd into a fine-mesh sieve set over a bowl. "It always clumped up and I got lemon scrambled eggs."

"Yeah, that happens sometimes," she reassures him. "Low and slow is what you want. You try and rush something like curd or custard, and the eggs cook too quickly instead of thickening up." He nods intently as he uses a spatula to shove the last of the curd through the sieve. "Right," says Susan. "While that cools, let's bake off those tart shells."

Twenty-five minutes later, with the baked tart crusts cooling on a rack, Chris calls out, "Lunchtime!," holding up a pair of bowls filled with pasta.

"You're a legend," Susan says, realizing—belatedly—that she's starving. She and Rab slide onto stools at the chef's table, and Chris sets the bowls in front of them.

Spaghetti aglio, olio, e peperoncino: spaghetti with olive oil, loads of garlic, and chili flakes. She stares down into the bowl, at the tangle of slick spaghetti and the bright red and orange pops of fresh, minutely chopped chili peppers. Breathes it in, that sharp, grassy-sweet smell of the garlic and the rich, fruity, green scent of the olive oil, and just like that she's back in his tiny kitchen in London, sitting on the countertop, giggling as he twirls the pasta around the fork and feeds it to her.

"You're not shy with the garlic," she gasped the first time she tried it. "Or the chili!"

"Too much?" he asked, withdrawing the next forkful.

"No, I love it!" She grabbed the hand holding the fork and directed it toward her mouth, inelegantly slurping up the pasta. It was addictive, that. Rich and comforting.

He grinned and kissed her, licking a tiny drip of oil off her bottom lip. "It's a sort of insurance policy," he whispered. "No one else'll want to kiss you after all that garlic."

She laughed, swatted him playfully, and finished the whole bowl.

He made it for her almost every time she stayed the night. It was *their* dish.

Was, she reminds herself sternly, swallowing hard, now. But she looks up at him, through her lashes, wondering if he's done this deliberately. Is this just his go-to dish? Something fast and easy to prepare, which he can throw together in a hurry, without thinking? Or did he make it because he knows the sort of memories it'll evoke? And if that's the case, why? Does he want to taunt her with everything she's stupidly given up, or remind her of how good it was, for a time? Or is it . . . something else entirely?

He's looking at her expectantly, facing her across the countertop. "Not hungry?" he asks, once her hesitation has become painfully obvious.

"No, just . . ." Unsure what to say, she dips her fork into the pasta, swirls it around, and takes a bite. Just as good as ever. He's added something—lemon zest, and perhaps some chopped anchovies, but it's still mostly about the heat of the garlic and the chilies, the decadent richness of the olive oil, and the silky handmade pasta.

"Almost exactly as I remember it," she says with a smile.

He cocks his head just a little. "Exactly?"

"Almost. You've made some changes," she allows, her smile widening. And then, before she can stop it, "Guess you've had some feedback over the years."

"No. Never made it for anyone else."

"Oh," she whispers.

The mist begins to rise again, until he clears his throat and turns his attention to some lamb chops he's trimming. "Most of the women I've known don't like that much garlic."

"No? But they were all right with the heat, I guess?"

He glances back up and smirks, then turns away and begins frying the chops in a pan.

Rab has inhaled his pasta, oblivious to their conversation. Now finished, he slides off the stool. "The missus is here, Chris," he says, jerking his head toward the front door.

Susan's heart seems to cram itself into her throat. *The missus?* She cranes her neck toward the glass door, confused. Surely she would have heard if Chris was married? Is this some secret wife he's had stashed away? Will there be some blonde glamazon at the door, waiting for her garlic-free lunch?

No, most assuredly not. Instead, there's a tiny, elderly lady with hair an improbable yellow-blonde color, pulled back into a bun. She's dressed in a purple cardigan with pearl buttons, black trousers, and sensible flat shoes. She's probably all of about five feet tall and roughly rectangular in shape. She has one hand cupped against the glass as she peers into the dark restaurant, looking for signs of life, no doubt.

Chris's head whips round. "Ah, she's early! Go let her in, Rab," he says, leaving the lamb chop to cook while he delicately arranges some fondant potatoes, glossy with butter, on a plate alongside roasted carrots and a mound of mushy peas.

Rab unlocks the door and lets the woman in.

"Thankee lad, that's a good lad," the lady says, reaching up to pat Rab on the arm. "How's yer ma?"

"She's awright," he answers, locking the door behind her.

"Comin' along, then? She must be gettin' big 'n ' all, now!"

"She is. Gran reckons it'll be another girl."

"Just so long's it's healthy."

Chris puts the chops on the plate with the veg and skitters out of the kitchen with it, bending to greet the woman with a one-armed hug. "Ya've caught me out, Missus Mollie!" he apologizes.

"Aye, well, I can see ye've got guests; a bit o' distraction's to be expected," Mollie replies, with a twinkling glance Susan's way.

"She's teachin' me tae bake," Rab announces.

Susan can't help but notice that his and Chris's accents are thickening considerably in this woman's presence, a phenomenon she's witnessed between staff members in her own kitchen. She once came across Gloria talking to the fish supplier in slang and accents so impenetrable she'd actually thought for a moment they were speaking Gaelic.

"Good on you, dearie," Mollie says in both Susan's and Rab's general direction.

"Lunch?" Chris brandishes the plate.

"Oh, aye, I think I will."

Chris leads Mollie to a seat near a window, about as far from the kitchen as the pair can get. He places the plate in front of one seat, then pulls out the chair for her and unfurls the linen napkin, as if he's a waiter and she the most highly prized guest.

"Rab," Susan whispers, as Chris seats himself across from Mollie and begins talking to her in a voice too low to be overheard, "who is that?" Some relative, perhaps? His mother returned from wherever she disappeared to?

"I think she's his best mate's mum," Rab answers. "She comes for lunch every Tuesday, when there's nobody about. He makes summat special for her, and they sit and chat. Sometimes she cries."

"She *cries?*"

Rab shrugs. "His mate's dead, I think," he elaborates.

"Oh." Susan frowns. "I thought his best mate was his sous chef."

"That's 'is best mate now, but that's"—Rab jerks a thumb in Mollie's direction— "the mum of 'is best mate growin' up."

Susan glances back over at the table. Mollie's talking quite animatedly, waving her knife and fork in between cutting pieces of meat and smearing it with mushy peas. Chris is laughing at whatever she's saying and then chipping in with something. She guesses they're trading memories. It strikes her as incredibly sweet that he'd do this for a lonely old lady.

"She's nice," Rab adds, watching them as well. "She talks to me sometimes when I'm here. I told her about my ma bein' up th' duff again."

"Do you have a lot of brothers and sisters?" Susan asks.

Rab nodded. "Four 'n all," he said. "Two each." He shakes his head. "It's a lot o' work, and Dad's away a lot. He works on the North Sea rigs, you see."

"Oh." Dangerous work that takes people away from their families for weeks at a time. She can feel the pressure on this young man's shoulders to help his mother while also trying to start a career and a life of his own. She takes her own bowl into the kitchen and pats Rab on the shoulder. "You must miss him. Must be rough when he's away." He lifts his head and she looks him in the eye and says, "You're doing a great job, Rab. You really are. You should be proud."

He nods slowly. "Thanks."

She pats him again and says, "Those tart shells should be cool by now. How about we make a ganache?"

By the time Mollie has finished her lunch, the tarts are filled: some with a decadent chocolate ganache, others with custard and glazed fruit, and the rest with the lemon curd. Susan finds some edible flowers in the refrigerator at the pastry station, and she and Rab carefully place one violet in the center of each lemon curd tart.

"Rab, you've done excellent work today," Susan compliments. "It's been a real pleasure working with you. Would you like to do it again?"

His face lights up and he nods. "Can we?"

"Of course!" She grabs a small plastic storage box and places one of each of the tarts inside. "Take some of these home—you've earned it!"

He glances toward Chris. "You sure it's okay?"

"He won't mind."

"Then . . . could I just take the chocolate ones? Ma'll like those best. She likes a chocolate nowadays. It's how I know she's 'avin' a girl. It were the same wi' my sisters."

"Take as many as you like," says Susan, picking up two other tarts and arranging them on plates. She thought it might be nice to give Mollie a sweet at the end of her meal.

With a smile, Susan approaches the table, but just as she reaches it, she realizes she's made a terrible mistake. Something has changed here. Mollie has pushed her plate away and her head is bowed over her hands, folded in front of her on the table. Chris, face contracted in pain, is speaking very quietly, seeming helpless. Susan stops and hovers a few feet from the table, unsure what to do. Turn and run back to the kitchen? That seems . . . strange. But coming closer feels intrusive.

After a few excruciating seconds, Chris glances up and notices her. The expression on his face is now plainly *What the hell are you doing?*

"I'm sorry, I-I-," Susan stammers, coming closer. As she does so, Mollie turns her head away and brings one hand up to further shield her face. "I thought you might like something for pudding," Susan finishes, feeling like a world-class tit.

"Just leave them," Chris orders sharply, warning her, with a look, to go. *Quickly.*

Susan jumps forward and puts the tarts down so fast the lemon one slides on the plate, tipping right over the side. The delicate pastry cracks in half and the lemon filling begins oozing onto the tablecloth. "Oh!" she reaches out to rescue it, but Chris swoops in first, roughly shoving the tart back onto its plate.

"Leave it—it's fine!" he insists.

"That's awright, dearie, thank'ee," Mollie says. A quiver in her voice betrays the emotions she's trying hard to conceal.

Susan backs away. "I'm sorry," she whispers, mortified. "Sorry!" She turns, flees back through the kitchen and bursts out the back door and into the August sunshine.

Chapter Eighteen
Too Close for Comfort

❧

"... so then I said, 'That's not on, and you know it, and you're just being a wanker now—'"

"Lauren! Little pitchers!" Meg claps her hands over the ears of the son nearest to her.

"Muuuuuum!" Ali wails, ducking away from her.

"He always was a wanker," Lauren's friend (Kate? Kell? Susan can't recall now.) responds, ignoring the murderous look Meg shoots her. Kate/Kell nudges a third girl with the elbow of the arm she's using to text someone. "Remember when we all went to Porty Beach after the Freshers Ball, and he dared Leila to jump off the steps? And she landed on some rocks and fractured her ankle and whacked her head, and then we made him come with us to A&E and he sulked the whole time we were there, even though it was his fault we were there in the first place? What a dick."

"Girls, will you *please* watch your language and—Hermione, I've told you time and again not to even *look* at that chicken! Out! Both you dogs! You are banished!" Helen herds the labs out of the dining room. Both cast mournful looks over their shoulders as they go, begging someone to intervene on their behalf.

"... Fascinating stuff, theater. I've always wondered how people do it. I mean, how do you manage to get so into so many different characters? Don't you get confused sometimes?" Russell wonders, stepping aside so the dogs can pass.

"But that's the genius of it, Russ!" Bernard leans over a platter of cold poached salmon. "That's what makes her *great*. It's why *everyone* wants to work with her, isn't that right, Kay? It's the same with Philip. It's why this show's going to amaze everyone—really amaze them, isn't that right, Kay?"

"Hermione!" shrieks Helen as one of the dogs streaks back in and makes for the chicken. "Lauren, I told you—"

"She got away from me, Mum! I told you she's impossible—you need to bring someone in to train her."

Susan can barely hear her own thoughts over the cacophony of the Cox dinner table. It's Wednesday, an unusual evening for a full-on family dinner, but Kay's play opens that weekend, and Helen wanted a "welcome to Edinburgh, Kay, dear," dinner before Kay's evenings were all spoken for. The weather has not cooperated: the previous day's sun gave way to a chilly, cloudy morning and then a chilly, rainy afternoon that barely tamped down the masses of people heaving up and down the city's streets. There's no crowd relief here either: Helen and Russell have invited loads of people, and they're all clumped around the buffet-style spread on the table, awkwardly holding plates, no one quite in a position to move them all into another room. So the dining room feels too full and too warm. The windows have steamed up; the children are bored and whiny; and the host and hostess, who should be the ones directing traffic, stand talking with their guests.

Besides Kay and the Napiers, the guests include Lauren's two friends, both switching between typing on their phones and eyeing Susan (at least, that's what they seem to be doing), three sets of neighbors, and a clutch of Russell's colleagues. Susan's found herself pinned in front of an immense bowl of three-bean salad, jostled on one side by the florid partner in an important law firm, and on the other by a bony academic, who asked what she knows about golf and the cognitive sciences. When she admitted she doesn't know the first thing about either, he lost interest and turned to the man next to him, who crowed, "God, Rory, have you seen what they've done to the front nine at Machrihanish? Bloody travesty!"

Susan gazes across the bean bowl and catches her aunt's eye. Kay looks pityingly back at her, then lays a hand on Meg's arm and says, "Meg, dear, you poor thing, trying to balance that baby and the plate. Here, let me help you. No, no, dear, I'll take the plate; you can take the little one. Let's just go on into the sitting room so you can sit down. Too hot in here for the wee ones anyhow."

"Oh yes, of course," Helen flutters. "Let's all go! We can spread out a bit!"

"I'm glad *someone's* concerned about *me*," Meg growls, shooting daggers at her husband, who only rolls his eyes.

"Everything okay?" Susan murmurs as William passes her, steering the two older boys ahead of him.

"Shipshape," he answers with a tight smile.

"I think we're going to go," Kate/Kell reports to the company in general. "You said Philip Simms was going to be here," Susan hears her hiss at Lauren as she passes.

"I said he *might* come, not that he *would*," Lauren flings back. "Oh, go on then. I'll text you later and we can meet up."

"Should we ask Liam?" the other one smirks.

"Do what you like," Lauren replies in a tone of studied disinterest.

As the others flow into the sitting room, Susan branches off and slips into the blissfully quiet kitchen. Hermione the dog follows and sits at her feet, looking up hopefully.

"Your mum won't like it if I give you something," Susan tells her.

The dog cocks her head and goes full mournful with the eyes.

"I won't tell if you don't," she seems to be saying.

"Oh, go on then." Susan tosses her a little piece of chicken, just as Lauren comes in.

"Ah, someone else who needs a moment of peace," Lauren observes, reaching into a tin on the countertop and retrieving a biscuit for the dog. "Sit!" Hermione's haunch hovers an inch from the tile. "Good girl!" Lauren tosses her the treat, then pulls herself up to sit on the countertop. "So," she says, waggling her eyebrows at Susan. "How're things with Philip?"

"They're all right" is Susan's evasive response.

"Just all right?"

"I'm sure Arion Nation will fill you in on all the details, if I won't."

"Oh, don't be like that! You still going to see him again? Your aunt says he's been talking about you ever since your date."

Susan grimaces, not liking the idea of Kay gossiping about her. To Lauren, of all people. It's almost making her reconsider agreeing to go out with Philip again, but she has to admit, he's fun to be around. He fortuitously phoned the night before, when she was still beating herself up about the debacle with Chris and Mollie. Philip had made her laugh, with a couple of stories about awkward fan encounters he'd had that day. They'd made him late and earned him a scolding from Kay that he termed "very maternal. I think she missed her calling as the mother of erstwhile thirty-something actors."

"She's got some erstwhile thirty-something nieces to make up for it," Susan pointed out before agreeing to a date—a definite date—on Thursday.

"I wish a movie star would come and sweep me off *my* feet," Lauren sighs. "Especially one like him, because he's both good looking *and* talented, and most of them aren't both, you know? I loved him in that last film; he's the only reason I went to see it. Of course, Liam said it was pretentious, but the critics loved it, so what does he know?"

"Ah, Liam again," says Susan with a teasing look. "He comes up a lot for someone you're only casual about."

"Only because he's always around." Lauren huffs. "He was with us in Berlin, and he was all right for a while, but then one night he had about five too many and started going on about the middle classes and how we're all cows or sheep or something, with our organic allotments and Waitrose grocery deliveries and just not really living or feeling or . . . I don't know. I tuned him out after a while. We all did. He's so boring when he's like that. Why can't everyone be a fun drunk?"

"Life would be so much better if they all were," Susan agrees. "So you two are through, then?"

"I don't know. Suppose so. I mean, I haven't sat down and had the big talk with him or anything, but who does that anymore? People just sort of go their own way, you know?" She sighs. "Maybe I should talk to him, though, just so there's no confusion. Do you think I should?"

"Yeah, Lauren, I think you should," Susan tells her quietly. "Confusion is . . . hurtful."

"Oh, Liam can't be hurt. He knows it's only just casual with us anyway." Lauren sighs again and kicks her feet against the cabinet. "Mum'll hate it. Dad too. They were so pleased when I got together with him because Liam's from setch a good feemily.'" She apes a nasal, cut-glass accent. "But honestly, he took me home with him one weekend, and I nearly wanted to die. His mother's a pill. She saw me looking at some painting in their breakfast room—that's what she called it, even though it was really just a dining alcove off the kitchen—and she said that of course the painting came from some ancient relative's Grand Tour. She thought I would be in awe of that, but really I was just thinking how ugly the thing was. And she's got some cousin—not even a cousin, a second cousin, or even further away than that—who's a lord something or other, and she never. Shut. Up. About. It. 'Oh yes, my cousin, Lord Suchandsuch, don't you know, he's *very* good friends with the prime minister, *practically* helps run the country, which is why he had to regretfully tell us he won't be able to have us to the villa in Lake Garda after all, because the PM's going to be calling an election soon, and my cousin simply *must* be at the beck and call of Number Ten. The sacrifices we all must make for our country!'" Lauren sticks her nose in the air and waves it around in imitation of this insufferable woman, and Susan laughs.

"You should go on the stage, Lauren," she says.

"Maybe I will. I'm young yet, aren't I?"

"Who's going on the stage?" Kay asks, sticking her head into the kitchen.

"Lauren, probably," Susan answers. "She'll be the most brilliant comic actress of her generation."

"I don't doubt it," says Kay.

"Comics, that's it!" Lauren brightens. "You and Philip should go to a show at The Stand! It'll be perfect—small, intimate, kinda dark, so you two can cozy up without causing too much of a fuss. If that's what you want."

"That *is* what I want," says Susan, who quakes at the idea of people staring at the two of them.

"There you are, then! If I don't become a famous actress, I'll become a famous date organizer. The world is full of possibilities!" Lauren hops down from the countertop. "Have you been sent to drag us in for Dad's big announcement?" she asks Kay.

"I have."

"Right, then, we'd better go. It's nothing terribly exciting—like I said, there's going to be a general election announced soon, and Dad's decided he's going to run for a Westminster seat. Sorry if I've just ruined the surprise."

"It's all right," Susan says, getting to her feet. "Guess we'd better put in an appearance, though."

"Yes, we'd better," says Kay, reaching out and patting Susan on the cheek as she approaches. "Smile, darling. I know you're tired, but you must practice your happy face."

"Must I?"

"Oh, Susan, are you all right?" Kay frowns, concerned. "You don't seem yourself tonight."

"Like you said, I'm tired."

"Hmm." Kay glances at Lauren, hovering nearby, waiting for gossip. "We'll be along presently, Lauren."

Lauren slumps and slinks away.

"Something you want to tell me, Susan?" Kay asks, drawing Susan farther into the kitchen so they wouldn't be overheard.

"No."

"Liar. Is this in any way connected with you going to Mr. Baker's restaurant yesterday?" Off of Susan's surprised look, she continues, "You know, Lauren can't hold a thought longer than a goldfish, dear."

"It's not that," Susan lies. "Not really. I made an ass of myself, that's all."

"Well, if that's all it takes to make you glum for more than a day, you need to practice it more. I spent most of my twenties and thirties making a complete ass of myself on a regular and daily basis. It helped me learn what not to do, but also made me immune to its effects. Try it, darling. Let go and be an ass!"

Susan laughs. "I can see why you and Philip get on so well."

"I want *you* and Philip to get on well. He really likes you, dear."

"I don't see why."

"Don't you? Oh, darling, we still need to work on you," Kay sighs, smoothing Susan's hair and smiling fondly at her. "You're wonderful, the best of all my nieces, and I'm not sorry to say so. Any sensible man would be lucky to have you. And an insensible man would be beyond fortunate. But try not to waste yourself on an insensible man. It really would be *such* a waste." She sighs again and pats her niece's hand. "Right, off we go to pretend to be excited that Westminster's getting another Tory. Happy face?"

Susan plasters on an enormous, false smile.

"That's my girl!

* * *

Chris feels like an asshole.

He tries telling himself that he shouldn't, that it wasn't really his fault—seriously, Susan needs to learn how to read a room—but he knows he's been unfair to her. He can still see her, standing there with her tarts in her hands, just wanting to do something nice.

And then he had to go and be an asshole about it.

This is new, the sensation that he's in the wrong and Susan right. And it kind of makes him wonder: Has he been an asshole to her a lot longer than he thought, and just didn't realize it? Has it taken the sight of her face falling as she stumbled around, trying to salvage an awkward situation, to make him realize that she isn't all bad and that he's been too harsh?

He was only trying to protect Mollie from embarrassment. The conversation had taken a turn he hadn't wanted: he tries to keep these lunches light and pleasant. If the subject of Sam comes up, he makes sure to tell a happy story. Something that makes both of them laugh. "Oh, aye, remember the time he tried some of your makeup out on the cat when we were six? The pair of us had scratches all over our arms for weeks, and you were fit to be tied when you found out we'd used all your eyeliner! How about the time he convinced that one fool boy in our class that there was buried treasure in the Meadows, and sent him off with a garden spade to start digging!"

"Remember how much he loved his lamb chops? Could eat a dozen in one sitting!"

That's what did it yesterday. Chris had forgotten about Sam's favorite food. It just happened that he got some beautiful chops from his meat guy and thought Mollie would like them. Turns out, it was the last meal she ever made her son. And Chris should have remembered because he was there. Not that he ate.

Yesterday, she ate her lunch, chatting as usual, and then got quiet, staring down at the empty plate, and murmured, "Sam always liked his meat with mash. You remember?"

He did. And then he remembered that last meal, and it flooded over him, this nauseating guilt and anger and powerful desire to grab the nearest chair and smash it to splinters.

And that's when Susan came over. Smiling. With her pastries.

For nearly twenty-four hours that anger simmered away, but the rush of service consumed him, leaving little room for anything else, and afterward he felt calmer, more philosophical about things.

And he felt like an asshole. *Feels* like an asshole.

They're all at the pub now for the post-dinner-service drinks. Most of the staff are gathered at a set of tables in the far corner, but Chris is at the bar, with Ginger lying beside him. He toys with his phone, wondering if he should send Susan an apology text.

As he considers it, Calum sidles up to him and comments, "You're about as much fun as a melted ice lolly."

"Sorry," Chris grunts. "A lot on my mind."

"Sure seems like it. How did Rab's lesson with the enemy go yesterday?"

"Ask him yourself. I was busy."

"Have it your way. Oi! Rab!"

Rab's head pops up from the mass of staff at the tables.

"Join us, lad, and tell me how it went yesterday. Did you learn anything we can steal? I mean . . . use to our advantage?" Calum winks at Chris.

"Yeah, I learned loads," Rab calls back, trying to extricate himself from the crowd. "I made a curd that didn't clump." He flushes with pride. The pastry chef looks surprised.

"He did very well," Chris confirms. "The tarts, Rab, were delicious."

Rab blushes even darker, until the rest of his skin almost matches his hair and birthmark.

"Will you have her back?" Calum asks Chris.

"I'm going to her place next," Rab announces. "She's got things to do in her own kitchen and wants to show me. I'm going on Friday. Is that"—he glances at Chris, shifting nervously—"is that okay?"

"Of course it is," Chris answers, patting the boy on the arm, hoping nobody notices he's cringing a little. Of course she'd want to have the lessons at her place now. Why would she want to come back to Seòin after how he treated her? And making that pasta dish, he now realizes, was almost cruel. Like he was trying to throw their failed relationship right in her face. It was just that he couldn't imagine making anything else for her. "Do what you like, lad. I want you to learn."

Rab looks equal parts relieved and uncertain.

"Ah, Christ," Calum mutters, gesturing toward the door.

Chris glances up and sees that Dan has just swaggered in. "Is there no other pub he can go to?" he wonders out loud.

"None other where he might find you," Calum points out, giving a fake smile to Dan, who waves enthusiastically and calls out, "All right, partner?"

"Not your partner," Chris murmurs as Dan saunters over, carelessly treading on Ginger's back paw. She yelps in protest and backs up against Chris's legs.

"Watch it!" Chris scolds the man.

"Ah, sorry, didn't see you there, boy," Dan says to the dog.

"Girl," Chris corrects.

"Oh yes, of course she is." Dan makes stupid faces at the dog, who glances up at Chris with a "how long do I need to put up with this idiot?" look before lying down again.

"What brings you all the way down to Leith tonight?" Chris asks him. "Thought you'd be busy getting your restaurant ready to open. Opens next week, right?"

"Oh, uh, we've decided to push the opening back a bit," Dan answers, trying to get the barman's attention. "Oi! Belhaven, please!"

"Have you now? You know what a pop-up is, right, Dan?" Chris asks. "It's only there for a little while. Time's a-wasting."

"It's all right—we've got it covered! We're just pushing it back a week so we can get ourselves sorted. Two weeks from Monday." He receives his beer and takes a swig.

Chris stares him down until Dan starts looking uncomfortable.

"The same night Elliot's reopens?" Chris confirms.

"Oh, is that their reopening?" Dan fidgets with the beer bottle and avoids all eye contact. Calum and Rab are now watching this interplay as if it's history's closest Wimbledon final.

"Come off it—you know it is," Chris snaps. "You did that on purpose."

"What do you care?" Dan asks, finally looking up, eyes flashing. "You said yourself you don't care about the place anymore. You're not still doing the daughter, are you?"

In another life, perhaps, Chris would have smashed that bottle (and maybe a few others) in that douchebag's face, then dragged him by his hair out into the street while his mates hooted encouragement in the background. He's sorely tempted to do so—and more! But he's keenly aware of the dozen of his employees watching, waiting to see how this'll go down. How their boss will handle the situation. He can't be splashed all over YouTube beating some fellow chef to a pulp, even if the guy does seem to deserve it. He can't mess all this up. Not again. A second chance is one thing, but a third?

So instead, he places his glass of beer down on the bar, very slowly rotates to face Dan full-on, and says in a low, even, absolutely deadly tone: "You're a right piece of shit, and you know it. Rest assured, that pop-up is the only restaurant in Edinburgh you will ever own or work in. You won't be able to get seasonal work in the most desperate chippie. So you'd better pack your bags and think about where else you want to live and work, and it better not be Scotland, London, or New York if you plan on staying in this business."

A long silence follows, and then Calum leans across Chris toward Dan and says, "This, I think, is the point where you piss off."

Dan drains his beer and hurries out.

Everyone watching collectively exhales as Chris picks up his phone and starts searching the contacts.

"Excuse me." A pretty brunette appears at his elbow, tossing back her hair so he can get a good view down the front of her tube top. "*Really* sorry to bother you, but my friend and I have a bit of a bet on. Are you the guy from *Outlander*?"

"No," crows Calum, "he's better! You should see what happens when you put a hand on *his* old stones!"

"Excuse me." Chris shoulders his way out of the pub, Ginger in tow, hastily texting Susan.

Chapter Nineteen
A Trick of the Light

❧

"That *asshole*!" Gloria bellows. She immediately follows that with a stream of Polish that needs no translation.

"I know," Susan sighs. "I hear you."

"That manky prick." Rey hands Susan her phone back. Chris's message still lights up the screen: *Dan has rescheduled his opening for 2 wks Monday. Thought you should know. I HAD NOTHING TO DO WITH THIS.*

This is important enough to have brought even Julia to the kitchen, and now she shakes her head and crosses her arms. "He did this on purpose."

"Gee, you think?" says Gloria, driving a chef's knife viciously through a head of cauliflower.

"It'll suck away all our press," Julia continues, ignoring Gloria. "All those journalists we invited—even if they go to both events instead of just choosing one, the story will be about pitting us against each other, not *our* reopening. All of *our* publicity becomes his."

I know! I know! Susan desperately wants to scream. Nobody's saying a single thing that didn't flash through her brain within twenty seconds of receiving that text. She probably moved through all the stages of grief in record time. (*"No, this can't be right.—What an asshole!—Maybe there's some way I can fix it. Can we reschedule?—Shit, no, we can't. We'll just have to soldier on and hope for the best.")*

"What about rescheduling?" Gloria suggests. "Move it up a night. Rey and I can manage, can't we, Rey?"

"Sure. What's twenty-four hours less of prep time?" He shrugs, as if that isn't actually a fairly significant ask.

"We can't reschedule. We've got press notices out, and Sunday's the last night of our aunt's play," Julia explains. "We need her and the other celebrities there if we're going to have *any* chance of getting coverage." She glances at Susan. "Philip's coming, right?" Her face says: *He'd better be, or I'm going to drag him here myself. I'll be* damned *if nobody sees all the work I've put into this place.*

"I think so," Susan answers evasively. She hasn't asked him yet. It feels a little bit like using him, especially now. But she does actually want him to be there, and not just for the obvious reasons, so . . . she'll ask tonight.

"We'll stick to the set date," she agrees. "But maybe we'll move it forward an hour. Start it at half five, and maybe we can get the journalists a bit tipsy before they go elsewhere. Or stuff them so full of food they won't want to go."

Julia rolls her eyes. "Half five? Nobody eats at that hour except toddlers and geriatrics. They won't show up, Susan!"

"Well, you suggest something then!" Susan snaps. "This is just how it has to be, Julia. I'm sorry. I can't force Dan to open on a different night, can I? Unless you can, this is what we're doing."

Julia shakes her head and huffs back upstairs, muttering about all her hard work going to waste.

"Are we agreed on the earlier time?" Susan asks Gloria and Rey.

"You're the boss," says Gloria.

"Your support is overwhelming," Susan grumbles, heading toward the pastry kitchen. Thankfully, it's bread day. She really needs to punch something for a while.

*   *   *

It takes about half a second for Philip to notice something's wrong when they meet for their second date.

"You all right? You look like your cat died," he comments, making a joking pouty face to mirror her own glum look. "Oh, shit, your cat didn't actually die, did it?"

Susan can't help but chuckle. "No."

She tells him about the reopening clash, and Philip cringes and comments, "Dick move. Seen it a dozen times with film premieres. I'm really sorry about that, Suze, but it'll probably be alright. Quality wins, right? Try not to think about it."

As if it's that easy. As if it's that easy to not think about the restaurant that might fail, or the fact that Meg spent the past forty minutes wailing over the phone about a sharp pain in her toe, or the ex-boyfriend who served her favorite pasta and alerted her to Dan's move but also seemed so angry when she tried to give his lunch guest a tart.

She does *try* not to think about it, though. None of this is Philip's fault, and it's not fair to him to put a damper on the evening just because things seem to be going a bit pear shaped in her life. So, she smiles, takes his hand, and speeds off in a taxi to a little bistro on Broughton Street. She tries not to mind when they're seated at a table right in the window overlooking the street, which is busy with festival-goers on their way to see *Oliver!* at the Edinburgh Playhouse just up the road.

"I don't suppose there's a more private table we could have?" she whispers to the waitress who seats them.

The waitress seems surprised and glances once or twice at Philip as she says, "Sorry. All booked up for tonight."

Susan tries not to think about her discomfort at being put on display. She tries not to notice the passersby who do double takes, point, and take photos with their mobiles.

Philip doesn't need to try: he seems completely unaware of the attention as he peruses the menu. "What're you in the mood for? I hear they do really great pasta here. There's one dish that has garlic and olive oil and chili and parsley that's really nice. I had it at this place in Rome, where some granny made all the pasta by hand, and I got to go in the back and watch her do it. Amazing! Just these sheets and sheets of paper-thin dough coming out of this machine she cranked by hand. Have you ever made pasta?"

"Yes." She tries not to think of her and Chris's early attempts with a machine they couldn't get to clamp properly onto the countertop. Chris had to hold the thing in place, leaning most of his weight on it to make sure it didn't shift all over as she tried to feed in the yolk-yellow dough, turn the crank and catch the smooth, leathery sheets that emerged. There was a lot of trial and error. They ate so much pasta they had to swear it off for a while.

"I should try making pasta sometime," Philip is saying. "I've got a machine—an electric one. I went out and bought it right after I met that old lady, but never actually got around to using it. I should. Think you could teach me to make pasta?"

"Um, yeah, maybe." Susan's distracted by a clump of teenage girls outside who are posing for selfies with Philip in the background. She tries shifting her chair back a few inches, hoping she can hide her face behind the menu posted in the window.

"So, what do you think? Should we get that pasta dish? Share it, Lady and the Tramp style?" He grins.

"I-I think I'd rather try the fish if you don't mind." For some reason, eating that dish with someone else feels . . . wrong.

"Suit yourself. Think I might just get one of the salads, then."

"No, get the pasta if that's what you want!"

"Nah. That's a bit much when I'm about to open in a play where I'm stripped to the waist in three scenes. People have certain expectations, you know, and if you show up with a muffin top, it's all over Twitter by the time the interval comes around."

"I'm sure you could work it off," says Susan as the wine is brought out and a taster poured for Philip.

His eyes twinkle over the edge of the glass. "Did you have anything in mind?"

Susan blushes and he chuckles, nodding for the waitress to go ahead and pour the wine. She does, then takes their orders and leaves them alone.

"Can I ask a favor of you?" Susan asks.

"Of course you can!"

"Will you consider coming to our opening?"

"I thought you'd never ask. I'd love to."

"Thank you."

He smiles charmingly, reaches across the little round table, and takes her hand. People outside are going a bit nuts now, and Susan retracts her hand, instead pressing her leg against his under the table, where it's hidden by the tablecloth. Philip grins and clearly takes that as an invitation, because he leans over and gently kisses her.

Susan forgets about the people outside. It's been ages since she's been kissed—what was it? Eighteen months? Two years? Barry, the forty-something solicitor with the overlapping front teeth she met online?—and it feels so *good*. It feels lovely to have someone seem to genuinely enjoy her company, to want to be seen with her, to touch her, to talk and laugh and joke with her. And she can't ignore the fact that the man is gorgeous and a splendid kisser—she can tell that much, even from just a brief embrace. But then, she playfully reminds herself, it's not as if he hasn't had plenty of chances to practice.

Finally, she doesn't have to *try* to think about something else.

Philip leans his forehead against hers and murmurs, "We could just ask them to box up our dinners and skip the comedy show."

Susan laughs throatily and is a little startled by how much she's tempted. But then the sound of someone's camera shutter going off (inside the restaurant this time) snaps her back to some sort of reality.

"Not tonight," she whispers back. "I'm starving, and to be honest, I could really do with a good dose of comedy."

* * *

They eat, then stroll up Broughton Street to The Stand, a close, bunker-like comedy club on York Place. With its low ceiling and basement location, it's a claustrophobic's nightmare, but Susan finds some relief in the knowledge that nobody will be able to get a mobile signal down here.

The backdrop on the tiny stage features the grim image of a grinning young boy dressed up as a cowboy, pointing a gun to his head, which Susan really hopes isn't going to set the mood for the rest of the night. Small, round tables around the stage are already fully occupied with people drinking beers and eating burgers and chips. The employee who checks their names against the ticket reservations list at the door tries not to look too surprised to see Philip and reassures them that more seats will be set up soon.

It turns out not to matter because a middle-aged couple with extra chairs at their table wave to Philip and shout, "You can join us, if you like!"

"Oh no, it's fine," Susan starts to say, even as Philip calls back, "Thanks!" and steers her over.

"I'm Bob; this is Sheila," the man introduces, reaching over to shake Philip's hand.

"Grand to meet you. Thanks for sharing with us," says Philip as he and Susan take their seats.

"Oh my God! I cannae believe it!" Sheila squeals. She has bleached blonde hair, an orange tan, and so much false eyelash on that Susan's amazed she can still comfortably blink. "I've seen every one of your movies," she breathes at Philip. "They're amazing! You were robbed at those Oscars, you were. I was ragin'."

"That's really kind, but Geoffrey put in an amazing performance," Philip demurs.

"Nah, never did like him much," Bob chimes in. Like his wife, his skin is an electric tangerine color. He laces his fingers behind his head and leans back in the chair. "Next year'll be your year, my lad." He reaches over and claps Philip on the shoulder. "Yer overdue."

"And what do you do?" Sheila asks Susan, turning toward her with a pleasant smile. Susan wonders if she's really thinking, "What the hell are *you* doing here with *him*?"

"I own a restaurant," she answers.

"You're not an actress, then? Oh, that's nice, you spend time with ordinary people," Sheila says to Philip. "Not snobby, like."

"Susan's an amazing pastry chef," Philip says. "She owns Elliot's, you know. It's reopening soon. You should try it."

"Oh, aye, we will," Bob promises with a polite smile that indicates he's only saying that because he has to.

"What do you like to bake?" Sheila asks. "I've been known to do a cracking summer pudding."

"I bake all sorts of things," Susan answers, relieved to actually be in a conversation she can contribute to (Bob is asking Philip about filmmaking). "How do you do your summer pudding? I sometimes put a little elderflower cordial in with the fruit when I'm cooking it, and use a good, stale brioche loaf."

"Do you? I'll have to try that. I usually just use a bloomer from Aldi." Sheila seems genuinely interested, and Susan feels guilty for having judged her.

"Did someone say summer pudding?" Philip asks, glancing over. "That's my absolute favorite. I'll bet you make a great one too," he adds, smiling at Sheila in a way that makes her giggle and blush right through that tan.

"Aye, she makes a good 'un, my Sheila," Bob confirms, patting his wife on the leg, making her smile and blush even more. "'s why I married her!"

"I married him because he can mend things," she says. "We met when 'e came over to sort out my plumbing."

"That's what she said!" he guffaws. Sheila laughs along with him. He reaches across the table and takes her hand. "Twenty years ago to the day, and I've never wanted to look anywhere else, eh?"

Susan hovers halfway between wanting to squeal like Lauren and tear up. She settles for a smile and an "Aw" as the lights dim and a spotlight illuminates the tiny stage.

Stand shows are a mixed bag of newcomers and more established comedians, four in all, doing brief sets, ushered along by a master of ceremonies. As the MC comes out, Susan tenses, wondering if he'll mention Philip, sitting right there in front of him, smiling, waiting to be entertained. But Philip goes unnoticed or, at any rate, is not singled out. She starts to relax, but then the first act comes out, points to Philip, and crows—"What's this? Am I being scouted? You'd better watch out, mate—I'll have your job!" He strikes a bodybuilder pose, which is meant to be funny because he's built like a beanpole. The audience titters encouragingly, recognizing a nervous newcomer, but that just serves to encourage him, and throughout his set he keeps coming back to Philip and making comments about all the famous actresses he must have slept with and was it really true what Gwyneth Paltrow said she did to her vagina? It gets so rough that people start grumbling.

It finally ends and the MC comes back out, rolling his eyes, and saying, "Well, all right, yes, there's a movie star–shaped elephant in the room tonight, and aren't we all just agog! But it's Festival time, people, and frankly, a movie star is the least interesting thing you're likely to see, right? There are a thousand shows put on by people so desperate for your patronage they'll balance a hippo holding a giraffe on the tip of their little finger while break-dancing on a high wire with no net. For *free*! Let's get excited about that instead, all right? This bloke doesn't need your attention; he's already buried in adoration and money."

Philip laughs and inclines his head. The room relaxes a bit, and the rest of the acts are much better.

Afterward, most of the audience rushes out (probably to update their social media feeds as soon as they hit the pavement, Susan guesses) while Philip, Susan, Bob, and Sheila follow more slowly. Bob and Sheila are chattering about the merits of a week in Magaluf and this really cracking resort they stayed in that Philip should look into, because it was beautiful and not at all pretentious, and people really did just leave you alone.

"I'll definitely have to look into it next time I'm down that way," Philip promises, sounding sincere. It gives Bob and Sheila a thrill, and they say good night and hug both Philip and Susan as if they're old friends, before wandering off, arms around each other's waists, in the direction of the garishly lit Omni Centre. Susan watches them go, a little wistfully, thinking of the genuine love and ease the two seem to share.

Philip reaches over and takes her hand, and they stroll in the opposite direction, taking the first left up North St. Andrew Street. It's just past eleven o'clock at night, so finally fully dark out, which means it's the perfect time to see the light installation in St. Andrew Square.

As they cross the tram tracks and enter the square, Susan gasps, "Will you look at that?"

The entire square is softly aglow from hundreds of spherical bulbs planted on stiff stems, like luminescent poppy seed heads.

They cover every last inch of grass in the square, and the lights slowly change from white to blue, to green, and back to white, the change staggered by section, so the square seems alive with rippling bands of light, like a tiny aurora borealis come down to earth.

It isn't the comedy show that makes Susan forget about all the things that are worrying her: it's this. This beautiful little oasis in the middle of a crowded city, the sight of which hushes the other people in the square and makes it easy to forget they're there. She looks up at one point and sees Philip, standing behind a section of lights that make him glow. He grins at her, clearly delighted by her delight. Swept up in it—the beauty of the lights and his smile and a need to feel wanted in an uncomplicated way—Susan rushes over and kisses him. Not a brief, soft kiss like at the restaurant, but like she really means it. She rakes her fingers through his hair and pulls his head down and feels his arm wrap around her waist and jerk her right up against him. She pushes the onlookers in the square from her mind, just for a moment, and concentrates instead on the feel of his hands and mouth. She wills a warm glow into being in her chest and tries to force it outward, to tingle in her fingertips and toes the way it used to, when she was young and . . .

She draws back, just a little, and something—a trick of the light, surely—makes Philip, just for a moment, look exactly like Chris, and it gives her a start.

He feels her movement, like a flinch, and frowns ever so slightly. "Something wrong?"

"No, just . . . no." She reaches up, pulls his head down, and kisses him again, but it isn't quite the same. She can't get caught up in it. Oh, it's nice. Really lovely, but different. And when they break apart this time, she only smiles sweetly in response to his suggestive grin, takes his hand, and steers them home.

Chapter Twenty
The Evening Ended with Dancing

∾

"You naughty girl, you!" Gloria greets Susan the following morning.

"What do you mean?" As if she doesn't know!

"You're a meme!" Gloria crows, holding up her mobile phone. Lighting up the screen is a gif of Susan, clinched together with Philip the night before, hands all over each other. Susan can feel the blush creeping up her neck. What was she thinking?

It's more than a gif, of course. She woke that morning to a text message from Lauren:

OMG, Susan, you're all over Arion Nation!

There was a link, which Susan was reluctant to click, but curiosity got the better of her. There were half a dozen pictures of her and Philip, accompanied by some very nudge-nudge-wink-wink text. Was that—she squinted at one of the pictures—was that Philip's hand on her breast? She didn't even remember that. But now everyone else would!

And it has spread beyond Rufus Arion's blog, of course. She's already ignored a phone call from *Hello!* magazine, and she's sure the *Daily Mail* will come knocking soon. Philip seems amused by the whole thing (*Oops! We were a bit naughty, weren't we?* he texted), but Susan is mortified. And she feels something else too, down deep in the pit of her stomach. Something she can't identify but definitely doesn't like.

"If I double your salary, can you forget you ever saw that?" she asks Gloria, only partly joking.

"Oh, come on! It's good you're getting out and having some fun," Gloria reassures her, tucking the phone into her pocket. "I'm not even going to ask how it was."

"I don't think you need to. You've got a front-row seat." Susan gestures to the phone. "You and the rest of the world."

"The price of fame." Gloria hoists a plastic tub filled with marinating chicken breasts and disappears in the direction of the walk-in.

Susan puts her things away and retreats to the pastry kitchen. She needs to get things in order before Rab comes and—Oh God. Susan freezes. What if Rab's seen all of this? What will he think? Will she be able to look this kid in the eye and teach him about the difference between the soft-ball and hard-ball stages of candy making without him losing it?

If he's seen any of the photos, gifs, or articles, he doesn't mention it, bless him. He's delivered downstairs by Julia, who waves to Susan through the pastry kitchen window, points to Rab, and says, "I think this one's for you?"

"Yeah, thanks, Jules," Susan says, coming out with a smile. "Hey, Rab, thanks for coming. I'll introduce you around. That's Gloria, our head chef—"

"Welcome!" Gloria calls back, waving with a pork chop she's working on.

". . . and our sous chef, Rey—"

"Word!"

Susan finishes the introductions, then shows Rab into the pastry kitchen. The boy, who responded to the greetings with fleeting smiles and kept ducking his head, seems relieved to be in a somewhat more private space.

"Today, we start with macarons," Susan announces. "The divas of the pastry world. They need a bit of careful, special handling, and they go to pieces at the least provocation, but when they turn out right, they're amazing and everyone loves them. I thought we'd do a batch of chocolate ones—what do you think?"

Rab grins. "Yeah. Sounds good."

They work away at it, the pair of them, Susan stepping back and letting him do most of the work, just as before. Once the macarons are mixed, piped out in neat little circles, and set aside to rest before baking, they move on to candy. Susan loves the miniature, multicolored, spade-like spoons that are often served with takeaway ice creams, and she got it into her head to cast some edible ones for the restaurant. She has no idea if it'll work—they might be too fragile to scoop properly—but figures they'll give it a go. While Rab keeps an eye on the melting sugar, she turns to other things.

"How's your mum doing, Rab?" she asks after a brief silence.

"Oh, she's awright. Gettin' big, so it's harder for her to keep up with the wee 'uns."

"Does it fall to you, then, to look after them?" she asks, thinking it must be a strain for him to do so after long days in the kitchen.

"Some." He goes quiet for a little while, then admits, "Mum worries a lot. About money 'n' that."

"Can't be easy with a large family," Susan sympathizes.

"Yeah. She wishes we could afford to move. She don't like some of the kids 'round us. One of 'em's got his eye on my younger brother. Not a good lot." He frowns at the bubbling sugar.

Susan watches and wonders if Chris knows all this. But then she thinks, *Of course he does.* This was the whole idea: taking on a kid who needs help. Giving a boost to those who'll most benefit from it, just as Elliot had.

"Maybe your brother can work for Chris too, when he's a little older," she suggests.

"Naw, not 'im. He'll be a mechanic, or summat. He's brilliant with cars and the like."

"Ah." Susan wonders if she can persuade her father to have a word with the man who owns the garage that takes care of his car. Then again, she'd probably have better luck with Russell. Surely he must know someone, and he'd probably be delighted to be able to say he helped a kid out.

"Rab, I want you to know that you're doing really well with me, and I'm glad to have your help." Susan smiles and pats him on the arm before sliding the first tray of macarons into the oven. "You can take some of the macarons home with you tonight, as a treat for your mum and siblings, if you like," she offers. "Only fair, since you helped make them."

Rab looks up at her with an expression so nakedly grateful she wonders if he's unaccustomed to even basic generosity. "Thanks," he says. "Thanks, that's really nice. They'll like that. They *loved* the tarts, you know." He smiles and Susan feels an incredibly strong urge to hug him. She doesn't because that'd probably be weird and teenage boys don't usually like to be hugged, do they? Even her eldest nephew doesn't seem to like it. Or, at least, he pretends not to. She grins back at Rab instead, but then the pastry kitchen begins to fill with the acrid smell of burning sugar.

"Oh, Rab, the sugar!" she cries, rushing over and yanking the pot off the burner. The entire bottom is now crusted with black gunk.

Rab backs away a few paces, wide-eyed. "I'm sorry, I'm sorry!" he gabbles. "I should've paid attention! I ruined it!"

"It's all right, Rab," she soothes. "It happens. You know how many batches of sugar I've burned? It happens in an instant." She snaps her fingers. "You don't think I'm just going to stop teaching you because of this, do you?"

The look on his face suggests that's exactly what he was thinking.

"Do me a favor, please, and take this to the dishwasher," she says, handing him the pot. "And when you come back we'll give it another go, okay?" He nods and takes the pot. When he returns, Susan steps back and lets him measure out sugar and water and start the burner back up again.

"Just make sure to keep a sharp eye on it once it passes two hundred and fifty degrees, because the temperature can spike really suddenly, and that's when you have to act," she advises.

He nods, staring intently into the depths of the copper pot.

"Nice," she says, as the sugar begins to slowly dissolve into a clear liquid. "On your way again!" She laughs and pats him on the back, noticing the tension in his shoulders ease just a touch.

* * *

By six thirty, the pastry kitchen feels very far away, and Susan is longing for it. At least there she feels competent. But instead, here she is, in front of the bathroom mirror, cursing and scrubbing away what feels like her twentieth attempt at putting on some credible eyeliner. Her poor eyelid is turning pink and irritated with all the effort.

"Argh!" she grunts, wondering if she should just give up, crawl into bed, and skip the opening of the play. But she can't do that: Kay would be terribly disappointed. And Philip too. And she wants to see it; she just hates the dressing-up ritual. Even as a child, she'd hated having Julia practice hair and makeup on her.

Speaking of Julia . . .

"Problem?" She'd evidently overheard her younger sister's exertions and is now leaning gracefully against the doorframe, arms crossed, smiling just enough to express amusement, but not enough to risk causing wrinkles.

"It's . . . this . . . thing," Susan answers, waving the eyeliner. "I can't get it to go on evenly. It's possessed!"

Julia shakes her head and holds out a hand. "Give it here and sit down."

Susan obediently plops down on the closed lid of the toilet, feeling ten years old again.

Julia bends down in front of her, cocks her head this way and that, narrows her eyes, and nods. "Close your eyes."

Susan does and feels smooth, sure strokes and something wet spread along her lash line.

"You wouldn't struggle with this if you wore it more, you know," Julia tells her, moving on to the second eye. "Practice makes perfect, and all that. Open."

"I don't feel like I have time for it," Susan says, flicking her eyes open. "And who cares what I look like when I'm in a kitchen, anyway?"

"Don't think of it as how you look to other people, then. Think of it as bringing out your best self. I wear makeup because it makes me feel pretty."

"You feel pretty because you look pretty to other people. So it's not really just for you, is it? You're dressing yourself up for everyone else."

"Just like you're doing now." Julia reaches for some blush and goes to work. "Or is it just one person you want to look pretty for?"

Susan colors and ducks her head.

"Don't do that—I'll smear. Well?"

"Yeah, I guess I want to look pretty for someone else."

Julia pauses with the blush and meets Susan's eyes. "And who might that be?"

"I—Philip, of course," Susan stammers. "Who else?"

"Did you know that Chris is coming tonight?"

"What? No. Why? How?"

"I think Lauren invited him."

"He's coming on a Friday night? That's one of the busiest restaurant nights of the week!"

Julia shrugs. "Take that up with him. But you're over him, huh? It's all Philip all the time now?"

"Yes, I'm over him," Susan answers with more conviction than she feels. "And he's definitely over me."

Julia smirks. "And Aunt Kay says I'm the bad liar." She begins poking around in Susan's makeup bag, pulling out lipsticks and testing them on the back of her hand.

"What's that supposed to mean?"

"I saw how the two of you were at that Festival. It was cute. But if I were you, I wouldn't give him another chance. He blew it, up and leaving like that when you were still so wrecked over Mum."

"Is that what you think happened?"

Julia pauses in her lipstick testing and looks up.

"Isn't it?"

Susan shakes her head. "I dumped him. Badly."

"Oh." She tucks the rejected lipsticks away. "The way Dad and Aunt Kay raged about him, I thought it was the other way around. And I thought he was a real prick for doing that, too."

"That's sweet," Susan says, surprisingly touched by Julia's sisterly feelings. "But what were Dad and Kay so upset about?"

Julia shrugs. "Ask them." She holds two red lipsticks up to the light and studies them.

Into the silence, Susan asks, "Do you ever think about Mum, Jules?"

A long pause, then: "I try not to." Julia shoves a lipstick back in the bag.

"Not at all? Not even the nice memories?" Susan can't believe that someone would—or would want to—eradicate their mother's memory like that.

Julia swallows. "We all have our ways of coping, okay, Suze? So spare me your judgment. You bake like you're trying to feed half the city, Meg buries herself in diseases, and I just try to move on and look forward."

"I'm sorry," Susan says quietly.

Julia blinks a few times, then turns to her sister, proffering the final choice of lipstick.

Susan reaches out and takes it. "Thank you." She stands and faces the mirror, tracing the lipstick over her lips. Julia steps back and watches.

"Is it getting serious, this thing with you and Philip? I mean, it looks it."

"Too new to tell," Susan answers, blotting and reapplying.

"Have you slept with him?"

"No."

"Will you?"

Susan's startled by the question and takes her time answering. "I don't know."

"You should," Julia tells her briskly, leaning toward the mirror and fussing a bit with her hair. "It'll do you good, I think, to get out there, be a little crazy. Who knows? You might like it." She straightens up and smiles another tiny smile. Susan smiles back, more widely.

"You're not half bad, you know that?" she says. "And your eye-liner game is spot on," she adds, looking at herself in the mirror. The face that looks back is, as Julia said, possibly the best-looking version of herself. Intense eyes, a subtle flush, and full, sensual, scarlet lips. She smiles again, thinking that Philip will probably like it and trying not to wonder if Chris will too.

"Don't make me blush," Julia says with a shrug. "We've got to work on your wardrobe, though, Suze. I mean, what you have on isn't too bad, although you really should invest in Spanx or something, but just about everything else . . ." She sighs. "Come on. We'll talk about it later."

* * *

The play is a triumph, an absolute triumph if Bernard is to be believed. He certainly claps the loudest at the curtain call, and shouts, "Bravo! Bravo!" when Kay and Philip step forward, away from the rest of the cast, and take a bow together.

"It's so marvelous having someone so talented in the family, isn't it?" Bernard says as they drift toward the exits. "We really are so fortunate the way such people seem to find their way to us." He smiles at Susan, which startles her a little. Is this the first time her father's been proud of her? It seems like it.

As they make their way to the chic bar where the opening night celebration is being held, Bernard chatters on about Kay and Philip and what a shame it was that Philip's last girlfriend seemed to have let herself go. "Used to be such a lovely, slender girl and then . . ."

Susan peels off from her family and makes for the bar as soon as they arrive.

"Champagne cocktail, please," she says to the bartender, who hands one over. A few sips and she's starting to feel like the bubbles are going right to her head, a delightful effervescence that brings on a smile and more relaxed stance. Another sip, and then she turns and sees Rufus standing beside her, dressed in a purple satin smoking jacket and yellow silk tie, grinning and looking her up and down, almost as if he knows what she looks like naked.

Her good mood evaporates.

"Didn't know you were on the guest list," she mumbles.

"It's my job to be on guest lists, Susan. Martini, please!" he calls to the bartender. "Stir, don't shake—bruises the gin."

Susan doesn't bother to hide her eyeroll this time. Not that Rufus seems to mind. He sidles right up to her as if they're friends, and props his chin up in both hands.

"You've been a busy little bee," he says, nudging her. "If I'd had an inkling of what a little wildcat you were, I'd have gone a *very* different direction with my interview."

"What? And missed out on having one over on both me and Chris Baker?"

"Oh, don't be like that—it was for your own good! You'd never have done that competition on your own, and he wouldn't have either, and it's done you good. You got loads of publicity. Don't lie—I saw the features."

He has her there. The win at the Foodies Festival has shone a greater spotlight on Elliot's. Two magazines have been in touch about doing features, and a travel blog asked Gloria for summer recipes. A national publication that Susan has been hounding has finally started to seem a little bit interested in covering them as well. And the journalists and critics invited to the reopening have responded very enthusiastically indeed. (Of course, that was before Dan introduced their conflict, so who knows what will happen now?) Still, she isn't going to give Rufus Arion the upper hand if she can help it.

"You don't know anything about me," she responds. "Maybe if you'd been honest, I'd have surprised you. But I can hardly expect above-board behavior from someone who takes his naming cues from the Nazis."

She expects him to be embarrassed by that, but instead he grins and says, "Stays with you, though, doesn't it, that name? You remember it. And that's the whole point, isn't it? We all just want to be memorable in a sea of other things clamoring for everyone's attention." He accepts his martini from the bartender. "If anyone should know that, you should. Don't think I don't know what this whole business with Philip Simms is. Cheers, my dear." He clinks her cocktail with the base of his glass and takes a sip.

Susan blinks at him. "What are you talking about?"

He cocks an eyebrow. "Wow, is it really genuine, then? I figured you were after publicity. I mean, the way you were acting in that park . . ." He chuckles. "Naughty girl! You do surprise me."

"Do I?"

"A little." He looks down at his drink and bites his lip, and his usual expression—half smug, half bemused—disappears suddenly. "Listen, since you say this is some genuine thing, and because you did me a favor with that Foodies Festival event, I'm going to do you one and give you a wee warning. Philip Simms is not quite what he seems."

"Of course not," she scoffs. "He's an imposter or a jewel thief, or he's got a secret family stashed somewhere—is that what you're going to say?"

"No, nothing like that. He's just not a particularly good person. He puts it on, I'm sure, but he's not. Just . . . be careful."

"And how would you know? Are you two close friends?"

He snorts. "No, certainly not. But I'd like for you and I to be friends. Shall we? If you say yes, I'll give you some good news."

"Will you, indeed?"

"I will. And you know what? I'll give it to you no strings attached, just so you know I'm capable of being decent. Seems your former chef's stunt with the opening has ruffled some feathers. He's been trying to gather backers to open somewhere permanently, but now no one will give him the time of day. Unless he makes an absolute splash at that opening, he's done. And I think we both know who you can thank for that." He glances toward the door, and Susan notices that Chris has come in.

She swallows hard around a lump that's suddenly climbed up her throat. She saw him in the theater, walking in with Lauren, who hung off his arm and chattered away. (Bernard muttered something about having a word with Russell about Chris and his daughter, which disgusted Susan.) But Susan convinced herself

Chris wouldn't come to the after-party. Surely he would want to go back to the restaurant, at least to check in and see how service is going?

But no, he's here, and something about her face has given her away, because Rufus's slithering smile makes a reappearance. "I think I'll be off now. Ta, luv!" He kisses her on the cheek, so quickly she doesn't even have time to react, and is gone.

Chris strides toward the bar, looking after Rufus's vanishing figure, and says, "Sorry to interrupt."

"Not at all, you're my savior," says Susan, scrubbing at her cheek with a bar napkin and taking a huge swig of her cocktail, finishing it off. "Better." She gestures to the glass when the bartender glances her way. "I'm surprised to see you taking a Friday night away from the restaurant."

"I have a sous chef I can rely on," he responds. "Also, CCTV in every corner of the kitchen, so I can watch their every move." He brandishes his phone. "Technology is a wonderful thing."

She giggles. "You're joking, right?"

"Maybe." He holds up the phone so she can't see the screen. "Ah no, not those microgreens, the purple ones. The purple ones!" he bellows dramatically, running a hand through his hair in mock frustration.

Susan laughs as she takes delivery of her cocktail, and he asks for a pint of lager.

"Seriously, though," he continues, accepting his beer with a nod of thanks to the bartender, "spending three hours watching a bloke sleep with his own mum and then gouge his eyes out is *so* much better than microgreens."

Susan giggles again and feels him watching her as he takes a sip of his drink.

"Champagne always made you giggly," he recalls, smiling.

"And beer always made you argumentative. Remember that time you and one of the line cooks at Regent Street got three pints in after a Saturday service and started debating what fruit would win in a fight if fruit were, in fact, able to fight?"

Chris laughs. "Oh, yeah. I went for pineapple because, obviously, pineapple would win—it's practically got armor on. What did he go for? Kiwi or something?"

"I don't remember, but you were both wrong. Obviously, coconut would win. Talk about something with armor. You want to drive yourself insane? Try getting any flesh out of one of those things."

"I have, and you're right. There was an episode of the show where we made the contestants fetch coconuts, and then they had to come up with some kind of a dish with them, but the only tools to hand were rocks and things. One guy concussed himself knocking them down from the trees; two needed stitches after their rock knives slipped; and one was so enraged after he finally got into the thing and found there's only a teensy bit of liquid in there that he nearly had a nervous breakdown. And then *I* tried the challenge and realized it was basically impossible and had *words* with the producer whose idea it was, and we had to scrap it and come up with something else. I bought everyone a *really* nice dinner that night."

"That was sweet of you," Susan says, unable to stop herself from cackling at the mental image of Chris going crazy on some beach over a coconut. "And I'll bet you put some of that amazing Scots slang to work with that producer too."

"Oh, aye, that I surely did. He'll still be scratching his head, the numpty."

* * *

Chris leans against the bar, chuckling, and watches her. She's more made up than he's ever seen her, and she looks good, but it's not a look he prefers. He thinks again of that long-ago afternoon in the park, with her Pimm's-stained lips. And more recently, at the

Foodies Festival, the way she looked as she turned away from the effusive judges. She was beaming in a way he hadn't seen since their earliest days together. Her cheeks were flushed from her exertions, eyes shining, hair curly from the humidity. She was glowing with excitement and success, and he was thunderstruck, thinking, *Goddamn, she's beautiful.*

Honestly, he can't believe that everyone doesn't find her stunning.

She glances up, catches him staring, and looks away, blushing. Chris clears his throat and takes another sip of his drink, casting about for something to say.

"How's Rab getting on?" he asks, grateful beyond measure for the kid's existence.

"Splendidly! He made some delicious macarons and little edible spoons. And learned all about the perils of sugar work."

Chris groans. "I don't even allow it in my kitchen. One mucked-up batch and the whole restaurant smells of scorched sugar all day."

"Ah, the drawbacks of an open kitchen."

He toys with his glass, then says, "Thank you for taking him on. I know you've got a lot on your plate these days, and having someone shadow you probably isn't the best or easiest."

"Not at all—I enjoy it! I mean, I did worry that it might be too much, but it's nice having an apprentice. Makes me feel like I'm accomplishing something." She smiles self-deprecatingly.

"You are accomplishing something," he reassures her. "And not just with Rab."

* * *

Susan feels heat creeping up her neck and across her cheeks. And again, it's hard to swallow. She shrugs. "If you can take the time to mentor a kid who needs it, then I can too. We all must play our part to bring along the next generation, right?" She sips her drink, then smiles playfully. "But I'm not going to give him that brownie recipe, so if this is some kind of elaborate plan, you can give up now."

"Aw, dammit!" He slaps the bar in pretend frustration. "You've found me out!" He breaks into a grin. "Well, I guess some things are worth working for."

Susan isn't sure what to say to that, so she just stares at him. And then an arm snakes around her waist from behind, and Philip is whispering in her ear, "Hey, baby. You look great! How'd you like the play?"

"Oh, hi!" She turns and hugs him. "You were brilliant! Really wonderful!"

"Aw, you're too kind." He kisses her and then seems to notice Chris standing there. "Oh, hello, I'm Philip," he says, extending a hand.

Chris takes it in a firmer grip than is strictly polite. "Chris."

"Oh, hey, you're Scottish!" Philip's face lights up. "You know, I've been thinking I might do a Scottish accent in my next role. Been working on it since I've been up here. What do you think?" He clears his throat and says, "Ocht, aye, we'll be off to the loch on a bricht mornin' eh?" He grins, seeking approval.

Susan wishes she could vanish into the floor.

"Can't wait to hear that in surround sound," Chris tells him, somehow—miraculously—straight-faced.

Susan begins to giggle but manages to cover it up as an inelegant snort. Chris glances at her and smiles.

"Aw, thanks, mate. What'd you think of the play?" Philip asks.

"It was good," Chris allows.

"Just good?"

"I'm no critic. High culture is not really my area, ye ken?"

"Oh, I ken. Huh, 'ken.' That's a good one. I'll have to remember it. Susan, do you have something I can write that down with?"

"Uh, no," she answers.

"Don't worry about it. I'll just remember. 'Nae bovver,' as they say up here, right?"

"That they do," Chris agrees in a tight voice. Susan once again begs the floor to open up and swallow her, remembering the cruel jests of the other chefs in London, all those years ago. Chris's hands clenching under the table as he struggled to control himself.

Philip is oblivious.

"Hey, what's that? Champagne cocktail? You mind?" Philip reaches across Susan and finishes her drink. "We'll get another in a minute, but first, you, milady, need a dance! You don't mind, Chris, do you?"

"No, I think she's done with me," Chris answers, looking away, drinking his beer.

Susan recoils at the unexpected sting.

"Thanks, mate!" Philip takes her hand and leads her to the dance floor. He pulls her close and murmurs, "I know this goes without saying, but you look absolutely spectacular tonight." The look in his eyes makes her swallow hard, and she tries to forget his incredible awkwardness with Chris just now. He was only trying to be friendly. She thinks about Julia and Gloria telling her she needs to move on and give someone else a go.

She responds with a sultry smile, shimmies up against him, and tries to put Chris out of her mind.

* * *

Ass. Hole! Why can't he seem to stop doing that?

Chris watches Susan turn away, face pinched in hurt and confusion. He watches the two of them press close together on the dance floor, a sight that causes a hard yank down in his stomach, until the view is blocked by Kay, who sashays over to the bar and takes the place so recently vacated by her niece.

"Hello, Christopher," she greets him, voice and smile as smooth and cool as a Siberian lake in wintertime. "I didn't expect to see you here."

"Lauren asked me. Insisted," he responds with his own frigid smirk. "And I thought it'd be good to widen my cultural horizons." *Just go ahead and call me some uneducated buffoon, you bitch! You can take your ancient Greek plays and shove 'em!*

"I do admire self-improvement," Kay says after ordering a gimlet. "And you seem to have come quite a long way since I last saw you. Well done."

"Thanks. I did it all for you."

"No need for that. I do wonder, however, if you do it for Susan? I hope not."

"Then your prayers are answered."

"I'm glad to hear it. Susan has moved on, you know."

"So I see." He glances toward the dance floor, where Susan and Philip are twined around one another as if no one else exists. He's starting to think he'll need something a bit stiffer than the beer.

"It's good for her. The poor girl's been through so much." Kay sighs. "We all want to see her happy. Don't we?"

He takes his time answering. "I hate to see her sad." He's had a lifetime's worth of that, and it still hurts to think about.

"Good. Then we're agreed." She sips her gimlet. "You really ought to thank me, you know, Christopher. In a sense, I did you a favor."

He stares at her, incredulous. Does she really believe that?

Kay shrugs. "Where would you be now if I hadn't done what I did? If I hadn't taken control of the situation? You'd probably be dead. Or in prison. Certainly not here." She gestures to the bar—a fancy one, with low lighting and premium booze and deep sofas where you can relax with your drinks and nibbles and trophy date. "And where would Susan be? You know I did what I had to do to protect her because I love her, and if you ever loved her, you'd see that and put it all behind you. I was, in a sense, the making of you both."

Chris smiles in wonder at the woman's gall, shakes his head, and finishes off his beer, snapping the empty glass back down on the bar. "Yes, Kay, I'm deeply grateful to you," he spits out. "I'm deeply, deeply grateful to you for sparing me a lifetime of Christmas lunches with Bernard, and opening nights of *your* plays, and barbeques with Russell and Helen, and glare-offs with Julia. I am *so* grateful to you. Thank you, from the bottom of my heart!"

Her haughty smirk never wavers. She just stares him down.

Chris spots Lauren in the crowd and waves to her. She dances over, throwing her arms around him and saying, "Here you are! Thought you were going to get me a drink?"

"I would, but they're lousy," he says. "Come on, let's go somewhere else."

"Oh, definitely! I heard the band on at The Liquid Room is really good! A friend of mine just sent me a video of them. Hang on . . ." She whips out her phone.

"Never mind, let's just go," Chris says. He hooks an arm around her waist, edges around Kay, and is out the door.

Chapter Twenty-One
The Morning After

❧

The room is too perfect. That's one thing Susan hates about posh hotel rooms: they're always too perfect. They have no personality to them. They're cold looking.

From her spot on the bed, she searches for it: that one little imperfection she knows has to be there. But all she can find are the ones created by two people in a hurry to get from door to bed: bright purple accent pillows strewn across the floor. A smear of vibrant lipstick on the snow-white duvet cover. An upended bedside table.

The shower's going, and a moment later the sound of Julia's tuneless humming begins to accompany the summer-rain sound of the water. Susan sets down the overnight bag she's brought and wonders if she should just go. She has things to do. Someone from the council is coming by to do a final sign-off on the building works (God help them all if anything isn't approved by this stage). Three ice cream bases need churning and flavoring, she's working out some kinks in a crème caramel recipe, and she needs to get Rab started on choux pastry.

The relaunch is just over two weeks away. Two weeks! And she still needs to finalize their pastry offerings, run interference with the press, and make all the tarts, cakes, mini pavlovas, jellies, and sauces they'll be serving. And here she is, sitting in a hotel room with her sister's clothes, like a porter!

"Jules, I'm gonna go," she calls.

"No, wait a sec," Julia sputters, turning off the water. She opens the bathroom door a moment later, releasing a cloud of steam into the room, wrapping herself in a thick, white hotel robe. She leans down, picks up the bag, and begins rummaging around in it. "Just want to make sure you brought the right things," she mumbles.

"Jules, I have things to do," Susan says, hand on the doorknob.

"I said just wait a second." Julia looks up at her sister and frowns. "What's up with your eyes?"

"I couldn't get the eyeliner off," Susan answers. She'd scrubbed and scrubbed and removed some, but she'd also irritated her eyelids and eyes so badly it looked like she had conjunctivitis.

Julia clucks and shakes her head. "We really need to work on you," she says, returning to the bag. "Oh, Susan, for heaven's sake!" She yanks out a pair of high heels. "What were you thinking?"

"You said you wanted the gray ones."

"Not *these* gray ones!"

"Julia, you literally have a dozen pairs of gray shoes. How was I supposed to know which ones you wanted?"

"Use your *sense*! These are *suede*, Susan, and look at the weather!" She flaps her hand in the general direction of the windows. Just beyond the sheer curtains, low, sulky silver clouds hover over the city. The roads and sidewalks are already slicked and shimmering with rain. "These will be *ruined*! Ugh!" She thrusts them back in the bag. "Never mind, I'll take a cab." She withdraws some lingerie from the bag and starts getting dressed.

"Whatever. Can I go now?" Susan asks, wondering if this faux pas will get her out of future walk-of-shame wardrobe summons.

"No, you may not. You're going to tell me about your night." Julia slips panties on underneath her robe, then goes to fetch a cup of coffee from the complicated-looking machine in the corner. She gives her sister a knowing look as she sips. "You and Philip seemed very cozy last night."

Susan blushes. She'd been trying to have fun, and she might have overdone it. Hard to say, really. She'd been pretty drunk. Her head is not thanking her for that today.

"So, did you and he finally . . .?" Julia smiles coyly.

"Obviously not, Julia, since I was home when you called me this morning."

"Well, not every guy lets a girl spend the night." Julia's smile is now a little smug as she goes back to her coffee.

"I wouldn't know how Philip feels about that."

"Oh God. You're just determined to be miserable and alone, aren't you?"

"What? No, of course not, I just . . . I don't know. I just wasn't in the mood." Susan toys with a photo on the wall; she's convinced it's crooked. A couple kissing under a bright red umbrella. Everything in black-and-white, aside from the umbrella.

"If you can't get in the mood with someone like Philip Simms, I don't see how you can get in the mood with anyone," Julia observes.

"You're quite generous about him, all of a sudden."

Julia shrugs. "I've moved past that. Obviously." She smirks.

Susan knows her cue. "And how was *your* night? Fun, I'm guessing." She glances around the room with a knowing smile.

"Oh, very. And he's proven himself to be a gentleman." Julia brandishes the cup of coffee. "Not all of them make you coffee."

"If he's such a gentleman, then where is he?"

"Early call at the theater."

"Ah. You going to see him again?"

Julia responds with a lazy shrug. "I might. We'll see. I haven't decided yet."

Susan watches her sister continue to get dressed, wondering what it's like to be able to keep sex so separate from deeper feelings. Casual sex never interested her. She needs intimacy in order to want to be intimate, and you can't go opening yourself up heart and soul to just anyone, can you? She's been trying to force it with Philip because it seems like she *should* want him, but Susan is now realizing it takes more than charm and an attractive face to arouse her.

"Right, then," Julia says, setting her empty cup aside and heading once more toward the bathroom. "Have to dry my hair and put my face on. You can go."

"Thanks" is Susan's dry response. "See you at the restaurant?"

"See you!"

* * *

The hotel's lift seems interminably slow, and Susan practically explodes through the doors and sprints toward the street. She's nearly there when a hand comes out of nowhere and grabs her wrist, yanking her back as a man's voice says, "What's the hurry?"

Susan whirls with a gasp, wrenching her wrist out of his grip, and is face-to-face with Philip. He's grinning, pleased and playful, apparently unaware of what he's done.

"That hurt!" she scolds, and the tone of her voice wipes the smile right off his face.

"I'm sorry," he says. "Let me get you some coffee or something to make up for it."

"No, I can't, I really have to go—"

"It'll just be a minute," he interrupts, grabbing her hand and almost dragging her into the nearby dining room. He takes her to a table right in the middle of the room, where everyone can see them. "So," he says, plunking down and spreading a crisp napkin over his lap, "what brings you here so early in the morning? Don't tell me I've been outplayed!" He laughs as if the very thought is a joke.

"Julia," Susan responds in a tight voice. "She needed a change of clothes."

"No kidding! Who was it? Oh, wait, don't tell me—she was practically salivating over Justin last night. Was it him? I'll bet it was. He can never resist a blonde."

"I can't say."

"Code of the sisters, eh? I admire that. None of my brothers can keep any sort of secret. They're worse than the press." He reaches across the table and takes Susan's hand, stroking it like it was a cat. "Wish it was you calling for a change of clothes this morning," he murmurs.

"Sorry," Susan says, glancing around to make sure no one overheard.

It could have been her. Philip was keen last night. "Why don't we take this party somewhere quieter?" he'd purred in her ear as they danced. And she'd thought about it; tried to convince herself it was what she wanted, but she just couldn't.

"It's not too late," Philip continues. "Why don't we get together tonight?"

"I don't know. It's really busy at the restaurant right now, with the reopening so soon. I'll probably be pretty knackered," she answers.

"Oh." He frowns a little and releases her hand. "Too bad. I mean, we don't have long before the play closes and then I'm off to London for a boot camp."

"Boot camp? Are you doing a war movie?"

Philip chuckles. "No, not that sort of boot camp. Singing and dancing. I'm doing a remake of *My Fair Lady* with Natalie Portman. We start shooting in Czechoslovakia next month."

"And who're you playing?"

"Henry Higgins, of course!" He smiles. "Who else?"

Susan tries, unsuccessfully, to imagine Philip as the irascible, middle-aged Professor Higgins. "I didn't know you sang."

"I don't. Not yet. But most of Higgins's songs are pretty much spoken anyhow. Natalie's got the really hard job—I wouldn't want to follow in Audrey Hepburn's footsteps." He chuckles. "It'll be good for us, though. Hollywood loves a musical. Look what *Les Mis* did for Anne Hathaway!"

Look what it did for Russell Crowe, Susan thinks, but outwardly she smiles. "I'm sure you'll be great. Listen, I'm sorry—I really do need to go." She rises and turns toward the door.

Philip springs to his feet and wraps his arms around her. "Say you'll come tonight," he insists. "Come on . . ."

"I can't," she tells him, firmly. "I have work to do too."

He seems surprised and maybe a little put off by her tone. He drops his arms. "Okay, fair enough. Still want me to come to the opening?"

"Of course I do." His little-boy-hurt look makes her feel equal parts guilty and infuriated. She tries to appease him with a kiss, which seems to work. "I'll call or text you, okay? We'll get together before then."

"I hope so." He resumes his seat and picks up his menu. "If you see the waitress on your way out, send her my way, will you?"

Chapter
Twenty-Two
Relaunch

⁓

Two weeks pass in a rush: they're a freight train, and Susan, Gloria, and the rest of the Elliot's staff are just clinging on for dear life, hoping to avoid a crash.

They've been working all hours, all hands on deck. The dining room is finally in good shape, all of Julia's special-ordered fixtures and chairs and sofas in their appointed places. Food's been served up for the waitstaff, who are drilled on every last ingredient by the head waiter. He occasionally stops and shouts to one of them, "What wine goes with this course? Name three, at different price points!" If they can't answer in under twenty seconds, they sit there with him for hours until they know that wine list and that food better than they know their own parents.

In the pastry kitchen, Susan churns out miniature cakes, leaves of crisp puff pastry, ice creams, mousses, breads, and dainty biscuits and chocolates. Chris generously sends Rab full time for the last week, and she's grateful for the help.

She's also grateful for the refuge of the kitchen: photographers have actually begun camping out at Moray Place and the restaurant, shouting questions at her as she runs past on her way to work.

"It's a bit tacky," Bernard sighs, looking out at them. But he can't help but strut down the front stairs every time he leaves the house, pausing to tell the press, "Now, now, my daughter's entitled to some privacy over her love life, is she not? And as a father, of course, I must protect that privacy, and I would never, ever discuss anything like a forthcoming engagement."

"Don't stop him," Julia warned when Susan shrieked after hearing what her father said. "You can't buy the kind of publicity the relaunch will get now."

And finally, it's here: the big night. Susan has just enough time to run home and change ("You need me to do your makeup again?" Julia shouts after her as Susan throws herself back out the door and into a waiting taxi) before she's back at the restaurant, plating up miniature desserts. In the kitchen, Gloria's turned up the music and is cranking out amazing dishes, shouting orders, keeping things moving. Rey slides tray after tray of delectable samples from the menu into the dumbwaiter, sending them up to the waitstaff, who hover, ready for the rush.

"Susan! Come on! Doors are open!" Julia yells, tottering half-way down the staircase on impossibly high heels.

Susan pipes one last rosette on a tart, wipes her hands, whips off her apron, and clatters upstairs, giving Rab a few last-minute pointers as she goes.

Elliot's is mobbed. So jammed full of people already that she can hardly get the kitchen door open to slip out and start mingling. Shoulders and elbows jab her as she passes, and the rising roar of conversation makes it almost impossible to make out what any one person is saying. The bartenders are whipping out drinks, making a show of rattling the cocktail shakers and pouring from a height into perfectly chilled glasses. The waitstaff somehow manages to circulate with their trays, smiling, pointing to the food, enticing everyone to try just a bite. It's disappearing fast; empty plates and trays go into the dumbwaiter and are returned to the kitchen, and more appear.

Susan catches sight of her father in the crowd, talking to some expensively dressed people, gesturing to the restaurant and then pointing to Julia and patting her on the shoulder. Julia smiles modestly and shrugs. *"Oh, this? No big deal. An* easy *project, really."*

Someone grabs Susan's hand and shakes it, and she turns to smile in the face of one of the judges from the Foodies Festival. He's saying something to her, but she can't make it out, so she just smiles and nods and thanks him.

Have they really invited all these people? It seems like more than she approved for the guest list. She notes the journalists and critics, family and friends, but there are other faces that are familiar but she can't quite place. And outside . . .

Dear God! Susan glances out the front window of the restaurant and blinks in astonishment. If it seems mobbed inside, it's *nothing* to the scene outside. A massive crowd has gathered, with photographers sprinkled among them, snapping away at people coming in. There are actually police there, doing crowd control. Every now and again, someone coming in pauses at the door, smiles, poses, and the crowd cheers a little louder. One of them is an actor on a ridiculously popular fantasy TV show. Susan didn't even know he was in Edinburgh. He definitely wasn't on the guest list.

"Did you invite all these extra people?" she asks Julia, pulling her sister aside from a group of young banker types in the "casual" uniform of jeans and bespoke shoes.

"No," Julia answers, jerking her arm away. "But be glad they're here—the press is all over it. Nobody'll bother with Dan tonight." With a smug smile and a pat on Susan's arm, she returns to her admirers.

Susan glances back out the window just in time to see Philip arrive. The crowd shrieks and pushes against the police holding them back. He smiles, waves, stops to sign autographs and submit to hugs from overzealous fans. He spots her through the window, grins, and gestures for her to join him. Susan shakes her head; the crowd doesn't want her, and the thought of going out there and making herself a spectacle makes her throat go dry.

A smarmy voice beside her remarks, "My, my, quite the turnout tonight." Rufus. Of course. He sidles up to her, arms clasped behind his back, and looks out at Philip and the crowd. "You've done a marvelous job, Susan, just excellent."

"Thanks," she says.

"Don't you want to go out and join him?" Rufus asks, moving a little closer. Susan crosses her arms and finds herself leaning away from him.

"No, I'm fine here."

"Don't blame you. I wouldn't want to be out there either. Not with him, anyway."

The way he spits the word "him" makes Susan turn toward him, frowning. "What'd he *do* to you? Why do you hate him so much?"

"I told you—he's not a nice person."

"You'll have to give me more than that."

"You know he dumped his last girlfriend for getting fat?"

Susan snorts. "I find that very hard to believe."

"Look it up, then. They were together more than a year, and then she put on weight for a role, and once the film was done, she had trouble taking it back off again. He dumped her four days before the premiere. No warning at all. By *text*. Some people are such cowards."

"I'm not exactly a stick," Susan points out. "And I happen to know there was more to it than that. You'll have to do better."

He shrugs. "He may have said there was more to it, but then, he would. He lost a bit of ground with fans when the story broke. So being seen about with you might be a way of rehabilitating his image." He smirks out the window. "Seems to have worked."

"I think you're just trying to create drama," Susan scoffs, trying not to think of all the times Philip's put the pair of them on display.

"Believe what you like, my dear. But he's a product and needs to sell himself. Angry people won't buy."

Susan rolls her eyes. "You just want a story. You want a big, dramatic breakup so you can blog about it."

"I wouldn't say 'no' if that's what you're offering."

"I'm not."

"I'm not surprised. You don't seem like the dramatic type." He sighs. "Can't fault me for trying, right?"

As she glares at him, Philip pops up beside her and grabs her arm, saying, "Come on! They want to meet you!"

"What? No, Philip, I—"

Too late. He's dragged her out the door to the front of the restaurant. Susan feels him shoving her toward the crowd, yelling, "Isn't she amazing? Come to her restaurant!"

She freezes, somehow managing to smile as the crowd roars and people shout things she can't make out. There are cameras and phones out, snapping pictures and recording. Philip wraps his arm around her shoulder and gives her a big kiss on the cheek. Girls in the crowd squeal. Susan wants nothing more than to retreat back inside, but Philip's arm is so tight around her, she can't move. The noise and the chaos and the crowd and the cameras are everywhere, and she thinks, *Oh my God, I'm in hell.*

* * *

She looks like she's being tortured, Chris thinks, just managing to make his way through the thicket of people surrounding the entrance to the restaurant. To him, Susan looks pale and overwhelmed, her smile brittle, body tense. He sees Philip throw an arm around her, and she stiffens even more. *Get off her,* he thinks fiercely. *Can't you see she doesn't like it? How can you not see it?*

He steps toward her, but a policeman blocks his path.

"Sorry, sir, but do you have an invitation?" he asks Chris.

Chris yanks his phone out and scrolls through his emails, searching for the invitation he received a week ago.

"Hi there!" a chipper voice to his right pipes up. He glances over and finds the journalist who interviewed him on the radio, standing next to him, searching her phone as well. "Didn't expect to see you here," she says, holding her invitation up for the policeman to see. "Not after what you said on the show. Have you come back around on Elliot's?"

Chris presents his invitation, and he and the journalist are admitted. "Elliot's is a wonderful restaurant, and I think Miss Napier and the chef will do amazing things here. They already proved it at the Foodies Festival. I have a huge amount of respect for them both. Feel free to quote me and tell everyone you know I said that."

"I will," she smiles, "if you get me a drink."

Chris senses the crowd simmering down, and he realizes that Susan and Philip have gone back inside. They're lost in the tightly packed mass.

"All right," he agrees, moving toward the door. Maybe he'll find Susan on the way to the bar.

* * *

Philip is stuck to her like a mollusk. He wraps an arm around her waist and keeps it there, steering her around the room, introducing her to his actor friends, all of whom are very smiley, very enthusiastic, and very firm with their handshakes.

"Great place! Great place!" they all chorus. "Great food! Great food!" they exclaim, even though she doesn't see a single one of them eat any of it.

No matter: other guests wolf it down. The flow of empty plates going back down the dumbwaiter increases. The bartenders shake,

shake, shake; the crowd gets noisier, the heat closer. Susan's face and hands hurt from all the smiling and handshaking. She's been too busy talking to people to eat anything herself, and she's starting to feel a little sick. When Philip finally lets go of her for a moment, she takes the opportunity to escape downstairs.

Gloria and her crew are winding things down; the sweets are going upstairs now. Susan stops by the pastry kitchen first, to thank Rab profusely for all he's done and reassure him that it looked great. He smiles, seeming extraordinarily relieved.

Gloria looks up as Susan comes back into the kitchen, and Susan grins.

"I think we did it!" she says.

"That's what I like to hear!" Gloria bellows, beaming, edging around the pass so she can give Susan a hug. "You okay? You look a little peaky."

"I just need a minute," Susan answers. "Are there any more of those potatoes left?"

"Kept a few back, just in case." Gloria hands her a plate. "All yours."

"Thanks." Susan retreats to the office and devours half the plate in seconds, enjoying the relative peace. But after only five minutes, Philip appears in the doorway.

"Here you are! Come on back up—there are some more people for you to meet!"

"I think I've met enough, thanks," she answers, more sharply than she means to.

He recoils momentarily, then steps inside, closing the door behind him. "Okay, we'll just sit here, then." He settles down on the extra chair.

Susan sighs and rubs her forehead. She wants to be left alone. "Why did you invite all those extra people?" she asks. It hadn't taken her long to figure out he was behind it: they were clearly all friends of his.

"I thought it was a party." He shrugs. "And you needed something to keep the press's attention, didn't you? This did it!" He shakes his head. "I thought this was what you wanted. I mean, isn't that why you wanted *me* here?"

"No," Susan answers. "I wanted you here because you're part of my life, and I believe in sharing important events with the people in your life." She throws back her head, contemplating the ceiling and trying to get her thoughts in order. "They're so radically different, your life and mine. You like this sort of thing, but I just want to be in a kitchen or arranging things behind the scenes. I'm better that way. I'm not at home in a spotlight."

"But you could be!" He reaches out and takes her hand. "You'll get used to it."

"I don't think so." She lifts her head and looks at him. He has a resigned expression on his face. He isn't even going to put up a fight. She wonders if she actually meant anything to him or if what Rufus said was true: that she was just a prop to help him win back fans. "Can I ask you something?"

"Yeah, sure."

"Were you really interested in me? Was this a real thing for you or—I don't know—filler? Something to do just while you were in town?"

He leans back and runs a hand through his hair. "Geez, Susan, of course I'm interested. You really think so little of me that you believe I'd use someone like that? Especially Kay Ashley's favorite niece? Do I seem crazy to you? She'd skin me alive and use the hide for a punching bag."

Susan snorts, despite feeling ashamed of herself for having accused him.

Philip sighs and leans toward her. "I think what you really want to know is how much commitment I was looking for here. And honestly? I don't really know. I mean, we basically just met, and like you said, I'm only here for the month. It's hard to know so early whether something's really worth a major investment, right?"

"Oh, I don't know," she murmurs, her voice catching a little. "I think you know, sometimes. And then it just seems easy. But sometimes we still manage to screw it up."

There's a long pause as he looks away. Then, "Yeah," he says, and she thinks his voice sounds a little thick too. "Yeah, I think I know what you mean."

She knows he's not talking about her, and she's fine with that. He looks back at her, and they share an understanding smile.

"We don't give men enough credit for having tender feelings," Susan comments, reaching out and stroking his arm. "We think it's only women who feel the sting and burn of a broken heart."

"We men don't do ourselves any favors," he says with a rueful smile and shake of the head. "We're supposed to be all tough and stoic, so that's what we are. We tamp it down, take it out on the machines at the gym or throw ourselves into work or whatever. We think emotion is weakness, until some of us get paid to show it, and then we get Academy Awards. Funny world." He chuckles.

"Strange world." Susan shakes her head. "Maybe that's the blessing and curse of being a woman: we're allowed—encouraged, even—to feel and express our feelings. We can get them out, but sometimes I think we get stuck in them too. We think about them so much that we just keep turning over and over all the things we did wrong and should have done differently, and how things could be so different and maybe better if we'd just . . ." She stops, unsure how to continue, as her throat closes and her eyes tingle painfully with tears.

Philip, his face pursed in an understanding grimace, rises and pulls her into a tight hug. Susan rests her head on his shoulder and draws in a deep, shuddering breath as he rubs her back the way Meg does when one of the boys is upset.

"I'm sorry he hurt you," he murmurs.

"He didn't," Susan responds. "I have nobody but myself to blame. And I probably always will."

They stand like that for another moment or two, and then Philip steps back and clears his throat.

"I know it's cliché, but I hope we can stay friends. Seriously."

She can tell he means it, and she's pleased. "I'd really like that."

He leans forward, pecks her on the cheek, and jerks his head toward the door. "I think I'll head out, if that's all right? Maybe out the back, so I don't draw attention by going?"

"Sure," says Susan. "I'll show you." She opens the office door and jumps when she finds Chris there, poised to knock.

"Hi," he says, looking embarrassed. "Sorry, I was being nosy and came down to see the kitchen. Gloria said you were in here. I wanted to congratulate you."

"Oh, thanks," Susan says, trying to pull herself together and wondering how much, if anything, he heard of her conversation with Philip.

Philip slips out of the office. "I'll find the way out," he says. "Take care, Susan. We'll talk soon."

"Good luck with *My Fair Lady*," she says.

"Oh," he responds with a roll of his eyes and self-deprecating smile, "thanks—I'll need it!"

He disappears into the kitchen, and Susan and Chris face each other in silence for a moment.

"You should probably go up," he finally says. "Take the kitchen staff; they deserve their moment in the spotlight. You all did great tonight."

"Thank you," she says, trying hard to read his face. Is it her imagination, or does he seem to be having trouble keeping eye contact?

"I'll see you up there," he says. He turns and walks away without another look.

* * *

Susan gathers the staff, brings them up to the dining room, and leads the guests in a round of applause. Then there are more handshakes, more smiling, pleased journalists promising write-ups, and guests promising to be back.

Bernard clasps her hand, smiles genuinely, and says, "You've done really well, my dear. Your mother and grandfather would be pleased, and so am I."

Susan blinks at him for a moment, then manages to say, "Thanks, Dad."

He releases her as Kay sweeps in, pulling Susan into a hug so tight Susan can barely breathe.

"You've done it, Susan! You've really done it!" she gushes. "Your mother would be *so proud*!" She looks around. "Where's Philip disappeared to?"

"He had to go," Susan replies, turning to embrace Meg and William, whom she notices for the first time are looking very sullen. "Everything okay?" she whispers to Meg, who just shakes her head and steps away. Susan holds onto her hand. "Let's get together soon, okay?" she says, frowning. "We'll have lunch or coffee or something, and a good talk." She can't help but feel like she's been neglecting her sister lately, with everything else that's been going on, and that worries her. Meg looks haggard, and William is refusing to make eye contact with anyone or stand within two feet of his wife.

The family drifts away, and Susan looks up and sees Chris standing at the bar with a half-drunk glass of beer in one hand. She tenses a little, remembering the awkwardness downstairs. But he lifts the beer in her direction, inclining his head in a sort of bow, and has a word with the bartender, who promptly pours a glass of champagne.

"You look like you need something to make you giggly," Chris says, approaching and handing over the drink. He seems more himself now, and she thinks, *It was all in your head, that awkwardness. He didn't hear anything.*

"Do I?" She takes the champagne and clinks the edge of his glass.

"You should be pleased—you had a great night," he says. "But you look like someone just kicked your dog and then ran it over."

Susan can't help but snort. "Thank you. That was . . . graphic."

"Well, if anyone should be looking unhappy right now, it should be me. I'm the one who's got bigger competition now." He grins. "And I couldn't be more pleased."

"Thanks," she says warmly. "That means a lot, coming from you."

He chuckles ruefully. "Yeah, guess I haven't been the nicest. I'm really sorry about that. Sorry I snapped at you the day you came to Seòin—I know you were just trying to be nice. And that comment at the party after the play . . ." He clears his throat. "It was uncalled for."

"Don't worry about it," she reassures him. "We all do hurtful things without meaning to. If anyone knows that, I sure as hell do."

"Well, you're not the only one who turns things over and over and over in their head long afterward," he says.

Oh my God, he did hear, Susan thinks, blinking up at him, trying to think of what to say next. He seems embarrassed, though, realizing what he's just blurted out. He's looking down at his beer, fiddling with it. So she decides it's best to let the comment lie.

At last, he clears his throat and asks, "At the risk of pushing my luck, would you be willing to consider trading support for support?"

"What do you mean?"

"I mean, I'm going to be appearing at the Book Festival next week, and I was wondering if you'd come." He drops his voice. "My publicist says I shouldn't worry, but I keep having nightmares about nobody showing up."

"I doubt that'll be a problem," Susan reassures him, remembering how the crowd cheered when he arrived that night, though he hadn't seemed to notice. Too busy talking to that journo he spent the next hour with at the bar. "But yes, I'll come."

He grins. "Thanks." He sips his beer. "So, are you all right?" His forehead is puckering in concern. "You didn't look . . . happy, when I saw you earlier. Or just now."

"I'll be fine," she reassures him. "Just a little tired, and overwhelmed."

"Yeah, I know how that is." He gestures to her now-empty glass. "Another?"

She wants to. She's tempted. She wants to get giggly with him. She wants it to be like it was, but at the same time, she reminds herself that this would just be a tease. It's a stolen moment, and things can't be like they used to be. They can be courteous; friendly, even. It's certainly an improvement over the hostility he used to show. But she can't get her hopes up—it would only crush her. He's just being polite; this is a professional courtesy, one chef congratulating another on a job well done. And it would be best for her not to try to make this more than it is.

"Thanks, but I think I'm all right with just the one," she answers.

He nods and polishes off the last of his beer. "Well, I'd best be off, then. Restaurant life is a busy one, and we both need our sleep, hey?"

"Yeah."

With one last smile, he turns away and is swallowed up by the remaining crowd.

And she is alone.

Chapter Twenty-Three
The Starving Artist

❧

The reviews are in, so glowing they're "practically radioactive" (Gloria's words). Susan's so relieved she almost cries when she reads them, the stress and anxiety of the past few weeks threatening to drench the chef's office.

"Hey, now, come on! You had more faith in us than that, didn't you?" Gloria asks, noticing Susan tearing up, even as she smiles, paging through the newspapers and printouts of online content. "You knew we'd get there in the end, right?"

No, actually, she hadn't. It's not that she didn't have faith in her staff, but with all their setbacks she'd started to feel like it would take a miracle for everything to come together.

Dan's place, on the other hand, has met with a collective shrug from the few critics who tried it. "About what you'd expect from a restaurant in a touristy area," one wrote, rather damningly. "Trying to be everything to everyone, but hitting the mark for no one."

Elliot's is fully booked for the next two months, and everyone is working flat out. They're serving lunch and dinner six days a week, and it's almost time to start planning and testing recipes for the autumn menu. In the back of her mind, Susan knows she should really step up the recruitment for a pastry chef—they've had some applicants, but none she was really excited about. And she has to admit, she's reluctant to hand over the pastry reins. She uses Rab's ongoing training as an excuse. She can't just pass him along to a whole other person, now, can she?

He's coming along beautifully: his puff pastry is a marvel now, and he's beginning to invent new dishes of his own. He and Susan are tweaking a cranberry linzer torte one afternoon a few days post-relaunch when her phone rings.

"Suze," Julia says from the other end, "I think you'd better come home. Meg's here, and I think I could use some backup."

"Why? Is she holding you hostage?"

"Just come home, okay? She needs something, and I don't think I'm the best person to give it."

The cryptic nature of the message sends Susan into a panic, so she reels off instructions to Rab while tearing off her apron, then leaps into the first cab she can flag down, and races home as fast as the traffic and crowds will allow.

"What's happened?" she shouts as soon as she's through the door at Moray Place.

Julia appears in the doorway of the sitting room. "For God's sake, Susan, calm down. No one's died."

"Well, what was I supposed to think? Where's Meg? What's wrong?"

Julia steps aside and gestures into the sitting room. "See for yourself."

Meg is lying prone on one of the sofas, face red and puffy, tears and snot streaming continuously.

"Oh, Meg," Susan murmurs, sinking onto the sofa beside her. "Sweetie, what happened?"

"I've abandoned my children!" Meg wails.

Taken aback, Susan asks, "Excuse me?"

"I just left! I just walked out of the house! I just left and came here!"

"Jesus, Meg, the kids are home alone?"

"No, of course not. They're with their dad!"

"Oh God, Meg, then what the hell are you talking about, you abandoned them? They're perfectly fine!"

"Are they? Are they really? William never notices when one of them has a fever. He doesn't know what to do when they get sick or need something. He doesn't know what Ayden likes to eat."

"I think he'll figure it out," Julia comments. "I mean, that kid eats dirt and dog food; it's not like he's picky. And Meg, can you use a tissue or something? The upholstery . . ."

"Can you make some tea or something?" Susan suggests sharply, glaring at Julia. Julia looks relieved to have something else to do.

"Okay, let's reel this back a little," Susan suggests, stroking Meg's hair and reaching for a box of tissues. "Did something happen this morning?"

"There was a fight," Meg sniffled, mopping at her face. "A bad one. I'd been talking to the GP about postponing some of Ayden's immunizations, or spacing them out a bit, because I heard that's better for them, and William's been so difficult about it, and he told me I'm just an idiot, and I'll end up killing our children or making them crazy, just like I make *him* crazy. And he said that *I'm* crazy, that I'm sick and I need help and everyone thinks I'm just a stupid mess."

"That was a terrible thing for him to say," Susan tells her. "And it's not true. We don't think you're crazy or a stupid mess. I certainly don't. You're just . . . well, you worry a lot, Meg. And that worries *me*. And I think it worries William too, and that's why he's saying these things. I'm not saying he's right," she adds hastily as Meg's face crumples anew. "I just think he's expressing his fear very, very poorly."

There's a long silence as Meg snuffles and sniffles.

"He doesn't understand," she hiccups. "He doesn't know just how easily a simple thing can become a complete disaster, does he? We understand, but *he* doesn't. And I'm—Susan, I'm *so tired*. I'm tired all the time because I'm on constant high alert, and I can't seem to stop it. Every time one of the boys gets a cough or I get a pain, I think, 'Jesus, this is it! All over again!' And when Andrew fell . . ."

She shifts onto her side, curling up in a fetal position, and renews her tears. "I felt like the worst mother. I try so hard to keep them safe and healthy, and then that had to happen! On my watch! And they all blamed me for it; you should have seen some of the looks Helen gave me afterward! It just kicked me into overdrive— I've had Ali at Sick Kids four times in the last month because he keeps telling me his tummy hurts, and they've run all sorts of tests and can't find anything, and they've started to say he might just be saying that because that's what he thinks he *should* be saying. So, either I'm making my own child crazy, or there really is something wrong with him and they just can't find it, and I don't know which one is worse!" She bursts into wracking sobs.

"Oh, love." Susan wraps her arms around her sister, squeezing as hard as she can, feeling guilty for getting so wrapped up in other things lately that she's barely had time for Meg.

"I-I feel like I've been trying to cope with all of this on my own for ages," Meg continues. "I mean, no one was there for me when Mum died. You had Aunt Kay, and Julia had Dad, and who was left for me? Just William, but he doesn't even want me!"

"Megs, honey, of course he does!"

"No, he doesn't! I heard him with you that one Christmas. I'm just the sister he settled for!"

Susan feels another guilty pang. "William was drunk when he said that; he didn't mean it. And I'm really sorry I couldn't be a better sister to you when Mum died. We kind of failed as a family back then, didn't we?"

Julia is hovering in the hallway, a tray of mugs in her hands, peeking into the room as if she's not sure she'll be welcome. Susan gestures for her to join them, and Julia sets mugs down on the table in front of both her and Meg.

"Meg, I made yours with extra milk and sugar," she announces, curling her legs under her and settling down on the carpet near Meg's head. Off Susan's startled look, Julia shrugs. "What? Mum used to say it's more comforting that way."

"I miss Mum," Meg whimpers, hauling herself into a sitting position and taking a sip of her tea. "If she hadn't died, I wouldn't be like this."

"If she hadn't died, a lot of things would be different," Julia observes, glancing meaningfully at Susan. "But she did die, Megs, and we have to muddle on as best we can, right? Try and un-muck things." She pats Meg on the knee and sighs. "I miss her too."

"Do you?" Meg shoots her older sister a skeptical look. "You never seem to."

"Like I told Suze, I try not to think about it." Julia shrugs. "But you know, Mum was the only person who didn't just tell me I was pretty. Well, except for you," she adds, looking at Susan. "She used to listen to me going on and on about design plans. Everyone else just seemed bored. She was the one who encouraged me to start the business. It's why I couldn't quite bear to go on with it after she died. I thought she was the only one who thought anything of me." Another glance at Susan. "But things are different now. And I don't want you talking about having no one, Meg. You've got two sisters, right? Come and talk to us, but, you know, without the hysterics. And there's something else that might help."

"Oh? What's that?" Meg asks.

"Well . . ." Julia clears her throat and sits up straighter. "You know that Susan and I saw someone after Mum died? A professional? Now, don't look at me like that—I'm not saying you're mad, but it did both of us a lot of good, wouldn't you say, Suze?"

Susan nods.

"There you are, then. It might help for you to talk to someone. And find something else to do besides just mothering. You need a hobby, Megs. Or a job."

"You say that like it's such an easy thing to do!"

"It *is* an easy thing to do," Julia insists. "Get out of the house and away from the kids. Get a new nanny and join a club. Take up knitting or—I don't know—get an allotment or something. Maybe Susan'll hire you at the restaurant!"

"I don't think Meg really wants to work at the restaurant," Susan interjects, "but there are plenty of other things to do. What about joining a choir? I miss you singing, Meg!"

Meg sniffles and stares down at her mug. "I do miss it, sometimes," she mutters. "I thought about joining one of the Edinburgh choirs, but I kept telling myself I was too busy . . . I don't know . . . maybe you're right and it'd be good for me to have something to do. I mean, Jules, you've been much happier and more interesting since you started redoing the restaurant. You actually seemed excited about it, and I haven't seen you excited about anything for years. Same with you, Susan."

"Thank you, sweetie," Susan says.

"Tell you what—I'm going to look into counselors, okay, Megs?" Julia offers. "I've a friend whose wife is a GP; I'm sure she'll know of someone. And I'm going to get you out of the house more. Let's make a standing date to meet for a drink—say, once a month or so. Be more family. You can come too, Susan."

"Aw, thanks." Susan chuckles.

"If you're not too busy," Julia adds.

"I'll make time," Susan promises.

Meg finally manages a wobbly smile. "Thanks," she says to both her sisters. "I'd like us to see each other more. Away from the rest of the family. Just us sisters."

"We'll be besties, just like in the movies," Julia comments with a wry smile.

The doorbell rings and Julia rises to answer it, returning a few moments later with Kay in tow.

"Oh, Susan, you're here!" Kay notes. "I thought I'd have to go to the restaurant to say goodbye."

"You're not leaving now, are you?" Susan asks. "I thought you were staying on until next week."

"Oh, I am, I am, but you've been so occupied lately." Kay takes in the mugs of tea and the tearstained face of her youngest niece and asks, "What's been going on here?"

"Just family drama," Julia answers. "Can I get you some tea?"

"That'd be lovely, darling. Susan, may I borrow you for a chat?"

"I know when I'm not wanted," Meg grumbles, hauling herself to her feet.

"Come on, you," Julia says to her. "We'll find some vegan something-or-other to cheer you up."

Kay takes Meg's spot on the sofa and looks meaningfully at Susan. "Now, my dear, I've had breakfast with a rather sorrowful young man of your acquaintance. What on earth happened to you and Philip? I thought you were going gangbusters, but the poor lad tells me it's all over."

"I'm sorry that he's sad," says Susan, "but it just wasn't right, you know? It was nice, it was good, but good just isn't good enough. I hope he's not too upset."

"Oh, he'll be fine, dear—don't worry. He'll be shooting in a few weeks and a little on-set romance will bounce him right back." Kay bites her lower lip. "Susan, my love, is it really that he wasn't right for you, or were you too distracted by someone else to give him a fair chance?"

"What do you mean?"

"You know exactly what I mean."

There's a sudden sting of tears behind Susan's eyes, and she glances away, pressing her lips together and trying to regain control of herself.

It's all the answer Kay needs, and she reaches out and hugs Susan fiercely. "Oh, Susan, my darling," she breathes. "I'm sorry. I'm so very, very sorry."

"What are you sorry for?" Susan asks.

"Just . . . I'm sorry you're sad, my love. You know I want more than anything for you to be happy, don't you?"

"I do. And I *am* happy."

"No, Susan. You're not. You're content, in a sense. But you're not happy. Not the way I want you to be."

"Well, there's not much to be done about that, is there?"

"Isn't there?"

"No. We—he and I, we're cordial, which is good. But he's not interested in me, and I don't blame him. I hurt him. I really, really screwed things up, and so he's moved on. It was a long time ago, and he has a very different life now. I should move on too, and I'm trying to; it's just a slow process. I'll get there." She smiles at her aunt in a way she hopes is reassuring, but Kay does not return it.

"Dear girl," Kay murmurs, "don't force it. Don't settle, for God's sake—that would break my heart. You're not content to give yourself by halves, and I admire that. I should have recognized it better ten years ago."

"Well, we were all pretty distracted."

"Yes, I suppose we were."

"Can we talk about something else now?" Susan begs, still feeling like she's teetering on the brink of bursting into tears. "Have you got a new role coming up or something?"

"Oh lord, you'll never guess! They want me to play Gertrude in a musical version of *Hamlet*. Can you imagine? Dancing around at my age? I told them I'd only do it if they doubled my salary and gave me top billing, and now they've come back and agreed. So now I need to come up with some other excuse not to do it. Don't suppose you could help me out there, could you?"

"No," Susan says, laughing. "I'm a terrible liar. But you're an actress; surely you can come up with something?"

"Yes," Kay muses. "I suppose I can."

* * *

"Chris, we have a live one!"

Chris's head snaps up. The distraction makes him pause in his stirring, until Calum bellows, "Watch that—it'll curdle!"

Chris yanks the pot off the heat just in time, beating the sauce with redoubled effort, simultaneously hissing to the hostess, "I thought you said we had no bookings at the chef's table today!" He has nothing prepped for the chef's table menu, and he'd planned to use this time to get ahead of some work for tonight's dinner. This is going to throw his whole afternoon off.

"It was last minute," the hostess replies. "She just walked in and insisted. Said she knew you and would have whatever you want to cook. You really want me to just turn someone away?"

Chris shifts to the side to peer around her, frowning. Knew him? God, not another friend of Lauren's? They come in giggling packs and barely eat a thing, just stare at him, take pictures of the food (and him) with their phones, and whisper among themselves while texting and updating their statuses. And once some right little shite of a boy in frayed jeans and shoes that must have cost five hundred pounds came along and made a point of looking bored and quizzing Chris on the provenance of every. Single. Ingredient.

"Because it's *very* important, you know, to be aware of where your food comes from and to make sure it's not irresponsibly sourced," the shite had mansplained, half to the girls accompanying him and half to Chris. "It's our duty, you know, to protect the environment."

Never mind that absolutely everything the kid was wearing was imported. Chris had never in his life taken such an immediate dislike to someone, which is remarkable considering he's spent his whole career in television and high-end kitchens, both native stomping grounds of obnoxious, pretentious assholes.

But the woman perched expectantly at the counter at the opposite end of the kitchen is not one of Lauren's preening friends.

It's Kay.

His teeth clench as she lifts a hand and waves, smiling. *Some nerve,* he thinks, *acting like we're friends.*

He'd like to tell her in no uncertain terms that she's not welcome here. That's the whole point of owning your own place, right? You can decide who stays and who goes?

Well, that's the fantasy. The reality is you can't turn away a paying customer. You definitely can't turn away a paying customer who's also famous. So he gathers up his knives in white-knuckled fists and approaches her.

"Hello, Christopher," she greets him, folding her hands on the countertop. She's settled her face into a blandly pleasant expression, and he wonders what she's really thinking. He figures you can never tell with a gifted actress. It's disorientating. He never has this problem with Susan.

"Afternoon," he responds, unleashing his full Scottish brogue for perhaps the first time since he left for New York. She can have his food, but she isn't going to get the posh, watered down version of Chris. She'll get the Full Scottish. "Chef's menu's no' available, I'm afraid. Ye'll have tae order from the menu or take what I can gi' ye now."

She keeps her eyes on him, and her mouth edges upward in the very start of a smile. "That's fine. Surprise me."

Without looking away, he reaches for a whole rainbow trout and, in one swift movement, whacks the head off it with his knife. Kay's smile widens and turns wry.

"Your restaurant's beautiful," she compliments, looking around as Chris gets to work.

"Oh, aye," he agrees.

"You must be very proud of all you've accomplished."

He grunts instead of answering.

She watches him work, then says, "I should have come in earlier, but the play kept me so busy. Still, I do love watching artists work. And you, young man, certainly are an artist."

He concentrates on arranging some sea bass sashimi, fanning the fish—sliced translucently thin—over the plate so it resembles whitecapped ocean waves. He finishes it off with an equally artistic arrangement of trout and delicate sauces, and hands it over. Kay spends a few moments silently admiring the plate, then takes her first bite.

"Oh yes," she murmurs, "you *are* an artist."

An apprentice appears to remove the tools he used for the fish, and Chris gets started on the meat course.

"I can see now," Kay continues a little louder, so he's sure to hear her, "why she's so enthralled by you. You *understand*."

He can't help it. He pauses in his cutting, and his shoulders tense. Enthralled?

Kay notices, but instead of commenting, muses, "It's astonishing, really, how food can turn one's head. I used to wonder what on earth my sister ever saw in that puddle of a man she married, and then I tried Elliot's food." She chuckles. "I think he wooed her far better than Bernard did. And while Bernard was a disappointment, I was never sorry that Elliot was such an important part of my sister's life. And Susan's. And yours."

Without raising his head from the meat he's working on, Chris looks her way. She's toying with a fork, blinking a little too rapidly, and tensing her lips.

"I wish you could have known Marie better, before she was so ill," she murmurs. "I wish a lot of things had been different. I think we both do." She looks at him now, and he returns his eyes to the food, swallowing hard and trying to distract himself.

"My niece is very important to me, Christopher. The most important person in the world. You know that, don't you?"

He laughs, a short, sharp bark. "I dinnae know any such thing," he says, jerking his head up to look at her. He forgets that he's still holding his chef's knife, which glitters in the flickering light from the grill. Kay's eyes drift toward it, and she gives him a look that seems to say, "Really?" He sets the knife down and walks over to the counter, leaning over it to hiss, "I think *you* are important to you. *You* are the most important person in the world. You care about *you*. And your *image*. You're just like the rest of 'em."

Kay actually cringes. "You cut me to the quick, young man. Please do not put me in the same league as Bernard." She spits the name. "And you're very wrong. I would have been happy—delighted—to have Susan stay with you if I'd really thought you were the best thing for her. Why do you think I'm here today?"

"I dinnae ken why you're here today." He crosses his arms. "So maybe ya'd better get tae your point, so I can get on wi' my work."

Kay sighs. "You are a prickly one, aren't you? All right, then. Susan is in love with you, Christopher. Very much so. There might have been a chance that she'd move on, but with the two of you sharing the same city, same circles . . . well . . ." She throws up her hands. "No hope for it now. Not even Philip Simms could tempt her! Imagine! Now, I must confess that I tried to steer her away from you because I know things about you, don't I?"

Chris purses his lips and looks away.

"And the things that I know . . . they aren't conducive to a healthy, lasting relationship, are they?" She cocks her head and purses her lips. "Can you really blame me for stepping in all those years ago? Susan was a wreck—you know that! And bless you, you tried to help her, but you were a wreck too, and you know it, so please don't try and play the wronged innocent. Yes, I interfered because I thought that it was best for Susan. Not for *me*, not for the family—for *Susan*. She had just suffered a devastating loss. Have you ever been in that position?"

He swallows hard, then nods, still not looking at her. Not trusting himself to. "Aye, that I have."

"So you know what it's like. She was in no shape to deal with what *you* were facing. And you were in no shape to deal properly with her grief. When you suffered your loss, were you truly in any condition to be a rock for someone else?"

He pauses, wishing there could be some other answer, but "No," he replies.

"There! You see?" She leans back a little in her chair, shaking her head, clucking. "I'll admit, I may have overdone things years ago. I felt guilty for not being there after her mother died. I was selfish, and when I came back I tried to fix everything as quickly as I could, and I failed to consider all the angles. I failed to realize just how much the two of you meant to each other. I thought it was just your average early-twenties infatuation. I made a mistake, and I want to right it because I want to see my girl happy."

She sighs. "Chris, no one else will do. Not even a movie star." She rises just enough to be able to reach across the counter and grab his arm, forcing him to really look at her. There's a fierceness in her face now that he's never seen before. It's startling, and he can't help but stare. "Listen to me: I see what the two of you are doing. I did it myself once. You're burying yourself in your work. You're letting it consume you because if you don't, then you'll have time to think about things and those things *fucking hurt*. Now, believe me, this is great for your career—I got an Oscar and a BAFTA out of it. But it's absolutely *horrible* for you and for the people you care about. You can't bury yourself in some distraction forever. You have to think those awful thoughts and feel those horrible, shitty feelings sometime."

Chris blinks at her, actually shocked into stillness to hear this woman cursing away, eyes blazing. The memory of it is definitely going to make watching her next refined period film a slightly uncanny experience.

Kay takes a deep breath, releases his arm, and sits back. She's calmer, but there's still that fire in her eyes. "Christopher, I need you to think—*really think*—about what you want. If you love her and are willing to give it another go, then please, please do so—I give you both my blessings a thousand times over. But if you've moved on—well, that would be a shame, but I understand, and she does too. She's already convinced herself that she can expect no more than professional courtesy from you, much as it pains her. But she'll survive. She'll find some kind of happiness in other places. A ghost happiness, never quite complete, but she'll convince herself it's enough. But please, Christopher, if you don't want to pursue anything with her again, then I beg you—don't parade yourself in front of her. Don't go thrusting yourself into her life unnecessarily. I know the restaurant world is a small one, so you won't be able to avoid each other entirely, but there are some steps you can take to be less . . . present in her personal life. I'm talking about Lauren."

He almost laughs: she need not worry there. He and Lauren seem to have reached a natural endpoint; they haven't spoken since the night the play opened. The pair of them went off to some club, where Lauren quickly located a group of friends (which included that pretentious little shite who pouted at the sight of Lauren and started to look downright belligerent when she began dancing with Chris. And no wonder: she danced around him like a strip club pole, and when the shite stomped out, she laughed, turned to her girlfriends, and seemed to forget Chris was even there.) Her life and his life did not intertwine well, he realized.

Oh, who's he kidding? He knew it all along. She's fun, sure, and she likes to be happy and be around people who are happy, which is nice and the sort of thing he needed. But her flightiness, her lack of direction or ambition, which once made her seem refreshingly carefree, just baffles and annoys him now. He can't wrap his head around the idea of being her age and having no drive to do *anything* useful. But then, he never had the luxury of indolence. He *had* to work, just like everyone else he knew. Except for Susan, and when she was Lauren's age, she was just as driven as him. She still is, and it makes him proud to see it and to see all her hard work rewarded.

Still, he's not prepared to yield an inch to Kay. He looks back at her and says, "You really havenae learned not to interfere."

"Clearly not. I'm sorry to disappoint Lauren, but she's young and free spirited, and she will recover quickly. And my first loyalty is always to Susan. So just . . . consider carefully, will you, please?"

He studies her and realizes after a moment that he's not looking at Kay the actress, but Kay the person. Kay the aunt and surrogate mother. Her face is open, and so like Susan's in that he knows what she's thinking and feeling, and that she means every single word of what she's said.

He can't process any of this just now. He has a full restaurant. Behind him, the kitchen buzzes, and Calum is issuing a stream of instructions to the other chefs and the apprentices. The phone rings at the hostess stand, and the waitstaff passes to and fro with full trays, empty trays, needing things. And the things he's tamped down, pushed away, locked up, tried to forget or bury underneath a hard crust of bitterness are seeping to the surface, like oil. Thick and dark, but bringing the possibility of hope. A slow trickle at first, which threatens to become an overwhelming gush.

He can't process this right now. He needs time. And quiet. A long walk with the dog, perhaps. But he won't get any of those things because Beth's coming in tonight, and they're overbooked for dinner, and he has the Book Festival tomorrow.

The Book Festival! He asked Susan to come. Will she? Or will she duck out, convinced, as Kay says, that she'll only be bringing more pain on herself? She said she'd be there, but was he, after all, asking too much of her?

Kay sits back down and waits, patient, recognizing someone going through quite a lot in a very compressed amount of time. When his eyes clear and he uncrosses his arms at last, she says, "Right. Am I going to get the rest of my lunch, then?"

Chris blinks. "You still want lunch?" He thought she'd done what she came to do.

"Of course I want lunch! You can't tease me with that excellent first course and not follow up. I'm a starving artist, my boy, and I can't wait to see what you have in store for me."

Chapter Twenty-Four
"I've Got a Story for You"

❧

For two weeks every August, the normally private Charlotte Square opens its gates to admit the literary masses. Huge white tents block views of the iron railings that normally keep everyone out, and picnic tables and pastel deck chairs circle the equestrian statue of Prince Albert in the middle of the lawn, inviting readers to relax with their newest signed novel. The tents fill with crowds to see every sort of author: high-flying politicos touting bestselling memoirs; writers of fantasy, chick-lit, sci-fi, young adult (and *every* possible combination of those). Authors and illustrators enthrall throngs of preschoolers and parents; up-and-comers present their work for appreciative and encouraging audiences. Books are signed by the hundreds and set out for sale in the inviting bookshop tents. People bask in the sunshine, when there is any, or gather in the café tent and grumble good-naturedly about the rain. They shake hands; gush, "I *love* your work"; add to their "to be read" lists, and leave carrying new hardbacks in handy Book Festival-branded tote bags.

To Chris, it feels strange to find himself in the midst of all this. He's never once been to the Book Festival. This rarefied square, surrounded by investment firms and the First Minister's official residence, never felt like a place where he belonged. Growing up, he and his friends always dismissed this festival as a place for posh folk. But now, looking around from a spot just in front of the café, he has to admit it's pretty nice, and friendly, though the Irn-Bru is definitely overpriced. It's a grizzly day, but there are still kids running around, clumps of people chatting over coffee and pastries, and one man in a navy jumper, doing a very Scottish thing and plunking himself down in one of the deck chairs, despite the weather, to read his new book. This change in perspective startles Chris. Is it because he's so different from that rough lad he used to be, or has he, as he has with other things, judged the festival a little too harshly? Hard to tell. Maybe both.

* * *

Inside the café, unaware of Chris outside, taking the measure of his future audience, Susan wonders if a slice of millionaire's shortbread is what she needs to really perk up. It was a full day at the busy restaurant yesterday, and today she spent the morning with her nephews, so Meg and William could have some time to *talk*, which they've been doing a lot of lately. Susan tells herself this is a good thing, even if it means she spent hours shepherding three excitable boys between Julia Donaldson and Barry Hutchison events. She saw the boys get their books signed, then handed them back to their parents (who returned from their brunch holding hands and looking like they had *not* been shouting, which is an improvement) and went in search of coffee. And sugar. She needs something because Chris's event is in an hour, and she doesn't want him to think she's bored when all she really is is exhausted. That's if he can even see her, from his spotlit perch at the front of the tent. He probably won't. All the same . . .

"Can ye no' just get a proper cuppa tea now?" the woman in the line beside her wonders aloud. Hands on her hips, she frowns at the array of fancy herbal teas on display.

"I think you have to ask special," Susan says, laughing.

"Course you do." The woman rolls her eyes. "Edinburgh," she grumbles good-naturedly.

"Not from the city, then?"

"Oh no, I'm Leith, born and bred. Put it behind me, though. I live near Aberfeldy now. I'm only here because my brother's got some event and, ya know"—she shrugs—"Family."

"I do know," Susan agrees. "It's nice of you to come. Who's your brother?"

"Chris Baker."

Susan starts. "Chris Baker! Why, then, you're Beth!"

Beth eyes her beadily. "And who're you?" she demands.

"Oh, sorry, yes, that was silly of me." Susan smiles and offers a hand to shake. "I'm Susan Napier."

Beth's eyes narrow, and she moves her hands from her hips to a tight cross over her chest. She looks Susan up and down very slowly. "So," she says at last, "you're the bitch."

Susan lets her hand drop. A few people crushed in around them overhear Beth and stare at Susan, as if to say, "Oh, so *that's* what a bitch looks like."

"Yeah," Susan agrees. "I guess so."

"Ya did a real number on my brother, ye ken?"

"I do. And I very much regret it, believe me. I was in a really bad place then."

"And what about the place *he* was in? All he was dealing with at your family's bleedin' restaurant, with that arsehole chef out to get him, and then you abandonin' him and your aunt firin' him and his best friend gettin' killed—"

"Sorry, *what*?" Susan cries, trying desperately to catch up. "My aunt fired him? Why? And his friend was *killed*? Is that . . . was that Mollie's son?"

Beth blinks at her, and her face changes. The rage leaves it, and now she just looks puzzled. "You didnae know," she murmurs.

"No! They told me he quit and left London. But that was after I completely screwed everything up and treated him like . . ." Susan closes her eyes, trying to collect herself. They seem to be drawing something of an audience now. People probably think this is an improv Fringe Festival thing. She drops her voice and leans toward Beth. "You're right: I was a bitch and I ruined everything, and I kick myself for it every single day, believe me. But what's this about my aunt firing him? She had nothing to do with the restaurant!"

"Best ask her that," Beth responds.

"I will!" Susan yanks her phone out of her pocket and dials her aunt's number as she and Beth step out of the line, all refreshment forgotten.

"Hello, darling!" Kay trills. "How's the Book Festival?"

"I need to talk to you," Susan replies. "Are you around?"

"I'm having lunch with some people on George Street. Could probably tie it all up in about half an hour?"

"Fine. Can you meet me here, by the café?"

"Is everything all right, Susan? You sound tense."

"There's something I need you to—"

"Susan!"

Susan jumps and Beth breathes, "Jaysus!" at the sound of Lauren's shriek.

"Susan!" In order to get a better view of the room, Lauren has climbed up onto the low dais where authors sit for book signings. She leaps off and races in Susan's direction. Her face is pale, eyes red and wide with fear. She grabs the hand Susan isn't using to hold the phone. "Susan, I *need* you!" she wails. "Something *awful* has happened!"

"We'll talk later," Susan tells her aunt, ending the call. Beth is watching this with some interest. Susan wraps an arm around Lauren's shoulder, draws her a little apart from the crush of people, and speaks in a soothing tone. "Hey, hey, it's all right. Whatever it is, we'll get it worked out. What's happened?"

"I can't, I can't," Lauren gulps. "Not here."

"Okay, okay." Susan glances around for a quiet spot.

Beth raises her eyebrows and says, "Think I'll be off now. Nice meetin' ya, Susan."

* * *

As Beth wanders outside, Chris is still there waiting.

"Thought you went to get tea," he says, noting she's without.

"Och, too much fuss." Beth shrugs. "Ye'll no' believe who I met."

"Oh?"

"Susan."

Chris's chest seizes. "Susan Napier?"

His sister nods. "In the flesh."

"Oh, Christ, what did you say to her?"

"I didnae say anythin'! What'd you think I'd do?" Beth scrunches up her face in annoyance. "As if I can't hold my own tongue! She's no' as bad as I thought she'd be."

"No," Chris agrees. "I may have given you a . . . poor impression of her."

"For sure you did! Gave her a fright, I did. And let slip about that harridan of an aunt of hers tossin' ya out. She didnae ken a thing about anythin'. I think her aunt's in for quite a hidin' later on."

"She didn't know they fired me? Because of my . . . problem?"

"Because of the drugs, Chris, let's no' mince words, eh?"

Several people passing or sitting at tables turn to stare, and Chris smiles nervously in a "Sisters, yeah?" kind of way. "What did she say?" he hisses, drawing Beth aside.

"No' much. Some girl with purple hair came runnin' over with a drama and dragged 'er off."

Chris frowns. "Purple hair? Was she about this tall? Young? Thin?"

"Sounds right."

"That's Lauren. What happened?"

"Oh, so *that's* Lauren, is it?" Beth shrugs. "Dunno what happened. Ask 'er yersel'."

"Where are they?"

"Went to find a more private place to talk. You know, I always thought these rich folk festivals were a bit borin' an' all, but this is better 'n the films, it is."

"Glad you're entertained," Chris grunts, rushing into the tent.

"Oy! Get me a tea while you're in there, will ya?" Beth shouts after him.

* * *

"Right." Susan steers Lauren through one of the side doors of the café tent. It opens onto a small alleyway near a general storage area filled with rubbish bins and huge jugs of water. Ignoring a "No Public Access" sign, they duck behind the café, taking refuge between two large stacks of boxes covered in blue tarpaulin. "Right, what's going on?"

"It's Liam," Lauren hiccups, somehow managing to fill that one name with an impressive amount of venom. "He and I—well, you know, we had a thing."

"So you've said. And you ended it. *Right?*"

"Well, sort of. I just hate breakups, you know? But I made it really clear it was over."

Susan nods, pursing her lips. "Okay. And how did you do that?"

"By making it kind of obvious that Chris and I were having a thing. The night the play opened, Chris and I went to a club where I knew Liam would be, because there were a bunch of my friends there. And I just sort of, uh, put on a show, you know? Like you and Philip were? Dancing?"

Susan closes her eyes for a few moments, grimacing internally. Is that really what she did? Put on a show?

"So what'd Liam do?" she asks, steeling herself.

"He—he had some photos I'd sent him a while ago, when we were still together. And he sent them to Rufus Arion! *Private* photos," she hisses.

Susan had already guessed as much. "Did he publish them?" she asks, horrified.

"No! Not yet, at least. But I'm sure he will, and when he does, it'll be the end for Dad's campaign, won't it? Upright family man Tory whose daughter's sending around nude selfies? Dad'll *kill* me! And Mum! I can't—how will they even be able to look at me? God, how could I have been *so stupid*?" She bursts into tears and drops her face into her hands. "And I'll b-b-be *humiliated*!" she adds. "Everyone I know reads that blog! They'll all see! It was just a bit of fun between him and me, back when things were good between us. I never—never—*never* thought he'd . . ."

Susan pulls her in for a hug, praying for patience, trying to figure out what to do here.

"Okay, it's okay," she soothes. "We'll find Rufus and work something out. You're sure he hasn't published them yet?"

Lauren shakes her head and holds up her phone. The screen shows Rufus's blog. "I've been refreshing almost every minute," she answers. "It's not up. I came here to see if I could find him—he's been posting selfies with authors on Instagram all day."

"Good. Let's go find him and get this sorted."

Lauren turns bright red and steps back, flattening herself against the railings, shaking her head. "Oh, I can't face him, Susan! Not after what he's seen!"

"This is *your mess*, Lauren!"

"I know! I know!" Lauren gulps. Great, fat teardrops start pouring down her cheeks, and she's breathing in that hitching, shuddering way that small children do when they're completely undone by their own emotions. It suddenly strikes Susan just how young Lauren is, and how Susan did pretty stupid things at this age too.

"It's all right," Susan reassures her, rubbing her back. "Just try to calm down, okay? And I'll see if I can find Rufus and get this sorted." Lauren didn't seem to be in any shape to face Rufus Arion.

"Thank you, thank you!" Lauren launches herself at Susan, wrapping her arms around her neck. "Susan, thank you so much! I knew you'd manage it!"

"It's all right," Susan repeats. "Just . . . mind what you send people from now on, okay?"

Lauren nods, then escapes around the backs of the tents while Susan ducks back inside. Her eyes rake the crowd, looking for Rufus, but the first familiar face she finds is Chris's.

He looks relieved when he sees her, and comes over.

"Is everything all right?" he asks in a low voice as soon as he reaches her. "Look, I'm sorry about Beth—"

"No, it's fine—your sister's great," Susan reassures him. "I'm sorry—I have to find Rufus." She tries to duck past, but a crowd waiting to have books signed blocks the way.

"Is this about Lauren? What happened?" Chris asks.

"It's fine, it's just . . . something I need to fix for her." She knows she looks frantic. Her heart is beating hard; her eyes still dart, searching the room.

Chris frowns in concern, puts his hands on both her shoulders, and looks her in the face. "Susan, please, let me help. You don't have to do *everything* on your own."

She looks up at him, and it feels like some hard nugget of resistance in her dissolves. "Okay. Help me find Rufus. Lauren says he's here somewhere. He's been posting pictures of himself with some of the authors."

He nods. "All right. Authors' Yurt, maybe? I'll get you in."

They set off, side by side, threading through the knots of people to a somewhat dark, oval tent set back from the square's main thoroughfare. Chris flashes a pass at someone at the entrance, and the two of them are ushered inside. Susan blinks for a moment, eyes adjusting to the darkness, and spots Rufus sitting at a table with a trio of crime writers.

"Well hel-*lo*," he says as Chris and Susan approach. "I'm guessing you two aren't here to talk about cookbooks."

"No, we're not," Susan says in a clipped voice.

"Didn't think so." Rufus excuses himself from the table and leads Chris and Susan outside and around the back of the tent. "I take it you've had a chat with Lauren," he continues, tutting and shaking his head. "Naughty girl!" he singsongs.

Susan doesn't even need to look at Chris to know he's clenching his fists. "You've been sent some private photos, and we want them deleted," she says, in a firm, even voice.

"They *are* naughty," Rufus agrees, slowly pulling a phone out of his pocket and scrolling through something on the screen. "I mean, I'm no saint, but . . . oh my!" He glances up at Chris and smirks. "You're a lucky man, Mr. Baker."

Chris makes a disgusted noise and growls, "Delete them now."

"Or what?" Rufus asks, looking bored. "You'll beat me up?" He tucks the phone away and turns to Susan. "You want me to bury this story? Then give me a better one."

Taken aback, Susan stutters, "But I don't—I don't have anything. What do you want? A story about the restaurant?"

"Oh, for God's sake, woman, of course I don't! Didn't you just date and dump Philip Simms? I'm sure you can give me a little something."

She's so repulsed she actually steps away from him, as if he might infect her. She's aware of Chris watching, waiting to see what she'll do. "You want a kiss and tell?"

"Of course I do, my dear. It's my stock in trade."

Save Lauren's reputation, or throw Philip under the bus. Susan knows that family should come first—that this should be an easy choice. Philip's famous; he'll probably come through this all right. He has paid professionals whose job it is to help people like him ride out scandals. And how big a wave could a story on a blog like Rufus's create anyway? But the whole idea is so ugly and sordid.

"No," she says. "Ask for something else. You can have anything you want on me, but not him. He's a decent guy. He doesn't deserve it."

Rufus's eyes narrow. "Are you sure about that?" he asks, slowly keying in his phone's password.

But then Chris steps forward and says, "I've got a story for you."

With identical looks of surprise, Susan and Rufus turn to him.

"Do you?" Rufus asks. "Is it a good one?"

"Very good," Chris answers, swallowing hard. "You could probably ruin me with it."

"Ooh, intriguing!" Rufus's eyes gleam.

Susan grabs Chris's arm and looks up at him, hoping her face says, "No! Don't play his game. Everything you've done! All the people who rely on you! Your whole future! Think about it!"

Chris looks back at her, and she recognizes the look from their London days. She used to see it when he'd had enough of the other young chefs' bullying and was preparing to take them on, however ugly it got.

"Can we go somewhere quieter?" he asks. "More private?"

"I live just around the corner," Susan suggests. "Moray Place."

"Very well, then," says Rufus. He bows low and gestures to her. "Lead the way, milady."

Chapter
Twenty-Five
Time Will Explain

Moray Place is empty, but as a precaution, Susan leads the others to the kitchen, so they won't be overheard if someone unexpectedly comes home.

"Oh, very nice, very nice," Rufus comments, looking around the gleaming room. "Your sister's work? I love the slate floor."

Chris catches Susan's eye and cringes.

"Should we get this over with?" he suggests, taking a seat at the table.

"Certainly." Rufus takes a seat across from Chris, sets his phone on the table, and prepares to press a button to begin recording.

Susan joins them, taking the chair at the head of the table.

Chris inhales deeply and places his hands, folded together, on top of the table. Rufus presses the large red button pulsating in the center of his phone's screen.

"I killed my best friend," Chris announces abruptly.

Rufus's eyes practically pop out of his head. "Did you indeed?" He leans forward. "Please, do tell me more!"

Susan wants nothing more than to smash his greedy face into the table.

Chris closes his eyes for a long moment, rhythmically clenching and unclenching his hands. "When I was working at Elliot's in London, I started taking cocaine," he says, looking toward Susan. There's something in his eyes that seems to be pleading with her. "A lot of us took it—it's not uncommon among restaurant employees. The long hours, the high pressure—it can be hard to keep up. But you know how these things go: the more you take, the more you start to feel you need."

Suddenly, Chris's behavior during the latter part of their relationship makes more sense. The lack of sleep, the manic talking. And she didn't think it was just the job that he needed to keep up with. He needed to keep going at full speed to help deal with her too.

"It was . . . not a good time," Chris continues. "I was half out of my mind. I wasn't the person I needed to be for other people." He looks at Susan again, and she shakes her head just a little, wishing she could hug him and tell him that that wasn't his fault. That he'd done what he could, and she knew that, but she'd expected him to take on too much. "I realized I needed to stop," he says. "I got rid of what I had, but during a random search at work, something was found in my locker." He shakes his head, and his lips and hands tighten.

Something was found. Or planted, Susan thinks, remembering the jealousy of the other chefs at Elliot's.

"I was fired immediately and told that the whole thing would be kept quiet if I agreed never to see . . . someone again. I told them they could take their threats and shove 'em."

Susan feels sick. Her aunt did this? Threatened Chris, to keep him away from her, even as she was gently persuading Susan to just give the relationship a little break for the good of them both? And yet, he'd still risked it. He'd risked the career that meant so much to him by trying to reach out to her. And she'd *ignored* him!

"And for the record, who was that someone?" Rufus asks, with a glance toward Susan, who blushed.

"I'm not going to say, on or off the record," Chris answers. "It's not relevant. She ended things with me the night I was fired and so had no bearing on what came after."

Susan nearly groans aloud. She couldn't have possibly known how bad her timing was, but . . . *Jesus.*

Rufus shakes his head. "Bitch," he hisses.

"I said *leave her out of this,*" Chris nearly shouts.

Susan jumps, but Rufus just raises an eyebrow and says, "All right. Moving on . . ."

"I came back home to Scotland," says Chris. "Not much for me in London. I was in very poor shape, not sleeping, not eating, couldn't figure out what to do with myself, sure my whole career was over." He shakes his head. "Twenty-something drama. Feels like the whole world's coming to an end. I stayed with my best mate. We grew up together, he and I. He lived next door to us, and his mum was sort of a mum to me after mine left. But he'd fallen in with some rough types. He was getting away from it when I came back. He'd gone legit, was learning a trade, seeing a nice girl, all that. But I, uh . . ." Chris blinks very hard, glances away, clenches his hands. The silence stretches, long and painful. "I felt like I needed something to help me. I was in a lot of pain." His lips thin and he looks deeply disgusted with himself. "I knew that he knew people. I asked him to get me what I needed."

Susan, too, blinks hard, and turns her head away. All this, at least in part, because of her. Because she hadn't had the decency to have an honest talk with him. To answer her goddamn phone.

"He went to meet with a dealer, and he didn't come back," Chris finishes, wiping a hand across his mouth and blinking quickly. "There was some dispute—something about the price, I think. They stabbed him and then buried him on a farm out in

Fife. His mother was frantic, searching, and then two months later they found him. What was left of him."

Susan emits a low moan.

"Did they catch who did it?" Rufus asks in a surprisingly gentle tone.

"Yeah. He was arrested for something else and led them to the body," Chris answers without looking at him. "He's jailed for life now, so there's that at least."

"And what did you do after that?" asks Rufus.

"I escaped. My sister came and dragged me off to the Highlands and kept me there for a while, straightening me out. She put me to work on her neighbor's farm, and I just channeled everything I felt into that hard, hard work. And then I traveled, picking up jobs along the way, learning what I could, and I wound up in New York, where I was lucky enough to get noticed and . . . that's how it went."

Another long, heavy silence. Both Rufus and Susan are frozen, feeling as if it isn't their place to break it. Chris refuses to meet either of their eyes, turning instead to look out the French doors into the misty garden.

At last, Rufus lifts a finger, stops the recorder, and says, "Well, I'm afraid I'm not going to publish that."

Chris very slowly turns to face him. Susan inhales sharply, relieved for Chris's sake, but fearful for Lauren's. With a flick of Rufus's thumb, the interview is deleted. "Calm yourself," he says to Susan. "For heaven's sake, I run a gossip blog, you two! A bit of fun, a place for people to blow off steam and have a laugh. This is"—he grimaces—"not fun. It's sad. And sordid. And nobody needs to read that." He looks up at Chris. "Least of all your poor friend's mum, right? I've a mum myself, believe it or not, and I wouldn't want her reading this sort of thing about me. Dredging up all those sad memories . . ." He shakes his head. "It'd be a shame, too, to lose your restaurant if people took against it. Not that they probably would—everyone likes a good redemption story."

"So what about Lauren's photos?" Susan demands.

"I was never going to publish those. I mean, talk about sordid. Also, distributing intimate photos without permission is extremely punishable nowadays, and I don't fancy five years in prison, thank you very much. Oh, and I wouldn't worry about that little shit Liam sending them to anyone else either. I put the fear of God into him, believe me." Rufus smirks. "If you're looking for a way to thank me, some free dinners wouldn't go amiss." He holds out his phone to Susan. "All deleted. You can see for yourself."

She gives him a wary look, then takes the phone and checks. No photos. "So, this whole thing . . ."

Rufus shrugs. "I thought I might get a story. Can't fault me for trying, right?" He tucks the phone away and stands. "Gotta get back, and"—he points to the pair of them—"I think you two should talk. Love your house, Suze!"

Once he's gone, Susan and Chris stare at each other for several seconds, not quite sure what to say or where to begin. Then, Chris's phone starts buzzing.

"Aw, bollocks," he mutters. "My publicist," he explains apologetically. "My event's starting soon."

"Right, you have to get back," Susan agrees.

"Yeah." He hesitates, then stands and moves toward the door.

Susan springs to her feet and grabs his arm. "Look, I don't expect us to be friends or anything—I don't think I even deserve to be a nodding acquaintance with you because I fucked up so completely, even worse than I realized, and I am so, so sorry, and I completely understand why you acted the way you did toward me, and I get it if you never want to see me again—that's fine— it's fine! I understand! I shouldn't be asking anything of you, ever, but if you could just know that I'm sorry. I'm so, so sorry. I acted like such a shitty child, and I swear, I had no idea that you'd been fired. I didn't know about that or the drugs or what my aunt did, not that that excuses my behavior." She pauses long enough to try to breathe, but her heart's hammering and her stomach's twisting and her lungs refuse to fill. "I know you're with Lauren now, and you must really love her to stick your neck out like this, so obviously I have no expectations or anything, but I was just wondering if maybe, someday, you could just . . . not hate me, at least? I don't expect more than that. I just want you to know that I'm sorry and please, please don't hate me!"

Chris is staring at her in some shock, trying desperately, it seems, to sort through this avalanche of words, but at that last he cups her face and says, urgently, "Susan, I don't hate you! *I don't hate you. I—*" His phone buzzes again, and he releases her face, dropping his arms and throwing back his head. He lets out an animalistic roar of frustration. "All right!" he barks at the phone, without bothering to answer it.

"I thought I hated you, okay?" he says to Susan, his words now pouring out, tumbling over one another in their rush. "I thought you'd just used me when you needed support, and then dropped and abandoned me when I needed you, and I resented that. All these terrible things happened in one big messy mass, and I stuck a face on all of it, and the face was yours, and that was completely unfair. But you're not . . . you're not this . . . person I thought you were. I built up an idea of what you were, this angry, bitter idea, but everything I've seen and known since we both came here made me remember that you're not this uncaring bitch—you probably care more about people than almost anyone else I know. But that anger was still there, in some form, so I kept lashing out, and I felt horrible about it, and I'm sorry. So maybe you could not hate me too?"

Susan laughs, a strange, garbled half laugh, half sob.

"And Lauren and I," he continues, "it's not . . . We're not . . . She's a nice girl, and I didn't want her to be hurt by some little rich kid shite with a grudge, but she and I—it was just my sorry attempt at a distraction. And maybe, yeah, another dig at you, and I'm so sorry about that, Susan. I'm sorry. I'm sorry!"

The phone again. And again.

"You should go," Susan says. "It's okay—we can talk later."

He pauses. "You're sure?" He looks a little scared, as if he's afraid she'll disappear in the interim.

"I'm sure." She squeezes his hand. "It's okay. Go. I'll follow after. I just need a minute."

He nods, squeezes her hand back, and leaves.

* * *

As soon as he's gone, Susan leans against a countertop, drawing in deep, ragged breaths, trying to slow her hammering heart. He doesn't hate her. He doesn't hate her! He might even—could she hope? Is it possible that all is not lost?

Her palms are sweaty, and her hands shake as she fills a glass with water and gulps it down. Her mouth is dry, knees gone to jelly, stomach still rebelling. What will she say when they speak later? What will he say? Can she hope to fix the damage she's done?

Can she hope?

Her phone buzzes, and a text message from Chris flashes up.

I've been a total asshole to you, and I'm sorry.

I've been unfair. Judged you. Thought you were cruel, even though I knew, deep down, that you weren't. Were never that. Never could be.

I thought you'd just stopped caring. Or never cared. I thought I was the only one who got hurt. And kept hurting.

Wasn't going to say this, but I heard you with Philip. Realized I was wrong.

I've lived in this agony too, knowing I did things that pushed you away. I didn't want to face it, but I know I did.

It's only ever been you. No one else will do. I tried to get away from you, but couldn't. Tried to pretend you didn't matter. Couldn't.

You are everything.

And I've done everything I can to push you away! So stupid!

Please, please. I

Nothing more. He must have arrived and been hustled into his event.

Susan only realizes she's been holding her breath when her lungs begin to ache. She lets the air out in a great whoosh, shaking all over, not sure if she wants to laugh or cry or dissolve into a puddle right there on the hated slate.

"You are everything.*"*

She bursts out of the house, so consumed she forgets to even lock the door. Her only thought is how vital it is to be with him, to eliminate the distance between them. She runs through the rain and presents herself, a damp and disheveled mess, at the Festival's largest tent.

"I'm sorry," the employee sitting there tells her, with a sympathetic grimace. "We can't admit anyone after the event's begun."

No!

Susan wants to scream or cry or do something, she's not quite sure what. All she knows is that she's let him down again. She promised to be here, and she's not. What will he think when he scans the audience and doesn't see her there? Will he think she just read those texts and chose to step away? God forbid! To lose him again—now! After he poured his heart out like that!

Now she knows what she wants to do: she wants to burst into tears.

Instead, she draws in as deep a shuddering breath as she can manage and shuffles back to the café to wait.

She's barely through the door when she hears someone calling for her.

"Oh! Susan! Suuuuuusaaaaaaan!"

Susan looks up, frowning, and sees Kay, standing near the bar at the back, smiling and waving to her.

"My, Susan, I've been waiting here for ages! Where have you been?"

The hysterics evaporate, replaced with a harsh, raw anger. Steeling herself, Susan straightens her spine, sets her face, and heads toward her aunt.

Chapter Twenty-Six
Half Agony, Half Hope

❧

"I had the most wonderful lunch at this little place down the street," Kay announces, setting aside the gin and tonic she's been sipping. "With my director and one of the producers for the play. They're thinking of pairing me and Philip up again. But don't you worry—my matchmaking days are over." She nudges her niece playfully, only to receive a stony face in return. "Oh, dear, what's put your nose out of joint?"

"Did you fire Chris from Elliot's and then try to blackmail him into staying away from me?" is Susan's blunt response.

Kay purses her lips and gets a look on her face that seems to say, "Ah, we're finally having *that* conversation."

"Yes, I did," she admits. "It seemed like the best thing at the time. It probably was."

Susan folds her arms over her chest. "Would you care to explain yourself?"

"Oh, Susan, darling." Kay reaches out and strokes her niece's cheek. "You were such a mess. We all were. I should have stayed around after your mother died, instead of leaving. I felt terrible about that, and even worse when I came back and saw the shape you were in. Don't you remember? Oh God, I hope you don't." She retracts her hand and grimaces. "You were leaning so heavily on that boy, so when your father came to me and told me the restaurant manager heard Chris had an issue with drugs—and before you ask, no, I don't know who told the manager about his habit—I knew something had to be done. The situation wasn't healthy for either of you. But of course my main concern was for you. You're my flesh and blood, Susan, and I will always fight in your corner. So, yes, I persuaded you to take some time away from the relationship. And I handled the situation with Chris. I knew Bernard certainly wasn't up to the task." Her lips tighten again, seemingly at the mere thought of his uselessness.

"You *threatened* him. It wasn't bad enough that you fired him; you *threatened* him so he would stay away from me!"

"I did. I said we'd blackball him in the industry. I didn't want him disrupting your recovery, and I thought the situation might help him clean up his act. And it did, apparently. He got his life sorted out quite impressively." She takes a deep breath. "At the end of the day, Susan, you were out of your mind with grief. You were slipping away from us, and I really didn't think that a junkie was the best person to have in your life at that time. I am sorry that I hurt you both—truly I am. I did what seemed to be the best thing at the time, which is really all any of us can do. I had no way of knowing how splendidly he'd turn out. Good for him, I say. Who knows? Perhaps my intervention was the making of him, in a sense."

Susan shakes her head. "You have no idea what your actions cost him," she says. "And mine." No one is blameless. After all, she's the one who broke up with him.

"I'm sorry," Kay repeats sincerely. "And I've told him that I'm sorry too."

Susan frowns. "When?"

Kay smiles and shakes her head. "Doesn't matter."

She looks over Susan's shoulder, and Susan follows her gaze. Chris's event has let out, and people are flooding into the tent. A peppy-looking blonde leads him to a seat at the signing table as fans, clutching crisp copies of his book, form a line.

Chris is pretending to smile and pay attention to whatever his publicist is saying, but at the same time he scans the crowd. Susan, standing frozen beside the bar, wills him to look her way, at the same time trying to force her legs to move. But even if they do— what? Will she run onto the dais and throw herself into his arms?

His eyes seek her out, settle on her, and his relief is visible in the sudden unstiffening of his posture. His smile becomes genuine, a warm beam that finally melts the ice in her legs, so when Kay gently nudges her and whispers, "Go on, then," Susan can move forward.

"Oh, oh, the line's this way," the peppy blonde informs her, steering Susan to a spot behind two women in flowery Joules jackets, already discussing which of Chris's recipes they'll make first. Susan looks helplessly up at Chris, and he returns the expression, and she wants to laugh hysterically at the absurdity of it: her, waiting in a line for what, exactly? And him trying to focus on signing books and politely answering questions and smiling for pictures, all the while darting glances her way, as if he thinks she might disappear.

And then she's in front of him, unable to speak, realizing she's on an actual stage, with people behind her still waiting for their books to be signed, and oh god, she doesn't even have a book!

"Oh, you've not bought your book yet," the blonde observes.

"It's fine—this one's hers," Chris says, plucking a display copy from a Pyrex stand near his right elbow. He scrawls something on the title page, closes it, and holds it out. "I hope you like it," he says, swallowing hard.

Susan accepts the book, still tongue-tied, and scurries off to the side. She closes her eyes, opens the book, and looks at what he's written.

I love you. I'm sorry. Have I ruined it?

And then Susan does laugh. A choking, relieved, nearly hysterical giggle that she can't control any more than she can control the tears stinging her eyes and pouring down her cheeks. She doesn't care that people are staring at her, some even backing away, apparently thinking she's crazy (which is fair enough). She only cares that Chris is looking at her, ignoring the hovering blonde and the poor man waiting for his signature. His face has an open, yearning expression that begs her for an answer. She grins, shakes her head, and mouths, "I love you too."

A massive smile erupts across his face, and she feels that flood of warmth again. Her own grin widens in response until she feels like her face might split, but she doesn't care, and she can't seem to stop smiling. Almost without looking, Chris signs the last book; then, ignoring his publicist's pleas, he leaps off the dais and grabs Susan's hand. Together, they duck through the side door and find themselves back where Susan last spoke with Lauren. Tucked away, among the tarpaulin-draped crates of books, slick with rain.

"I know we need to talk about things, lots of things," he chokes, "but I just—"

Susan grabs his face, pulls his head down, and devours him.

And that kiss is *everything*. It's love and regret and apology. Passion and sex, friendship and promise. It's want and need and yearning and heat and shivers that they both feel shuddering through their bodies. It's ten years' worth of kisses, all crowding into one embrace as the pair of them rediscover each other: the curves of their mouths and bodies pressed close, the insistence of hands and tongues, the hearts hammering in concert, and the silent, mutual promise that there is more—so much more! and better!—to come.

When they finally part, Susan looks up at him with a teasing smile and says, "You're not just doing this for the brownie recipe, are you?"

"Ah, you caught me!" He laughs, then kisses her again and again and again, and when they pause once more, she notices the flush creeping up his neck, the mixture of frustration and desire in his eyes.

Clinging to him, she says, in a throaty voice: "Your place or mine?"

"Well," he answers, with a devilish smile, "yours is closer, but mine doesn't have your father or Julia in it."

"Right," Susan laughs. "Yours, then."

Together, they hurtle through the crowd, through the gates of Charlotte Square, bellowing in unison, "Taxi!"

Epilogue

So, this is it, Susan thinks in satisfaction.

Cupping her mug of early-morning tea, she looks around the flat: the walls newly painted a sunny yellow, which compensates for the misty day outside. Fat pillows and a warm blanket and Ginger, snoring on the sofa. Photographs hung, a vase of daffodils on the counter—the place looks like a home now. She loves returning to this every day, and Chris does too. She can tell.

It was such a relief to leave Moray Place, which emptied surprisingly quickly. First her, then Julia, and now Bernard's leaving. He announced, over the end-of-Christmas-dinner port, his intention to sell.

"It's just a bit too much," he sighed. "Especially now Julia's gone. She and I talked it over, and I think I might take a little pied-à-terre in London. So many people have been inviting me to stay with them on holidays—did I tell you *Sir* Miles Cadogan has asked me on a skiing week in January? Anyway, it seems a bit silly to keep such a big house when I'll only be there a few weeks out of the year, don't you think? And it's just *so quiet.* I long for a bit of life about me. Julia knows a place near Canary Wharf she thinks will suit. Of course, I'll miss you two terribly," he added with a mournful look at Russell and Helen, who smiled tolerantly back, "but I'm sure when the next election comes around, you'll be joining me down south. The voters will have come to their senses by then, surely?"

"One can only hope," Russell agreed. "If at first you don't succeed, try, try again!"

"Hear, hear!" Bernard cheered.

"How nice you'll be near Julia again," Helen commented. "Though I'm sure you'll miss Meg and Susan and your grandchildren terribly." She looked meaningfully at the girls. Susan returned a wry smile.

"That goes without saying, of course," Bernard said, turning to his girls. "But you're all so grown up now, you don't need dear old dad, do you? I must find some way to fill my time, and we must do what's best for everyone, eh?"

It *was* for the best. Bernard does not love Edinburgh. He whines about the weather and the slippery cobblestones and the crowds of people who are "such a bother. All these *tourists* everywhere!" He wonders why Meg's boys aren't better behaved. He doesn't shoot or play golf or read, so he has nothing to speak to anyone about, and no one invites him on any recreational excursions. He's better off in London.

Susan didn't mind putting a bit of extra distance between herself and her father. He barely spoke to her for days after he heard she broke up with Philip, and when she told him she was back together with Chris, he looked horrified. Though, it seems that wasn't entirely down to snobbery.

"Oh, Susan, are you sure?" he asked as she prepared to move out of Moray Place. "Is he really the best person for you? He has . . . weaknesses, you know."

"I know all about that, Dad. It's not a problem for him now."

Bernard's face pinched, the most expression she'd seen him make in years, and Susan was shocked to realize her father was actually concerned about her.

"It'll be fine, Dad," she reassured him, reaching out to embrace her father for the first time in . . . she didn't even know how long.

He was surprised by it and took a moment to react, but then patted her on the back, and when they parted, he blinked quickly, looked away, and said, "Well, at least he was on television. And perhaps he'll do it again soon. Why just be a chef when you can be a celebrity chef?"

And just like that, he went right back to being Bernard.

It's March now. A dreary month almost anywhere. Susan sips her tea, contemplating the weather. It's not raining, really; it just looks like the rain clouds have descended, leaving everything perpetually damp. The cobblestones are slick and treacherous. Meringues are off the menu indefinitely because they turn into a soft, sticky mass within minutes of coming out of the oven. But no bother, Susan has plenty of other ideas.

Today is a workday. Tomorrow, Julia comes up from London, so she and Susan can sift through what remains at Moray Place and decide, at last, what they each want to keep and what can go. Bernard has already had the things he wants sent to his new place in London. Julia did it up for him and had it photographed for a spread in *Elle Decor*.

Julia's much in demand now. The work she did at Elliot's caught the eye of one of the better-known guests, who asked if she could come have a look at his dining room. She did, and soon she was redoing all the public rooms, and then the bedrooms, one of which she now enjoys on a more personal level. She limits the number of clients she takes on, insisting that doing so really allows her to focus on each one's needs. Exclusivity breeds demand, and she prices accordingly.

So she'll be up to pick through the remains, and then she, Susan, and Meg will have their monthly dinner and drinks, and catch up. Meg will undoubtedly fill her elder sister in on how utterly adorable her new therapist is (Susan, of course, has already heard it all many times) and how he *really* seems to *listen*. Whether it's the looks or the listening, he seems to be doing Meg a world of good. She hasn't tried a fad diet for months, and the boys have stopped worrying they're going to die.

Susan remembers that Meg has a choir concert in two weeks and wonders if she can persuade Julia to make a special trip north to see it. Bernard is a lost cause, but Kay will surely be there. She is, after all, taking some time off to relax and be with family, and she seems especially committed to the latter bit. She comes up to visit every chance she gets. She's put in a mighty effort with Chris, and it seems the ice between them is thawing, slowly, although Susan is sure the past and everything that happened will always lie between them.

Lauren will probably come too. Probably. She has less time on her hands now she's back at school and actually applying herself, having been scared straight, to some extent, by her near miss with internet infamy.

Rufus wasn't joking when he said he'd put the fear of God into Liam. The boy was so remorseful about sharing the photograph that he'd shown up at Lauren's to apologize in person, only to find both of her parents there, demanding some sort of explanation. Once they got it, *they* put the fear of God into the boy as well. Russell bellowed that he'd telephone Liam's father and every single person he knew to make sure the boy never got hired anywhere if he even so much as *thought* about telling someone about those photographs.

Liam, stammering, handed his phone over. "Keep it, just keep it!" he gabbled, racing back out the door. He transferred to another school, and that was the last of it. But Helen wasn't taking any chances and kept Lauren on a tight leash now. So it was probably for the best that Russell lost the election.

The sound of Chris shuffling out of the bedroom breaks her reverie. He joins her in the kitchen, blinking and rubbing his face. His hair is wild, and he has a two-day red-gold stubble that she rubs affectionately when he approaches.

"Thought you might sleep in," Susan croons, pouring him a cup of tea and topping it up with milk.

"Ta," he croaks, drinking. "Meeting with the business manager at nine," he explains.

"Ahh. Let me guess—your very own line of nonstick spatulas." They exchange playful smiles.

"Tartan ones, of course. For the international market," he jibes back before dropping a kiss on her cheek and wandering over to the window to drink his tea and look out at Leith.

They've been living together—officially—since October. It happened so gradually, neither of them even seemed to notice. She brought over a few necessities, and he quietly made room in his drawers for them. By the end of September, she realized she hadn't spent a single night at Moray Place for more than two weeks. And two weeks after that, Chris, frowning into the sitting room area, said, "I think it's time for us to buy a new sofa."

And that was pretty much it. The joint choosing and purchasing of a sofa—something they both liked and wanted to live with—was the deciding factor. Susan brought the rest of her things, and that was that.

"When are you two going to get married?" Kay is now asking, echoed occasionally by Meg.

"No time for that now," Susan always answers. Both of them were playing to full houses—she at Elliot's and he at Seòin. Gloria has done some television cooking specials on Saturday mornings; Chris is being wooed by the producers of another cooking competition show. There are talks of cookbooks on both sides, and merchandising on his. Chris Baker could very well become a brand.

It's hard, but they make sure to set time aside for the two of them. Tonight is their night. Seòin is closed, and Rab will hold down the pastry fort at Elliot's.

"Breakfast?" Susan offers, setting a pan on the stove. It's one of her grandfather's—no one objected to her taking most of the pots and pans from Moray Place when she moved out. Chris's home kitchen was so poorly equipped it had become an ongoing joke with them.

"Aren't you a chef?" she'd giggled, that long-ago day they cleared the air and came back together. After hours of energetic lovemaking, they realized they were famished, and of course Chris wanted to make *their* pasta dish. But five minutes of desperate searching through his kitchen cupboards yielded only a single tiny saucepan, a bottle of olive oil, and three withered cloves of garlic.

"I cook everything at the restaurant," he sheepishly explained. Susan pulled him close and kissed him, and for a while they forgot about the pasta.

But even lovers must eat sometime—and visiting sisters too, something the pair of them became very much aware of when Beth burst in, looking for sustenance at the end of a long day at the Festivals, and caught the pair of them.

Everyone froze, blinked a few times, and then Beth said, "I'll just go down the chippy, hey? Back in forty minutes. *Exactly* forty minutes. And I'll take the dog with me as well." She scooped up Ginger, shielding the dog's eyes, as if she was in danger of being corrupted. By the time she came back, everyone was slightly more presentable, and Beth turned it into a joke that Susan readily bought into, so it was less a painfully uncomfortable memory and more one that just made everyone laugh, especially once they were a few whiskies into an evening.

Susan smiles at the memory as she gets to work beating eggs for breakfast. Chris abandons the window, sets his mug in the sink, and wraps his arms around her waist from behind, nibbling on a bit of bare flesh between the edge of her shirt collar and the base of her neck. The stubble tickles tantalizingly.

"We could start date night early," he whispers. She closes her eyes for a moment as her stomach quivers and she feels a throb between her legs—a sensation that falls in that delicious spot between pleasure and pain.

"I'd love to," she murmurs back, turning to face him and wrapping her arms around his neck. "But Rab'll be here soon, and I don't think he's quite as likely to laugh certain things off as Beth is."

"Humorless little bastard," Chris murmurs, lightly kissing her forehead, temples, chin, neck, nose, and finally lips.

"Mmm. It's my own fault for suggesting he come by so we could toss ideas back and forth on the walk-in," she says. "So blame me, if you like."

"I do blame you, for stealing him in the first place," Chris answers, nibbling her bottom lip. "That was mean."

"He could have stayed at Seòin. He *chose* to be my apprentice."

"You made him an offer he couldn't refuse! The promise of a job as head pastry chef?"

"That's right! You couldn't match it, so I win. Ha!"

"We'll just see about that. Maybe I'll tempt him back someday."

"Maybe you will. We'll just have to see which one of us he likes best."

"In the meantime, you'll have to make your theft up to me."

"And how should I do that?" she purrs.

"I can think of a few things," he responds. "But since Rab's going to be here any minute, why don't we just start with making the brownies tonight?"

"Already ahead of you," she promises. "And we can discuss the other things later."

"We'd better." He kisses her again, smiles suggestively, and heads toward the shower.

Susan helps him on his way with a playful smack on the bum, then drinks her tea as she pours the eggs into the hot pan.

Watching them turn into curd-like clumps, she swallows hard and realizes she probably should have started with dry toast.

Chris doesn't know yet about the baby.

She'll bring that little announcement out later, after the meal. With the other sweet things.

Acknowledgments

So much love and thanks to my incredible husband, Adam, who supported me through the whole writing process with hugs, cups of tea, words of encouragement, and thoughtful manuscript commentary. Also, to our sons, Jamie and Alex, who provide so much joy and motivation, even on the worst writing days.

An immense amount of gratitude to my parents, Janine and Michael, and my grandmother, Jane, for nurturing my imagination, cheering me on, and always being willing to listen to my stories.

And to Diane Alder, the wonderful teacher who encouraged a shy eleven-year-old girl to write. I still remember her saying, with certainty, that I'd be published one day. It's teachers like her that can really make a difference in a child's life.

To the team that brought this book to the world: Steven, my agent, whose unfailing good cheer, encouragement, and persistence is truly astonishing. Faith, my editor extraordinaire, who championed this book and knew just what to do to make it better. Melissa, Madeline, Ashley, and the rest of the team at Alcove Press, who made my introduction to the publishing world such a joyous one. I thank you all, from the bottom of my heart.

Acknowledgments

And finally, I would be most remiss if I didn't raise a glass to the incomparable Miss Austen, whose thoughtful, funny, touching stories continue to enthrall and inspire readers and writers to this day. Without her, and without everyone else mentioned here, this book would not have been possible.